THE LAST MARINE

A LAST HERO NOVEL

CARA CRESCENT

CRESCENT BOOKS, LLC

For my dad.
And all our other heroes,
of whom, we often ask far too much.

Acknowledgments

While writing a book tends to be a solidary experience, a multitude of people are needed to see the project in print. I'd like to thank my critique partners, Marissa John and Aedyn Brooks. My family and friends editors Jean & Yelena. My copy editor, Dorrie O'Brien. And the amazing ladies at Killion Group, Inc. for my cover art and formatting.

1

—— ◆ ——

WASHINGTON, D.C. 2265 A.D.

Griffin Jude Payne.

That's what they'd call him now. They always referred to political assassins by three names. Christ, his parents must be rolling over in their graves. They certainly hadn't raised him to be a murderer.

Griffin stood still amid the dense crowd with his spine straight and his hand clasping his wrist behind his back. He'd donned his dress blues for the occasion. He'd even dared to come into town a few hours early to clean and shave and have his hair trimmed. This was for his unit.

He was the last, and since one man had no chance of succeeding in a campaign against a whole army, he planned to take out their leader. Everything he'd done in preparation for tonight had been carefully planned. Precisely executed. He refused to give anyone a reason to claim him insane.

Still, the whole mission was too easy. Security hadn't swept him for a weapon despite how he'd dressed. Maybe this was all too new for them to have noticed. Only a week had passed since the U.N. had absorbed the world's military forces.

And euthanized those unwilling to cooperate.

Tonight's event was being held on the mall before the towering U.N. building. At one time flagpoles had surrounded this area—one for each member state. All those flags were long gone now. The pale-blue-and-white flag of the United Nations waved and snapped alone in the brisk November wind. A simple stage had been erected with a lone podium and a holo-projector behind it, projecting a two-story, full-color hologram of the U.N. flag.

Where the hell was security?

He forced slow, easy breaths through his nose as he surveyed the crowd of smartly dressed civilians eagerly awaiting U.N. Prime Minister Alfred Parnell's speech.

Of course they were eager. They waited for the man who had been instrumental in creating the first global utopian society. They adored him. Worshiped him.

Hell, he had, too, before he'd learned the truth.

Before he'd witnessed U.N. Blue Helmets frag his base.

The U.N. wasn't the same benevolent international organization it once was. Oh, the mission statement still spoke of peacekeeping and international cooperation, blah, blah, bullshit. The U.N. was about utopia.

Which meant getting rid of the undesirables.

The lights dimmed and the crowd erupted into applause as a spotlight lit the stage. The sound chased his heart rate higher. Almost time.

Alfred Parnell walked onto the stage with his wide, shit-eating grin. Alfred's brother, Randolph, followed with Alfred's alien wife. Damn. He didn't like the idea of the woman being on stage, but she must be as bad as her husband to be smiling along with the rest of them.

He could do this. He needed one clean shot. Then he'd drop his weapon. The Blue Helmets wouldn't be able to kill him if he was unarmed. Not in front of this group. Not in front of the holo-cameras. It would be too public, tarnishing the peaceful façade the Parnells had toiled so hard to create.

Briefly, he considered taking Randolph down, too. Alfred witnessing his brother shot seconds before his own demise would be a fitting justice. But none of the intelligence he'd gathered suggested Randolph was a threat. Aside from displays of familial support, he showed no aspirations in the political arena. Hell, some of what he'd uncovered suggested Randolph was psychologically fragile.

No. This needed to be seen as a specific mission for justice, not some random act of violence. He'd kill Alfred, drop his weapon, and they'd have to take him into custody. After a very public trial, they'd transport him to Asteria. Asteria was his goal—that's where they'd shipped his younger brother.

He just needed to stay alive.

"I'd like to show my appreciation by having all our young service men come up. Come on up, boys, so we can give you a round of applause."

Griffin couldn't believe his good fortune. His chances of surviving tonight increased tenfold. The people around him clapped him on the shoulder, urging him toward the stage. He made his way down the crowded aisle, tucking his arm tight to his body to feel the reassuring presence of his sidearm.

Mingling in with the Blue Helmets—the U.N. soldiers wore light-blue uniforms and distinctive blue headgear—he didn't stop like the rest when he reached the bottom of the steps leading to the stage.

Alfred Parnell's curious gaze locked onto his.

Griffin's heart slammed hard in his chest. His blood pulsed in his ears. *Think of Lucan, alone on a violent, alien planet.* "We forged ahead with each decree, killed like your hired guns." His voice didn't carry far, but the Parnells damn sure heard him singing his version of the Marine's Hymn. "From ships at sea to each air base, we died in your bomb runs." Griffin reached the top of the stage. The applause died as those in the audience tried to hear. "You banned our kin from life on Earth, but I'll wash your sins clean."

For the first time, Alfred's gaze swept Griffin's uniform, the blaster holstered at his hip. His eyes widened in alarm.

"I'm nothing more than you made me, I'm the last U.S. Marine." In one clean sweep, Griffin pulled his weapon, fired once, and dropped his sidearm as he lifted both arms high over his head.

Alfred took the photon-blast between his eyes. He was dead before the first audience member screamed. His brother Randolph dove for cover, leaving Alfred's wife standing alone on the stage with Griffin. She'd jumped a little when the blast went off but didn't try to hide like the others. She stared at him with huge lavender eyes.

When the Blue Helmets jostled him to the ground, he didn't resist, he kept his attention trained on the brunette. Something about her was off. She didn't scream or cry. She didn't even look to see who he'd shot. Her worried gaze stayed with him.

The Blue Helmets secured his arms behind his back and wrestled him to his feet. After checking on Alfred, Randolph Parnell stood and faced Griffin. "You killed him." Rage twisted his thin face into an ugly sneer. "I'm going to make you pay for this."

Griffin smirked. "Careful there, Parnell. Wouldn't want anyone seeing your monster."

Randolph waved them away. "G-Get him out of my sight."

Medics ran onto the stage as the Blue Helmets dragged Griffin to the nearest hovercar and headed across town for booking. Everything had gone as he'd planned.

A public service announcement bell sounded over the radio.

"Hey, turn that up." The driver pointed to the radio. "I bet it's about the shooting."

Griffin straightened in his seat the best he could with his hands cuffed behind him and leaned forward to hear better. Parnell was going to make an announcement so soon?

The sound of applause died down, replaced with Randolph's voice. "It is inevitable, I'm saddened to say, all saints are martyred far too young. Today we will grieve for my brother and weep that, for all the greatness he brought to these United Nations, this was his reward. And tomorrow. Tomorrow I will continue to work tirelessly toward completing his vision of peace for these United Nations. Prime Minister Alfred Parnell may have died tonight"—Randolph paused—"but his vision will endure through me."

Applause and cheers erupted.

Griffin slumped back in his seat. What had he done? His gut twisted into a sickening knot and bile rose to the top of his throat. . . . No, damn it. Tonight wasn't supposed to end like this. Alfred was dead. Alfred was the one with the dream of Utopia. His damned dream was supposed to die with him. None of the intelligence Griffin had gathered suggested Randolph was anything more than a leech riding on Alfred's coattails.

But tonight Randolph reminded him more of a hungry shark in blood-tinged waters.

He wouldn't rest until the public knew what the Parnells had done. He'd have an opportunity to speak at the trial. If the jury didn't listen, he'd steal a ship and return with those who'd been shipped off the planet. They wouldn't be able to ignore all their voices.

Damn it, he would be heard.

New York, 3 months later.

"Say something, damn you."

Prudence Angelica Parnell paced in front of the holo-projector—the single non-essential object in her room. The Parnells preferred a minimalistic lifestyle. At least, for her. The white walls and floors gave her room a sterile atmosphere. Her toes curled into the carpet when she paused to stare at the hologram.

In the hologram, Master Chief Griffin Jude Payne was strapped to a gurney-cage the court officers had propped up in front of the witness box. The contraption looked uncomfortable, painful even, though the reporters claimed it wasn't. The trial for the murder of Alfred Parnell had been ongoing for three months and Chief Payne hadn't spoken a single word during the length of the trial. Occasionally, he'd nod or shake his head to maintain an air of competence. A couple of times he grunted.

His apathy was killing her.

When he shot Alfred, she'd thought everything might turn out all right. Everyone would be safe. A hero had arrived. But if anything, Chief Payne's actions had made things worse. Randolph Parnell had the public's sympathies now. He could do no wrong. And he was so much worse than Alfred.

The one thing Chief Payne had accomplished was to provide her with an opportunity to escape. With Alfred dead and Randolph needed at the trial, she'd had plenty of time to prepare. Tomorrow, when he returned to Washington for Chief Payne's sentencing, she'd be boarding a ship to Asteria.

The door flung open and Randolph strode in.

Prudence eyed him. He'd never entered her private room before. "Is there something you wished to discuss?"

He closed the door and leaned against the jamb, folding his arms over his wide chest. He was a big man, with much more muscle and mass than Alfred. He kept his black hair oiled in place and not a wrinkle marred his gray suit. "I have a couple hours before I leave for Washington." His dark brown gaze flicked to the hologram. "Ah, you're following the trial. What do you think?"

She clasped her hands in front of her, trying to ease their tremble. What did she think? She thought the trial was fixed.

She couldn't understand why Chief Payne wouldn't speak. He didn't appear to be drugged, his eyes were clear and full of wrath, but something wasn't right. The whole thing was a joke. But she couldn't say any of that to Randolph. "I think he'll be found guilty and transported."

"I wish I felt as confident." He pushed away from the wall, removing his jacket and laying it across the foot of her bed. "Since the bastard won't talk, I'm worried they'll call for another psych eval and find him incompetent." He yanked on his tie, loosening the knot. "The longer this carries on, the more chaotic and ineffectual the government appears."

A sickening knot formed in her belly. He held the same delusional beliefs Alfred had. She was half Lythonian and females from Lython were known for their gifts. The thing was, the gift wasn't theirs to use, but rather for their mates. To her it was more of a curse, one that had completely ruined her life.

"That's unlikely." Prudence walked to the window and looked down on the city, wanting to get as far away as possible, wishing she was in one of the hover cars zinging past. "They already evaluated him." She needed Randolph to believe he would win. That he didn't need her or her gifts to help his cause. "They found Chief Payne to be competent and he's done nothing to suggest otherwise."

"Yet he won't speak."

"His eyes are clear and he responds non-verbally when he wants to. It's—" She turned, noticing he'd removed his shirt and undid his buckle. Alfred had forced his attentions on her on their wedding night. Is that what Randolph planned? Was he not even going to wait for their nuptials? "It's clear he's following the trial. Besides, even if he is found incompetent, he'll still be transported. Why does it matter?" Her gaze slipped past Randolph to the door. She'd never make it, and even if she did the guards downstairs would stop her and bring her back. There was nowhere to run.

"Utopia is built on a foundation of trust, consistency, and the belief that those around you are striving toward the same peace you are. The very unpredictability of illness, crime, poverty—they chip away at the basic structure of our new society. Insanity by its nature lacks consistency, therefore it cannot exist here."

It sounded odd to hear him mimic his brother's words. Had Alfred lived, in time, he'd have shipped Randolph away with all the rest.

Randolph smiled. "I find I am unwilling to risk the trial on luck when I can have assurance through you."

When Alfred died, she'd thought she was free but no sooner had they buried him than Randolph announced their engagement to the public. "You promised to wait until after the wedding."

He strode over to stand in front of her. "I need you tonight."

"You cannot steal my gift." Her voice shook, lacking the note of confidence she wanted in her tone. "It has to be given freely."

He stepped closer, the musky scent of his cologne surrounding her. He cupped her throat with one hand, his thumb nudging her chin up until she met his gaze. "Don't lie to me. Alfred was no great orator. No one listened to him before he lay with you."

Heat flooded her face as her body released a healthy dose of adrenaline. He knew. Alfred must have told him his crazy ideas, about how, after he'd fucked her, her gifts made people listen to him. He had been fanatical in his belief that she bestowed the power of persuasion to him, as her mother had done for her father. And while he'd only touched her that once, he'd kept her under tight supervision to ensure she didn't give her gifts to anyone else.

But he'd been wrong.

Alfred may have forced her to marry him, to lie beneath him, but he couldn't force her to take him as mate. Nor would Randolph. She still carried her mating marks, and they would be on her belly tomorrow no matter what Randolph did to her tonight.

"You Lythonians think you're so smart, trying to keep your gifts secret. You can't hide such things from the U.N. You gave Alfred the ability to persuade the people. Now you'll give it to me."

A tremor ran through her. She had fought Alfred. Randolph she couldn't. After so many punishments by his hands, she knew what he was capable of—and all of that had happened before witnesses. Here, alone in this room, she couldn't imagine what Randolph might do. She tried to back away, but his grip on her throat tightened. He jerked her terrycloth robe off her shoulders with his other hand, revealing she wore nothing beneath. As soon as the cold air hit her body, her nipples tightened and she hated it. Despised the idea he might take it as a sign of acceptance. Of excitement.

She tried to cover her body.

His fingers tightened until she dropped her hands to her sides.

"Please don't." He enjoyed strangulation. Waterboarding. Suffocation. *Do what you want to her, but don't let her die,* Alfred would say.

"Don't flatter yourself." Randolph's face twisted in disgust. "I'm doing this so I'm successful tomorrow, and for no other reason. Do you honestly think I'd choose you when I could have anyone I wanted?"

His fingers flexed and she couldn't help the tear sliding down her cheek. "Of course not." *No one wants an alien like you,* Alfred would say. *You're disgusting. Useless. Ugly.*

"Do you think I'll derive any pleasure from having someone as cold and frigid as you beneath me?"

Oh, yes. Alfred had told him everything. *It's like fucking a knothole in a frozen tree.*

"Do you?"

His fingers tightened until she couldn't speak. Couldn't breathe. She shook her head.

"You're skinny." His expression stated plain enough that he found her lacking. "Your breasts are too small. You have no ass, and your eyes are disgusting. Close them."

Alfred hated them, too. *They're the color of a day-old bruise,* he'd say. She shut her eyes.

"Undo my pants."

She pressed her lips together, determined to refuse him. Black dots and bright pinpoints of light checkered behind her closed lids. Her lungs burned. She'd pass out soon. Or die. Either would be better than sex with Randolph. *Sex? Say it how it is. It's rape.*

She fisted her hands at her sides, resisting the urge to claw at his hand.

Her head went fuzzy and her lungs strained with the need for air. Randolph released his grip around her throat and her traitorous body inhaled a deep, painful breath.

His hand squeezed again, his breath rough against her ear. "We can do this all night."

I can't fight. If I fight, I'll be in the infirmary tomorrow instead of escaping.

The threat of repeated strangulation extinguished the last spark of her resistance. That, almost more than what was about to transpire, brought fresh tears to her eyes. She'd been raped once before. This just happened to be a different body doing the deed. What pained her was her inability to protect herself. She was weak. Pathetic. Why couldn't she be stronger? Fight harder? Get angrier? Instead, a paralyzing numbness washed over her. It slowed her heart, suspending her emotions. She went blank, as if her spirit disconnected from her body and became a dispassionate observer.

"Don't make me ask again."

Prudence wrenched open his fly, pushing his slacks down over his narrow hips and under her gaze, his half-erect cock deflated, testament to how unappealing he found her.

Leading her by the throat, Randolph forced her onto the bed. "Spread those bony knees."

She complied. She didn't struggle as he mashed his flaccid dick against her most private place. She didn't fight his hand tightening at her throat. She turned her gaze to the holo-projector and focused her blurry vision on the silent man facing trial, distancing herself from what happened to her body. She wondered, if maybe, if somehow Chief Payne might have shut down, too. Just like her.

They faced different demons hundreds of miles apart.

But tonight, they'd be silent and stoic together.

Her and her almost-hero.

2

As soon as the door slammed shut, Prudence allowed herself to cry, keeping her face from the pillows so her lavender tears didn't stain the white pillowcases. She couldn't even say why the full-body sobs shook her so hard this time. In the end, Randolph couldn't get it up. By the time he returned to try again, she'd be long gone.

She didn't understand Earthers. From what her mother told her, men never treated women in such a way on Lythos. Maybe because they knew they would never get their mate's gift until they won over their woman's heart. Or maybe they were better men. They would never use a woman this way.

Mating was sacred on her home planet. Celebrations were given upon the exchange of a gift—and it was an exchange, the male would receive a gift he needed to better support him and his mate and the woman would get the gift of a new life—a baby. Deep down, despite everything, even she still harbored some hope. Women with lavender eyes always bore daughters and she'd love to have a daughter.

Forcing herself to rise, she went to the window and stared down to the drive far below. Randolph would leave soon. The first faint hues of dawn poked through the skyscrapers, lighting the thick, green lawns and vegetable gardens growing on platforms outside the windows of each floor. Most days, she found the sight beautiful and inspiring. The tall buildings were vertical greenhouses for all intents and purposes, layered with various shades of emerald and jade and dotted with a rainbow of flowers.

Today, the street far below held her interest. The main entrance to the Parnell compound stuck out several hundred feet, allowing her to see the front entry. A limo pulled up, hovering over the drive.

Prudence palmed away the wetness blurring her vision and rubbed her puffy eyes. She waited, pressing her face to the glass. Randolph appeared ant-sized when he emerged from the building, but she was sure that was him. Thomas, the driver, wouldn't dare open the back door of the limo for anyone else.

Randolph would be on his private transport to D.C. within the hour.

This was it. This was her chance.

A sudden onset of tremors shook her from head to toe so hard even her teeth chattered. Fresh tears welled in her eyes. There was so much she had to do. She couldn't forget any of the items she'd planned to take—there would be no general store on Asteria—and she couldn't take anywhere near the amount of gear she wished she could. If she walked out of here with more than one bag, security would become suspicious.

The enormity of what she was about to do hit her full force.

This was why she cried.

Why she shook.

What she'd endured at the hands of the Parnells and society as a whole was a known quantity. The adventure she'd chosen to embark on was not. Security could get suspicious and alert Randolph. The Blue Helmets at the spaceport might recognize her. The ship could crash. She might die at the hands of Scarecrows moments after disembarking on Asteria.

Or she might succeed.

Truth be told, she couldn't decide what she feared most. What would success look like? Would success be living alone in a small cabin in hostile territory? Would she find a community? Friends? Would she grow old never being loved or holding her daughter?

She'd never find out if she didn't get moving.

Prudence took a cleansing breath and wiped her eyes. She crossed the room with purposeful strides and flung aside her closet door. She had stacked the shopping bags holding her supplies in the base of the closet last week. She didn't reach for them, she stood there staring at the symbols of her freedom, paralyzed.

Don't touch them yet. Don't tarnish them with the smell of Randolph still on your skin.

She had to hurry. Barry was on shift now, and he had a soft spot for her. He wouldn't scrutinize her too much, not like the other guards. She flipped on the shower, jumping in before the water had a chance to warm and scrubbed herself. Five minutes later, the water was blazing hot, the bathroom smelled of eucalyptus and her skin was red, but clean. Every time her hands stroked over her neck, pain radiated down her back and across her collarbone. Her movement wasn't hindered, nothing was broken, but she wasn't surprised when she stepped out of the shower, wiped her hand over the mirror, and caught sight of the black stains around her throat.

Dripping all over the floor, she returned to the closet, and started shoving her supplies into the brand new duffle bag. Barry wouldn't question the bag—she'd been taking goods to the Sisters of Charity for the war orphans once a month for the last six months. She left out a box of black dye and a pair of scissors and rammed them into her purse before dressing and shouldering her pack.

Calm down, Pru. They're going to take one look at you and know something's wrong.

Her throat! She returned to her closet and grabbed a hat and scarf from the rack and donned them.

Downstairs, she exited the elevator and walked toward the front entrance, clutching her bags.

Barry smiled when he saw her. The burly black man always had a smile for her. She had no idea why he worked for the Parnells—he was far too kind—but he'd always been here. "Mrs. Parnell. Off to do your good works?"

She had to crane her neck back to look him in the eyes which made her wince. "Yes. The Sisters are expecting me today. How's your wife, Barry?"

Barry's expression grew concerned.

Prudence's breath caught. Had she given herself away?

"Alda's doing real well. Thank you for asking." His lips thinned. He took the bag with her gear and began walking toward the front doors.

Her whole body grew tense, wanting nothing more than to snatch the bag back. Her future was in there. Instead, she forced herself to stay calm and walk by his side. "And Jast?"

"Oh, well, now, he's doing okay. Been a little rebellious lately, and Alda's real worried." He shrugged. "Me, I think it's the age."

The other guards watched their every move, their heads turning to watch their progress. "He'll be all right. He's always been very respectful to me."

He held open the lobby door. "Here you go, Mrs. Parnell."

She stared at the limo and for one heart-stopping moment, she thought it was Randolph's.

Barry winked. "I saw the elevator coming down, so I called the car up."

"Thank you."

He handed off her bag to the driver, who held the door open for her.

"You'll be back in time for lunch?"

Halfway into the limo, she paused. "Actually, I . . . I thought I might join the Sisters for lunch today. They always ask, and I never have the time."

He nodded, holding her gaze. "All right, then. I'll tell the cook."

"Goodbye, Barry."

He waited until the driver stepped away and leaned down to look her dead in the eye. "You be real careful now, you hear? Be quick, be quiet, and be invisible."

The breath stalled in her lungs. Her heart slammed against her ribs. *He knew.*

Again, the large man winked. "I got your back, like you've always had mine."

She managed a shaky nod, and a whispered, "Thank you."

Barry closed the door and when the car pulled away from the curb, she turned to stare out the back window. She'd never thought of Barry as an ally before. Nice, yes, but not a friend. Not someone who'd risk Randolph's wrath for her. She lifted her ha nd in a small wave.

He didn't raise his hand in return, but he gave her a tiny nod of acknowledgment.

The rest of the trip was uneventful. The Sisters allowed her into their sanctuary and loaned her the use of a room to dye her hair and change her clothes. She cut off most of her waist-length, honey-brown locks, leaving her now black hair just below her chin. The Sisters helped her create an ID with her new look and one of the nuns gave her a ride to the New York spaceport.

"I'll pray for you, child," Sister Agnes said from the driver's seat. "This is poor timing in my opinion. You'd be better off waiting until next week when they launch the new *Apollo*."

Tonight would be *Genesis V*'s last flight. *Apollo*, named after the first space shuttle, would begin service next week. They said *Apollo* would be able to make the flight in less than half the time *Genesis V* did. "Next week I may not have the ability to leave." Next week she'd be getting married if she stayed.

"I know." Sister Agnes shook her head. "That's why I'm driving you today, but you be careful and remember to purchase the cheapest seat on the flight."

Prudence smiled. "No problem there, Sister. I don't have much money of my own."

She stared out the window for the rest of the ride, as if seeing the city for the first time. Heat billowed from beneath the hover-cars racing down the roadway. Even early in the morning, the city bustled as society members dressed in bright colors crowded the clean streets winding in and out of the garden-tiered skyscrapers. Maintenance drones patrolled the walkways, making repairs, grooming the foliage and sweeping away the autumn leaves. New York was beautiful. Spotless. Crime-free. Poverty-free. Illness-free. All the people walking the street had someplace to be, a job, a home, and a specific place on the tiers of the new U.N. society. No one limped, no one needed canine assistance, and no one wore holey, dirty clothes. There were no street performers, panhandlers, or police, just brightly dressed society members hurrying to do their part for Utopia.

Sister Agnes pulled up to the loading dock. "We're here."

Prudence jerked her head in the other direction. New York spaceport was massive, over three times the size of the historic JFK International Airport. Two-story glass buildings surrounded three sprawling launch pads. Yellow-and-white lines dotted the tarmac and spaceport employees roamed the area in hover-carts and on foot. Only one ship was docked—*Genesis V*. It wouldn't leave port until midnight. But, with a little luck, she'd be able to board now, and Randolph wouldn't think to look for her here until she was long gone.

She scooted to the opposite side of the car and leaned forward long enough to kiss the Sister's cheek. "Thank you for the ride."

"Go with God, child."

3

She shouldered her bag, slipped out of the car, and stared up at *Genesis V*. The ship was old and wore the battle scars of a decade's worth of space flights. The ship stood almost fifty stories tall, yet only one floor of the craft was designated for passengers with purchased tickets. The rest of the ship would be filled to bursting with exiled humans.

Prudence wound her way through the crowd and purchased her ticket. She didn't have enough for a private cabin, nor even for a semi-private cabin. The bulkhead was full and for long, heart-pounding moments, she didn't think anything she could afford was available. Her hands started to sweat and she wiped her palms on her jeans.

The cashier turned back to her after checking the flight log. "I've got one pod left down in the barracks. You'll have one roommate from what I hear, but no one else wanted the pod."

"Why?"

He snorted, dragging his hand down his chubby face. "Can't say why. I need to sell the ticket, lady."

"Can you tell me if it's safe?"

"The pod is in perfect working order. Now, do you want it or not?"

She wet her lips. What was she doing? She couldn't afford to be picky. "I'll take it."

After she had her ticket grasped in her hand, she used the last of her money to purchase lunch and spent the afternoon sitting on the floor in the terminal, people-watching. Every time someone raised their voice, she jumped, thinking she'd been found out. When 11:30 PM rolled around, they allowed paying passengers to board the ship. She went straight to her quarters, which turned out to be a room used to transport prisoners, and let herself in.

The whole room was white and stainless steel. Two pods were in the room and one sat in an upright position. There were no windows and only the one door.

She approached the horizontal pod. The life-links lay in a neat bundle to one side and she sent up a silent prayer of thanks to the Sisters of Charity for helping her research how they all worked. Down here in the barracks, there would be no stewardess to help her hook up.

The door opened so hard it hit the wall and bounced back, startling her. She stared wide-eyed as a man stumbled through, Blue Helmets on either side. He was bound at the hands and feet with shackles connected by a short chain, which severely restricted his mobility. Once inside, he stopped and glanced up.

Griffin Jude Payne.

She should have known. His sentencing had been this morning and Randolph wouldn't have wanted him hanging around until the *Apollo* flight next week.

They must have permitted him a shower; droplets of water clung to his clipped, blond hair. He didn't wear prison garb. They'd supplied him camouflage cargo pants and a pea-green tee. It wouldn't do for the general public to realize the U.N. shipped convicted felons to the same planet as the sick and the poor.

His eyes met hers and lit with recognition. Neither her short hair, nor the hurried black dye job appeared to have fooled him. She froze, waiting to find out if he would give her away.

The corners of his mouth went down, but he remained silent.

The two Blue Helmets muscled him over to the upright hibernation chamber. They didn't need to use the kind of force they did. He didn't struggle.

Until they tried to enclose him inside.

Chief Payne threw his shoulder against the door and head-butted one of the Blue Helmets. The man slumped to the ground.

The other soldier punched Chief Payne in the face. He reeled back with a grunt and the Blue Helmet slammed and sealed the door.

Prudence's hand flew to her throat. "You're leaving him in here? With me?"

"If you wanted a private cabin, you should have paid for one." Out of breath, the Blue Helmet glanced at Prudence. The heat left his tone. "He can't bother you, miss, he can't reach the release with his hands cuffed. Not while he's vertical."

She gave him a shaky nod and as soon as he dragged his partner out, she locked the door behind them. Goddess help her if they brought her any more roommates.

She kept her gaze on the now occupied hibernation chamber as she edged toward hers. He should already be falling asleep, but he wasn't. His intense sea green stare followed her across the sterile silver-and-white room. Did they expect her to undress with him watching?

She turned her back to Chief Payne and removed her hat, scarf, and jacket, taking her time folding them. With a glance over her shoulder, she noted he was still awake. His patrician features were schooled into the stoic mask she'd grown to know so well through the holo-projector. She took off her shoes and socks, storing them in the compartment under her chamber. Waiting was risky. If she wasn't locked into her chamber when they dropped life support, she could go under before securing all her life links.

A thud came from behind her and she spun around, her hand flying to her heart.

He hadn't gotten free.

His forehead was planted on the glass. His lips moved, forming one word: Please.

Please what?

His gaze dropped as he stared at something in the chamber, before shooting back to hers. He repeated the action, trying to communicate with her. His expression searching, intense.

She approached his chamber, getting close enough to peer down into the pod. His life support links hung loose at his side. No wonder he'd fought the Blue Helmets. They'd planned to let him die in there.

His head hit the glass, drawing her attention. Again, he mouthed one word. Please.

Her heart slammed in her chest. He wanted her to open the chamber. What if he attacked her like he did the Blue Helmet? Despite being cuffed he'd proved to be dangerous. She'd witnessed him kill with no remorse and the fact that he refused to speak at his trial didn't exactly endorse his sanity.

But could she live with herself knowing she'd let him die?

She looked up into his sea green eyes. "Don't hurt me."

A small smile curved the corner of his lips, softening his features. He shook his head.

She reached out and pulled down the emergency release on the side of the chamber. The air hissed as the air-lock opened. His lips parted and he sucked in a hard breath.

"You couldn't breathe?" She stared at him in horror.

He shook his head.

The Blue Helmets hadn't hooked him up to the life links or activated life support. That must have been three or four minutes. If she'd hesitated any longer . . . . "I'm sorry. I didn't realize." She should have. She'd studied these chambers and how they worked in preparation for this trip. A mask delivered oxygen to the occupant of the air-tight chamber.

His chest heaved with each breath and she thought she heard him say, "'S'okay," but wasn't quite sure.

Before she lost her nerve, she reached into the pod and untangled the life support links. This wouldn't be easy with him cuffed and clothed. The peripheral parenteral nutrition line would be easy enough to attach to his bare arm, so she did that first. She wrapped a band around his biceps, found his vein and slipped the needle in. "Is that okay?"

He nodded.

"No pinching? The vein doesn't ache?"

He shook his head.

Why wouldn't he talk? "I've got to put the electrode pads on you, or your muscles will atrophy."

He nodded.

"Um, I'm gonna need to—"

His hand twisted around and he unbuttoned and unzipped his cammies. Her face flamed, but she knelt and pulled down his pants. She'd just escaped one man, and here she was, kneeling in front of another with his pants around his ankles. She forced herself to pay attention to what needed to be done, placing electro-pads on his calves. Huge bruises covered his muscular legs. "Who did this?"

One tawny brow lifted. The chains linking his cuffs and shackles jangled as he reached his hand toward her. The tip of his finger traced down her throat in a gentle caress that left her shivering. A foreign flutter settled into the pit of her belly—nothing unpleasant, just strange. She wet her lips as she stared into his eyes.

He stroked her throat again reminding her of her question.

She jerked her hand up to cover the dark stains circling her neck. With everything else, she'd forgotten the bruises Randolph had given her. In the grand scheme of last night, they seemed inconsequential. Randolph had done this to him, no doubt in an effort to make Chief Payne talk. And when he wouldn't, Randolph had come to her. Well, soon they'd both be far out of Randolph's reach.

She shook her head and got back to work. Each of the electrodes needed to be placed over major muscles. She attached them to his thighs and calves and then blushed all over when she needed to reach up the tight boxers he wore to attach them to the hard globes of his glutes.

When she stood, she pulled his pants up, careful not to snag any of the wires. But there was no way to re-button them. Not with the massive erection straining against his underwear. All the breath seemed to leave her lungs. "I, uh, think you'll be more comfortable if I leave these loose."

He didn't look at her, but gave her a curt nod.

The electrodes that went on his arms were easy enough, but then she needed to lift his shirt to place those that went on his chest and abs. She stared at his dog tags, trying to ignore the wide expanse of smooth skin stretched over thick muscle. He hissed in a breath when she grazed a large bruise on his ribs. "I'm sorry. Almost done." How could he even stand? He'd been badly beaten. Interesting the bruises were confined to areas his clothing covered—that reeked of true Parnell style.

She went back to work, sliding her hands under his shirt and reaching up to attach the remaining electrodes to his back. It almost felt like a hug, bringing her flush against the hard muscles of his chest. He had a pleasant scent; musky and male. His skin was warm and smooth. Her nipples tightened and she blushed.

Damn it, she didn't like men. Especially not violent men. As soon as she finished, she stepped away. "Goodnight, Chief Payne."

His gaze, laced with surprise, shot back to hers.

"Yes, I recognize you." She hesitated, almost thanking him for trying. True, he didn't succeed. He had made things worse, but he was the only person who'd ever tried to make things right. In the end, she placed her hand over his heart and smiled. "I'll see you in six months."

He gave her a clipped nod in response.

She slipped the clear plastic breathing mask over his face, activated life-support, pushed the door closed, and sealed him inside.

The ten-minute alarm went off and she dashed back to her own chamber, pulling off clothes as she went. When she'd stripped down to panties and a tank, she folded her belongings and tucked them under the pod.

The whole ship rumbled as the engines ignited and as she settled into her pod, she realized Chief Payne stood in his. That couldn't be good. When he lost consciousness, he'd slump down and undo the life-links she'd attached.

She leapt up, returned to his chamber, and studied the markings on the side until she found a button showing a picture of the chamber with an arrow pointing down. Hitting it, she stepped back as the entire chamber began to lower, catching his expression of sleepy-eyed appreciation. Through the fogged breathing mask, his lips parted in a silent thank you.

She returned to her own chamber, stepping on something sharp. "Ouch." Grabbing hold of her sore foot, she hopped over to lean on her pod. With a baleful glance around, she found keys lying on the floor. No doubt those two Blue Helmets would be looking for these later. She picked them up, and took them with her into her chamber.

Getting the electrode patches on Chief Payne had been much easier than doing her own. She twisted and turned, working herself into bizarre positions to get all her electrodes in place. She wasn't sure she had the ones on her back right, but they would have to do. She inserted the peripheral parenteral nutrition line needle into her arm and laid back as the five-minute alarm went off. Prudence hit the self-close button and put on her breathing mask as her chamber sealed shut. Her eyelids grew heavy as the chamber cooled, and she tried to relax.

In six months, when she woke, she'd have a brand new life. A brand new her.

She'd learn to be strong and smart and never be beholden to anyone again.

As she drifted off to sleep, her thoughts turned to her roommate.

For a convicted murderer, Chief Payne was nice.

Handsome, too.

4

New York, Five Months Later

"We're being attacked."

Randolph Parnell set his knife and fork down on his plate, sat back in his chair and stared at the young Blue Helmet who'd made that asinine pronouncement. He owned Earth's military. He'd deported all those people who didn't appreciate Alfred's vision, relocating them to Asteria.

With a wry smile, he glanced at his partner and head of security, Donald Bronsen. "He must be drunk."

Bronson smirked before taking a bite of steak.

Randolph turned his full attention to the Blue Helmet lieutenant providing his report and cocked his brow.

The Blue Helmet's Adam's apple bobbed as he swallowed. "No, sir. Rebels *are* attacking. It's happening all over."

Impossible.

Bronsen cleared his throat, his handsome face lit with a wry amusement. "All over the compound?"

"No, sir, not yet." He shifted his weight. "All over the world."

With a shake of his head, Bronsen pulled out his Saph-link, a thin, flexible piece of Sapphire, and unfolded the device for use. Good. Bronsen would find out what was what. He had been Alfred's head of security for years and Randolph had learned a lot from him.

Randolph turned to the Blue Helmet. "And what have these rebels done?"

"It's an organized attack." The young lieutenant rushed to impart his news, his worried gaze darting between Randolph and Bronsen. "There was no warning. Stations have already fallen in Tel Aviv, Hertfordshire, St. Paul, Phoenix, Tokyo, Ho—"

Bronsen cleared his throat, drawing Randolph's attention, his expression flat, serious. He nodded in confirmation.

Randolph's patronizing cynicism dissolved and a sickening knot tightened in his gut. This couldn't be happening. Not now. Not when he'd finally had a taste of a peaceful, ordered life. "But who? Who organized the attack?"

"Military orphans." Bronsen let his Saph-link fall to the tabletop; the device folded in on itself until once again it was small enough to fit into a pocket.

Randolph had a horrific vision of parentless children bludgeoning his soldiers to death, but no, that's not what the lieutenant meant. He meant all the soldiers who were left without a military. When they'd disbanded the various branches and bombed the remaining bases, he'd assumed some soldiers would escape, but he'd never envisioned there'd be enough to organize and fight back. Not like this.

His head jerked twice. He could feel himself unraveling, losing his careful mastery over his body. Reaching out one unsteady hand, he aligned the unused utensils still lying on either side of his plate.

"We knew this was a possibility." Bronsen's calm gaze captured his. "We'll deal with it."

Randolph inhaled a slow breath. *They would deal with the rebels. Everything would be fine. He'd put everything into order once, so everything should fall back into place quickly.*

"We've had some contact with the rebels, sir," the Blue Helmet said. "They claim they're answering Chief Payne's call."

White-hot fury blazed through him, begging for release. *Almost everything. Like one, misplaced domino, Chief Payne caused chaos amid functioning order.* He slammed his fist down on the table "That son of a bitch made no call. He couldn't even speak at trial. I made sure of it." He'd had total control over the trial. There hadn't been any surprises, despite the fact he hadn't been able to secure Prudence's gift.

"Maybe not, sir." The Blue Helmet's doe-brown eyes shifted away. "But the people heard his song the night he assassinated Alfred. The rebels sang his hymn while they attacked." The young Blue Helmet wet his lips. "The attacks are being broadcast."

"Holo-projector, on." Randolph stared at the hologram everyone in the world was watching.

Smoke billowed up from his stronghold in Honolulu. The bodies of his soldiers—distinguished by their bright blue helmets—lay amid the wreckage. The rebels, wearing a conglomeration of uniforms from disbanded militaries, held up their weapons, cheering for the holo-cameras, singing that fucking song.

His eyes blinked hard, repeatedly. He tried to stop the tics, but couldn't. He couldn't focus. He'd never been able to amid chaos. "We can't go back. I can't go back."

Under the table, Bronsen's hand settled on his knee. "Lieutenant, thank you for your report. You're dismissed."

Randolph had always been against Alfred's idea of Utopia. In the early years, he'd wanted nothing to do with such foolishness. He'd been sure Alfred would fail.

But his brother had been brilliant. Once Alfred gained traction with the members of states, of countries like Kenya, Nepal, Chile, and Greece, things started to change. Those countries shipped away prisoners and their national debts began to lower. Other countries took note and one by one they ceded to Alfred. The U.N. took over governing, putting decades'-old wars to rest. The world had grown too big for self-governing nations. The governments had all become corrupt. Even in countries like the U.S., citizens had become so polarized, no agreements could be made. The political climate grew worse year after year until even the great countries had no recourse but to accept Alfred's leadership under the U.N. flag if they wanted to survive.

Some thought breaking the nations into smaller governments was the answer. But no, Alfred had the right of it—one global government was the answer. One mission. One set of laws. Life was better now.

And Randolph would be damned if anyone threatened that. He thrived in the new world Alfred created and he knew, without a doubt, Alfred had built this utopia for him.

"We're too close to achieving what we set out to do." Randolph shook his head, trying to disguise the tics jerking his head to the side. "We can't go back. It would be far worse than before. Can you imagine?" There would be chaos and infighting. There would be no peace. No order. "Nothing got done before Alfred took control. It was just a matter of time before we annihilated ourselves." Most days, impending Armageddon had been all he could think about. But now, things were better. Now he could breathe.

"No one wants that." Bronsen stood and pulled him into his arms. "These rebels, they don't know what they want. We'll get rid of them."

"We can't go back. Nothing made sense before the U.N. took control. Alfred fixed things, lined everything up like dominoes." Perfectly ordered. No surprises.

When he'd taken over as the U.N.'s Prime Minister, he'd felt invincible. For the first time in his life, people looked to *him* for leadership, instead of Alfred. People listened to him.

Then Prudence left.

He hadn't cared at first, lying with her was a trial he'd had no stomach for. The way she'd stare at him unnerved him. He never felt in control when she was around. He'd decided since society had accepted him as their new leader and no one had challenged him, he didn't need to subject himself to her. But lately, fewer citizens came to his rallies. He'd heard what almost sounded like criticism from local media. Lately, he'd wondered if he needed Prudence and her gifts, after all. "Has anyone found my fiancée?"

"Are you sure you want to go that route?" Bronsen's green eyes bored into his. "I know how difficult you found the whole ordeal."

"People aren't listening." His neck popped as his head jerked to the side.

"You could hand things over to me for a while. I'll make them listen to you."

Randolph shook his head. "It's too far gone for that. No matter how much I hate the idea of fucking her, we have to find her." He would not go down in history as the Parnell brother who had failed. He'd held that title long enough.

"I know where she is." Bronsen's large hand stroked his back, comforting. "The day she left, she went to the Sisters of Charity. The Sisters wouldn't talk at first, but I . . . persuaded them to tell us where she went."

A shiver raced over Randolph. Bronsen was a master of torture and he'd taught Randolph everything he knew. He was only sorry he'd missed the chance to watch him work. "And?"

"She boarded *Genesis V* to Asteria. She'll arrive in about a month."

"What?" That couldn't be right. Why would anyone want go to that godforsaken planet? The trip took six months. Even *Apollo I*, its successor, was excruciatingly slow, taking a full four weeks to get to Asteria. His concerned gaze tangled with Bronsen's. "I'll n-n-never g-get her back in t-time."

Bronsen frowned. "You will calm down."

How? How could he possibly? Everything was falling apart. He pushed away from Bronsen.

He'd only taken a couple strides before Bronsen slammed Randolph against the wall, wrenching his arm against the small of his back. "Better?"

The world came into sharp focus. The firm pressure of his lover's weight, the pain from where his shoulder had collided with the wall—all if it grounded him. Randolph nodded.

"I haven't seen you like this in a long time. Are you taking your meds?"

Randolph tried to push away. He'd quit taking the Haldol. It made him fuzzy and with everything so calm, so ordered . . . . "I didn't need it."

"You do. You don't want the others seeing you like this, do you?" Bronsen rubbed his stubbly cheek against Randolph's hair. "You take your meds and I'll have you in Asteria in two weeks."

"How?"

"You've heard what they say—technology doubles its advances every six months." Bronsen bit his ear, sending a sharp pain shooting through his head. "The *Orion I* hasn't been publicly announced yet, but she's fit for a maiden voyage. We'll take a crew and a few soldiers."

Randolph grunted, reveling in his lover's solid embrace. "That's still too long. The war might be lost by then." He had no desire to be parted from his lover, but perhaps he should send Bronsen to retrieve Prudence and stay behind to ensure the Blue Helmets did their job.

"No one needs to know you're gone." Bronsen twisted his arm higher, almost to the breaking point, leaving Randolph panting. "The rebels had surprise on their side today. That's no longer the case. The Blue Helmets will rally; you'll call on the citizens of Earth to do their part. While we're away, you can stay abreast of what's happening while remaining safe from the war. We'll be back long before the rebels reach this part of the country, if they ever do. If you need Prudence at all, you'll need her after this little uprising has finished."

Bronsen's reasoning was sound. His military leaders were on guard now. They would rally. They had to. And the speeches he made in the aftermath would be the most important. He'd need to reclaim the faith of all Earthers amid blood and destruction—the antithesis of Alfred's dream. He needed Prudence if he wanted to be successful. "Do it. Get everything ready. When can we leave?"

Bronsen swung him around, pressing Randolph tight between the wall and his body. His mouth slanted over Randolph's, demanding, urgent. "Tonight. We'll arrive a couple weeks before *Genesis V*. We can stand at the arrivals gate and snatch Prudence up as she disembarks. We'll be back before anyone misses you."

Randolph nodded. Bronsen always knew what to do. Every time he began falling into the gaping abyss of madness, Bronsen always brought him back.

5

Griffin jerked awake with a gasp.

Flames engulfed the doll, the dainty plastic face melting into a gruesome death mask.

He shook his head, trying to clear his mind of the horrendous images.

Jesus, his jaw ached. Somehow, in the back of his mind, he'd hoped the pain would be gone by the time he woke, despite the spiked wires sealing his jaw closed. He opened his swollen eyes and tried to rub away the sleep, but the chain between his leg irons and cuffs prevented the movement.

Outside his chamber, puffs of smoke curled across the ceiling and for a heartbeat, he thought he was still captured within his dream. Was the ship on fire? Impossible. Life support, and therefore oxygen, should be limited to the hibernation chambers during flight to prevent such catastrophes.

Maybe it was his eyes. They were grainy, the lids heavy from sleep. He blinked several times to try to clear his vision. To his right, he spotted the bright-red hatch release. He rolled to his side, tucking his legs up as far as possible within the chamber's tight confines. He stretched his arms out, arched his back and strained toward the button.

Almost.

He tried again and this time, he managed to hit the edge of the button. It was enough. The hatch opened, hissing as the airlock released. The acrid scent of smoke assailed him.

He sat up, ripping the needle from his arm and detangling himself from all the electrode wires.

The ship *was* on fire.

Emergency strobes flashed and somewhere outside the room a siren blared. The smoke carried a bitter note of burnt plastic. The hibernation chambers should have released on their own during an emergency, waking their human occupants. Life support had turned on, they must be close to Asteria, but then why didn't the hibernation chambers open on their own?

Christ, he needed to get the hell off this ship. When they'd brought him aboard, he'd made note of the escape pods. There was one down the hall from this room.

He swung his legs over the side and dizziness assailed him. Weakened from hibernation, his stomach ached from lack of normal food. He stood, fighting off sickness, easing his weight onto legs that hadn't been used in a long while. His cuffs made moving difficult, forcing him to hunch over while he shuffled along on trembling legs.

The smoke grew thicker in the room and the lights blinked out, leaving the emergency strobes to light the way. Survival instinct urged him to the escape pod, but his gaze lit on the second hibernation chamber. He hesitated.

Go on, Payne, leave the Parnell woman and get the hell out of here.

God knew what kind of terror she'd bring to the unfortunate souls of Asteria. Why was she even here? Seemed pretty damned convenient she happened to occupy the same room as him. Did Randolph send her on some kind of mission to ensure his delivery to Asteria? He took another step toward the door, but paused, indecision plaguing him. *You never let harm befall a woman . . . unless she's trying to kill you.* His father's words echoed in his mind, driving a foul curse between his teeth. She hadn't tried to kill him. Yet.

Damn it, he couldn't leave her. Not after she saved him. Hell, maybe she'd be good leverage when it was time to go home. Randolph Parnell wouldn't want his fiancée harmed. She might keep him from being blown out of the sky upon his return to Earth.

He pulled the emergency release for her chamber. She was sound asleep, her black-dyed locks spread out around her. She wore nothing but panties and a skimpy tank which left little to the imagination and holy hell, she was a beautiful woman. He sat on the edge, pulling his legs up so he had enough chain to reach into the pod. He strained against his restraints, easing the needle from her arm and detangled her from the electrode wires.

Only after a lot of uncomfortable, awkward maneuvering did he happen to see the keys. They appeared identical to those the Blue Helmets carried. How did she come to have them? He leaned forward until he'd sprawled across the width of her chamber—thighs over one edge, shoulders over the other—bowing his back until he managed to reach them. Going through, one by one, he found a small cuff key, released himself from his bonds, and stuffed the keys and the cuffs into one of his leg pockets.

He stretched his back and rubbed his chaffed wrists. Ah, yes. That was better.

The smoke grew thicker, changing from white, wispy clouds to a dense gray fog. Breathing became more difficult and he lifted the hem of his shirt to cover his nose and mouth. Why the hell wasn't the woman waking up on her own? He leaned into the pod and patted her cheek.

She jerked awake with a gasp, those lavender eyes staring at him with incomprehension, then widening in horror. "You."

Yeah, him. Damn society misses couldn't even be appreciative when a base-born rescued them. "Gotta get out." He spoke through clenched teeth, the barbs locking his jaw shut ripping into his inner cheeks and tongue making each word agonizing.

Her gaze darted around the room. "What did you do?"

He lowered his shirt and pulled a face. Seriously? He'd been asleep like everyone else.

Pink stained her cheeks. "Sorry."

Griffin slid off the pod and grabbed her clothes, thrusting them into her hands. While she dressed, he snatched up her bag and—the damned thing was heavy as hell. Did she pack her whole closet? He grabbed up her shoes, took a med kit off the wall, and unlocked the door.

"Where's the escape pod?" She held the sleeve of her sweater over her nose and mouth, muffling her words and leaving only those wide, lavender eyes visible.

He took hold of her hand and went out into the hall. No one was around; whether the other passengers had already fled, or still slept in their chambers he couldn't say. Orange light flickered at the far end of the smoke-filled hallway. By some miracle, the escape pod was still there. They didn't get move more than a couple steps before another door swung open and three Blue Helmets came barreling into the hall, halting on sight him.

"Freeze."

Like hell. The fuckers weren't armed—their side-arms were locked up in-flight. He released the woman and allowed instinct and years of training take over. He grabbed the two closest by their throats and knocked their heads together hard enough to crack helmets. As they crumpled to the ground, he kicked out at the last, slamming his foot down on the bastard's knee. The Blue Helmet screamed as he dropped to the floor. Griffin grabbed him by the shirt, lifting him long enough to punch him in the throat. The Blue Helmet didn't make a sound when he slumped down next to his comrades.

The bright orange light at the end of the hall grew brighter; flames licked up the side of the passageway.

Hell, should he try to find Peggy? Parnell had held his neighbor hostage during the trial, threatening him with her death should Griffin say anything he didn't like. He wasn't even sure she was on the ship, though, and they needed to get out of here quick. He turned to grab the woman.

She flinched away.

They didn't have time for this shit. He scowled, motioning her closer.

She shook her head.

Griffin strode over and hauled her over his shoulder. She was fast becoming more irritation than she was worth. He opened the hatch and lowered her inside. The small one-person craft had a small space to store essentials and one seat with a three-pronged seatbelt.

He'd have to find a different pod for himself.

She stared up at him with wide, terrified eyes, stopping him from closing the hatch. "I don't want to go alone. I don't know what to do."

Less than a minute ago she didn't want anything to do with him.

Tears spiked her thick, dark lashes. "Please."

Shit. He pushed her into the seat.

"Come with me." She became as tenacious as an octopus after crab meat, her hands grabbing at his, while he tried to shake her off long enough to strap her in.

He slapped her hand.

She reared back with a shocked gasp.

He shook his head, securing the straps over her chest, latching them into the three-pronged buckle and pulling them tight. As he turned to leave, he heard the click of the belt.

The woman lunged forward, hitting the button to close the hatch, sealing them together inside.

Did she have any idea what she'd done? There was one seat. *One seatbelt.* And two of them in a small, cramped, very hard pod that was about to make a brutal emergency landing.

Jesus H. Christ, she was a lunatic.

She shrugged. "You don't know if there are any more pods."

He had no opportunity to respond. The vessel ejected from the ship, throwing them both to the floor.

Griffin checked the display panel while he got up: It showed the image of a pod with a little dotted line headed for Asteria. That line grew shorter by the second.

They had maybe five or six minutes before they landed.

He shoved her belongings and the med kit into the storage bin. Then stared at the flight seat.

"Can I help with something? What do we—?"

Griffin scowled her into silence. He was pretty damn sure she'd done quite enough.

They had two choices. Either he strapped her down, probably killing them both as his body was flung around the pod, or he took the seat and secured her to him, hoping to hell he could hold on to her during impact.

Damn it! He pulled her bag out, found a couple of sweaters and shoved the rest back in the storage bin. He took the seat, strapping himself in and motioning her to sit on his lap. She backed away. What was she thinking? He yanked her into his lap, grateful she was such a tiny bit of a thing. He tied the sweaters from her bag around her middle, and used the cuffs he'd kept to secure her to the seat. With a little luck the padding would prevent the chain from cutting through her when they landed and he wouldn't emerge from the vessel covered in blood and regret.

The distance counter on the wall ticked off the miles, the number growing smaller and smaller. They could die in the next few minutes, but that didn't stop his dick from taking notice of the woman in his lap. She wriggled, trying to get comfortable and he almost moaned as that sweet little backside of hers snuggled up tight to his groin. He wrapped his arms around her, and crossed his legs over her extended ones.

The woman was chanting. Praying, rather. For herself most likely. Typical for a Parnell.

Her face nestled to his neck and her arms covered his. She laced her fingers with his. She must be scared as hell because society misses like her did not touch the riff-raff.

The pod jolted and bounced as they began their decent into Asteria's atmosphere. The craft filled with the noise of a dozen trains barreling down on them and the temperature spiked.

On the monitor, flames surrounded the pod in the animated display, the little dotted line was almost gone now. The noise diminished.

Five dotted lines left.

She continued to pray, her voice rising and her fingers squeezing his.

Four lines left.

Now that he could hear her clearly, he was stunned.

Three left.

"Dearest goddess, keep us safe. Let no harm befall us. Dearest goddess . . . ."

Two.

She was praying for *them.*

6

The lavender sky matched her eyes.

Griffin stumbled out of the escape pod, his boots sinking into soft, glittering black sand. His jaw throbbed something fierce and dried blood caked his nose. He must have hit something hard during the landing. Probably that crazed female's thick head.

Where the hell was she? There was a beacon on the pod and he wanted to be hell and gone from here before Blue Helmets showed up to rescue the pod's occupants. He scanned the barren landscape, seeing nothing but an endless sea of black sand. In the far distance, jagged mountains spiked up from the horizon, impossibly high and unwelcoming.

The sun here didn't shine a warm, happy yellow, but glared a stark and cold white. Its light brightened Asteria with the same harsh illumination of a surgical lamp in an exam room.

He returned to the pod long enough to check for, and retrieve, the small cache of emergency supplies stocked in the compartment under the seat and stuff them into his pockets. It wasn't much: a few packets of pain killers, some antiseptic swabs, two small, boxed waters, and four protein bars. The Parnell woman had taken her pack and the med-kit.

Damn her anyways. He needed that kit to get the wires out of his mouth. Hell, he supposed he needed her for the task, too. He'd passed out when they'd put the damn things in and he wasn't so arrogant to assume he wouldn't lose consciousness when they came out.

This time when he exited, he walked around the other side of the craft. Several tall, cylindrical, multi-colored buildings rose up in the distance from the barren landscape. The sun glinted off their flat metal roofs. That wasn't a spaceport. It was an outpost. Those buildings were manned by . . . who? Blue Helmets? Locals? Criminals?

She must be headed there. He set out at a quick clip. The lunatic female probably thought she'd find civilization. Maybe she would. This is where the Parnells sent the poor, the ill, and the non-compliant. The outpost could be a town of normal, average citizens, trying to get by. His brother, Lucan, might even be there.

What concerned him was the fact they'd sent *him* here. He doubted he was the first convicted felon sent to Asteria, though the U.N. denied doing so. The prison he and Peggy had been housed in had been empty and the U.N. was publically opposed to the death penalty. All the criminals must have gone somewhere. He didn't buy into the idea that crime had vanished with the implementation of Parnell's vision.

He slowed at the edge of the settlement. The place appeared to be a ghost town at first glance; the whole area was eerily quiet. The buildings had been patched together with scrap from the earliest flights to Asteria. The nine silo-like buildings sported no windows. Why? Was the climate here so harsh? Did Asteria have predators aggressive enough to break through the glass? Or were these buildings left over from an era of atmosphere building?

He knocked on the first door and, when he received no answer, he slipped in. The place was sparse. It was a home of sorts, but more in line with a barracks than a residence. No art or knickknacks decorated the place. The only splashes of color were the battered squares of ship-siding that had been repurposed to create walls, floors, and stairs. He found a barrel serving as a nightstand on the second floor, and a makeshift hammock with a few rumpled blankets thrown across it. A crate that was off to the side held a holey pair of shoes and a few sets of shabby clothes. One was a prison-orange jumpsuit. Well, that answered one question: At least one man in this town was a felon.

Whoever lived here didn't have much, but he had an old blaster—*had* being the operative word, because now the weapon belonged to Griffin. He tucked the gun into his waistband at his back and slipped outside. As he entered the next building, somewhere nearby, a chorus of male voices rose in excited shouts.

He'd found the woman.

Walking in here had been a colossal mistake.

Prudence had wanted to find help for Chief Payne. Unable to rouse him, and too weak to lift him, there hadn't been any other option. She couldn't leave him unconscious in the desert overnight, and she'd be damned if she'd stay out there alone with him.

But there was no help to be found here.

This building must be the cantina. Half a dozen round tables sat around the room. Men squatted on stools, barrels, and buckets and stood clustered in groups of two and three. A long counter made of the same sheet metal as the building ran the length of the back of the room and several bottles of what looked to be liquor were lined up at one end.

The dirty, shady-looking men filling the space hadn't responded to her plea for help. They had stared. At her. By the look on their faces they hadn't seen a new person in town in some time. Or, maybe it was females they hadn't seen in ages.

Some aspect of their too-bright eyes made her edgy—made her hair stand on end as if she faced a ravenous pack of wolves instead of a group of human beings. Her heart rate increased as a healthy dose of adrenaline encouraged her to flee.

"Sorry, gentleman." She forced a smile, gripped the strap of her pack tighter and backed toward the door. The biggest of the lot, an old, grizzly male moved to stand. "No, no. Please don't get up."

He didn't grant her request.

And her exit was blocked.

She came up hard against someone, jumped, and spun around. Another male, this one with a deep scar cut into his cheek, stood between her and the door. Stumbling back, she bumped into another man. Ugh, they stank.

"Where'd you come from, darlin'?"

She turned on her heel to find the owner of that question. The older man. White streaked his hair, silver gleamed off his front tooth and there was a distinct coldness to his blue eyes.

"I am in the wrong place." She swallowed. "So sorry to disturb you nice gentlemen."

"Oh, I wouldn't use the word disturb, necessarily." Silver Tooth's grin broadened. "Though you are doing something profound to me."

Laughter erupted in the tension.

"I'll go." She tried again for the door, but others had circled around and no one moved to get out of her way. Hungry eyes roamed over her. "Please."

"Now, darlin', as long as you're not difficult, we'll make sure you have a real nice time."

Several murmurs of agreement rose from the crowd.

"You don't . . . . You don't want me." She folded her arms around herself and shook her head. "I'm diseased. Contagious. That's why they sent me here."

His silver tooth flashed as he grinned. "You're in good company."

It took her a moment to understand his meaning. They didn't care because they were already sick. Her stomach churned. Desperate to escape, she stomped on Scarface's foot and when he moved, she ran past him. The door was in sight. Only a few more feet to freedom. She reached her arm out, ready to grasp and pull the handle once she reached it.

Someone grabbed hold of her hair and yanked her to a halt.

Prudence screamed. Pain lanced through her scalp. She pressed her hands to her head, trying to keep him from tearing her hair out.

The men seized her, holding her by the arms and legs. They lifted her in the air and her gut bottomed out. Oh, goddess, she was going to be sick.

Shouts of excitement rose as they carried her deeper into the room.

Prudence fought, kicking and scratching, trying to twist out of their relentless grips. All the while she prayed for divine intervention. She'd escaped playing whore to Randolph. She'd rather die than to play one for this lot. Her heart slammed in her chest as they hauled her onto one of the dirty tables and yanked her legs wide.

A loud crack reverberated through the room, silencing everyone. The hands pawing her paused and all eyes swung toward the sound. Chief Payne stood in the doorway like an avenging angel, blaster in hand. He pointed to her and motioned her over.

Prudence attempted to rise, but the hands restraining her didn't move.

Another crack issued in the room and this time the man pinning her arms jerked back. One small, black hole appeared in his forehead. As she stared, a tendril of smoke rose from the hole and he fell to the ground. Ah, goddess be blessed, he was dead. Her stomach cramped and bile threatened to choke her. Chief Payne had killed him.

No. Chief Payne rescued me.

Dragging in a deep breath, she sat, glaring at the man holding her legs. He released her, raising his arms in surrender. Prudence slid off the table, staggering as she applied her full weight to her shaking limbs. Part of her wanted to run. To hide. Another demanded vengeance. The sickening knot in her belly roiled into a violent anger she'd never experienced before. Pulling herself to her full height, she took a step closer to the old codger who seemed to lead this pack of wolves. Her hands fisted.

"No." Chief Payne shook his head and motioned to her again.

There was no give in his command, no doubt she would obey. She resented him—his confidence in his supremacy over her—despite the fact he had rescued her. Briefly, her eyes narrowed on the silver-toothed leader, but the moment of fierce anger had passed. Tremors returned with staggering force. She darted through the males, pausing once to grab her bag. When she reached Chief Payne's side, all she wanted to do was lean on him, seek comfort and reassurance.

Goddess preserve her, was she mad? He was a male, and as violent as the rest.

He didn't spare her a glance, just jerked his head to the side, indicating she should leave. Would he kill them all? Prudence gave the men in the room one last, cursory glance before turning her back on them and walking outside.

When the cool, fresh air blew over her, the reality of what had almost happened hit. Tears poured down her cheeks. She doubled over and gagged. This was supposed to be her chance to be independent. For years, she'd dreamed of making her own way and growing stronger.

How stupid was she? Nothing was different here. *She* wasn't different here.

She couldn't take anymore. She wanted away from all of them. So she fled. She ran straight out of the filthy outpost and kept going until her legs wouldn't carry her any farther.

Griffin waited until the woman was outside before turning his attention to the men. He probably should have followed her out, but he needed information.

"Weapons aren't allowed in city limits," the big ugly one said. "She your woman?"

Griffin nodded once and despite what a pain-in-the-ass she was, realized he wasn't wholly averse to the idea. With an internal shake of his head, he braced himself for the pain speaking caused. "Is anyone else in this settlement?"

Big Ugly shook his head. "Just us."

Relief washed through him. His brother wasn't with these miscreants. With a little luck, Lucan had found somewhere safe, surrounded by others like him. "How far to the next town?" He swallowed a mouthful of blood, hoping to hell he didn't look as shitty as he felt. Showing these assholes weakness would not be wise.

"Seen ships flying over, landing on the other side of the mountains. You'll never make it. Your best bet is to stick around here with your woman."

Yeah, and he'd bet a full day wouldn't pass before he died in his sleep and she became the camp whore.

An older man with thick white hair, snorted. "No one survives outside town. The Scarecrows'll pick you clean before you get far."

Scarecrows? Hell, if his mouth wasn't throbbing so bad he'd ask what they were, but he didn't have the capacity for chit-chat right now. They were talking in circles and he was pissed as hell he needed to repeat his question. "Where's the closest town?"

Several of the men laughed. "Clear 'cross the desert out to the west, or past the mountains in the south."

"What's north and east?"

"Unexplored territory."

Griffin eyed the men. He couldn't tell if they spoke the truth or not. What the hell was he doing? Nothing these assholes had to say could be trusted. He motioned with the gun to the back of the room. "Over there." Once they complied, he walked to the counter and hopped over. There wasn't much by way of supplies, but he found a backpack with a blanket, a couple tools, night goggles, salt, and some fruit. He grabbed a bottle of liquor for good measure and stuffed it in the pack.

Beggars couldn't be choosers.

On his way out, he paused long enough to lift one of the bar stools and slam it over the counter, breaking off a leg. He took the thick piece of wood with him. Backing out of the room, with the gun trained on the men, he pulled the door open, exited, slammed it shut and rammed the broken stool leg into the door handle. That chair leg wouldn't hold them long, but it bought him some time.

Seconds later, the door rattled as the men tried to get through.

Griffin turned to grab the woman. She was gone. Only the deep, aching throb in his mouth kept him from cursing a blue-streak. He lifted both arms to the alien sky, silently asking whatever god might be up there, *Are you fucking kidding me?*

The wind had picked up, creating little whirlwinds and rearranging the black sand. If he didn't hurry, he'd have no chance in hell of finding her.

Behind him, someone rattled the door violently. The stool leg held in place. For now.

He scanned the ground, searching for footprints. He'd expected she'd return to the pod—the one familiar place on this planet—but he couldn't find any sign she'd gone that direction. He circled all the way around before seeing her footprints. There. Due east. If those men had spoken the truth, she was headed straight into unexplored territory. Then again, they could've lied. He would've in their situation.

Griffin shouldered his stolen pack and ran into the desert.

7

Someone was following her.

Prudence's heart was trying to gallop right out of her chest via her throat. She pressed her back up against the sharp stone outcropping and went still.

Everything had gone silent. She heard no more footsteps, no heavy breathing.

The brisk wind swept over the desert floor, dragging the sand into an ever-changing landscape. Whirlwinds carried the black stuff into the air in miniature tornados.

She eased to the side and peered around the stone. Whatever she'd heard had gone. With a sigh, she closed her eyes and leaned back against the rocks. When she opened them a scant second later, she screamed.

Chief Payne had found her. With the quick grace of a predator, he grabbed her arm and clicked something around her wrist. A handcuff. The other end was already secured around his arm.

"No!" She wrested her hand away, inadvertently pulling him closer. "What are you doing? Why are—?"

His hand clamped down over her mouth. "Shut it, lady. Those friends of yours might come looking. So decide, them or me."

She stared at him in dawning horror. After everything she'd gone through to escape Randolph Parnell, after barely avoiding being gang-raped, he was going to do the deed. He was no better than the rest of them.

He turned away, which yanked her arm forward and, as he crouched to sit with his back to her, she almost ended up with her face plastered against his backside. Something in her snapped and she shoved him. He did a face plant in the dirt, the cuffs linking them dragging her forward, too. She landed on top of his back, fisted her hands and punched his head and shoulders, kicking him as hard as she could.

With a swift, powerful roll he pinned her beneath him, his palm once again covering her mouth. She struggled. One of her hands ended up between them, but she punched and pushed at him with the other until with a curse he released her mouth and squished her other hand between their bodies, too.

He glared down at her, speaking through clamped teeth. "Have I hurt you?"

"Yes! You're hurting me now."

"Before you attacked me, have I ever hurt you?"

Her mouth opened to scream yes, but his expression shifted, his eyes narrowing. She shook her head.

Griffin got up, dragging her with him. "Sit." He motioned toward the rocks she'd huddled against earlier.

She did as he said, shaking so hard she wasn't sure how she'd have the strength to fight him again. He wasn't like the Parnells. He was larger and more muscular than even Randolph. And he wasn't like that pack of ruffians, either—he was controlled, calm.

He sat on his haunches next to her. "Spread your legs."

She gasped. "What?"

With a loud sigh, he grabbed her knees, thrust her legs apart and lay between them. Before she got past her shock enough to fight, he pressed his shoulders between her thighs and rested the back of his head on one. He held his hand up with some kind of tool in it. "Wire cutters."

She looked down at him and he smiled—grimaced really—and she gasped again. His teeth were bloody and thin barbed wires crisscrossed over and between them.

"Okay?"

Okay? No, it wasn't okay. No wonder he didn't speak during the trial, he probably couldn't. "You—" She shook her head. "You want me to cut them out?"

He nodded.

"I don't know what to do."

Griffin reached up and undid the cuff from her wrist. She almost sighed in relief, but before she could, he had the cuff around her ankle, instead.

She glared.

He showed her the keys before tossing them several feet away. "Don't. Hurt. Me."

Prudence snatched the wire cutters. "I'm strong. I could drag your dead body that far."

The corner of his mouth tilted up and he shook his head. "Weak."

She bristled at the insult. The man could hardly speak, every word must be excruciating, yet he thought it was important enough to tell her he thought her weak. "And you're stupidly brave to goad me when I could cause you unspeakable pain."

His gaze shifted away and his throat rippled as he swallowed. Hard.

Master Chief Griffin Jude Payne was scared. Of her. That was a bit of a revelation. True, he appeared to be in a vulnerable position. But was he? She'd seen the way he moved, all coiled power behind easy movements until he chose to strike. Then he was quick as hell and twice as deadly. Back on the ship he'd taken down three Blue Helmets in less than a minute. He might not like being in this position, but she wasn't stupid enough to assume him vulnerable.

Still, he hadn't hurt her, not really, even though she must have caused him pain when she punched his face. "But I won't." She waited until his sea green eyes searched hers. "Because I'm a better person than that."

He spread his lips and she used her thumb to help push his full lower lip out of the way. The wires pulled tight against his teeth, the little barbs pointed out to do the maximum damage to inner lips and cheeks. She snipped the first wire, groaning as the cutters slipped and gouged his gums. A bead of blood welled. She was doing more damage than good. "I'm so sorry." Tears sprang to her eyes. "I can't do this. I'm gonna hurt you."

With his un-cuffed hand, he reached up and wiped her tears. "Worse if you don't."

Prudence sniffed and wiped the backs of her hands over her eyes. She could do this. If she wanted to be a pioneer on Asteria, she'd have to treat injuries from time to time. What were a few nicks in the face of split skin every time he tried to talk?

She moved to the next wire, but he caught her shaky hand in his. "Breathe."

She took a deep breath and nodded. Huddling over her task, she was all too aware of her breast snuggled against his face as she maneuvered the cutters around the next wire. Her lips thinned as her nipples tightened and something deep in her stomach sprang to life. Her body was ridiculous. Here she was, a mouse with a wounded lion sprawled in her lap, waiting for her to make one wrong move so he could gobble her up.

This was not the time to be aroused.

She never got aroused.

She sounded like she was in the throes of passion.

Griffin bent his knees, planting his feet flat on the ground to hide his budding erection. With each snip of the cutters, she moaned in sympathy. He could imagine a hundred different ways he wanted to make this gorgeous woman moan and not a damned one of them involved sympathy.

He must be in a bad way if his errant body responded to dental work.

"The front ones are loose. I need you to turn to the side."

He held her gaze for a moment, willing her to understand how much he was trusting her. How much she'd regret betraying him. Turning, he placed his cheek to the soft pad of her thigh. He could smell her, eucalyptus and musk. His cock jumped in anticipation.

She pulled his cheek back and the cutters, warmed by her hand, slipped toward his back teeth. *Concentrate on that. The pain. The thought of freedom. Wanting this woman goes against everything you believe. She's a Parnell, for Christ's sake.*

But there wasn't much pain. She executed each cut with care, removed each wire gingerly to prevent further harm.

What is her name? He had researched the Parnells. He remembered her name had a double P—P Parnell. Something old fashion. Petunia? Paris? Portia?

"This one's going to hurt. The wire is too tight; I'll have to snip it up by the gum."

He slipped his arm under her leg and flexed around her to keep himself from jerking away at a critical moment. Smooth metal scrapped his gums. The woman tensed. Snip. He relaxed with a sigh as she pulled out another piece of barbed wire and bent back to her work.

How long had it been since he'd been between a woman's thighs? Since before his last tour, at least. He'd buried his parents on his last leave and that was what, two years ago, plus the six months travel time to Asteria? So, too long. That's how long it'd been.

She stroked her hand down his face. "Other side."

Griffin rolled over and wrapped his arms around her other leg the best he could while cuffed to her ankle. This was going to be a bitch. Once she made the last cut, she'd have to pull the big one out.

Jesus, the Parnells were sadistic bastards. He hated the lot of them. *All of them?* Yes, damn it. This one may be convenient and beautiful, but she was still a Parnell. He wouldn't hurt her if she behaved, but he damn sure didn't have to like her.

"You can make noise." She cut another wire and moaned. "I won't tell anyone."

He almost laughed. She'd hear him make some noise all right. Right after she finished with these external wires. When that last one came through his tongue, he had no doubt the pain would unman him. Parnell and his buddy Bronsen had taken great pleasure in reminding him he'd passed out when they pulled the damn thing through. Those barbs hurt like hell.

"Almost done."

If only.

"There." She started to tug on that last wire and he gripped her wrist to stop her. He took a moment to stretch his stiff jaw. The joint screamed in agony after not being used in the last nine months. After opening and closing his jaw a few times, he opened it as wide as he could and stuck out his tongue so she could see how the wire had been pierced through.

She stared into his mouth, her eyes reflecting the horror of what she saw. Her head started to shake from side to side and she reared back as if to flee. He lifted his hand to stop her.

When she met his gaze, he nodded once. "Oo at." Great. He sounded like a drunk toddler.

Holding his tongue against his teeth, he parted them enough so she could pull the wire through. He made a jerking motion with his hand to show her he wanted her to rip it out fast.

"Chief Payne, I can't."

He nodded once and lay his face in her lap, flexing his arms around her leg. He was done discussing the matter. It needed to be done and she'd better get on with it.

The wire tugged at his tongue a couple times as she wrapped one end around her finger. His heart hammered in his chest and sweat broke out on his brow.

"One."

He wanted to tell her to get it over with already.

"Two."

Damn, this was going to hurt.

"Three."

She screamed.

Griffin didn't make a sound.

"Chief Payne?"

His grip on her leg would leave bruises. His face pressed into her jeans and a shudder ran through every tensed inch of him. For a heartbeat or two, he didn't appear any tougher than a toddler, with his eyes screwed up tight and his whole body seeking some kind of feminine comfort. She dropped the wire cutters and wrapped her arms around him best she could. "It's all over now. All done. You were very brave."

When he released her leg and pushed back, she sat back to accept his gratitude.

He glared. He sat up, turned away and spit blood on the ground.

No more little boy, just a surly, testosterone-filled, badass now. When he tried to stand, she pulled the chain linking them together. "Come here. I have a med-wand."

"'Ow ma'y?"

If he'd been difficult to understand before, now it was almost impossible. "Just the one, but that's all you need."

"'Eep it."

"Goddess save me from prideful males. You need it. I don't." She pulled the thin silver wand out of her backpack. "Come here."

He shook his head, and spit again. She glanced down at the bloody bit of wire she'd pulled out of him. Three jagged spurs jutted out at various angles. His tongue must be shredded.

The chain linking them tugged at her leg as he tried to stand. Tried being the operative word. He dropped back to his knees, his eyes rolled back and he slumped face-first in the sand. Men. At least he'd landed closer to the cuff key.

Prudence collected her bag, slipped the wire cutters inside one of the pockets, and set it next to Griffin. The little tool might come in handy again. She scooted past Griffin, careful not to tug on the chain linking them, to see how close she could get to the key.

Not close enough.

She tried lying on her belly, her cuffed ankle extended toward Griffin, and stretching her hands toward the keys. She almost giggled in glee when they jangled beneath her fingers. It took her awhile, but she nudged them closer until she could wrap her fingers around them.

Prudence unlocked herself, then Griffin. The cuffs and keys went into her pack. They might come in handy, too.

Now, for the dangerous part. Kneeling next to him, she rolled Griffin onto his back. He was a mess—his cheeks were swollen and blood dripped from his mouth. She slipped the med-wand between his parted lips. The scanner clicked on, assessing the damage and beeped twice when finished. She withdrew the device, calibrated the wand as the scan suggested and put it back between his lips.

Griffin moaned when the device clicked back into action. Med-wands were handy tools, but painful. It took several minutes before the med-wand clicked off. She set it down next to him and used the edge of his shirt to wipe away the last few droplets of blood beading on his lips. She had to pull his shirt all the way up so it bunched under his armpits to reach his face, and that's when she noticed his tattoo—the eagle, globe, and anchor over his heart. The mark of a Marine. She traced the outline of the anchor.

Her father had been a Marine. That's how he'd met her mother. Daddy would be so upset by what the Parnells had done. She missed him terribly but was glad he wasn't around to see the country he loved so much fold without even the flicker of a fight. Her father had raised her to respect and depend on Marines. They were true heroes. Now Chief Payne was the last.

He was a beautiful specimen of a male. Lean and muscular, with the face of an angel.

Yes, well, the Christians' Lucifer was an angel, too. That didn't make him trustworthy.

Marine or not, she couldn't rely on a male. Prudence forced herself to stand. She came to Asteria to be free. To be independent. To find her courage. Not to be further manhandled and abused.

She surveyed the desolate landscape. This was her new home. She'd studied every scan she could find on the place, learning about the plants, the animals, and the natives—the Scarecrows. The native creatures didn't come into the desert.

She didn't have much to worry about out here but the sun. And men. But once she reached the mountains, then she'd need to be careful. Either she'd die out there, or she'd become the woman she'd always wanted to be.

With one last glance at Chief Payne, she said a prayer for his safe-keeping and headed out into the Black Desert.

8

Randolph Parnell paced the length of the arrivals gate at Asteria spaceport.

This wasn't good. This was not good at all. All his grand plans to continue Alfred's dream were unraveling. Back on Earth, forty-six percent of his strongholds had been commandeered by the rebels. In some areas of the world, his own men had turned on him, switching sides and joining the rebel forces.

He needed Prudence. But *Genesis V* had yet to arrive. They'd lost contact a little over an hour before *Genesis V*'s scheduled landing. He glanced at Bronsen, who was speaking to spaceport security. Their words were low and urgent, their faces drawn into serious masks, making anxiety claw at Randolph's insides. Bronsen said he'd take care of everything. He already had men searching. If Prudence survived, they'd find her.

Whatever this was, whatever had happened, it must be because of Chief Payne. The man was a walking disaster. He should've killed Payne while he had the chance, but he hadn't wanted to tarnish the sterling reputation Alfred had created for the U.N. Chief Payne wouldn't be so lucky when their paths crossed again.

Bronsen turned and strode over to Randolph, putting an arm around his shoulders and guiding him off to one side where they wouldn't be heard by the others. "The ship is dead in space. There was a fire, which gutted most of the craft before the flames broke through the external bulkhead and the vacuum of space extinguished the fire. Fifteen escape pods were ejected. They landed all over Asteria's Southern Hemisphere. It'll take some time to determine who landed where."

Randolph pressed his fingers to his eyes to stop the rapid-fire blinking. That particular tic was driving him insane. "What's the likelihood Prudence is on one?"

"Pretty good, actually."

Thank God. As long as she lived, he still had hope.

"Both her and her roommate's life-chambers opened prior to the craft losing power. The escape pod outside their room did eject. There's an excellent probability they were on board."

"Can't we track their pod?"

Bronsen frowned. "Had the ship still been intact, yes. But we lost the beacon tracking device when *Genesis V*'s AI systems shut down. All we have to go on is the demographic feeds sent prior to the system crash."

"Damn it." Anything could happen to her out there and then what? How would he convince the people of Earth they needed him, that they wanted Utopia, that the rebels were all criminals? "What about the roommate? Anyone we know?" Hopefully someone who could get her to civilization safely.

Bronsen grimaced.

"Well, who is she with?"

"Chief Payne."

Randolph cursed and pushed away from Bronsen, his eyes blinked so hard, so fast they were starting to water. "It's him."

"Jesus." Bronsen pulled him back, glancing around before pinning Randolph with his gaze. "Quietly."

"Some—" Bronsen squeezed his fingers and Randolph lowered his tone. "Somehow, all of this is because of him." He pressed the heel of his free hand to his eye, willing his lid to stop with the infernal twitching. "How the hell did he meet Prudence? Has she been fucking him this whole time? Is that how he got the rebels to fight for him?"

Bronsen shushed him. "Don't let anyone see you upset. Breathe, baby. I have no idea, but my best guess is that all of this is coincidence."

"Bullshit."

"We had him in our custody during the trial, Randy. Prudence never got near him. She couldn't." His frown deepened. "Why are you acting like a jealous lover?"

Bronsen didn't understand. Chief Payne had gotten his intelligence from somewhere. From someone. And where did Prudence get the idea to board *Genesis V*? And the money? She was far too meek to come up with such a scheme on her own. The bastard killed his brother and now evidence pointed to Prudence helping with the assassination. "I'm not jealous, I'm pissed as hell. What if she conspired with Payne to assassinate Alfred?"

Bronsen's eyes widened, his expression suggesting he'd never considered the possibility.

"I'll be damned if that bitch makes me out for a fool. If she had anything to do with this Rebel uprising, anything to do with Alfred's death—" He swung around, not wanting anyone to see the emotion choking him. How could she? After all the time and energy they'd spent bringing her into the height of society? She was an orphan, a base-born, and an alien. She should be thankful they paid her any attention at all.

Bronsen forced him to stop his pacing and cupped his face in his hands. "We're going to get them both and when we do, Prudence can watch while we show her what we do to traitors. We'll make Payne talk and if she had anything to do with Alfred's death, she'll wish she was dead."

9

He was going to kill her, if she wasn't dead already.

Griffin kicked the used med-wand, shattering it against the rock outcropping. Blasted woman. What the hell had she been thinking to waste the damn thing for this? For him?

The desert night offered no answers, just a deep, dark, unsettling stillness. There was no moon to light the sky. Even the stars looked dimmer here than on Earth.

Damn. He had no idea what to expect out there. His plan had been to research Asteria from the comfort of prison. Yeah, right. If he hadn't been in court, he'd been being tortured. Questioned. The months he'd spent in that prison were a blur of pain and disillusionment. If he'd been skeptical of people before, now he was goddamned cynical.

Griffin ran his hand down his face. His perfect, healed face. Not even his tongue ached anymore. Part of him was grateful, but mostly he was pissed. His had not been a life-threatening injury and med-wands were not exactly abundant out here. What would she do if she got injured?

He walked back to the dim outline of the rocks and found his pack. Praise Jesus, at least she wasn't a thief.

It's back to two for two, buddy. You saved her twice, she saved you twice.

Even. He didn't like even. He'd much rather have her in his debt. He dug through the pack he'd stolen until he came across his weapon. He stuck the blaster in his pants at the small of his back. Then he dug some more until he found the night vision glasses. He slipped them on and the desert lit up a bright lavender.

Like her eyes.

To hell with her eyes.

Why are you planning to go after her, then?

Was he? He wasn't even sure which way she went. Away from that outpost, no doubt, but that left three directions. She didn't give him the sense she was lost. It had taken him almost two hours to catch up to her yesterday and in all that time she'd headed in a straight line.

But she's alone. Down one med-wand.

His damned conscience was going to drive him stark-raving batshit crazy. He scanned the desert floor until he found the grooves of her footprints in the black sand. "Gotcha."

She must have some clue where she was headed as determined as she was.

He walked out into the desert night with confident strides, secure in his belief she couldn't have gone too far. But as the night wore on and the horizon lit with dawn, he began to wonder how long he'd slept. Aside from an occasional footprint, he saw no sign of her—or anyone else. The desert was barren, the wind shuffling the sand the sole sound. He saw no birds, no reptiles, no people. He was alone. The thought brought him up short, unsettling him. How long could they survive out here in the baking sun with no other life to support them? There were no animals to hunt. No plants to eat. No water. The challenge of continuing to cross the desert became daunting, indeed. So much so, that like any sane man, he considered going back.

But if all this made him nervous, what must the woman be feeling? She must be terrified. If he could find her, she would no doubt be grateful and gladly tell him everything.

Griffin pressed on, sometimes jogging, but mostly walking, conserving his energy. He'd wait until tonight to drink one of the boxed waters. In the cool darkness his body would be able to retain the liquid for a while.

By the time he caught up with her, it was almost dusk and he heard her long before he saw her. She'd made it clear across the desert flats and into what he'd begun to think of as enemy territory. She was damned brave. Or crazy as a feline snorting catnip.

From a distance, with the desert heat wafting up from the sand and making objects in the distance appear to move, he thought he'd seen people walking ahead of him. They were rocks. The haphazard black outcroppings jutted up in strange, thin octagonal shapes resembling large crystals except they held no beauty. They did, however, carry an echo: When she screamed, the sound bounced off the rocks, comming from everywhere and nowhere all at once.

Griffin pulled his sidearm and froze, listening for any other sound. There was a shuffling and a thud. Softer, the sound didn't echo as much and he zeroed in on her location, setting off at a sprint. When she screamed a second time, his heart leapt in his chest.

Had she run into more locals? Wild animals? He barreled past the rocks, dodging this way and that. He was closer. He could hear her sobbing. Moaning. Adrenaline surged through him as the urge to kill, to protect or die trying, swelled through him. Griffin ran past one last stand of stone and came to an abrupt halt.

She was sprawled on the ground with something pinned beneath her legs, pounding the living hell out of it with a rock. "Die, damn you." Crying in earnest, her swings grew weaker by the second and the moaning creature wasn't going down without a fight.

Was that a scarecrow? He strode over, aimed and fired a laser in its brain. At least he hoped that's what he hit—both ends of the creature looked remarkably similar.

Prudence skittered backward over the hot sand. He might say she cowered, but her chin still jutted out mutinously. She appeared ready to fight, but unsure of how to proceed.

"What the hell is it?" He waved the gun toward the creature.

She shrugged, wiping at her face with the back of her hand. "Dinner."

"Dinner? I thought you were—" He paced away, clicked on the safety and shoved his weapon under his belt. When he heard her scream . . . . He'd never experience a terror so acute. "I thought you—" No. There was no way in hell he'd admit he had been worried. Terrified, actually, that the single living person he knew out here was dying and, once again, that he'd been left to survive alone. Christ, he didn't even know her. He strode across the space separating them.

The woman got to her feet, edging away. Not this time. She wasn't going anywhere. He hauled her up against him. Every inch of her compact frame pressed tight to his, causing his mind to scatter and his anatomy to focus. What the hell had he wanted to say?

She tried to jerk away. "What are you doing? Why're you even here?"

Oh, that's right. He narrowed his gaze and gave her his meanest scowl. "The next time I hear you scream, if you are not in true jeopardy, you will be when I find you."

"I thought I was alone." She tried to push away.

He shifted his hand until he cupped her ass, pressing her close and she froze, those lavender eyes widening. "Lady, you never assume you are alone. Survival 101: There is always someone bigger, stronger, faster, or smarter than you watching."

She lifted her chin, but her bottom lip trembled. "Is that a threat?"

"It's a truth." Feeling his body start to shift to life, he released her abruptly. "Why were you crying? Are you hurt? Did it bite you?"

She shook her head. Her gaze shifted to the creature and her eyes filled with tears again.

Good God, she was as leaky as a broken faucet. "What the hell is wrong with you?"

"I never had to kill anything before, okay?" She sniffed. "I didn't— I have no food."

Rage flared inside him. He paced away, unable to look at her. She didn't belong here. She was sophisticated, a society miss, and there was something intrinsically innocent about her. That she had thrown away a part of her innocence to fill her stomach infuriated him. The fact that she'd proven to be strong enough to do the deed made him admire her. He didn't want to like anything about her. He couldn't decide which part of this whole scene pissed him off worse.

"Jesus. What are you doing here, lady?" He waved his arm to encompass the alien world around them.

"I—I wanted to be a pioneer."

Her voice was small, hushed, but even if she'd shouted, he still wouldn't have thought he'd heard her correctly. "A pioneer?"

Unable to meet his gaze, she nodded.

Oh, he couldn't believe this shit. "*A pioneer.* What the fuck do you think pioneers do? You think they walk off the ship and stroll up to the local McDonalds? Have a nice, piping-hot droid-made meal? There is no civilization on Asteria, lady. You want to eat, kill something. You want to survive, be prepared to defend yourself." He turned away from her hurt expression and motioned toward her kill. "Let's get it cooked." With a glance around, he realized there was nothing they could use for fuel—unless she was carrying something to cook with. Had she put herself through the hell of killing for the first time and not have a way to cook it? He stared at her, eyes narrowing. No, she was smarter than that. "Were you planning to eat it raw?"

She didn't respond, but the way her grip tightened on her pack told him everything he needed to know.

He'd underestimated her. Again. Back on *Genesis V*, when he'd lifted her bag he thought she'd packed the thing full of fripperies—make-up and clothes, maybe a few dozen pairs of shoes. When he opened it and pulled out those two sweaters, he hadn't seen anything to make him think otherwise, but now . . . . "What's in your pack?"

"*My* stuff."

He shrugged off his pack and sat down cross-legged in the hot sand next to her kill. He reached in and pulled out one of his apples.

She turned her nose up.

Christ. He took out the saltshaker.

This time, her gaze lingered on his offerings briefly, but in the end, her eyes shifted away and her grip tightened on her bag.

What the hell did she have in there?

Obviously more than him and suddenly, with great urgency he wanted to find out what. With a heavy sigh, he reached in his bag and pulled out one of his boxes of water. He held it up, then set it next to his other offerings.

The tip of her tongue darted out to moisten her lips.

Ah, yes, I've got you now, my pretty. "Come on. I'll share, if you share."

She wiped at her face with the back of one dust-covered arm, dragging her eyes from his offerings to look at him. "How do I know I can trust you?"

"I've got a blaster, lady. If I wanted to make a tactical acquisition, I could've killed you and already been halfway to my meal."

Her face twisted in indecision.

She would share, damn it. "What's your name?"

"Pr—" She coughed and lowered her thick, black lashes. "Angelica."

Prudence. He remembered, now. "Liar."

"Chief Payne, I am not a liar. I—"

"I could give a shit less why you're lying. What's it going to be, Angel?"

She stomped over and plopped down on the other side of her kill. "I caught it; you skin it."

He arched a brow. "Knife?"

She reached into her bag and drew out an old Swiss army knife. He took the tool and her kill a short ways away to take care of the task. The creature appeared to be a cross between a seal and a caterpillar the size of a house cat with coarse, tan fur covering its fat, segmented body. His gaze kept roaming to Prudence, curious about what else she had in her magical backpack. She was turning out to be a fucking Girl Scout over there. Maybe she packed for camping as opposed to a new life in society, after all.

She pulled out a small camping stove, flipped it over and began reading the instructions.

Griffin breathed a sigh of relief. They'd have to hack small chunks of meat off the creature and cook as they ate, but they'd eat. Once he'd skinned the beast, he cut it in quarters and handed them to her one at a time.

She didn't talk while she worked, which was fine with him. Gave him time to study her. Her face and arms were bright red from sun exposure. He'd have to keep her in the shade for the next day or two else she'd get sun-poisoning. And that might be tricky since she didn't trust him.

Each of her movements were graceful and economic, though her hands shook. And every time he moved, she flinched. Nothing showy, just a tightening around her eyes, her shoulders. Maybe she had cause. Before they'd set sail to Asteria, her whole throat had been black and blue. He wouldn't be surprised if Randolph beat her. The son of a bitch wouldn't have patience for a spirited woman. Maybe she'd gotten sick of his shit and left.

Still, she'd been married to Alfred. In all the pictures he'd seen of her she always wore the same happy, polished smile. Odd. Now that he'd spent a little time with her he noted that there wasn't a whole lot polished about her. True, she was a society miss, the quality had been bred into her bearing and tone. But a true society lady wouldn't kill for food no matter what. She wouldn't come to Asteria willingly, nor wipe her face with the back of her arm. She sure as hell wouldn't share a meal, much less air, with someone like him.

Nothing about Prudence Angelica Parnell added up and he didn't like that at all.

Prudence finished cooking the first piece of meat. The smell alone had her mouth watering and stomach grumbling. She offered the morsel to Griffin, hoping he'd stop staring.

"You go ahead, Angel. Give me the fork and I'll get the next one started."

The gray meat burned her fingers as she pulled it off and handed him the fork, but she wasn't letting go of her prize. She bit into the morsel, which was rubbery and bland and tasteless. It was wonderful.

Griffin's eyebrows popped up. "Good?"

"Mm, oh. It's horrible." She swallowed. "But I'm starving."

He laughed and she paused mid-bite. His whole face changed with a bit of humor. Those green eyes sparkled with mirth and the hard planes of his face softened with his smile.

He handed her the saltshaker. "Where you headed?"

Prudence forced her gaze away, focusing on seasoning her food and taking another bite. "Better. Thanks." She refused to look at him, but his stare bored into her and her stomach roiled. What did he want? She finished chewing and swallowed. "The settlement out near the spaceport, Diamond Fjord. Why are you following me?"

"Now, don't go flattering yourself, Angel. I happen to be going the same direction."

Heat flared in her cheeks. Of course he wasn't following her. She was nothing. The only reason he might want her was for her gift . . . but perhaps he didn't know. The way he dismissed her indicated as much. And, as he mentioned, he was armed. If he wanted to attempt to steal from her, food or sex, he could have done so already. Relief washed through her, but a strange surge of disappointment over the fact he held no interest in her soured the small victory. But why would he be interested in her? Chief Payne was a beautiful male and she was . . . alien. Skinny and small-breasted with eyes the color of a day-old bruise. Males never desired her. They coveted the gift she held. Shame of her lack of attributes made her turn away, despite her hunger.

"Here." He nudged her shoulder and held out a second helping. "Go on. I'm still building up my courage."

She took his offering with a rueful smile. "I didn't take you for the squeamish sort."

"Squeamish, no. Guess I'm waiting to make sure you don't keel over."

Prudence wheeled around with a gasp.

Chief Payne held up his hands. "A joke. I'm joking." He let out a soft chuckle. "Jesus, hasn't anybody ever teased you before?"

She bit her lip and regarded him. His body appeared relaxed and she found no malice in his eyes despite his heartless comment. He was . . . teasing. She remembered watching such activities in school, but had never been the recipient. At least, she didn't think so. Alfred and Randolph often said mean things, but their eyes never danced with mischief like Griffin's. "It's a child's game to tease, is it not?"

He snorted. "Maybe. But grown-ups do it better." He winked.

He winked?

Prudence picked up the saltshaker and sprinkled her second piece of meat, eyeing the box of water. There had been a two-ounce packet of water in the med-kit, but she'd drunk that halfway through the day and goddess help her, she was thirsty.

He caught her staring at the small box. "No water until you're done. We're sharing it, and the way your face keeps wrinkling up with each bite, I'm betting you'll be happy to wash the taste out of your mouth."

What? She thought he would give her the whole box in exchange for half the meat. "You didn't say we were sharing it."

"I did."

Her gaze flicked to the green fruit next to him. "What about the apple?"

"That, too." His eyes narrowed, hardened. "Half of what you had out, for half of what I had out."

Interesting how specific he was. Did that mean he had more in his bag? Maybe more water he'd be willing to share later? She bit her lip. "I guess that's fair."

"Damn straight, it is."

She took another bite so she wouldn't have to respond. Politeness demanded she thank him. The water he offered was worth more than everything in her pack. But she feared if she showed him any gratitude, he'd take advantage.

"You know anything about this place?" He finished cooking his first piece and set it on the edge of the stove while he started the second.

"We're in the Black Desert."

"That's original." He scoffed.

"There were volcanoes in this area at one time. Then Asteria went through a flooding period. The sand is what's left of the lava flows. That's why it glitters in the sun."

"Thanks for the geology lesson." He shifted, leaning back on one elbow while still keeping his second piece over the stove. "What about the natives? Animals? Plants?"

"They did very little research on Asteria before the Expulsion."

His scowl was fierce. "Expulsion? Is that what you call it when they throw away half the population?"

The term *was* offensive—bringing to mind a body purging itself of impurities, instead of the mass-exile of human beings. But she hadn't created the term. Deciding against defending herself, she kept the conversation moving forward. "Most of the plant life can be found in the plains and mountain areas. They tend toward darker colors than on Earth—reds, navy blues, blacks."

"I don't suppose you know what's edible and what's not?"

She shrugged. She had a field guide to Asteria in her pack, not that she'd be sharing that information. Most likely, she'd end up minus a field guide if she did.

"What about life?" He picked up the cooked meat and tore a too-big chunk off with his straight, white teeth. His cheek bulged. "What the hell are Scarecrows?"

His table manners were appalling. "There's one type of humanoid creature here; the first exploration crews called them Scarecrows. No one knows much about them other than that they're deadly."

He reclined back on his elbow, making his shirt lift enough for her to see the dusting of blond hair dipping into his cammies. She jerked her gaze up as he took another giant bite. "Why's that?"

"Do you always talk with your mouth full?"

"I'm multi-tasking, Angel." He paused chewing long enough to pouch the food in his cheek and scowl. "I didn't go after your table manners when you inhaled that first piece."

Prudence looked away. He was right. She had no reason to take him to task other than he left her feeling unsettled and off-balance. "The Scarecrows murdered the first exploration crew. Second one, too. After that, NASA said the planet was uninhabitable and banned further exploration."

"Until your hubby came along."

He started in on his second helping and she busied herself turning off the stove and putting her supplies away. He was correct. Alfred saw no problem with exiling potential enemies of his dream to this inhospitable planet.

"So where are they, these Scarecrows?"

"They live in the mountains where food and water are abundant."

"You do realize if you keep going in the same direction you're liable to walk right into them."

She bristled at his sarcasm. "Yes. I'm aware."

"Well, seems to me it would've been easier on everybody if you offed yourself on Earth."

She froze, staring into the backpack that contained everything she owned. Maybe she should take exception to his heartless words, but she couldn't. She could only consider them. On Earth, she had been suicidal. No doubt about it, she'd prayed for death. But when the idea to go to Asteria had entered her mind, all that had changed. She knew the risks—they were as abundant as the individual grains of sand making up the Black Desert. Asteria was by far much harsher than even the most inhospitable places on Earth. The storms were violent. The wildlife aggressive. The locals, murderous. There was every possibility she wouldn't survive.

But here, on Asteria, there was every opportunity she might.

"At least I know what I'm getting into." She shrugged. "You knew they'd transport you, did it occur to you to do a little research before you, uh, purchased your ticket?"

His eyes narrowed into unnerving slits. "There wasn't time. I would've lost my opportunity. I spent all my time between watching my base get fragged and shooting your loving husband searching for my family and researching yours."

"Maybe you'd have better served your loved ones if you'd continued your search."

"I am. My brother is here. Committing a high-profile felony was my ticket to continuing my search." He leaned forward. "Since I'm military, I've been tagged. Had I tried to purchase one, they'd have killed me like they did all the other military who refused to work for the U.N."

All military personnel were tagged with locator beacons so if they went missing in action, they could be found. Still, his reasoning was spurious. "Alfred wouldn't condone murdering anyone."

He scoffed. "Yet your beloved signed off on the orders."

She shook her head. "He wasn't my beloved."

"And yet you were always at his public appearances, smiling away like a proud, happy wife."

As if she'd had a choice. "All I'm saying is the order couldn't have come from Alfred. Randolph, yes, maybe even one of his commanders, but not Alfred."

"After everything that's happened you still can't see what Alfred was, can you?"

Why was he being so argumentative? She had no control over the Parnells. "I do know what Alfred was. Much better than you ever could. When I say that he didn't sign off on those orders, it's not because I agree with his vision or think him incapable of violence. It's because he wouldn't sign a kill order. Doing so would go against his fundamental beliefs. Torture, yes. Imprisonment, yes. Banishment, yes. Killing, no. His brother, however, would have no qualms about mass murder. You'd have been better served to shoot Randolph."

"Yeah, well, hindsight's twenty-twenty and all. I should've killed them both."

Unbelievable. Did he use his gun to solve all his problems? She shook her head. "You're nothing like what I imagined."

"Oh? Why's that?"

"I thought—" Emotion choked her. What a fool she'd been. To think of all the time she'd wasted watching his trail. Praying for him. He was as violent and uncaring as the Parnells. She stood, shouldered her pack and headed out.

Griffin blocked her path. Backed her against a boulder with a few predatory strides. "Finish it." Her traitorous body responded to his nearness despite the menacing scowl he wore. "You think I'm some lunatic? Some murderous sociopath? Or some dumb soldier who can't string two words together?"

She shoved against him, but he wouldn't budge, immovable as the giant rocks jutting out of the sand around them.

"I want to hear you say it." He scowled. "Who did you think you were sharing a meal with?"

"A hero."

10

Griffin staggered back a step. She couldn't have stunned him more.

And she wasn't through. Prudence Parnell squared her shoulders and took a step forward, prodding him with her index finger. "I thought you were a Marine." Poke. "A hero. I thought you shot Alfred in hopes of a more promising future for everybody. But no. You"—she jabbed her finger into his shoulder each time the word "you" crossed her lips—"weren't sacrificing yourself for a higher cause. I'm sorry for what they did to you, wiring your mouth shut like that, but you could've still spoken up at trial. You chose not to. You didn't care about all the people suffering. All you were thinking about was what you wanted. And in the end, after everything is finished, you made everything worse."

Something very small and very fragile withered inside him. Had he thought he'd hit rock bottom already? Hell, that had been a little outcropping of pride, suspending him from the big plummet. The force of her accusations crumbled that last foothold, sending him reeling into an abyss of self-loathing.

He hadn't just failed, he'd made everything worse.

For a few terrifying seconds, the only tangible thing around him was the blaster pressed against the small of his back. The metal was warm from the desert and the damn thing stuck to his sweaty skin, taunting him. *You should have died with the rest of your unit. Every breath you're taking pollutes the air around you, buddy. Do it—stick that warm, sweat-slicked barrel between your lips and squeeze the trigger. You won't feel a thing.*

His hand seemed to agree. Twice he reached for the fucking thing. Twice he dropped his hand to his side. He was a fucking coward—he just wasn't sure if he was a coward for thinking about blowing his brains all over the Black Desert, or if he was a coward for being unable to rid the world of his sorry hide.

Marines don't give up. They don't give in. They never leave a man behind.

Prudence's hand flew to her lips and she backed away a step. "I shouldn't have said that. None of it." She continued to search his face and if her expression was any indication, she'd read every one of the damning thoughts in his. "Whatever you're thinking, don't."

Out of every accusation she'd made in the last five minutes, the sympathy in those eyes of hers was what sent his hackles up. "Oh, no." He stalked forward, crowding her. "You don't get to do that. What's said is said. The thing is, *Angel,* I don't believe you."

Her face screwed up in an expression of disbelief. "What?"

He'd be damned if he buy into her lies about Alfred's innocence. The bastard *had* signed kill orders and he'd personally rewarded those who carried them out. Griffin had been the recipient of one of those damned rewards. If she was lying about Alfred, maybe she was far more involved in everything than he realized. "You heard me. I think you're up to this whole stinking mess to your eyeballs. I think you know exactly why I didn't talk at trail."

"Oh? Why's that?"

"They had my neighbor. If I said anything they didn't like, they said they'd kill her."

Prudence lifted her hand to her mouth. "I'm sorry."

He shook his head. "I don't buy it. I don't think you wanted me to succeed, I don't think you ever thought me heroic but I do think you're trying to fuck with my head so I don't continue my mission."

"What mission? The Marines are gone. The Army, Navy—they're all gone. Don't you get it? We're light-years away from Earth. You failed. *There is no mission.*"

"There's *my* mission. I'm gonna find my little brother. I'm gonna rally the exiled, acquire a ship and return to Earth to start a revolution. I haven't failed, lady. *I haven't even started yet.*"

Her lavender eyes widened with each pronouncement. She pressed into the rough rock behind her as if willing the solid surface to absorb her into its stony embrace. "You're insane. You'll never even get close to a ship. The Blue Helmets will shoot you two hundred yards out."

He leaned down until they were nose to nose. "But they won't shoot you."

***

What was it with men?

She'd gone from bad, to worse, to diabolical. Alfred wanted her gift. Randolph wanted to intimidate her and steal her gift. Now Griffin wanted to use her in exchange for a ship. Then what?

He'd end up dead and she'd be right back where she started.

Chief Payne possessed an aura of desperation and madness. Today was the first time she'd glimpsed it, and while frightening, she didn't think any of it was directed at her. Those tumultuous emotions were reserved for himself and seeing him hurting broke her heart a little. Like when that terrifying expression of self-hatred had passed over his face, dimming his eyes and sending a shudder through him. She hadn't missed the way he had kept reaching for his weapon and with that particular look on his face, she didn't imagine he had planned to use it on her. No, she didn't think he presented a direct danger to her, but he intended to hand her over to Randolph and that would be worse.

"I'm not going back." She must have said those words twenty times if she'd said them once. She'd yelled, cried, pleaded, and she shouted some more.

And Griffin sat there like an immovable, uncaring lump. The most response she'd gotten out of him in the last couple hours were uncivilized grunts. He had his back against one of the crystals, his arms braced on his knees and though he sat motionless with his eyes closed, she had no doubt he was wide awake. She'd been loud enough to wake the dead back on Earth.

She paced. "Chief Payne, I want to talk about this. I. Cannot. Go. Back."

One sea green eye opened. "You are turning out to be a typical society miss with your goddamned whining."

Prudence stared at him in the twilight. A drop of sweat ran down his temple. Her gaze followed it down his chin, his neck, until it disappeared beneath his collar. A shiver raced over her skin. Was he teasing her again? She was an alien to the Earthers; no part of society had ever embraced her. "That's funny because none of the society misses I've met thought I had a lot in common with them."

It was true. She'd always gotten along better with servants and shopkeepers than any of the women the Parnells mingled with. She was too thin for any of the current fashions to look good on her, which was a check against her. She spent more time staying abreast of current events and studying foreign cultures than keeping on the up-and-up about celebrities and society, which was another mark against her. And she was a hybrid—born of an alien and a base-born Marine—a huge no-no in society's circles.

He shifted and let out a long, beleaguered sigh. "Ah, what's-a-matter, the crème de la crème of the world wasn't good enough for you? Don't worry, Angel, you'll be a goddamned celebrity when you get back. Everyone will be vying for an interview with the woman taken captive by assassin Griffin Jude Payne."

Prudence opened her mouth to defend herself and then snapped it closed. He thought she was one of *them*. She almost laughed, would have had her situation been less precarious. How many years had she spent lamenting society's antipathy toward her? How many years had she tried to fit in to no avail? And Griffin was convinced she was one of them—she could see it in his absolute refusal to even acknowledge her.

Well, this was awkward in a life-or-death sort of way. He wanted to use her to get a ship, but she wasn't so sure Randolph would take the bait. He may blow them both away. By this time, Randolph must have figured out society followed him because they wanted to, not because of her gifts. He'd realize he had no need of her. But if she told Griffin that, then he'd demand that she tell him about her gifts, which would put her in a whole other kind of jeopardy.

Why were men such horrible creatures?

"Lie down and go to sleep."

She planted her hands on her hips and glared.

"Lady, you don't want me to ask again."

No, she didn't doubt that for a moment. "You're a bastard. An absolute bastard."

His scowl darkened and she went straight to her pack and lay out her sleeping mat. She refused to lie down. She sat on her mat with her back to one of the crystals jutting out of the ground. "Why are you being like this?"

He shook his head and so much time passed, she didn't think he would answer. When he did, his voice was low and his beautiful eyes filled with pain. "I witnessed everything I loved blown to pieces. Men and women I fought with, risked everything with, gone in one bomb blast. And why?

Because they loved freedom more than the ideal of a perfect, unattainable society."

Sympathy for him overwhelmed her. She was alone in the world. She'd stood on the outside, watching everything in the world change. She couldn't imagine being in his position, standing in the middle while the U.N. systematically destroyed everything around him.

The thing was, Alfred's dream had started out innocent enough. The nations had been warring for decades, fighting over resources, religions, ideals. It had become obvious that Earth's people would not survive much more. When the U.N. stepped in, the nations didn't have much choice but to bow to their whims. War-torn, bankrupt, and struggling to support their citizens, the nations folded one by one. The problem was, the Parnells' solution ended up being far more damaging than the problem.

She was staring at proof of that.

Chief Payne was suicidal. She couldn't mistake his haunted, pain-filled gaze for anything other than what it was. She'd seen that look too many times in the mirror. She'd wounded him when she'd blamed him for making things worse, twisting the knife into whatever guilt he already carried.

Prudence lay down and gave him her back, her heart aching with regret. She'd finally learned to fight back, but in doing so, she'd hurt someone she wasn't too sure deserved her wrath.

He lay down beside her, trapping her between outcroppings of stone and his body. "The Parnells took everything from me: my brother, my unit, my corps, and my country. I did what I did for them. Not just for a ticket here. Not with any aspirations of being anyone's hero."

Maybe he wasn't the hero she first thought, but he was still the only man who'd made an effort. And no one deserved to experience such pain.

"I want it all back. You . . . ." He leaned over so his words brushed against her ear, sending shivers over her skin, "you're going to get it for me."

Renewed anger burned through her sympathy with the force of a forest fire.

They'd see about that.

Griffin woke to the glare of sunlight probing his lids. The sand was hot beneath his body and he had a crick in his neck from using his pack as a pillow. He stretched and opened his eyes.

"Goddamnittohell!" He jumped to his feet, trying to look in every direction at once.

Prudence was gone.

How the hell had she gotten past him? True, he'd been relying a bit on her realizing she needed his help, but *fuck*. He grabbed his pack and slung it over his shoulder, scanning the ground for footprints. They'd been all over their campsite last night, so it took several minutes before he found what he needed. There. She was still headed straight into Scarecrow territory. The woman was stubborn as a mule grazing on stinkweed. Depending on what time she left, she could be miles away already. He set out at a run, his stomach grumbling in protest. He'd intended to share that damned apple with her, but not now.

A hundred yards out, he stopped and swore. He'd thought they were coming out of the desert, but glittering sand spread out before him like a great black ocean for as far as his eye could see. Not even the slightest breeze shifted the sand or cooled his skin today. He had a clear view of Prudence's footprints headed straight into the wasteland and disappearing into the shimmering horizon where the heat wafted up from the ground.

The fool woman would cook out there with her fair skin and dark hair, she'd already had one hell of a sunburn. By the end of the day, she'd likely have sun poisoning and wish to hell she hadn't wasted her sole med-wand on him. She had no water. No food.

She was fucked.

Unless you find her in time.

Griffin cupped his hands to his face, trying to see past the glare. The ground was flat and dark as a forest pond. He saw no movement—there was nothing out there to draw his eye. She must have hauled ass last night. *Why wouldn't she after you told her you were going to use her as a hostage?* He shouldn't have made the threat. He had no intention of carrying it out. But damn it, what she said last night . . . it hit far too close to home and as a true soldier, he fought back.

But he never expected her to do anything that might put her life in danger. What the hell was she running from? Him?

He'd be doing her a favor, returning her to Earth. If she wanted to leave Randolph, fine. No law said she had to marry the S.O.B, but wandering around Asteria alone was not a good alternative. Besides, if he had his way, Randolph would be dead soon after they returned and she wouldn't have to worry about him anymore. She could live out her life safe in the embrace of society back on Earth.

Damn it. He shouldn't have made that threat.

She was being hunted.

That adage about Marines never giving up was proving to be true. Griffin was tracking her. Every now and again she'd pause and look back the way she came and every time she saw a heat-misshaped splotch in the distance. The heat rising from the desert floor made it impossible to discern her pursuer's identity, but she had no doubt it was him.

Oh, part of her wanted to run right back to him. This hike might be easier with someone to talk to, someone to depend on. But Chief Payne was a tortured soul and she wasn't so sure it would be wise to get close to him. When she'd left during the night, he'd been dreaming in his restless sleep and it had been impossible to miss the tears on his face, glistening in the moonlight.

Prudence paused, took off her pack and set it down.

Somehow, she needed to get out of this desert and find water. With her skin blistering and sore, she lost more energy every hour. The map she had couldn't be drawn in proportion. The cartographer must've taken liberties with the size of the Black Desert, assuming no one would be foolish enough to attempt to traverse the barren wasteland.

But she wouldn't give up. She'd rather die out here than go back to Randolph.

Prudence shouldered her pack, wiped the sweat from her brow and set off again.

11

Randolph brushed off a bucket and sat to watch Bronsen work. He didn't trust himself to do the questioning; he was far too angry. Bronson, though, always kept a tight leash on his temper.

They'd located the pod Prudence had been in; she'd left a couple of sweaters behind he recognized. They had also found traces of blood in the pod, but after analysis, they'd discovered the blood belonged to Chief Payne. As far as they knew, Prudence had landed safely.

Except, she was gone.

Black Desert Outpost was the logical next stop. The buildings were the only sign of civilization near the escape pod. They must have come this way, but so far the denizens of the outpost weren't being cooperative.

Bronsen, with the help of a few Blue Helmets, had three men strung up by their feet, their arms tied behind their backs and their heads swaying a bare inch from the floor. He sat on a stool in front of the three men and watched their faces grow red as the blood pooled in their heads.

One of the Blue Helmets walked over and placed two large buckets of water on either side of Bronsen.

"Now, boys, as you can see there are three of you and only two buckets here." Bronsen smiled. "That means one of you gets to live."

The men glanced back and forth at each other.

"So, let's see who here is going to be talkative today." He leaned forward on the stool. "Has a woman come through here in the last week?"

The big one in the middle stretched his lips into a semblance of a smile, revealing a silver tooth. "A woman? Why didn't you ask? Sure, a woman came through here."

Randolph shook his head. They'd been asking about Prudence since they'd arrived. The ex-cons who lived in BD Outpost made it clear they wouldn't talk to Blue Helmets. These men . . . these men were the reason he had to succeed. They represented everything he hated. They were criminals. Dirty. Sick. They were manipulative and dishonest.

Bronsen's attention traveled to the man on Silver Tooth's right, then to the man on his left. "You boys don't want to play?"

"It's like he said," the man on Silver Tooth's left said. "She came through, what, two or three days ago. Her and her man."

Bronsen pushed one of the buckets toward the man on Silver Tooth's right and a Blue Helmet shoved it under the man's head. The water came up to his chin.

Both Silver Tooth and his chatty friend watched in horror as the other struggled, water splashing out of the bucket. He'd have upturned the pail by now had the young Blue Helmet not held it in place. The man's struggles slowed, then stopped. It was all over in a handful of moments.

Randolph wet his lips. He loved this, the absolute total control. The brutal truth of pain and death. They were two facts of life that never changed, never lied. And these men, these thieves, liars, and murderers, they deserved the ultimate punishment. He'd never agreed with Alfred's demands that these people be sent off-planet. They needed to be annihilated. Only then could there be true order.

The Blue Helmet regarded Bronsen. "You want him revived?"

"No, thank you." His attention turned to the two prisoners. "One bucket is still in need of a head. So, she came through two or three days ago. What did she look like?"

Both men spit out their answers frantically. "Black hair, tiny bit of a thing." Silver Tooth shouted at the same time the other stammered, "Short hair, purple eyes, real purdy."

Randolph harrumphed. Not even ten minutes had passed and they were already turning on each other. They had no pride, no compassion for their fellow man. These men were selfish. Bronsen easily wielded all the power in the room. He was by far superior to these ruffians. Randolph shifted in his seat as his body began to respond to his lover's show of dominance.

Bronsen glanced back at Randolph and winked before turning back to the prisoners. "Was she alone?"

"Big fella with her," Silver Tooth said. "Shot one of my boys."

"Yeah," the other agreed. "He stole a pack with a bunch of our stuff. Ran off with some of our booze and our shaker of salt."

Chief Payne was a thief on top of everything else. He was no better than these lot.

Bronsen nodded. "Good. You're both doing real well. Now, which way did he go?"

The two men shared a look. "Don't know," they said at the same time.

Randolph shifted in his seat, his cock growing hard.

Bronsen slid the second bucket to the young guy on the left, who started screaming as the Blue Helmet approached, twisting and fighting as the young soldier placed the bucket under his head.

"That's my son," Silver Tooth's cry ripped through the room, the anguish in his voice palpable. "That's my boy."

Randolph pressed his hand to his cock. His heart raced and his breathing jacked up a notch as pleasure shot through him.

Bronsen got down on one knee in front of Silver Tooth. "Then talk. Tell me what I want to know."

"The son of a bitch locked us in here!" Silver Tooth yelled, staring with wide, teary eyes as his boy struggled. "It was windy, by the time we got out, there weren't any tracks. We checked out the pod, but anything worth something was gone. They were nowhere around."

Bronsen nodded to the Blue Helmet who pulled the kid up and moved the bucket out from under him. The young man sputtered and coughed.

"What else can you tell me?" Bronsen forced Silver Tooth to look him in the eyes. "Did they talk to each other while they were here? What did he take with him?"

Silver Tooth bawled in gratitude. "Thank you. Thank you. He had a blaster. Said the woman was his. He was looking for someone, asked if there were any other men in the outpost. Took a pack, some food, liquor, and night goggles."

"You did good, big guy." Bronsen stood. He removed the bucket from under the dead man, nodded to the Blue Helmet. They both stuck their buckets under the two prisoner's heads at the same time.

Randolph moaned as he watched father and son find their ultimate truth together.

12

He admired her.

Yeah, she was still a pain in his ass, but damn, the woman was tough as week-old rations. He'd followed her for the last two days, staying close enough to watch, close enough to help if she needed it, but far enough away to keep her from noticing him.

He had no desire to deal with a wounded female, but he couldn't allow himself to interfere unless she needed help. It took him six hours to catch up to her, and by then, he was angry. Furious, actually. He'd hung back, wanting to avoid a confrontation until he'd had time to calm down. But, as he'd walked behind her, watching her silhouette waver in and out of focus in the heat-baked distance, he got curious. What would she do now? How did she expect to survive? How far was she willing to take this little suicidal streak of hers?

There weren't many full-grown men trained in survival who would walk out into the desert not knowing where they were going, or how to get to resources. The fact that she'd been going in a straight line, only stopping to rest when the sun hung at its highest and most deadly point in the sky, told him that not only did she have a plan, but she also had grit.

Her embarrassing second attempt at catching dinner informed him she didn't have a clue what she was doing, nor did she have a weapon other than the Swiss Army knife.

Lastly, he knew she was hurting. Whether physically, mentally, or emotionally, he couldn't say, but when the skies grew dark and he had no visual, he'd close the gap between them and off and on throughout the night he'd hear the occasional sniffle, the random sob. The first night, he thought she was afraid. He kept expecting her to come flying back in his direction screaming his name. But she didn't. She kept right on trekking, no doubt leaving a trail of tears in her wake.

Part of him wanted to shout at her to stop with that nonsense—crying stripped her body of needed water. But if he were to tell the truth, out there in the pitch of night, stepping one foot in front of the other in the stifling heat with nothing but those mournful cries to follow, he may have let fall a tear or two as well. The sound of her hurt damn near broke his heart and made it impossible to ignore his own pain. At night, with nothing to distract him, he couldn't hide from the faces of his past. He couldn't shy away from his punishing thoughts.

A time would come when he'd be called to account for his sins, when he'd either have to find a way to redeem himself or succumb to the bitter hatred roiling inside him. As he followed Prudence, their walk for survival sometimes felt more like a pilgrimage toward his atonement. Hopefully, at the end of this walk, he'd find Lucan. Certainly, at the end, he'd find the spaceport. One way or another, soon after, he'd either die, or find relief in destroying Randolph Parnell.

But for now, there was no relief.

There was just the walk. And as time went on, his admiration for Prudence's tenacity, strength, and endurance grew.

A screech rent the air above. Griffin paused and, shading his eyes, scanned the lavender sky. A large green bird coasted overhead; its wings held out steady as it circled. His first thought was grim: A carrion eater. But as he watched the bird's graceful flight, he realized this was the first he'd seen. He'd been starting to think there might not be any birds on this godforsaken planet, but perhaps the birds avoided the deep desert, staying closer to more temperate regions. Staying close to food, water, and shelter. He checked out the horizon. There was nothing to see, not yet, but if his theory proved true, they'd be coming upon more hospitable land over one of the dunes in the distance.

He refocused on Prudence. She was getting tired. He could see it in the way her shoulders sagged and her head hung low. Her steps had grown less sure since midday, and she stumbled more often. The urge to stride over, pick her up, and tell her he was damn proud of her almost overwhelmed him. But she wouldn't accept him or his praise. She still had fight in her and he wasn't sure how to apologize. So he was biding his time.

Above him, the green-plumed bird was startled out of a graceful arc, squawking and darting away.

What the hell had scared it?

Prudence's mind was consumed with the crazy male following her.

"Why doesn't he take over?" She flung her arm out to the side as she muttered to herself. "That's what men do, isn't it? They take. They manipulate. They control."

So why did Griffin insist on hanging back?

She was about to swing around and shout her question, when the sand in front of her shifted. She stumbled to a halt and leaned forward, staring at the glittering black grains. Had she imagined the movement? The ground appeared still and solid now. But, as she lifted her foot to take another step, a whole, curved strip of sand about four feet wide jerked to the right. The ground shook and a howl filled the desert twilight. The howl triggered something in her brain, reminding her of a creature she'd read about: Sandhowlers.

She jumped over the shifting strip and ran. With every step her feet sank into sand that seemed to want to suck her shoes right off her feet. She'd gotten a dozen feet or so when something wrapped around her ankle, tripping her. She fell flat on her stomach, the hot sand chafing her chin. The thing around her ankle tightened and flexed. It was a glistening, coral pink tentacle. Tiny pink appendages sprouted from the tentacle, and even tinier appendages sprouted off them. They all whipped around, searching for purchase, independent of one another.

It must be a Sandhowler, a creature that burrowed below the shifting sand—a giant snake-like beast that could grow to be three hundred feet long. The worst part, she'd read, was the mouth. One whole end of the Sandhowler split open into four toothy lobes which could pull prey into its mouth.

She rolled to her side and kicked out with her other foot, trying to dislodge the appendage that had her within its grasp. She stomped down on the thin tentacle, scraped the sole of her shoe against her ankle, everything she could think of to try to dislodge it from her leg.

Goddess, protect me.

She searched the horizon for Griffin. He wasn't moving. From this distance, with the sun in his eyes, he couldn't possibly see what was happening. He was too far away to be much help at all. Even if he started running now, the Sandhowler could gobble her up before he even got within shooting range.

The Sandhowler began dragging her foot below the surface of the sand, with slow, steady pressure.

Oh, no. Goddess, please no. Not like this.

She flopped to her belly to use her hands and other foot to try to stop her descent, but the sand offered no solid handhold and she lost more ground. Sand, hot and scratchy, spilled into her shoe as the Sandhowler pulled her foot beneath the surface. This wasn't happening. *Goddess, no*! She hadn't survived Alfred, Randolph, a ship fire, a room full of ravenous fiends, and this horrible desert to be taken out by an overgrown snake in the middle of nowhere. Twisting, she pulled off her pack and grabbed the folding knife in the front pocket of the bag. Her hands were slick with sweat and sand and her fingernails were down to the quick from rooting around under the occasional boulder for roots or signs of water. She couldn't grasp the tiny indent to pull the blade out.

Griffin must have realized something wasn't right. He strode toward her over a distant dune, shielding his eyes from the sun.

"*Helllllppp*!"

He paused, then set out at a sprint.

The Sandhowler had dragged her foot below the surface of the sand. Her mind filled with the image of the creature gnawing on her leg, its teeth snapping right through the bone as it tore off her foot. She had to get the thing off her before the rest of it showed up. She went back to work trying to get the knife open. Her hands shook, but she got the blade up. She cupped her hand, scooping the sand from her foot so she could see what she was doing, slashing at the appendage. The only visible part of the creature was that small tentacle wrapped around her leg. She cut it again and again until she hacked through.

The wounded tentacle receded and another howl rent the air, so loud and deep it vibrated inside her. The ground rumbled, causing individual grains of sand to jump on the surface. She pulled her pack back onto her shoulders and stood. She held up her hands in a signal for Chief Payne to stop.

He stopped.

The book she'd read said the Sandhowlers found prey by feeling them pass over the surface of the sand. If they both held still a little while, the creature might leave.

The rumbling continued.

Maybe even increased.

She waved Chief Payne away and turned to flee in the opposite direction. After a few strides, the sand began to slide under her feet again. Shifting toward the place she'd been, slowing her progress as she fought the tide.

The rumbling grew into a cacophony. The Sandhowler breached the surface amid a great eruption of sand.

Prudence backpedaled. The Sandhowler's thick, pink body rose segment by segment, its tentacles spread out, each with smaller appendages growing from those, giving the creature the lacy, ornate quality of a leafy sea dragon. Unlike the cute sea creature of Earth, the Sandhowler's body was as wide as an old elm tree and for a heartbeat or two, the creature shaded her from the sun. The four lobes at the end of its head split apart and the Sandhowler roared.

Beneath her, the sand began sinking around the Sandhowler, filling the spaces below where it had just been. Flopping onto her belly, Prudence grabbed at fistfuls of the grains to keep herself from being swallowed up by the sifting earth.

"Angel, run! Get out of there!" Griffin's voice was still so far away. He ran to her in long ground-eating strides, but he wouldn't reach her in time. The report of his gun sounded small and flat over the howl of the creature and the static rain of sand.

The sand slowed. She crawled as fast as her shaking limbs would carry her, terrified the creature's mouth would descend and bite her clean in half. "Oh, goddess, please keep me safe. Goddess, please—"

A shadow fell over her. Time was up and Griffin was too far away to help. She was on her own.

Prudence gripped the blade in both hands and rolled onto her back.

The Sandhowler rose high above her, its fat, pink body glistening in the sun. This creature was young, a baby—there were just three sizes of tentacles sprouting from its body. From what she'd read the adults could sprout hundreds of tentacle-buds.

She hacked at anything that came close. Slashing the appendages that whipped the sand next to her and stabbing at those trying to grasp her legs. The Sandhowler reared back in response. She scooted away as fast as the shifting sand would allow. The air grew so oppressive with heat and dust each breath she took felt like it stagnated in her lungs. Her eyes burned from the sand and sun. Her heart thudded in her chest and her overexposed skin burned from the chafing sand. Each movement took more and more energy, making her increasingly lethargic.

Another flat blast of Griffin's gun sounded in the distance.

The Sandhowler dove for her. The lobes of the creature's mouth spread wide, revealing the corrugated ridges of its inner mouth and rows upon rows of teeth.

Oh, goddess, I'm gonna die. I'm gonna die and I'm not ready. Not yet.

She held her arms straight up, knife pointing to the creature and waited.

The Sandhowler drove itself right onto the knife, coming down until her elbows gave out. For terrifying seconds she didn't think she'd done enough, the Sandhowler was still coming for her.

The creature flung its head back, whipping its head to the side, trying to dislodge the blade. Prudence held onto the knife and went flying through the air to land in a heap on the hot desert sand. She glanced back in time to see the creature sink below the surface with a wounded roar.

Griffin slowed his approach, holding his arms out to the side as if to say, *What did you do now?*

I don't need him.

Prudence dragged herself up onto shaky legs. Her ankle burned from cuts, now dirty and caked in sand.

I am not weak.

She wanted to be gone from here in case the Sandhowler's momma showed up. She needed every ounce of determination to ignore her thirst, her hunger, and her pain, but she grabbed her pack and started walking again. Sort of.

Behind her, Griffin cussed profusely. He always cussed. He was crude. Belligerent. Uncivilized.

She didn't need him. She didn't need anyone, damn it. She was a strong, independent woman.

Now that the danger had passed, her body began reacting to the adrenaline. The shakes set in, her empty stomach roiled, and tears blocked her throat. Half a dozen steps and she dropped to her knees again. It might have been the most humiliating experience of her life, to fall on her knees while *he* watched. Griffin thought she was weak—he told her so—and she'd proved him right.

Unable to look at him, she kept her head bowed when he approached. His dusty boots appeared in her line of vision. He waited for something—an apology or an admission of failure—she wasn't sure, but she refused to give him anything of the sort. She waited for his teasing and taunting. Held herself braced for whatever bit of nastiness he spewed.

"Don't fight me, sweetheart." He bent down and lifted her into his arms. Perhaps the desert dried up his reserve of set-downs.

Prudence wrapped her arms around his neck and buried her face beneath his chin and even after four days on Asteria sweating and dirty, somehow, he smelled good.

A hot lump burned her throat and she had to choke out what she needed to say. "You don't have to tell me, I already know."

He rubbed his cheek against hers as he started walking. "What's that?"

Why was he being so gentle with her? "That I'm weak."

13

—— ◆ ——

Weak?

He'd never met anyone as strong. He might be in better shape than her after three days in the desert, but he'd been trained. He was used to going without. He was used to tough treks. She was soft. Small. She had no training or practice. He wasn't so sure had their positions been reversed if he would've fared so well.

"I'm weak."

Anger simmered in his gut. She'd taken down that . . . that . . . whatever the hell it was all by herself. She was bleeding from one leg and both shoulders. Damn it, he wished to hell they still had that med-wand. His arms tightened around her. "Don't say it again. You defended yourself against that thing. I couldn't get to you in time. The fucking sand kept sliding under my feet and this old blasters got no goddamned range. You were amazing, so don't you call yourself weak."

"Why not?" Her lips moved against his skin as she spoke, sending shivers rolling through him despite the heat. "You've said it yourself."

He had. He'd been trying to goad her into doing minor surgery on him at the time, but he'd never apologized. "I was being an ass. You're not weak. Neither of us will say it again."

She scoffed, or sniffed, he wasn't quite sure which.

"I'm serious, Angel. I'm shooting the next person who says you're weak and I always keep my word, so don't test me."

She pulled away enough to look at him, her face was dirty and tear-streaked, those lavender eyes wary and watchful. "Why are you being nice?"

He snorted. "I'm always nice. Besides, you're bleeding—I never tease people who are bleeding."

Tears welled in her eyes. The tiny drops were tinted lavender, too. It was like watching a fairy princess weep.

"Christ, don't do that." He looked away, unable to bear the thought of being the cause.

She sniffed. "What?"

"Don't cry, damn it." He lifted her higher in his arms, balancing her weight more evenly while he treaded sand. His legs were starting to burn like hell, but he'd be damned if he'd set her down. "You'll make me cry, too."

A startled laugh jolted through her small frame. Low, and husky, the sound went straight to his groin.

For the first time in days, a smile curved his lips. "Come on, now. Tuck you face under my chin and be still. My big ol' head will give you some shade."

She did as he asked, but he still felt wetness on his neck and chest. He couldn't say if tears or sweat caused the moisture. "For a society miss, you've got brass."

"I keep telling you, I'm not society. My mother was alien and my father was a Marine."

She had denied being society before, but he hadn't believed her. "A Marine? You were raised in the grunt class, too?"

She sniffed. "Went to public school and everything."

"Really?"

"Until my parents were killed in the Chicago attack. From then on, I lived in an orphanage."

"How the hell did you end up with the Parnells?" He tried to pull away enough to see her face, but she tucked her head beneath his chin.

"Alfred picked me out of a line up. Just lucky, I guess."

Lucky? Maybe when Alfred had been alive, but based on what he'd seen, luck had nothing to do with her time with Randolph. At least she'd only been subjected to the brute for three months before she'd run away.

He crested the dune and there, not a hundred feet away an oasis sprawled in the sand. "I'll be damned."

Prudence gasped, and a wail tore through her. "I was so close. I would've made it on my own if I'd kept going."

She was killing him. "Stop it. Everything's all right. Everybody needs help now and again." He headed straight into the soft-hued foliage and into a rainbow of pastels. The sun glinting off all those colors dazzled his eyes after staring at so much black for the last few days. The trees weren't anything like they were back home. Here they had spiked layers like a palm tree, except they looked more like opaque, glittery diamonds than any kind of bark he'd ever seen. The layers went from the base of the trees all the way up, growing smaller and smaller down to the thinnest branches. The leaves were wide and cupped, spanning the range from deep reds to pastel blues and yellows. If he'd ever bothered to imagine what the biblical Eden might be like, he might have pictured this. A clear, red-tinged pond sat in the middle. The water looked deep, might even go all the way up to his neck, and it appeared empty of wild life. He pointed. "What's the red? Is it safe?"

"It's from Deridium deposits. The mineral is safe, we've been using it in antiseptics on Earth since its discovery, but—"

"Good." They could both use some antiseptics for their sunburns and cuts. He walked straight into the water, shoes, clothes, Prudence, and all.

"No." Her arms tightened around his neck and she shifted in his arms until her legs were wrapped around his chest. She seemed to be trying to climb right up to balance on his head. "I—I can't."

"You're fine." He coaxed her arms from his neck so he could breathe again. "I'm not letting you go." His words didn't have much effect. She still clung to him, her hands fisting clumps of his shirt, her breath coming in needy little gasps. "Close your eyes and hold your breath."

"Why?"

"I'm gonna dunk us."

"No, don't—"

She came up sputtering, sobbing and fat, lavender tears dotted her cheeks. "Oh, please don't. I won't resist. Don't drown me. I swear I won't—"

What the hell? Griffin gave her a hard shake, but her eyes weren't focused, they were wild with fear. Her hands had white-knuckle grips on him—one at the nape of his neck and one at his chest, she didn't seem to realize she had skin as well as shirt fisted in her hands.

"Sweetheart, I'm not gonna drown either of us. I'm standing. We can't drown. I just want to get the dirt off that sunburn of yours."

The way she stared at him tore at his heart. Had she almost drowned as a kid?

"Hey, look at me."

Her eyes met his, but she wasn't seeing him. "Don't put me under. Don't drown me. I can't breathe." One of her hands went to her throat clawing at her skin. He pulled her hand away from her neck and remembered how bruised her throat had been on the ship. What all had Randolph done to this woman?

Randolph and his buddy Bronsen had led several waterboarding sessions in the prison with Griffin as their star attraction. They'd tie him down to a slanted table, cover his head, and pour water over his face. They'd hold him there, let him struggle while his sinus filled with water. Then, they'd hold him there some more until that water backed up, dripping down his throat into his lungs. After a while he wouldn't be able to restrain his need for air, and his body reflexively sucked the water deeper into his lungs as he attempted to breathe. Water burned like hell when it filled his lungs, especially if was ice cold. But nothing was worse than being brought back, knowing one of Randolph's fucks would give him CPR and flush the water from his lungs, give him time to catch his breath, time to remember every detail of what happened, then do the whole thing over.

He pulled his arms between them and cupped Prudence's face in his hands. "Angel? Look at me." He had to repeat his request several times before her gaze focused. "When I was in prison, Randolph and his cronies used to do something called waterboarding, do you know what that is?"

He didn't need her to answer. Her eyes dilated in stark terror and her breathing increased until he feared she might hyperventilate. She moaned low in her throat. "Please, please, don't."

That son of a bitch had tortured her. He cursed. When he found Randolph his death wouldn't be quick like Alfred's. Randolph would suffer. "I will never do that to anyone." He gave her a little shake and bushed her hair from her face. "I will never do that to anyone. Not even my worst enemy. Do you understand?"

"Y-You . . . ." Her eyes blinked as if she were having trouble focusing.

"I'm not gonna dry-drown you. I swear to God. I swear on my parents' graves."

"But . . . y-y-ou had . . . ."

"Sweetheart, I swear to you, I might be a bastard, but I would never, ever do that to anyone."

"He did that t-to y-you?"

Alarm bells went off in his mind. Why the hell did it matter to her? He gave her a quick nod.

Prudence launched herself at him, wrapping him in a full body hug. "S-so sorry."

His face twisted as a burning lump of something awful parked itself in his throat. Tears pricked the back of his eyes and he blinked them away. Those days were over. They were light years from Randolph, Bronsen, and the prison. There was no reason for tears now. His response to her tender apology shocked him so much he almost shoved her away. But he couldn't, because he had no doubt she'd been through the same and if she thought he needed comforting, that meant she needed it more. So Griffin bent his knees, bringing them both lower so the water covered the teeth marks on her arms and returned her embrace. The thought of anyone subjecting Prudence to the same torture he'd endured from Randolph made his gut twist.

"Tell me."

Her quiet demand sent a bolt of terror through him. No one talked about torture. Not those doing it, and not those subjected to it. Torture was grim, disturbing. "No." He softened his statement with a little squeeze. Lifting his hand out of the water, he stroked his palm over her cheek, trying to wash the dirt from her sunburned skin without upsetting her. She allowed him several passes and then let him shift her to his other shoulder so he could get to her other cheek while she rested her face against his wet shirt.

Her breathing calmed and her body relaxed against his until he thought she might have fallen asleep. He leaned back, resting his shoulders on the edge of the pool and let the cool, healing water lap over them. He liked her. Maybe that made him a traitorous wretch, her being a Parnell and all, but he couldn't not like her. Not anymore.

"I hated coming to."

Griffin pulled away to see her face.

She allowed him a quick glance, then pressed her face back onto his shoulder. "I always had a moment of panic right before I inhaled. My heart would be pumping so hard I could hear it in my head. And when I sucked in that breath, I could hear the water whoosh into my body as the pain started—the burn, and that horrible ache in my chest. But right before I died, I always had this split second of peace."

The tremors coursing through her body seemed to jump right into his. Griffin swallowed hard. He knew what she was talking about and he loathed that she understood such a thing. After the third or fourth time, he had started looking for that brief glimpse of peace, started hoping he could stay with it. He'd dream about it. While it didn't sound so bad when he referred to that moment as peace, that moment was the split second everything shut down except his brain. The peace she spoke of was a silent heart. Still blood. Waterlogged lungs. That peace was the split-second before the electricity in his brain fizzled out. Dreaming about those quiet seconds, hoping for them, was a special brand of sickness. A madness only a man captive and tortured could comprehend. But *she* knew.

"Next thing I knew my chest was on fire, my eyes felt like they'd popped out and got rammed right back in my skull and everyone stood around watching. Eager to see it all again."

And if he used her as a hostage, if he got his ship at her expense, he'd be sending her right back to hell. No wonder she'd run from him. Bowing his head, he rubbed his cheek to hers. "I didn't know."

She stayed quiet and still, letting him comfort her, allowing him to take comfort for himself and for the first time in as long as he could remember, he experienced a true connection. A communion.

He'd be damned if Randolph got near her again. "You lied to me, Angel." He kept his voice soft and rubbed his chin on the top of her head. "You didn't come here to be a pioneer. You came here to escape."

"I came for both. I've got a fighting chance here. I have opportunites."

And he'd threatened to take all that away. "Turn around, Angel." He disentangled her limbs from him and urged her to lay her head back on the crook of his arm and float. "I want your cheeks in the water. Put your head back and relax. I'll keep you from going under."

With her muscles so tense, her body kept sinking until he gave her his other hand to hold on to. One of his arms supported her, the other lay between her breasts as she clutched his hand in both of hers. He tried not to notice how see-through her tank-top was. The white material had turned a mottled gray from the black sands, but the dirt didn't make the thing any less transparent. There was no mistaking the dark circles of her areolas or the tight points of her nipples.

His body grew hard and aching, making him hate himself a little more. She was tearing him up. He liked her, wanted her. But she had been married to his enemy. This attraction had to stop. Maybe they'd bonded over their mutual dislike of Randolph, but she was still Alfred's widow. Equal parts of him wanted to protect her and scare her away, because as much as he resented her, he was starting to fall for her, too.

No. It was just the proximity. He pulled her up. "That should be good."

"Thank you."

"No problem."

She lifted her hand and placed her palm over his heart. "Do you understand now? I can't go back."

Griffin looked away. "I told you, I didn't know."

"Are you still going after a ship?"

He had to. He couldn't leave the people of Earth at Randolph's mercy. He couldn't leave those stuck here on Asteria against their wishes without hope. He had made everyone's lives worse. He couldn't live with himself until he made things right or died trying. He nodded.

"Then it doesn't matter. You'll draw their attention. You'll bring them here."

Prudence pushed past him and clung to the side of the pool, going hand over hand until she reached a point she could put her feet down, and climbed out.

Griffin followed. "What do you want me to say? That I'm giving up? That I'm going to leave them to Randolph's generous mercy?"

She whirled around. "Haven't you ever considered that the Earthers might like the way things are?"

"No."

"Maybe you should."

Christ, he was in trouble. Her clothes clung to every soft curve, nook, and valley of her body. He wanted nothing more than to kiss her into submission and make her stop taunting him. "No. That son of a bitch did something. Did he drug the water? Brainwash them? Bribe them?"

"None of the above."

He pulled himself out of the pool and stood in front of her. "Don't lie. I've been in the U.N. files. There were all kinds of pages blacked out with references to Alfred preparing things for the 'persuasion of the masses.' That's what those documents said—of course the part describing *how* he persuaded the masses had been redacted. You've got to know—what did he do?"

He was like the rest of them in every way but one—her body reacted to his.

As furious and upset as she was, she couldn't help but stare at the way his shirt plastered over his muscular physique, nor could she get the feel of him out of her mind. Moments ago, she'd had her whole body wrapped around his. She still might had he not started spouting nonsense.

"Alfred had some weird beliefs. Kind of like Hitler believed he'd gain power from religious artifacts and President McKinley believed a red carnation worn on his suit gave him luck. Even though each of those men truly believed in those things with their whole hearts, neither of them were true."

Griffin let out a laugh, but there was no humor to it. His eyes darkened. "Why are you still protecting him?"

She threw up her hands. "Why can't you believe me?"

"Because I've seen all your pictures." His gaze dropped, lifted, and then dropped again. "You standing there with Alfred, or Alfred and Randolph, smiling away for the holo-cameras. You looked happy in all those photos. Hell, you married the son of a bitch. Fucked him night after night. You gonna tell me you didn't?" He stepped closer.

Prudence flung herself back, out of reach. "Can't we have a civil conversation?"

He wasn't even making an effort to look at her face now. He stalked closer. "I'm not civilized."

That was a fact. Everything about him screamed feral. She glanced down to see what he stared at. The water had turned both her white tank-top and white bra to see-through. She covered herself with her arms. She intended to give him the set-down he deserved, but his finger grazed along her collarbone and her breath caught.

"Do you miss having a lover?" Those sea green eyes of his fixed on her lips. "I think you're as passionate as I am. You're just better at hiding it."

A shiver raced over her and it had nothing to do with the cool water still drying on her skin. "I'm not." Passion had never been a part of her life. "I don't like sex."

"Then he was doing it wrong." He stood so close, the heat from his body sent gooseflesh lifting on her skin. "You must miss some of it. The cuddling?"

She shook her head. "There was no cuddling."

"The kissing?"

"No. There was no kissing."

He grinned. "The feel of a hot tongue slipping through your curls?"

Her hand went to her straight, short hair.

"These." He leaned in enough to let his thigh brush the juncture of her legs.

The intimate touch and the heat in his eyes made her nipples tighten in response. A breath shook out of her.

"Mm. You like that idea. I do, too."

She tried to focus, tried to remember what all men wanted. Certainly not her. Never her. "You just want my gift."

One tawny brow lifted and he focused lit on her lips again. "Oh? What kind of gifts do you give?" The tip of his tongue dampened his lower lip, then he bit it.

Something sharp and aching rose deep in her belly. Heat swamped her cheeks. That horrid place between her legs grew damp. The way he looked at her made her feel wanted. Desired. And he didn't appear to know anything about the legend of Lythonian women. That errant finger tracing lines along her collarbone and shoulder slipped lower, dipping down the V of her tank, between her breasts.

She sucked in an erratic breath. "I like respectable men."

"You were married to one of those and engaged to another and look where it landed you. Here." He stepped closer. "Alone." He lifted her chin, forcing her to meet his heat-filled eyes. "With me."

"I don't like you."

He rocked back on his heels, closed his eyes, and inhaled deeply. "Maybe not, but your body does."

The rogue was scenting her like a dog. She gasped.

"Come on, now, Angel. Don't go getting offended. I like your scent. I can't wait to bury my face between your legs."

She pressed her thighs together, trying to stop the ache.

"And you know what? I won't be civil. I won't dine. It'll be a goddamned feeding frenzy and I won't stop until you pass out from the pleasure."

Her entire body shook with the force of his words. She felt sensations in places long forgotten and vehemently hated. Her response to him terrified her. Not so much because the sensations were new and strange as much as because she knew they could never lead anywhere good. She wasn't like other women. She'd disappoint him and he'd hate her for it. "I won't." The look on his face suggested he didn't believe her. She shrugged. "I can't. I'm frigid."

The teasing glint left his eyes as he searched her face. She could almost feel his ardor wane. No one wanted a frigid woman. No one wanted to be with someone who couldn't respond. Whatever drove Griffin to pursue her, it wasn't worth enough for him to desire her, knowing she'd be unresponsive. She lowered her lashes, unsure what the pang in her chest was. Did she care? She came here for independence, to become her own person. The last thing she needed was an entanglement with Griffin Jude Payne.

Swallowing past the lump in her throat, she tried to slip past him, but that wandering hand of his cupped her throat. She froze at the feel of his fingers curling around her neck.

"I forgot." His words were somber, almost an apology, and his hand slid up to tangle in her hair. He pulled her head back until she stared up into his eyes. "I don't think you're frigid, Angel. You just had a shitty lover."

Maybe. She hadn't liked either of the Parnells. Still, she had no desire to try. She feared she'd discover the Parnells had been right about her. Her lips parted on a protest lost against his hungry mouth. He was right, there was nothing civil about him. About this. His mouth was hot and spicy, his lips firm and his tongue did not beg entrance. He swept right in and took.

She gripped his shoulders, meaning to push him away, but instead found herself clinging to him.

"Kiss me back, Angel." He nipped at her bottom lip. "You know you want to."

Prudence almost lunged at him. There was something different about him. Something that made her joints go liquid and her belly get tight. Even when she fought with him, he made her breasts tingle and her pussy ache. She kissed him, wanting nothing more than to find a way to curl up right inside him and *feel*.

His hands moved, gliding up her damp arms, pushing them higher until her arms wrapped around his neck. His hands slid back down her sides until he gripped her ass and dragged her against the insistent bulge of his arousal. She let her head fall back, gasping, focusing all her attention on where their bodies touched.

Why him? Why did her body come to life for him?

All these years she'd longed for a hero, some pretty knight in shining armor who'd romance her with sweet entreaties. She wanted polite. She wanted tenderness. She wanted safe. Griffin was none of those things.

He suckled her earlobe into the heat of his mouth, his erratic breath echoing in her ear and sending shivers rolling over her flesh. There were no sweet kisses, instead he marked her throat with teeth, scored her flesh with hot, bruising sucks.

Needy, uncouth noises broke past her lips. Sounds she didn't recognize. Sounds that made her blush.

Without warning, his big hands gripped the backs of her thighs, spreading them as he lifted her and pinned her against the closest tree.

She rubbed her core against him, needing the friction, needing more. Shivery bolts of pleasure raised goose flesh on her skin and made her inner muscles clasp with wanting.

His hands were on her face, fingers dragging over her lips, dipping into her mouth, teasing her into suckling them.

She wanted him. Oh, goddess, she *wanted* and that terrified her. Despite being able to feel desire for Griffin, she still expected the end result to be disappointing. Embarrassing. Painful. She took a deep breath and pushed away, stumbling when he allowed her her freedom and lowered her to her feet.

He reached out to steady her. "Easy there."

Prudence smoothed her hands over her shirt, looking everywhere but at him. "I-I didn't come to Asteria to be manhandled and bossed around. I came here for independence. For choices. Not for anyone to force me—"

"Hey, now. No ones talking about forcing anything, Angel." He drew in closer, tipping her chin up so she had to meet his gaze. "You telling me you don't feel the chemistry between us?"

She shook her head. She refused to lie.

"Good." He wet his lips. "Then I'll wait civilized-like until you're ready to do something about it. You just say the word."

He moved away and she felt bereft. She crossed her arms over her chest.

"You cold?"

She nodded.

"You got any other clothes in that bag?"

She had a couple extra bras, underwear and socks, but nothing that would keep her dry and clothed. She shook her head. "I forgot to grab the sweaters from the escape pod."

He tossed her a button-down shirt from the pack he'd stolen and while she stood behind a bush to change into his shirt, Griffin shook out the sleeping pad she'd left last time they slept together. "Come over here if you want to get warm. I won't debase you. Our clothes will dry soon enough, then we'll both be wishing we were back in that pond." He lay down with his back to her, leaving plenty of room on the blanket for her to lie down behind him. After she changed, she scooted into the place he left between him and the wall and lay on her back, staring up at the stars.

The heat from his body helped her relax. What it might be like to lie beneath someone who cared for her. He'd been so gentle with her when she freaked out in the pond. She felt liked they'd bonded a little. Then he'd ruined it with his rubbish.

If he ever worked through his troubles, Griffin might be the kind of man she could love. As they lay there together, she discovered she wanted to ease and reassure him the same as he'd done for her. She just wasn't quite sure how to go about it.

The sky here was different, as alien as the planet itself. The stars didn't sit in the same positions as they did on earth. They weren't even the same stars. "I always thought the stars were set. That it didn't matter much what night sky I looked at because they'd all be the same."

His response was terse. "They aren't."

Her gaze shifted to his back. Did he speak of the sky, or men? "No. I guess it'll take some getting used to, though."

He let out a long, heavy sigh and rolled over, pulling her up against him. "There's time."

She didn't dare show any visible reaction, but inside, she smiled. He'd wait. He'd let her get used to the idea that he wasn't Alfred. Or Randolph. That Griffin was his own man, with his own needs and his own ideas of what being with a woman should be like. And maybe, she'd be able to help him heal a little in the meantime. "Good night, Griffin."

"'Night, Angel."

Prudence let herself drift off to sleep, but every time he moved, she jerked awake. She wasn't used to sleeping with a man and when he started dreaming, she was wide awake. The moonlight lit his face, making the tears on his lashes sparkle as he grew restless. She couldn't ignore him tonight.

Not after knowing he'd been through the same horrors she had. Not after he'd held her through her panic.

Raising up on one elbow, she placed her palm flush to his cheek. "Be at ease, warrior. All's well here."

He pressed his face into her palm and for a few blessed moments he slept quietly.

What tortured him so? Something drove him. Something bad enough he was willing to die over it.

But even if he succeeded in his self-imposed mission and killed Randolph, would it be enough? Would he feel redeemed from whatever ate away at him? Or would he keep going?

14

Two days later, Prudence had to re-evaluate her expectations of Griffin's patience. He was stalking her like a predator.

They'd left their little paradise the next morning and discovered that small oases dotted the remainder of the desert. They'd just set up camp at the third one in three days. She also discovered some edible root plants that liked to grow near the water's edge. Griffin wasn't a huge fan, he complained about the lack of meat, but the roots kept their bellies from grumbling.

She felt his gaze on her. Felt cornered by the way he kept circling their little camp, doing this or that, but mostly watching.

On his thirteenth trip around the perimeter, she'd had enough. "Sit down."

"Only if you sit in my lap."

A very unladylike growl came from low in her chest.

He chuckled. "How 'bout a game?"

Her eyes narrowed. "A game?"

"Mm. I found a travel kit in that bag I pilfed. There's a deck of cards in it."

A simple card game might be nice to pass the time. At this point she'd do anything to keep him from stalking her. "Fine. If it'll keep you from prowling around camp, let's play." She settled herself in the grass and waited while he retrieved the cards and joined her. "What game?"

"Poker."

She arched her brows. Her father had enjoyed playing poker, but he often had to teach those he played the rules of the archaic game. "That's rather old-fashioned, isn't it?"

"Poker never goes out of style." He grinned. "I played a lot while on tour. It's pretty much the only game all the guys in our unit could agree on. We'd play for snacks, smokes, booze, whatever we had handy."

"We don't have anything to bet with." If he thought she'd bet the items in her bag, he was howling mad.

"Don't we?"

She harrumphed.

"Seems to me, you want something and I want something. You think you want me to leave you alone—"

This was ridiculous. "I'm not sleeping with you."

His intense gaze locked onto hers. "And I want fifteen minutes of kissing you wherever I want."

Her mouth went dry and parts of her that should want no part of any of this burgeoned to life.

"What's fifteen minutes of foreplay against a lifetime without me bothering you?"

She bit her lip while she thought it over. Fifteen minutes of kissing him? She'd thought of little else since the last time. She'd come to like him over the last few days. He'd lost that wild air of desperation she'd glimpsed while they shared their first meal. His teasing had turned sweeter. Most importantly, he'd never harmed her. Never tried to take advantage. She'd grown to trust him. She just wasn't sure she trusted him in this. He always had conditions where she was concerned. Her eyes narrowed. "Just kissing?"

"I promise I won't stick any of my hard bits into any of your soft bits."

The rogue. "Any?"

The corner of his mouth tipped up in wry amusement. "No fingers, no toes, no nose, no uncivilized cock." He leaned back on one elbow, looking, at first glance, relaxed. On second glance, she realized his muscles were tensed. Coiled to strike.

Fifteen minutes against a lifetime free from his advances? She was curious if he could arouse her with such ease a second time. Fifteen minutes of kissing would give her a chance to enjoy his attention for a little while without any expectation for later should she lose, but if she won . . . she'd be free from the uncertainty. Free from the possibilities. "Okay."

His grin spread into an evil smirk and he sat up to shuffle the cards.

He wasn't a beginner. That was clear in the way he handled the cards. He fanned them down against the grass, then up against the bridge of his fingers, never faltering in the quick, graceful movements. What might it be like to have those clever digits play on her skin? In her soft bits? She snapped up her five cards and sorted them—jack, queen, ace of hearts, three of spades and a four of diamonds. If only the goddess would see fit to throw her a King.

"I dealt, bets already placed. How many cards?"

She agonized for long seconds. Should she discard the ace for a chance at the king? She discarded the four and the three. "Two."

He dealt her two cards. Her heart stuttered in her chest—two fours. She had a horrible hand, had she kept the four of diamonds she'd be in a better position, but this was a losing hand if ever she saw one. She met his gaze—his intent, hungry gaze. There would be no renegotiating bets. What had she done?

"Dealer holds."

Griffin appeared negligent about the whole thing, reclining back on one elbow, his cards face down on the grass. She wasn't sure he'd even checked to see what cards he held.

He grinned. "I'll show you mine, if you show me yours."

With a hard swallow, she put her cards down.

"Two fours, not bad." He winked at her as he laid down four tens. "But not quite good enough."

Oh, did he look pleased with himself. A nervous flutter of anxiety erupted in her belly. "We could play three out of four."

He glanced past her into the horizon. "Sun's setting. No time."

She gathered the cards up and put them back into the box, resisting the urge to throw them at his head. Once the cards were put away, she took a deep breath and leaned forward, offering him her face.

That infuriating grin returned. "No."

"No?" She sat back on her heels. He played for a kiss, she was paying up, what was the problem?

"Stand."

With a curious glance, she complied.

"Very nice." He reclined back on his elbows. "Now, unbutton my shirt."

Her gaze shot to the black tee-shirt pulled taut over his chest.

The low rumble of his amusement rolled over her. "My shirt . . . that you're wearing."

If he thought she would renegotiate, he was delusional. "You said kissing."

"Exactly. Me, kissing you, wherever I want. I figured you wouldn't let me undress you. Wasn't part of the bet, now was it?"

And I want fifteen minutes of kissing you wherever I want.

Her mouth went dry as the Black Desert. "I thought you meant location."

"Mm-hm." His lazy gaze hit her lips. "Location." Her breasts. "Location." The V of her jeans. "Location."

She propped her hand on her hip. He'd tricked her. "Chief Payne—"

"Griffin."

She narrowed her gaze. "Fitting. Both names."

He chuckled. "Just so you know, my fifteen minutes don't start until my lips are on your skin."

With a growl, she turned around and unbuttoned his shirt with angry motions. She should be happy—she'd gotten what she wanted, after all, but part of her was terrified. The part of her that knew her body didn't behave like other women's. She was frigid. Both the Parnells had reminded her often.

She slipped her bra off through the sleeves and removed her shoes and jeans. Luckily, his shirt came almost to her knees, covering her. There would be no getting out of this little bet and she only had herself to blame. Goddess help her, he'd see how skinny she was. How small her breasts were. The nervous excitement vanished, leaving her with a knot of dread wound tight in her belly. With one last prayer that this Marine was everything her father claimed a Marine to be, she composed herself. Distanced herself. She wrapped the garment tight around her body and turned, keeping her eyes focused on the horizon.

He stayed silent so long, her composure almost slipped. She wanted to scream at him to get it over with.

"Come here and lie down."

She followed his command with all the emotion of a robot, lying down and placing her hands flat on her stomach. Still and silent, she waited for the pain. Literally, she supposed.

Why didn't he get it done?

One warm hand wrapped around her foot.

Her foot?

She refused to look and see what he was doing. He must be messing with her. Was he examining her skinny legs? Her knobby knees? What set down would he give her?

He lifted her leg, bending her knee and something hot and wet slipped along her ankle. Open-mouthed kisses burned over her skin. His lips only touched her ankle, but her joints loosened as pleasurable tingles raced up her leg to pool low in her belly. The hands she had placed on her stomach, curled into the fabric of his shirt.

He drew a thin, wet trail up her calf to the base of her knee with his tongue. How did she feel that one stroke all the way in her breasts, her stomach and her pussy? She inhaled a deep, controlled breath.

"You're a bit of a thing, but you're all legs, Angel. Gorgeous legs."

Gorgeous? He lied. She'd always been told her legs were too skinny, her knees knobby.

He traced the seam of her knee with that errant appendage of his and a shiver raced over her, lifting the hair on her head. He followed the path of her inner thigh, kissing, licking, nipping until he paused so close to her core that his cheek brushed her pubic curls. He sucked a spot on her thigh until she felt a tiny pinch. When she jumped, he backed off, soothing over the spot with the flat of his tongue.

She squirmed. She couldn't help it. Her body had taken on a life of its own, making her want to strain toward him. He was so close to her core. . . . He wouldn't. He couldn't. He skipped over her center and started down her other thigh.

Her breath whooshed out of her lungs on a shaky sigh. She tried to go back to ignoring him, she wanted to stay dispassionate, but all her nerve endings seemed to gather and pool under his lips, trailing after his mouth like tiny puppies seeking scraps. He got all the way down to her ankle, then disappeared.

Was time up already? Had he realized how ugly she was?

A shadow fell across her face and she heard his heavy breath a scant heartbeat before he suckled the pulse at the base of her neck. Her breath came out in a harsh exhale. He took his time, begrudging not one inch of her throat his attention.

Confusion clouded her mind. He didn't act like a man disgusted with her body. But then, if he was enjoying her, shouldn't he be rushing toward the deed? He had her almost naked and sprawled before him; why didn't he take her? Instead, he nipped, suckled, and kissed. Goddess, she'd never define a kiss the same. This was no bruising, violent act of ownership. This was passionate, needy, and desperate. His kisses weren't just about lips. They were about tongue, teeth, and harsh bursts of air buffeting her skin. They were lovely.

He drew her earlobe into his mouth and then disappeared again. The next place she felt the wet heat of him was her breast. Where had the shirt gone? Her fingers dug into the soft, thick grass as he pulled her nipple into his heat. His tongue battered her, sending sparks of need coiling deep in her belly.

The tone of his voice dropped low. "I take back what I said."

What? What did he take back?

"It's your breasts. They're perfect."

A pleased warmth heated her flesh.

"Your nipples are hardly a shade darker than your lips." He licked her other breast. "Every time I look at you now, I'm gonna remember this." He drew the tip into his mouth. She arched off the ground, shaking her head. She didn't want him to remember this. Did she?

Her nipples tightened further as he scraped his teeth down her ribs, leaving her moistened breasts to the evening air. She squirmed and writhed when he found each of her ticklish places, teasing her into response. Her breath caught and held as he traced her mating mark with his tongue.

She let out a low, keening moan when he returned to her core, spearing his tongue through her curls and lapping at her. White-hot heat blazed over her flesh and her hips rose off the ground. Something deep in her belly wound tight. That wicked tongue of his found her entrance and sank inside her—his softest bit in her softest bit. The rogue. Everything inside her wound tighter, straining toward something.

"Look at me."

She shook her head. He'd ruin it. He'd embarrass her. Punish her. And she was enjoying this, damn it.

"Let me see those beautiful, lavender eyes, Angel."

She couldn't refuse that request. Regret, yes. She was sure she'd regret obeying him. Her pride, her need for someone to see beauty in her had always caused her no end of pain. Still, she raised herself on elbows and looked at Griffin.

Face half buried between her thighs, those sea green eyes of his didn't waver once as he tongued her closer to something profound.

Orgasm? No. She'd never had one before. Not even when she tried on her own. Frigid women couldn't find release. Except, she hadn't liked the Parnells. So maybe . . .

His eyes sparkled with mischief. He sucked her clit into his mouth and her whole world shattered into stardust. A cry burst from her lips and she shuddered, her legs flexing around his head. Her heart pounded in her chest as the last ripples of release rolled through her. Goddess bless him, he'd done it. He'd given her an orgasm. She held on to the experience, held on to him and sent up a prayer of thanks. Maybe it wasn't the same as reaching fulfillment during intercourse. She had no delusions she'd be able to experience such heights during the pain of sex. But the gift he'd given her left her awed.

His eyes gleamed, growing hungrier. He lunged up her body, forcing her back into the grass and settled between her thighs. "Taste." His open mouth came down on hers, his tongue barging past her lips without waiting for permission and he fed her, her desire.

She tried to avoid him, fearing she'd be repulsed, but he wouldn't let her. Her scent, her taste laced every exhale, each thrust of his tongue and beyond that was his.

"Christ, you're good." He plunged her mouth, arousing her anew. "Salt and sweet and musk."

She fisted his hair in her hands, kissing him back.

Somebody had fucked over his Angel. Probably those goddamned Parnells.

When she'd first lain down, her eyes had gone distant and her expression blank. He'd seen that same look too many times on the battlefield. He sure as hell didn't like seeing it on her face. He'd almost told her to get dressed again, but he didn't suppose that would do either of them much good. Now that she'd relaxed for him, she was passionate as hell and all the sweeter for the effort needed to woo her. Much more and he would burst right out of his pants.

Prudence was the antithesis of her name. She didn't possess a prude bone in her body, or she wouldn't by the time he finished showing her how things should be between a man and his woman. This wasn't enough. This was nothing but a tease, foreplay to set the stage. He wanted more.

His mind filled with the dirty, sordid acts he wanted to perform on her. With her. Be the recipient of. He wanted those pouty lips of hers sealed tight around his dick. He wanted to come on her breasts, marking her as his. He wanted to sink deep into her heat. Wanted her tight walls flexing around his shaft, milking every last drop of his seed. His cock grew painfully hard, and with each flex of his hips, chills coursed down his spine, gathering at the small of his back.

He could have her. Her arms had wound tight around his neck and her legs circled his waist. She met him halfway on each flex of his hips. And, damn it, he wanted her. His hand flexed in her hair as he fought the urge to reach down between them and unbutton his pants. Yeah, he could have her. But she wasn't ready. If he took her now, she'd never lower her guard around him long enough for him to have her again. And he had no doubt he would want her again.

"Time's up." He needed every ounce of discipline to push off her. He stared down at her startled expression. Well, hell. She hadn't expected him to honor his word. "You say the word if you want more."

Her pink tongue darted out to wet her lips. "I—"

"Say it any way you want. Tell me to fuck you. Tell me to make love to you. Ask me to come to you. Anything, sweetheart. Give me anything."

"I can't." Her back arched, her body seeking contact, but her eyes still held a note of wariness. "Take what you want."

Everything in him wanted to pounce. To claim. To possess. But that look and tone spoke of resignation, not demand. He wasn't Parnell, damn it. He didn't want her resigned to lie beneath him. He wanted her demanding his attention. "No."

Pushing away from her was one of the hardest things he'd ever done. He turned, scanning the landscape as he waited for his body to catch up to the change in mood. "Why don't you go bathe? I'll stay here. Give you some privacy."

She didn't say a word, but he sensed her gather her clothes and leave.

Griffin let his head fall back and took a deep breath. He pictured his high school math teacher. His grandmother's best friend. His obese, balding, male neighbor who lived across the street from his family when he was a kid. The old man had some kind of sinus issue and there were always boogers in his mustache.

Nothing worked. His dick, it seemed, wasn't keen on giving up the idea of release.

He glanced back toward the pond; Prudence was nowhere in sight. Her clothes were gone—well, everything but her panties. She'd dropped those near the end of the path to the pond. She must've slipped into the water by now. He could sit in the deepest part and the water only came midway up his chest in the shallow pond. On Prudence, the water must come all the way to her neck, but the red-tinged liquid was clear—he'd have a full view of her willowy frame and small, pert breasts.

His erection was going nowhere with thoughts like that.

He unbuttoned his pants, folded up his shirt to get it out of the way, and leaned back against a boulder. Closing his eyes, he took his dick in hand and imagined Prudence sprawled out before him like a feast. He recalled the heady scent of her musk, her nipples, a shade darker than her lips and those soft, brunette curls between her thighs. In his mind's eye, he imagined her saying the words he needed to hear: "Please, Griff, take me now."

15

She couldn't find her panties.

Prudence held Griffin's shirt in front of her and snuck back toward camp, hoping she'd dropped them somewhere this side of the bushes. Just her luck, they were two feet inside the clearing. Great. Where was Griffin? She poked her head around the foliage and froze, her breath catching.

He stood with his legs braced apart, leaning back against a large rock. He had his shirt folded up, revealing tightly packed abs and a thin dusting of blond hair leading from below his navel down to meet his pubic hair. He'd lowered his pants enough to release his cock and stroked himself off.

She shifted, squeezing her legs together to squelch the tingle there. Goddess bless him, he was a beautiful male. Not pretty. Beautiful. She loved the way his muscles bunched and flexed as his hand rode his length. She'd never done that for a man, never circled her fingers around a cock and stroked, petted. She watched closely, trying to learn what he liked, wondering what he might feel like in her hand.

Or her mouth. Would she lick him like he'd done to her, or suck him into her mouth? He was much bigger than the Parnell brothers, but not even the thick width of him doused her smoldering desire.

His head rested back on the rock, eyes closed, lips parted. His breathing grew erratic. Who did he imagine? Someone back home? Maybe an old lover or a famous model? A woman with the large breasts and lush curves popular in society? He picked up the pace, his hand a blur of motion, stroking, twisting, and rubbing over his thick, dark head. His low groan reached across the campsite and hardened her nipples. Thick jets of cum spurted from his cock and his knees seemed to go a little weak. "Ah, Christ, Angel."

Prudence's eyes widened. Did he imagine her? Or did he give all women that nickname? Reluctantly, she hurried away from her position and went back into the cool water. She'd finished bathing, but she needed a little time before she tried to look him in the eye. If she did so now, she'd blush over the memory and he'd know she'd been watching. She splashed some water over her cheeks, but it didn't expel her blush, nor the other heat coursing through her nether region. Glancing back toward the campsite, she slipped her hand under the water and between her legs. Her folds were slick with desire and as soon as she slipped a finger between, a jolt of pleasure arced through her.

Never had that happened before; it was like he'd flipped some hidden switch inside her, making such things possible.

Maybe if she could make herself climax on her own, she wouldn't be so afraid to try sex with Griffin. She couldn't imagine how it might help. Sex was painful, nothing like the slick glide of a tongue, or the soft stroke of fingers. Sex hurt and she couldn't fathom how any woman could find climax amid such agony. Besides, her one time with Alfred had left her sore and aching with sharp pains between her legs for days and Griffin was much bigger. She couldn't imagine the pain he might cause.

She trailed two fingers along her cleft, circling the bud above her opening. Something dark and hollow opened inside her belly, sending out shockwaves of shivers. Experimenting, she circled the little nub, pressed her fingers to it, and scraped her nail across the little bump. The whole while she imagined those tight muscles of Griffin's and those penetrating green eyes staring into hers.

She opened her eyes and stopped still. There, not four feet from the edge of the pond stood the strangest creature she'd ever seen. Its barrel-shaped body stood on four thin legs, and an undersized, graceful head sat atop a stout neck and the thing's deep blue fur had thick black stripes.

Food.

She didn't know what it was, some kind of mammal, but it looked a heck of a lot more appetizing than the last creature they'd eaten. She had nothing to kill it with. Her stomach rumbled as she shifted her weight to her knees.

The creature lifted its head.

It would bolt if she tried to move. "Griffin," she whispered, hoping he could hear her. "Griff." She had to repeat herself half a dozen times before she saw him. She lifted her hand in a staying gesture and pointed to the creature.

When he didn't do anything, she turned to see what he was doing.

He stared back.

"Food." She pointed again.

His gaze wrested to the side and he withdrew his gun. He crept closer to the creature, but his attention kept straying back to Prudence.

What was he doing? "Kill it."

Griffin leaned to the side, aimed around a tree and fired once. The creature dropped to the ground.

Prudence jumped up with a whoop. "You did it. You got him. We're having meat tonight!"

Griffin continued to stare at her and he didn't appear happy at all.

"What's wrong?"

"I—" He motioned back to the clearing, then motioned to her. "And now—"

Prudence glanced down, in all the excitement, she'd forgotten she was naked. She squatted in the water.

"I can still see." He growled. "You're killing me. You know that, right?"

He tromped back toward their camp, leaving Prudence to wonder what his problem was.

Their trek the next day was easier with bellies full of protein. They were leaving the desert behind. Today, dark-blue grass and small stands of trees dotted the sand. The watering holes became more frequent, as did shade. They could see the edge of a forest in the distance that reached up into the jagged mountains.

Griffin had hardly looked at her the night before and today he'd been uncharacteristically quiet. She'd glance at her companion occasionally, a little unsettled by his comfort with silence. She wanted to understand him better—what drove him on this suicidal mission he'd set for himself. She understood the frustration of seeing everything you knew and loved change. She understood his unhappiness with the Parnells' twisted vision of utopia, but they were free from that now. Why couldn't he let it go?

As the sun started to fall in the sky, he motioned toward a thick growth of trees. "We'll camp there. Looks like there's water." He shielded his eyes from the sun. "Might reach the base of the mountains tomorrow."

"The spaceport is beyond the mountains."

"Good. I'll want a nice, long look at the place."

"What is your plan? Do you even have one?"

He shrugged. "I have an outline of one. Find my brother, commandeer a ship, and return to Earth. Hopefully with enough people to start a rebellion."

"That's an outline?" Sounded more like a movie tagline to her.

"A rough one, yeah. Look, in case you didn't realize, all information on Asteria's spaceport is top secret. It's not like I could pull out my Saph-link and look up the floor plan for the spaceport here or determine how many soldiers are stationed on Asteria."

Silence fell between them, not a comfortable one like before, but a quiet born of tension. She didn't want to insult him; she'd come to like him. She worried about him. "So you are planning to take some time to observe how things work at the spaceport?"

"Well, yeah." His tone was rife with sarcasm.

"And your brother, you know where he is?"

They'd reached the stand of trees he'd indicated, and he held a low-hanging branch out of her way so she could step through. "Look, I know I might not find him. I guess my hope is that the majority of the people sent to Asteria will stay together—safety in numbers. It's logical." He scanned the area while he spoke, looking for wildlife or people. He always remained watchful. "The more people who live in the same area, the more experts there will be to provide services to the rest of the population. These people are used to living in a network of other people, my assumption is that they will gravitate toward continuing that way of life here, too." He pointed off to their left. "Water's that way. We'll camp over there."

She followed him through shrubs and trees. "I caught a glimpse of a report on Asteria last year. There are two main settlements about a day's travel from the spaceport and several smaller settlements dotted around them. I doubt much has changed since then; they haven't sent as many people in the last year." He offered her his hand and helped her over a small outcropping of rocks. "What's he like?"

"Who?"

"You're brother. You haven't even told me his name."

He set his bag down near the edge of the water and stretched. "Lucan. He's different."

"How so?"

Griffin lifted his hand, running his palm over face and head. "I don't know." He sat down, leaning back against a tree. "He was always the smart one. Got good grades. Could remember everything he read, everything he saw."

She sat next to him. "He had a photographic memory?"

"Yeah. My parents would take us on vacation and I always took pictures of everything, everyone we met. But not Lucan. We'd get back home and a month later I'd walk into his room and he'd have pencil sketches and chalk drawings all over his walls." He shook his head. "Exact replicas of the places we went. People we saw."

She smiled. Griffin didn't sound resentful of his brother's gift, more like awed. "Did he go into the military like you?"

"Nah. Lucan's a little . . . . Well, let's say I got to play big brother quite a bit. I guess the flipside of all the amazing things he could do was that he got picked on a lot." He shrugged. "He outgrew it. Once he was in his teens, he'd work out with me whenever I came home on leave and got big enough that no one dared mess with him anymore, but he didn't have the stomach for fighting. Guess I wouldn't either if I had perfect recall of every man I killed in the name of corps and country."

This was as close as he'd come to talking about his service. Maybe it was rude to ask, but the military was such an integral part of his life and she wanted to know him. "Do you regret it?"

"What? The military?"

She nodded.

"No. Yes." He shook his head. "I don't know." He released a long sigh. "It's one thing to kill those who are trying to kill you, or infringing on others' rights, or who are euthanizing their people. There was a lot of that going on during my first tour. Everybody fighting everybody. For land. Religion. Wealth. Power. But then Alfred came on stage and everything changed. I just didn't realize it yet. None of us did. I kept following orders, doing what needed to be done, not knowing I'd changed sides." He let out a string of curses. "I was working for the oppressors, corralling people into spaceports and taking out compounds. The people would beg and cry and I was deaf to their pleas. I worked for the United States of America, damn it. We protected the weak and defenseless. They wouldn't have sent me for any other reason than protecting rights and freedom."

His voice broke and he quit talking. She'd never considered how the U.N. had communicated their takeover. Everything had been peaceful. One by one, countries had handed over the reins. She'd always assumed those countries communicated the change to their soldiers, but now she wondered.

He plucked a long blade of blue grass and twirled it between his fingers. "The U.N. started coming 'round more often, looking for volunteers to become Blue Helmets. No one at my base was interested. Then the government placed a hold on all leaves those last two years and blacked out all communication to home—said the situation abroad was urgent. But see, they were sending us after more and more families. They were asking us to cart away pregnant women, the elderly, the sick. When I started asking questions, my CO told me to mind my place."

"But you didn't." She bumped her shoulder against his. "You're not the type."

He refused to look at her and for a terrible moment she thought she'd guessed wrong. Then, he shrugged. "Every day I'd take my Saph-link out of scanning range from our base. Sit up in the hills and try to figure out what the fuck was going on. All the news reports talked about the governments giving up power to the U.N. to stop the fighting. The thing was, I was stationed in Africa. There was no fighting. There weren't many people left to fight. We were shipping them off by the thousands, being told it was a humanitarian evacuation." He snorted. "Supposedly the water had been poisoned, causing those who drank it to fall into dementia and insanity. We were to kill anyone who resisted on sight. It was weird. I mean right up until the orders came down we were all drinking the damned water. Nothing was wrong with us."

She couldn't imagine being so far from home with nothing to depend on but a faceless voice passing down orders.

"Jesus, there was this school—boarding school or orphanage." He shook his head. "I'm not even sure what—but the place was filled with kids and nuns. They didn't want to come with us. Kept telling us there was nothing wrong with the water, that they'd all been drinking it."

"Oh, no."

He sniffed, blinking his eyes as he looked away. "They seemed fine to me. All appeared hale and hearty."

She didn't want to hear this. "You don't have to tell me."

"I do." Anger flashed across his face, making her want to scoot away, but she held her ground.

"I want you to understand. See, my CO wanted to follow orders. He was there supervising another unit and I had my unit. We're all crammed tight into this little schoolhouse and the discussion got heated. There were kids crying. The nuns were weeping, begging for mercy. My CO called me a traitor, threatened courts martial to me and anyone who sided with me. Sowhen he gave the order to fire—"

She put her hand on his shoulder. "Griffin—"

"When he gave the order to fire, I shot him."

She stared back. That hadn't been what she'd expected to hear. She didn't understand why he was so upset. He did what he needed to do to save the innocent.

"All hell broke loose. My unit opened fire on his unit right there in the fucking schoolroom." His gaze bored into hers. "I killed my own men, Angel. Men I'd known and fought alongside for years. I killed them all right in front of those kids. That night, I knew someone would be coming for me. I knew word had gotten out. But when I left to search the 'Net for information that night, I had no idea they'd frag the entire base."

Goddess help him. He was carrying so much guilt and most of it wasn't his. "That wasn't your fault. You have to know that. The bomb runs didn't have anything to do with you. They were losing control. Alfred sent the order to disband the bases. I suspect Randolph twisted the order to destroy the bases." Somehow, she'd never understood how, the Parnells' had managed to keep the bombings from the media. Very few knew. Military families had been exiled long before the order had gone out.

"Why didn't you do anything?" He got to his feet. "I mean I'm trying to understand, but you had access. You could've leaked information. You could've done something."

"You think I didn't try?" She got to her feet, refusing to let him tower over her. "Why don't you tell me, Griffin, what lengths would the Parnells go to, to protect their dream?"

"Any and all." He looked away.

"Yes. The only time they didn't have me under surveillance was in my room and even then, I'm not so sure I had any privacy. I tried to sneak out documents. I tried to transmit documents. I tried anonymously tipping off the media. The information never got where I intended it to go and I always got caught. You know what Randolph does to anyone who goes against the Parnells. He was fanatical in his loyalty to Alfred."

"All right." He reached out to take her hand in his.

She snatched her hand away. "I watched guards die. Servants, too. Anyone who tried to help me became a target.

I got to where I wouldn't talk to anyone in private and kept to the most mundane of conversations in public. Yes, I may have smiled in those pictures you're always throwing in my face, but I smiled because I knew someone would get hurt if I didn't. Maybe me. Maybe whoever drove the limo that day. Maybe the cook who served us dinner. I had no way of knowing. So I smiled."

"Enough."

"No." She frowned. Who was he to say when she'd said enough? "I'll decide when it's enough. You wanted me to understand, well, you're going to, too."

He walked right up into her personal space, crowding her back. "I get it. You don't have to keep on."

His scowl was fierce, his body shifting from side to side in agitation. For the first time, she wasn't scared of him. She'd always thought he wanted to intimidate her when he did this. But no, he was seeking attention like an over-sized, ill-mannered puppy. Offering himself to make up after their argument—scowling at the possibility of rejection, but putting himself within her reach if she wanted him. The epiphany floored her. Determined to test her theory, she placed her hand over his heart. He stilled and though he made no sound, something vibrated through his chest, reminding her of a cat's purr. She allowed herself a small smile. This big, belligerent soldier liked to be petted.

"Ask me, Angel."

She had no doubt what he wanted her to ask. His stormy eyes filled with heat and his voice dropped low. And she wanted from him. She wanted his kisses, his lips on her skin, his muscular body snug against hers. She just didn't want the rest—the pain, the crushing disappointment. She shook her head. "I can't."

16

She may have said no, but her body swayed toward his when she did.

He wet his lips. "Then play a game with me."

A rueful smile spread on her lips. "I already know that particular trick, Warrior."

"Different bet this time."

She bit her lip in indecision and before she could say no again, he rushed to get the new bet said. "If you win, I'll leave you alone for the rest of our time together." He was making a promise he wasn't sure he could keep, but he had a better-than-average chance of winning. The cards were marked. "If I win, you get fifteen minutes of kissing me anywhere you want."

She released a breathy little sigh that tore straight to his groin. Her body leaned toward his. Then she came to her senses and straightened. "Oh? And if you win, how do I know you'll let it go at that?"

He grinned. "I know you still have those handcuffs. I could hear them clanking around in your pack."

A furious blush stole over her cheeks. "You're being silly. I wouldn't even know what to do."

He stepped closer. "Angel, you could get me off just looking at me."

She gnawed on her bottom lip so hard he was sure she'd have a sore spot come later. "And if I win, you won't do this anymore?"

He lifted his hand and drew a cross over the back of her hand, which still rested over his heart.

"This is the last time?"

"Last time." She was bending. She might not like the idea of taking a screwed-up soldier for a lover, but she wanted him.

"Get your cards out. Let's get this over with."

He shook his head. "First, I need to know you can shoot."

Startled, her wide eyes locked with his. "What do you mean?"

"If I'm handcuffed and someone comes around, you're gonna need to defend us."

Her brows drew together in a frown. "And you'd trust me to do so?"

"Yeah." A bright smile spread across her face, making him feel like a goddamned hero and he wasn't even sure why. Was she pleased because he thought her capable, or pleased at the prospect of getting hold of his blaster?

She pulled away and wiped her palms over her thighs. "Show me."

Griffin pulled his weapon out and held it up. "This thing's damn near an antique but it gets the job done." He flipped the gun on its side in his palm and pointed to a tiny button near the grip. "You see this here? This is the safety, and it needs to be pressed all the way in if you want to fire. Are you a lefty or a righty?"

"I'm right-handed."

"Good." He pulled her in front of him and placed the gun in her hand. "Now, when you're pointing at something, if you decide you need to shoot, the safety is right here." He placed her thumb over the button. "You can keep your finger on the trigger, and thumb the safety up all at once. Go on, try it."

She depressed the button with her thumb.

"Good. Now, these babies have a bit of a recoil, so use both hands. My mom used to wrap her left hand over her right wrist to help brace her arms."

She mimicked the position.

He grunted. "Almost. Keep your right elbow locked and your left elbow bent, that way you keep a straight shot. There you go. Now, fire into the water."

Prudence lowered the blaster and stared at him over her shoulder.

"There's nothing living in there. Go on. I want you to feel the recoil."

He stood behind her, helping her line up the shot. "Keep both eyes open and keep the sight on what you're shooting at." He used his body to give her something to brace against.

A laugh shook her frame. "Goddess save me, I'm nervous."

"That's good. Always have a healthy respect for firearms. Breathe." He lowered his face closer to her ear. "Relax."

She held her position while she worked at steadying her breathing. Her thumb slid across the safety, and her finger tightened on the trigger. She fired. Her whole body jolted back into his, but she kept her arms straight.

He nuzzled the hair back from her ear. "Real good, Angel. Now, next time, what'll you do different?"

She turned her face to his. "Brace my feet apart, one a little behind me so I can lean into the recoil."

Her lips were a hair's breadth from his. Her shaky exhalations caressed his face. He wet his lips. "You're a quick study."

She blushed at his praise, her lips parted.

His body screamed at him to kiss her.

No. Keep her trust, buddy. You'll get your chance tonight.

He moved away, trying his damnedest to focus on all the business they needed to take care of before they played. "Go on. Go take your bath. I'll prep dinner." They didn't have much. A bit of leftover meat from last night and a couple of those stringy root veggies.

"But, I thought . . . ."

His gaze lit on her face and from the fierce red staining her cheeks and the way she wouldn't meet his eyes, he realized she thought he'd given up. He strode back to her, crowding into her space and lowered his face. "Dinner first. Dessert later."

He kept his mouth bare inches from hers, hoping she'd take the bait, lean in and kiss him. Her breath came fast, and a tremor wracked through her.

"You're very confident you'll win."

"Go on. Might as well wash your clothes while you're at it. Looks like we'll be moving into cooler territory soon. You can wear my shirt while your things dry."

She swayed toward him, but came to her senses at the last possible second. She gave him a nod and moved off toward the pond.

Griffin let out an unsteady breath. That woman had him twisted six different ways to Sunday. *Patience, buddy. She'll be worth the wait.* Of that he had no doubt. His concern wasn't whether they'd be good together, he was fast getting worried they'd be so good together he'd embarrass himself.

The rest of the evening was wrought with tension and by the time he left her behind to take his turn in the cool water, he feared he'd allowed her too much time to think. She was jumpy as a dormouse in a wobbly room full of bowling balls. He washed himself and his clothes quickly and threw a blanket around his hips. He couldn't be more obvious, but he didn't want to give her any excuses not to explore him as she wanted.

Tonight would tell him everything he needed to know. Either she'd be as curious of him as he was of her, or she'd walk away. The whole prospect of what may or may not happen had him on edge. He was putting himself at her mercy, and while part of him was calling himself ten types of fool, another part kept saying this was how it had to be with her.

The sun hung low on the horizon when he walked back into camp and tossed his clothes over a bush to dry. They had enough light to get through one hand of cards.

Prudence sat near their packs, cards unboxed and lying in front of her. The sight caused him to pause. Had she taken a good look at those damned cards?

"I'm no good at shuffling, so I left that for you."

She shook like a leaf in the crisp November breeze, but her expression held no sign of anger. Griffin sat, tamping down the twinge of guilt for cheating her, and shuffled the deck. *You're not making her play.* No, he wasn't. He didn't browbeat or threaten her. She chose to play because she wanted an excuse to touch him without having to admit she was attracted to him. That made him feel better about deceiving her. He tossed out five cards for each of them and lifted his hand.

He had two pair—tens and kings. He surveyed the back of her cards. *Shit.* His heart set to galloping in his chest. He was going to lose. The blasted woman had a full house—three kings and two jacks all lined up like perfect little soldiers. He almost tossed down his cards in defeat, but then she'd know what he'd done. "How many cards?" *None, idiot. She's got a perfect fucking hand.*

Her eyes snapped up at his surly tone and her head cocked to the side. "Are you all right?"

"Mm."

Her chin lifted, her gaze remaining steady on his. "I'll take three."

For a heartbeat or two, he stared. "What?"

"Three." She held up the center three cards in her hand, and set them in the discard pile face down. "I want three cards."

His hand shook when he pulled the top three cards from the deck and tossed them in front of her. He couldn't look to see what she had. She tried to throw the goddamned game and with his luck she'd still beat him.

"Dealer takes one." He dropped his odd card down and drew a six, leaving him no better and no worse than he'd been. Heart pounding in his ears, he wondered at his reaction. Yeah, he wanted her, but that didn't explain the anxiety crawling under his skin. Wanting sex didn't equate to the crushing disappointment he'd felt a moment ago when he'd thought he'd lost, nor the elation of watching her try to throw the game. Why the hell had this become so important to him? Whatever was going on with him was a hell of a lot more than wanting.

"What do you got, Angel?"

She lay down a flat hand. She'd traded everything for nothing.

For him.

He laid down his two pair, unsure if he felt ashamed or grateful or awed that she'd pretty much cheated, too.

For him.

Gathering up the cards and stuffing them into their box, he held his breath waiting to see what she would do. Maybe she knew what he'd done. *Had she set all this up just to call him out for cheating?* She'd worn his shirt again. The damned thing came down to her knees so he couldn't see if she wore anything else when she leaned over to grab her pack. Suddenly, he was nervous.

The sun had dropped below the horizon, giving him the benefit of twilight's shadows, but he discovered he was worried. He'd planned things this way so she'd have the benefit of darkness to hide in, hoping she'd be less shy. But he found he needed it, too. For the first time in his life, he was worried he wouldn't please a woman. That was an unsettling thought. One he didn't like one bit.

Keys gripped in one hand, shackles in the other, she bit her lip in indecision.

When he was in prison he vowed he'd never let anyone put cuffs on him again. Yet here he was about to allow the widow of his enemy tie him up. He wet his lips. "Now, don't you lose that key."

Her whole face lit up with her smile. "I didn't think you weren't scared of anything."

Oh, he was scared.

She knee-walked over to him. "Lean forward."

Putting his hands behind his back, he waited for her to cuff him and when that second click resonated in his ears his heart jumped in his chest. Good God, he'd lost his mind. He cleared the thickness from his throat and leaned back against the tree. "I'm all yours for the next fifteen minutes." But when he met her gaze, he wished he'd kept his damned mouth shut.

Her whole body shook, her eyes were wide, dilated. "Close your eyes."

Now he started shaking, too. Eyes closed, hands cuffed behind his back, she could kill him as easy as kiss him.

She shifted, kneeling over his lap, her inner thighs enclosing his and his cock jumped to life, straining up toward her heat. He expected her to snuggle down into his lap and kiss him, but she leaned forward, instead. Her shirtfront brushed his face as she held his head to her, hands in his hair, cheek rubbing the top of his head. A shudder ran through her and infected him. This might be the most tenderness he'd experienced since he'd been a kid. He told himself he didn't need or want any such thing, but then why did he rub his cheek against her, seeking more. Her clean scent filled each breath and when her hands cupped his face and her lips pressed to the top of his head, tears pricked behind his eyes.

Good God, what was it about this woman? Why did she affect him so profoundly?

She trailed her mouth down his forehead, over his cheek until her lips were close enough for him to capture with his. He thrust his tongue toward hers, desperate for her taste, frantic to get inside her any way she'd allow. Leaning forward, he chased her flavor as far as he could.

Prudence sat back, breathing hard, studying him in the twilight.

Damn it, he shouldn't have rushed.

She pushed him back with one hand. "This is my fifteen minutes."

"Thirteen." His breath shuddered out of him.

The lavender of her eyes seemed lit from within as she followed the path of her hands over his shoulders and down his chest. Butterfly soft, she brushed her fingers over his nipples, driving him insane. His cock, already hard and aching, jumped against the confines of the towel.

Her gaze dropped and she bit her lip.

Please, dear God, let her take me in hand.

She leaned in, mouth to the pulse at his throat and rotated her hips against him.

Shivers darted out from his groin. He moaned.

Pulling her hands away, she set her fingers to the buttons on the shirt she wore. The whole time, her hips flexed, squeezing his cock between their bodies, riding the bulge of his erection. She pulled the edges of the shirt wide, leaning in to kiss him, letting her hardened nipples stab into his chest. Thrusting her tongue into his mouth, she moaned. She grasped his neck, his shoulder, gasping in breathy little sighs.

He flexed his hands in the cuffs, wanting for all the world to put his hands on her hips and drag her against the length of his cock. Wanting to cup those gorgeous breasts. Wanting to sink deep into her heat. "Harder."

She nipped his lip and he almost cursed when she slowed her pace. She sank low on his lap and dragged herself across the bulge of his erection in one long caress.

His nuts drew up tight as pressure built. "Christ, you're gonna make me come."

"Isn't that the point?" She tweaked his nipple, sending a shockwave through him.

He needed every ounce of control to keep his body in line. She had him wound so tight he wasn't sure how much longer he could wait.

Her thick lashes lowered as she watched her hand stroked over the towel. "Can I . . .?"

Ah, God. "Yeah."

Getting to her knees again, she pulled the towel from around his waist. She sat back on his legs, watching as she curled her fingers around the base of his shaft. "Your skin's soft. Hot."

He sucked in a breath, closing his eyes and letting his head fall back. Her hand was warm and her grip tight, sending pleasure roaring through his loins on her first stroke. Her other hand joined in the play, squeezing his head, rolling her thumb over the slit on top.

"Angel, I think . . . Ah, Christ." He couldn't catch his breath, never experienced anything as erotic as this woman exploring his body. The way she watched for his every reaction, the way she responded to him, growing aroused from his pleasure. His fifteen moments of bliss were over, he was sure. He intended to remind her and he had no doubt it would kill him when she stopped. "I think the time's—"

She kissed him, her tongue tangling with his in an erotic love play while her hands set a rhythm he was powerless to resist. Her whole body rocked against his, her nipples chafing his chest. The scent of their desire mingled in the humid air. His body tensed, and his orgasm struck like a thunderclap, bombarding his senses and escaping on a hoarse shout.

He opened his eyes.

She swiped her finger across her semen-smeared belly and stuck it in her mouth to taste him.

Just like that, he grew hard again.

She was gorgeous, bathed in moonlight, his shirt hanging open over her small frame. "Undo the cuffs."

Without a word, she picked up the keys, reached around him and undid his constraints. Rising to her knees, she moved to get off him and he stayed her with a hand to her wrist.

"Ask me." He sounded desperate, needy.

Her gaze darted to his lap, eyes widening when she saw him already hard again.

"Say the words."

"I—" She licked her lips. "I—"

Griffin released her. "Never mind." He stood and strode off to the pond, hoping the cool water would abate his erection.

What the hell did he expect? After the things he told her today he was surprised she even wanted to touch him. He hadn't even skimmed the surface of his misdeeds.

Prudence stared after him, anger and disappointment warring inside her. He'd waited this long, he couldn't hold out a few more seconds? Why couldn't he understand how difficult this was for her?

She had begun to believe he wanted *her*.

Sweat trickled down between her breasts, the sensation lifting the hair on her arms. She shifted uncomfortably. Bringing Griffin to orgasm had been the single most erotic experience of her life. Hearing him gasp and moan, breathing in his musk, feeling his muscles bunch and flex under her and tasting him. Her whole body was one throbbing, aching mess. He did this. He made her believe he wanted her. He made her start caring for him. He made her want him despite her fears.

Well, he was getting her.

She got to her feet and marched over to the water's edge, dropping shirt and panties behind her.

He didn't turn at her approach, so she dipped her foot in the water and splashed him.

Griffin whirled around, anger written in the lines on his face. "What?"

"You're an impatient ass." She stepped into the water.

"And?"

She took a deep breath. "I want you." As soon as the words left her mouth, she jerked back, surprised she'd gotten them out.

He started wading toward her.

"Wait." She held up her hand, trying to stay his advance, but he didn't stop until her palm flattened against his chest and pressed between their bodies. "I'm afraid of disappointing you. What if—"

His mouth crashed down on hers, his tongue stroking and teasing hers. Prudence wound her arms around his neck, rubbing her breasts against his chest. This part she liked. She leaned into him, loving the contrast of the cool water compared to the heat radiating from his body. His whiskers chafed her lips and chin, and left a hot, tingly trail as he made his way down her throat, nipping and sucking at her skin.

A fresh surge of desire throbbed deep in her belly. She arched her back, lifting her hips to his. Why couldn't sex be this blissful?

He lifted her, drawing one puckered nipple into his mouth, stroking his tongue against the turgid tip. All her attention zeroed in on that one point, reveling in the blissful shivers racing under her skin. He ran the uneven edges of his teeth along the tip, making her gasp before he pulled away. "You worry too much." He licked her other nipple and suckled until she clutched his head in her arms, moaning from the intense sensations. "I told you I'd take care of you." He pulled her thighs up to wrap around his hips. "You remember?"

"Yes." The tip of his cock teased her entrance while he suckled and nipped at her breasts. Her pussy pulsed and clenched as if trying to grasp hold of him. Part of her wanted to let herself sink down on the broad head of his cock. A more prominent part of her was still terrified.

It wasn't his cock that slipped past her nether lips, but his fingers. Her arms tightened around him, expecting pain, but a shiver of pleasure tripped up her spine. She released a shuddering breath. First one digit, testing and teasing her inner walls, then a second, thrusting in and spreading wide on the descending stroke.

"Relax, Angel." His ragged breathing buffeted her breast. "You're too tight."

With her legs spread wide and wrapped around his hips, she had no way to escape his sensual assault. His fingers stretched her, easing in and out. She held on, riding out the pleasure, the hollow, aching emptiness inside her growing ravenous. "Griff, please."

"Please, what?" His stormy green eyes looked black in the moonlight, his expression stark as he waited, fingers buried deep inside her, flexing.

Prudence took his face in her hands. "Make love with me."

"I thought you'd never ask." His lips twitched into a wry grin. "Hang on to me, Angel." He waded to the edge of the pool and carried her out of the water.

She bit his earlobe, nuzzling his neck until he reached their campsite and lay her back on the blanket. He didn't give her time to grow nervous, lowering his weight over her at once. The crisp, wet hair on his legs tickled her inner thighs and the cool metal of his dogtags fell between her breasts as he kissed her neck, his mouth hot and damp.

Prudence clutched his head in her arms, keeping him close and arching against him. The scruff on his jaw chafed and teased her skin, making her writhe under the assault of so many new sensations. He eased down her body, pausing to suck a nipple into his mouth, before licking his way lower and thrusting his tongue into her navel, his tags dragging down her torso in his wake.

She'd given him permission, why didn't he mate with her?

Teeth nipped at her hipbone making her muscles cramp and tense. "Griffin?"

"I got you."

That he did. He spread her thighs wide, hitching them over his shoulders and dove for her core.

A shout escaped her lips at the first brusque buss of his lips on her clit. His fingers thrust into her and she tensed, expecting pain. There was none. His slick tongue slipped over her clit, the rough brush of his stubble bristled against her nether lips and his fingers pumped into her. There was nothing sweet or polite about what he did to her. He was urgent. Demanding. Even a little rough.

But she didn't hurt.

Her back arched off the ground, she couldn't catch her breath, couldn't take any more and yet urged her body deeper onto his fingers, tighter to the seal of his lips. Waves of shivery pleasure raced over her skin, tightening her nipples, lifting gooseflesh on her skin, and raising the hair on her scalp.

Frenzied. He'd told her once that their joining would be frenzied. She'd imagined a quick, painful rut. But he hadn't meant they'd be rushed, he'd meant the sensations, the emotions of their joining would be intense and tumultuous. He was right, pleasure warred with uncertainty, fear with sweet need. In this moment, she felt more than she could ever remember feeling before. Her mind grew crowded with questions, with shock at each new ripple of pleasure.

She could bear whatever pain their joining brought if this was the precursor. She should be terrified, but his strong arms anchored her in place, reassuring and steady. And whenever fear began clawing its way into her consciousness, she lifted her head and met his unwavering, confident gaze.

As long as he didn't lose hold of the tight reins of his control, they'd be fine. She'd be safe.

Slow, intense pulses began building inside her. Goddess bless him, he was doing it again. A low moan reverberated through her body as she drifted toward that magical place. Release burst upon her, stealing her breath, blinding as pleasure throbbed through her. Griffin's hard length covered her body, he still had one of her legs drawn over his arm, holding her wide beneath him. The broad head of his cock pressed to her entrance and stopped.

"Tell me you want me."

Fear began to crowd in on her enjoyment, but seeing him holding rein over his own desire, his face pulled tight, expecting and bracing for her rejection made her brave. She wanted to please him by giving back some of what he'd given her. She wanted to join with him. "I do. I want you."

He pushed into her on one long thrust, the width of his cock stretching her, filling her near to bursting.

She stared up into his eyes, shocked to her core. "It . . . It doesn't hurt."

"What?" He reared back. "That's what you've been afraid of?" At her nod, he cursed.

Prudence pulled him down for a kiss, hiding from his questions. He didn't need to know. No one ever needed to know what her marriage had been like or what Randolph had done.

The generous man in her arms set her free from all that. And as he started to move, thrusting in and out of her body in thick, slick glides, something warm and fragile built in her chest. Tenderness swamped her, bringing the sting of tears to her eyes. She held him close, stoking him, running her fingers through his hair, trying to find a way to touch him the same way he'd touched her.

She was driving him insane.

Her hands were never still, stroking and grasping his sweat-slicked skin, her mouth wild under his, her toes curling into the back of his leg. Christ, her sweet, tight pussy clutched around his shaft on every outward stroke as if trying to hold him inside.

The scent of their desire mingled in the humid air and her breathy sighs and husky moans urged him on.

His control hung in threads. His whole body shook as he forced himself to go slow, to be tender when all he wanted was to thrust as deep into her wet heat as he could get. The desire to possess, to own and to claim warred with his need to protect and ease her. He rotated his hips against her and felt the sting of her nails on his back as her inner walls clung to his shaft. Heat simmered in his loins, drawing his sac up tight to his body and sending tendrils of pleasure rolling through him. Jesus, he was close. Too close.

He pulled out of her, and she cried out.

"I just need . . . I need a minute." He released her leg and shifted so he could take one of her nipples into her mouth. She had beautiful breasts, a handful with pert nipples he loved to run his tongue over. He dragged his open mouth down her belly, letting her feel his teeth on her skin, and smiling as she twitched and shivered beneath him. He ran his open palm over the birthmark on her stomach, licking the outline until she gripped fistfuls of his hair to bring him back where she wanted him.

Getting to his knees, he pulled her toward him until her ass hung between his thighs.

"What are you—?"

He pressed his cock back into her depths. "Watch."

Her eyes opened and she lifted onto her elbows, her attention zeroing in on where their bodies joined. Her desire coated them both, glistening in the moonlight, her opening stretched wide around him.

Griffin stroked his thumb to her clit, circling, rubbing. Her eyes widened and fixed on his hand, watching his every move.

"You're beautiful."

His gaze shot to hers.

A soft smile curved her lips. "The way your body moves. The way your muscles bunch and flex."

Pleased by her praise, by how freely she gave to him, he paused, a little guilty about how they came to be in this position. "I cheated you at cards."

"I know." Her lips twitched. "I cheated, too."

He sucked in a hard breath. He'd known she'd cheated, but her confession, so easily given, shocked the hell out of him. He thrust into her, making her gasp. "Come for me, Angel." She tightened around his shaft. She was close and he wanted her to come before he did. His thumb grazed over her clit and he pinched the little bud lightly.

She fell back on the blanket, her body arching.

Griffin grinned. Prudence Angelica Parnell had a dirty streak in her. Maybe she didn't realize it yet, but she liked him a little rough, a bit coarse. He found that quality sexy as hell. He gave into his need to increase their pace, pinching and plucking at her clit. Her head tossed from side to side, her moans and gasps coming more urgent now. "Come for me, Pru."

Her whole body tensed, her thighs squeezing around him as her inner walls broke into pulsing release around his cock. He lowered himself over her, thrusting hard, sealing her lips with his, and chasing her orgasm with his own.

Starbursts of euphoria erupted inside him and he shouted, sinking deep within her tight sheath.

His heart pounded in his chest. Something happened there, something strange and new and terrifying. Something well beyond a physical release. He tried to roll away, sure his weight must be crushing her and desperate to escape, but she held on, ending up sprawled over him. All those sweet, tight curves snuggled up close.

"Christ, Angel."

Had he really imagined he could fuck her without losing a part of himself? Prudence had touched him in odd ways since the day she stood facing him on that stage. She intrigued him. Infuriated him.

She made him want her.

And now he wanted more.

Griffin Jude Payne wrapped his arms around her. How the hell was it possible to be so close to her and still have her so far out of reach? He stared up at the stars peeking through the trees, cursing himself. She had been correct—not all starry skies were the same.

Not all men were the same.

Some deserved a woman like Prudence.

And some were assassins who'd ruined the world.

17

Spent and sated, Randolph dropped to his belly, Bronsen's weight pressing him to the mattress. The only sound in the room was his thundering heart, their labored breathing. The scent of their lovemaking laced the air. Bronsen nipped his shoulder and shifted his weight to lie next to him.

Randolph didn't move. He was content. His tics had stopped for the moment. His thoughts were calm, focused. All this would be over soon. Even now, ships were out, scanning the surface of Asteria for signs of Prudence. The Blue Helmets would find her.

Bronsen stroked his hand down Randolph's spine. "I'm worried about you. You've been so stressed lately."

"I'm fine. Or I will be, once we have Prudence."

"You know, Randy, you could turn things over to me for a while." Bronsen's warm breath brushed his ear, making him shiver. "Not anything permanent, just long enough to set things to right again." His hand stroked over Randolph's ass. "We could head home, you and me. You could make a public announcement. I'll take care of the Rebels, get everyone on our side again. You know I'd do anything for you."

It wasn't the first time Bronsen had made the suggestion. In some ways, it was tempting . . . Bronsen was good at making things right. But he needed to do this. He had to finish what his brother had started. After all, Alfred had done everything for him. "No. I can do this. We need to find Prudence. Once we have her, the people will listen to me again."

Alfred would've wanted it that way.

Sometime during the night, Griffin shook Prudence awake. She stared up at him through groggy eyes and a fogged mind. "Morning already?" She wasn't sure why she asked the question, the skies were still lit by moonlight, the air was cool.

"There's a ship coming."

A ship? They were rescued? They could fly to the spaceport in comfort and . . . . She glanced back toward the low rumble of the craft. A thin line of red light almost a meter long scanned over the ground below. They were searching for signs of life. They might even be searching for her. "Oh, no."

"Come on." He took her hand and pulled her up. "We can hide in the water; I already stowed our stuff."

Prudence glanced back and sure enough all their belongings were out of sight. The ship floated closer, the surrounding trees bending low from the wind caused by the ship, the red scanning lights lit the ground where they'd been sleeping.

Water enveloped her foot; she paused. What was he doing?

"I need you to trust me, Angel." He cupped her face, whispering in her ear. "The water will keep us hidden from the scanners."

Oh, goddess. He must be whispering because he feared they were scanning for sound, too. "How?"

His lips thinned into a half-hearted smile. "High school science—water refracts light." He drew her deeper into the pool. "We'll have to stay below the surface until they pass."

She backed away, shaking her head. "No."

"Yes. I don't know why they're here. Somehow, I doubt it's for a failure like me. It's your choice—Randolph and the ship, or me and the water."

Prudence didn't even think, she threw herself into his arms.

"Watch the light." He lowered them both down to their chins. "When it gets close, hold your breath and stay under until the water gets dark again. Understand?"

"What if I can't hold my breath that long?"

His mouth brushed her ear. "I'll keep you safe, Angel."

The red lines of light approached, edging right up to the pool before sliding back the other way.

"They'll scan the pond on the next pass. Take a deep breath as soon as it hits the edge of the pond."

Heart hammering away in her chest, she wrapped her arms tighter around Griffin. The trees bowed and the water rippled and splashed around them as the ship hovered overhead. The red beam swung back their way, crawling over the ground, the rocks, the trees and shrubs, right up the edge of the pond.

Prudence inhaled a deep breath and Griffin pulled them both down. As the red light passed over them, their eyes met.

She put him in danger by being near him. If they found her—found them together—Randolph would kill Griffin.

The beam passed overhead, but instead of moving on, it came back. Pressure built in her chest. Her lungs began to burn and her panic built. Had they been seen? Griffin believed the water would protect them, but how could he be sure? Anxiety crawled under her skin as the beam passed over, lighting the water around them for what felt like an eternity. Her lungs ached, burning with the need for air. She tightened her grip on Griffin. *Please, Goddess, give me strength. Don't let me do anything stupid.*

But she needed air.

Old fears unfurled inside her. Her body would inhale soon. Her oxygen-deprived body would start to shut down, she'd begin to lose consciousness and, as her mind became scattered, she'd reflexively pull in a long, deep breath of water. It would burn. Her lungs would seize as they tried to expel the liquid which would make her suck in even more water.

They were both going to die.

Griffin fisted his hand and placed the circle of his thumb and forefinger against her mouth.

She didn't understand.

He nodded, putting his fist to his mouth and tipping his face up.

He wanted her to use his hand like a straw. Goddess bless him.

She tipped her head back and he lifted her until she could take a fresh breath of air through his fist. She inhaled a deep breath and pulled herself down, keeping herself submerged by holding on to the rocky edge of the pool, while Griffin took a fresh breath, too.

The red scanning light passed again. This time, it moved on. Griffin found her arm in the dark water, gave her a squeeze and urged her up. They broke the surface at the same time, both taking deep, quiet breaths, unsure if the ship just scanned for life, or if they were scanning for sound, too.

His lips grazed her ear. "You got something you need to tell me?"

She didn't know what to say. Griffin was the first man to ever want her for herself. She had no desire to complicate things by telling him about the gift she carried for her mate. She had no desire to explain why Randolph wanted her or how he meant to use her. She also didn't want to lie.

"Remember I told you President McKinley wore a carnation for luck?"

His cheek brushed hers when he nodded.

"I'm his carnation."

Griffin backed away, his brows drawing together. "What do you mean?"

"Randolph thinks I . . . bring him luck."

"But why?"

"Because Alfred thought I brought him luck and Randolph has always wanted everything his brother had."

He shook his head, looking off into the distance. "I think they're gone." His gaze returned to her. "For now. We need to beat feet, though. We'll be better able to hide from the scanners in the forest where there are lots of plants and animals." He started to climb out of the water, but Prudence grabbed his hand, afraid he was angry with her.

"Maybe they're not looking for me."

He sank back down next to her, taking her face in his hands. "If you'd gone missing on me, I'd want you back." He kissed her, slow and sweet. "Except I wouldn't have sent someone for you. I'd have come myself."

Goddess bless him, that was the sweetest thing anyone had ever said to her. "I don't want you to get hurt." She couldn't stand it if anything happened to Griffin. In a very short time, he'd come to mean so much to her.

"I'm not gonna." He bussed her lips again and started out of the water. "Come on. We need to get moving before the next one comes along."

"You think there will be more?" She searched the sky.

"In the Marines, when we searched for someone important enough to use scanners for, we always did so in waves of three, about an hour apart."

Prudence followed him back to their campsite and shouldered her pack. They hiked all through the night and sure enough, about an hour apart, scanning ships flew overhead, forcing them to hide in the ponds dotting the landscape. It wasn't until dawn, when they'd reached the base of the mountains that Griffin relaxed.

"Let's take a break and eat."

"Shouldn't we keep going, at least find the next pond?"

"Nah." He set his pack down and sat on a stump. "Those scanners don't work worth a shit in the daylight, especially if it's hot." He lifted the edge of his shirt and wiped the sweat from his face. "We'll be all right until tonight."

Prudence put her bag down and stretched her back, wishing she could do the same with her legs without being too obvious. After so many days of walking, or maybe because of their lovemaking last night, she felt stiff and sore in places she'd forgotten she had. She sat down in the soft blue grass and started looking through her pack for the root vegies she had left over.

"What about this?" Griffin held out two fist-sized brown objects.

"Where'd you get them?"

He pointed up. Above them, the branches of the trees were loaded with the stuff. "You think it's edible?"

She wet her lips. *Goddess, she'd give just about anything for something sweet.* "Let me check." She dug to the bottom of her pack, opened the plastic container holding her treasure, and pulled out the field guide she'd guarded so zealously.

Griffin's eyes widened. "Is that—?" He reached forward, then snatched his hand back. "Is that a . . . book?"

Prudence smiled. "A real book, printed on paper and everything." Had she been worried he'd take it from her? He appeared terrified by it. "Mm." She ran her hand over the cover. "I had it printed for this trip." With the rise of electronic media, using products that contributed to diminished natural resources had gone out of fashion. Products like books had become more expensive until the average citizen couldn't afford them. Eventually, people forgot about books, satisfied with electronic print.

"I've never seen one."

"Printing is a dying art." She opened it, paging though to the section on plants. "I'm friends with the Sisters of Charity. The nuns have strong feelings about certain things, one being the need for the printed word. They have this theory that someday all our knowledge might be lost if our networks go down. They don't like the idea of all the print books in the world being in the Global Gallery, inaccessible to the masses. I guess their paranoia turned out to be a good thing for me. I never owned a Saph-link—not that one would be much good on Asteria."

"Can I see?"

She held the book out to him and he shook his head as he scooted off the stump to sit behind her. "You hold it. I just want to look."

Prudence leaned back against the strong wall of his chest and paged through until she found pictures of tree fruit. On the fourth page in she found an image of a fruit similar to what Griffin had. She held the fruit next to the page. "Berriegranate. It's edible." She glanced at him over her shoulder, but he appeared to have forgotten about the fruit, all his attention on the pages of the book.

"You know my favorite part?"

He dragged his attention from the book. "What?"

Keeping her eyes on him, she lifted her treasure to their faces. "Smell."

They both inhaled a deep breath of the intriguing scent of printed paper, woodsy, and a little bitter. They shared a smile. "The Sisters are a bit rebellious. They still have an old press down in their basement and make copies of books they think are worth preserving. Sister Agnes took me down into their vault once. They had books from long ago and they all smelled different. She said it depended on what type of tree pulp the pages were pressed from, the type of glue and ink, and where it'd been. She said they picked up scents like clothing does."

"Hm." He nuzzled the side of her neck. "Odd how the damn thing brings on a sense of nostalgia when I've never even seen one before."

"The sisters taught me how to make them."

The low rumble of his laugher rolled through him. "A pioneer, huh?"

Yes, she had told him that she wanted to be a pioneer, but even pioneers needed books. She grinned. "Why not? Why can't we have books on Asteria? Why can't we do away with the bans on non-Christian religions, eradicate the social classes, and start over?"

Griffin's expression grew serious. "There's some things that don't change, Angel."

"Why not? The only reason something can't change is if people don't want it to. That's why I didn't want to stay on Earth. People seemed to like the way things were. I didn't. I want to have an altar in my home dedicated to Dydona. I want to print and read books. I want—" She almost told him she wanted to be with him. Almost. But her feelings for him were too new and undefined. She knew she wanted him. She knew she liked to be with him. She cared for him. But was all that enough?

"I guess we'll find out what's what when we find civilization. We'll see what the people of Asteria want."

"And if we don't like it, we can always start a new town."

He searched her face for a moment, something stark and pain-filled in his expression. "We better eat, Angel. We can't hang about all day." He picked up one of the brown fruits and moved back to his place on the stump.

"What's wrong?"

He took a bite of the fruit and motioned to the book. "What else does it say in there? Anything about the Scarecrows?"

Prudence wanted to continue the conversation, but knew he wouldn't cooperate, so she let it drop. For now. "I've read that chapter a hundred times. The Scarecrows live in the mountains." She picked up her piece of fruit and wiped it with her shirt. "They live in caves and use echolocation to hunt."

"They're blind?"

"Seems so. Nocturnal, too. Doesn't slow them down, though. They can fly and they're quick. The fool who wrote this book says he survived by staying in their caves at night." She let out an unladylike snort.

"Sounds reasonable."

She stared. "Are you crazy? This is the same author who says the Black Desert is about half the size of what we endured."

He shrugged. "Think about it, they all leave to hunt and we're safe until dawn."

"Oh sure, we just have to sneak past them not once, but twice."

"At least we'll know where they are. Better than making camp out in the open and jumping at every little sound. You have a better idea?"

"Goddess preserve us, you're insane."

"Oh, lady, you don't know the half of it."

Prudence reared back. "We're back to that, are we? I'm just 'lady,' again?"

Griffin got up. "I'll be right back." He walked off to get away from her for a few minutes.

What the hell were they doing? For a few minutes there they were cozied up, sharing a moment over a book that he would remember for-fucking-ever. There she sat, talking away about changing things. About not needing social classes. Making it sound like they were going to be together forever. She was making *plans*. And him, dumb-ass that he was, listened. Thought, *yeah, you know, she's right. We could live here, the two of us happily-ever-after.*

Bullshit. Horseshit. Scarecrow shit. Shit. Shit. Shit. Griffin sat down and hung his head. He wasn't supposed to care. He never gave a damn about the women he slept with and, damn it, they never gave him a second thought, either.

Why the fuck was she different?

She crawled right under his skin and snuggled up 'round his heart. Now what? *Now you do what you gotta do. You find your brother, you get your ass back to Earth and you make things right. Leave her here, take her there, either way you can't let her make plans until you get your honor back.*

"Griffin?"

"Yeah, I'm coming." He dragged his hand over his head and down his face. *Priorities. He had to keep his priorities straight.*

18

Griffin kept his gaze locked on the entrance to the cave.

The sun drifted below the horizon and, weapon in hand, he waited to see if anything was going to come out.

Behind him, Prudence had a shaky-handed death grip on his shirt. She was furious with him for this, but he'd be damned if he would sit out here in the open letting the Scarecrows pick them off like fish in a barrel.

Bit by bit, the lavender sky turned royal purple, deep violet, and then black. The stars appeared and the first of three moons rose above the treetops. Hell, when he'd first arrived, he didn't think Asteria had a moon. Every other night since, a new one popped up.

His legs grew stiff and ached from squatting. He turned to Prudence. "We picked an empty cave. Come on, let's get inside before anything sneaks up on us."

She let out a long, shuddering breath and opened her mouth to say something, but her attention jerked to the side. "Look."

There, to the side of the cave, one of those blue-and-black-striped creatures grazed in the blue grass. Griffin's mouth watered. They'd nicknamed the creature zeblu and it was delicious. "Stay quiet."

Griffin made his way closer, Prudence right behind him, easing around the bushes for a clear shot. The zeblu moved off to one side to graze in a fresh batch of blue grass, leaving nothing but the tip of its nose visible.

"Christ." Griffin got back to his feet, sneaking closer to the mouth of the cave. Pressing his back against the stone surrounding it, he leaned around to take the shot. He lifted the gun.

Fluttering filled the night air.

The blue-and-black-striped zeblu lifted its graceful head, its ears perking.

A loud screech made Griffin freeze. The noise reverberated, sinking straight down to his bones and in its wake the flapping became almost deafening, a thousand wings beating simultaneously, echoing in the entrance to the cave. The zeblu darted away, and a big, gray blur flew out of the cave, followed by half a dozen more.

Griffin jumped back, trapping Prudence between him in the wall. Watched in awe as the creatures lifted their dinner high in the air. More winged creatures joined the first and tore the bleating zeblu into several pieces. Blood rained down. A ragged leg dropped, landing near the mouth of the cave with a meaty thump.

Scarecrows. Dozens more erupted from the mouth of the cave, taking to the skies in search of food. Griffin's gut twisted as one circled back and landed not four feet away with its back to them. The creature bent down to retrieve the leg that had fallen from the sky. Wet smacking mingled with the sound of flesh being torn from bone. Griffin reached behind himself and squeezed Prudence's hand, hoping she understood they were in peril.

Of course she knew, she hadn't wanted to do this from the get go. If they survived, it'd be a long while, he was sure, before she let him live this down.

He released her and she slipped the open Swiss Army knife into his hand.

A bird took flight from the trees behind them and the Scarecrow turned around.

The humanoid creature had leathery wings spanning from wrists to ankles like a bat. The fingers and toes resembled a bat's, too, with thin, clawed appendages extending out from its limbs. That's where the similarities ended. He'd always found bats to be cute, but there was nothing flattering about the Scarecrow. Its brownish-gray skin had the texture of a burlap bag. The eyes were tiny and black and the ears nothing more than holes in the side of its bulbous head. The sole feature of note was its mouth—a long black slash across its face.

The scarecrow tipped its head from side to side.

Neither one of them had moved. Neither made a sound, but something had captured the Scarecrow's attention.

Griffin gripped the blade tight and studied the odd creature. He'd rather avoid using the gun—the sound might draw others. If he needed to, he'd go for the throat. Maybe the ear. If it was an ear, he'd have a direct-connect to the brain, providing his blade was long enough.

The creature stood before him.

His heart jumped in his chest and a healthy dose of adrenaline flushed into his system. He hadn't even seen it move. One second it had been there, now it was here, so close he could smell its rotten breath. *Breath.*

The sound of their breathing had drawn its attention. Griffin held his, praying Prudence would notice and do the same.

She didn't.

The scarecrow opened its mouth, revealing rows of jagged, rotten teeth, and screeched. Hell, it must be trying to get a bead on them, trying to see them through echo-location.

Griffin's muscles tensed with his weapon held between him and the scarecrow. If push came to shove, he'd fire, but how many more would he attract?

The creature opened its mouth again, and this time Griffin struck, ramming the blade into the creature's ear.

He didn't kill it.

The fucking thing screamed, the sound different from the noise it had made before. Thin, clawed hands reached for his neck and blazed a fiery trail down his chest, shredding shirt and skin.

He wrested the blade from the Scarecrow's head and thrust the knife into its neck. The Scarecrow fell to the ground, thrashing wildly, and Griffin leapt onto it, stabbing into its throat and face until its arms fell limp to the ground.

The Scarecrow had black blood. He tried to wipe the sticky, foul-smelling stuff from his hands, but all he managed was to spread it around more He swiped at his face with his upper arm, and his sleeve came away black.

Damn it, he needed to get it off before Prudence saw.

"Griffin."

He refused to turn to her. "Get in the cave." He had to get the blood off. If she saw him like this she'd know. She'd see how comfortable he was with killing. She'd know he had horrible secrets.

"Come with me."

The sound of flapping wings drew his gaze to the sky. Four of the creatures had returned to investigate. Griffin reached behind him for Prudence. "Get in the cave, stay against the wall and don't breathe if they get close."

Her hands pulled at his shirt, urging him up.

He waved her away. "Go." He got to his feet, following, but keeping his eyes to the sky. He'd be damned if she'd get hurt on his watch.

One of the creatures screeched.

Griffin froze. After a heartbeat or two, he moved again, easing back.

It screeched again.

Shit. He froze, but knew he'd been caught. If the thing had half a brain in its head, it'd realize he'd moved.

The Scarecrows swooped down, encircling him.

Griffin lifted the blaster. If he was going, he would go down fighting. He shot the closest, swinging around and stabbing his blade into the neck of the second. For a split second, he thought he might make it. He brought the gun around, ready to shoot the third, but the Scarecrow knocked the gun from his hand, leaving long claw marks across his arm. He ripped his blade out of the second one's neck, slashing out at the third. He gouged deep into the thing's boney chest.

Behind him, the second Scarecrow still moved, its clawed hand closed around his ankle. The third grabbed hold of his wrist. A vision of that blue-and-black-striped zeblu being torn apart flashed through his mind, except in his mind's eye, the creatures ripped *him* to pieces.

A blast lit the night.

The Scarecrow holding his arm released him and dropped to the ground. He spun around, stepping on the other's arm, and coming down on it with the knife, stabbing until it let go.

Prudence still held the blaster in jittery hands, ready to shoot again if needed, lavender tears rolling down her face.

He stood. He was covered in blood. His. Theirs. And the way she stared at him—as if he were one of the Scarecrows—he knew beyond a shadow of a doubt that she was seeing him for who and what he was: A killer.

He needed to get her inside where they'd be safe for a while, but he feared startling her if he moved. Holding his arms out wide, he dared a step closer, his gaze flicking up to check the sky before returning to hers.

She jumped at his movement and for a heart-stopping moment, he stared down the barrel of his own weapon.

A shudder ran through her. She blinked. Her arms dropped to her sides, and she ran to him, throwing her arms around him.

Jesus. She wasn't afraid of him. The wave of relief that washed through him left him trembling. He gathered her into his arms and carried her into the cave. He found a place to sit and held her close. "You're all right, Angel. We're fine."

She squeezed her arms around his neck and cried silently.

Christ. He leaned back against the wall and held her tight. Why wouldn't she say anything?

Her whole body quaked with heart-rending sobs and it gutted him to think somehow he was the cause. "Say something. Yell at me. Curse me. Anything." He rocked her, unable to sit still any longer. "Goddamn it, please, Angel. Tell me what's wrong with you."

She sniffled, pulling away to look him in the face. Her eyes were red and swollen, her face tear-streaked and she was furious. "What's wrong with me? I thought I lost you. They grabbed you and I thought . . . ." A shudder ran through her. "I remembered what they did to the zeblu."

He gave her a shaky nod. "Me, too."

She kissed him, her fingers twined punishingly tight in his hair. He got just a taste of her before she pulled away and got to her feet, pacing deeper into the cave. "Instead of asking what's wrong with me, why don't you tell me what's wrong with you? I'm so upset with you, I can't even look at you right now. You could've died, you stubborn ass." Each word snapped with anger, but she kept her voice the barest whisper. She came back to him and planted her hands on her hips. "Get up. You got us in here, now let's see where we are."

Griffin got to his feet, ignoring the pulls and twinges of his torn skin. He didn't think any of his injuries were life-threatening and he'd be damned if he drew attention to them and added fuel to the fire. It'd be bad enough when she realized Scarecrow blood now covered her, too.

Women. Why'd they have to get so damned emotional? Wasn't like he was the first one to come up with this plan. The cave was empty. They were safe until morning. Why the hell couldn't she be appreciative of the fact they were both still alive?

He followed behind her, deeper into the cave. Two-dozen feet in, the moonlight stopped and everything grew black as Scarecrow blood. "You got my pack?"

She shoved the pack at him without a word. Holy hell, this was going to be a long night.

He dug around until his hand clamped over the night-goggles and slipped them over his face. The ceiling of the cave must've reached twenty or thirty feet up, bowl-shaped, with thin, worn scars from where the Scarecrows nested. Somewhere in the back of his mind came the unsettling realization that if they creatures nested up there, the base of the cave must be covered with their shit. Slowly, he lowered his head.

The floor was moving. Worms of all sizes slithered and snaked over the mushy, dung-covered ground. Some were tiny and thin as fishhooks, others were the length of a snake.

He took Prudence's hand and started backing away, but a light toward the back of the cavern caught his attention. Brighter than moonlight, the light came from a hole in the opposite wall. "I'm gonna go check something out."

"Not without me."

Yeah, right. Like she would walk over all that. She didn't even want to be there. "The floor—" He paused his explanation. If that light proved to be a safe space, he'd need to get her over there one way or another. "—is dirty. Why don't you let me carry you?"

She snorted. "Keep moving, Warrior. I'm fine."

"Well, all right, then." He cleared his throat. This would be amusing. "If you're sure?"

"I'm sure."

"Come on." He started walking toward the light, his feet sinking into the squishy floor. One of those worms slithered over the toe of his boot and he kicked it across the cave.

Prudence grasped hold of his shirt. "What's on the floor? I can't—I can't see."

"You don't want to know, Angel." He kept going.

She squished herself against his back. "Can't we go any faster?" Her voice edged up out of a whisper. "Something's crawling on me."

He turned, picked her up and bushed the worms from her feet, all the while keeping his steady pace. "Does this get me out of the doghouse?"

"No."

He paused and her arms wrapped tighter around his neck. "Griffin Jude Payne, don't you dare drop me."

A chuckle broke from his mouth. "Christ, you are a piece of work, lad—"

"And don't you call me lady."

"What would you prefer?" Something squishy crunched under his boot heel.

"Angel. I like it when you call me Angel."

"Then act like one."

Her gasp echoed in the cavern.

19

He reached the light and bent down with her in his arms to look through the man-sized hole situated waist-high on the wall. Inside, the stone floor was clear of critters and shit and a pool curved around the far wall. "Get in." He lowered her enough that she could crawl through without putting her feet down on this side. Then he pulled off the goggles and followed her through, pausing to dust the critters from his boots.

The stones glowed. Not all of them, but long flowing veins of iridescent stone wove into the gray rock walls. Stalactites hung from the ceiling and stalagmites poked up from the ground around the edges of the cave, streaks of luminous minerals swirling through the cone-shaped formations.

"It's beautiful." Prudence stared into the pool. The rocks made the red-tinged liquid glow.

At least after a bath he wouldn't have to worry so much about infection. The claw marks stung like hell, telling him the cuts were caked with dirt and sweat and God knew what else.

She turned and her eyes widened and she let out a gasp. "You're hurt."

"It's nothing."

"I'll decide."

There was no avoiding her unless he wanted to go sleep with the worms. It was as if she'd suddenly grown twenty arms, no matter which way he turned, there she was, prodding his wounds. "Jesus, lad—"

Her eyes narrowed.

"Angel."

She tugged at the remnants of his shirt. "Take this off, or at least what's left of it."

He pulled his shirt off, trying not to wince at the tug and burn of torn flesh. Thick gashes crossed his chest, the centers of the cuts wider than the ends. "I'll go for a swim and be fine. The water is antiseptic, remember. You first. Go on, you're covered in blood."

"Stop. Enough with the 'women first' philosophy. You're hurt and you probably need stitches on some of those. Get in the water." Her eyes blazed with annoyance, but her hands were undoing his pants. "This is the exact reason why I didn't want to do this. Look at you." She lifted her hand to wave at the gashes over his chest and arms. "You're a mess. What if you get an infection?" She knelt and started taking off his shoes. "Lift your foot."

He complied while he tried to figure her out. He couldn't remember ever having anyone yell at him while they undressed him before. Was she coming around to admitting she was wrong?

"Look at how red and swollen your skin is around those cuts. You may as well have served yourself up on a silver platter. All you missed was putting an apple in your mouth. This was the most reckless thing I've seen you do."

"Reckless?" He yanked off her shirt, dropped it to the floor and went after her pants.

"What are you doing?"

Her hair swung forward to cover her face as she looked down at where his hands worked on her pants.

"You're getting in the water. No need to be shy, Angel. I'm pretty damn sure I've licked every square inch of your body." He hooked his fingers into the waistband of both jeans and panties and dragged them down her legs. "Now, let's talk about reckless. Reckless would be camping out in the open. Maybe having a fire, roasting some zeblu meat, falling asleep and snoring." He pulled her foot up, removed her shoe and removed her pant leg. "You know, sending out an open invitation for dinner."

"You don't know that." She scowled.

Her hand clasped into his hair for balance while he attacked her other shoe and finished getting her clothes off. "You, Angel, should be thanking your lucky stars I'm around. You'd be dead by now without my particular brand of recklessness."

She stood in front of him like an avenging angel, fire in her eyes, chest heaving, and hands fisted. Five-foot-five of pure sensuality and biting anger. "I'm not the one bleeding all over the floor." She stomped over to the pool and lowered herself into the water. She turned around and glared at him, tears glistening on her lashes. "I'm not the one who almost died. You shouldn't have put yourself at risk." She turned around and busied herself washing away the blood.

Griffin wanted to shout. To pound something. To . . . argh. Infuriating woman. He sank down into the water, hissing when the liquid came in contact with his cuts and started bubbling like peroxide on an open wound.

There. Concentrate on the pain.

Dunking down, he wet his hair and scrubbed his skin clean. But time and again his gaze returned to Prudence. She kept her back to him, shoulders stiff. He didn't like her yelling at him, not even whisper-yelling. He didn't like being on her bad side. *You shouldn't have put yourself at risk.* Was she worried about him? Was that why she got so angry?

He waded over to her and slipped his hand onto her hip. "Are you still angry?"

"Yes."

This wasn't like her. There had been plenty of times she should've gotten mad at him, but she hadn't. Why had this set her off? They hadn't had a whole lot of options.

Pressing his lips to her shoulder, he tried to gentle her. "You know there wasn't anything else we could do."

Softer this time. "Yes."

"I didn't try to start a fight with them. You know that, right?"

"Yes."

"So explain to me why you're so upset." He trailed his lips up her neck to nuzzle below her ear.

She rubbed her cheek against his clipped hair. "Because I've fallen for you."

Ah, God, he was in trouble. Elation burst through him, leaving him shaken but smiling. "And that's bad?"

"Of course that's bad."

Of course. He was a soldier. A killer. He had no honor. He'd left the world worse off for his presence.

She turned to face him. "You've got this whole 'save the world' mentality going on and maybe for a while I fooled myself thinking you were all talk. But I realized today it's not. No matter how crazy, how suicidal, once you say you're going to do something, your goal is as good as done."

He searched her face. "I don't get what you're saying."

"I'm saying I want you to forget about returning to Earth."

Backing away, he shook his head.

"I want you to stay with me."

Christ.

"I'm saying I want you to consider what could be done here, instead of trying to fight for something on Earth that people don't seem to want."

"I can't let it go."

She covered her face with her hand and turned away. "I'm not enough."

"Not true." He came back to her, unable to allow her to think that. "Angel, I'd love nothing more than to play house with you."

"Play house?"

Damn it, he couldn't say anything right. "What I mean is, I can't think of the future until I settle the past." He put his arms around her and drew her back against him. "I can't give up on trying to put things right. It's my fault."

"No, it's not. You're not that powerful."

Her words were like a slap in the face. He understood what she meant, there were more people than him involved in fucking things up, but unlike the rest of them, he needed to redeem himself. He needed to believe he had the power to do so. He stepped away from her. From someone else, that might not even have phased him. He'd have ignored it. But from her, holy hell, that hurt.

"I'm sorry." Prudence pressed her face to his back. "I'm scared I'll lose you after just finding you and I couldn't stand it. I couldn't stand living here with nothing but memories."

"And I need someone to believe in me."

"I do. You've proven time and again to be smart and resourceful." She kissed his back. "I know if anyone could make things change, you're the one. I'm not sure any of them want to change. Do you understand the difference?"

"I can't believe that." He turned around and let himself sink in the water so he'd be face-to-face with her. "I can't believe everyone is that far gone. I have to imagine there's still some good out there. That people are still flexible and tolerant, because otherwise, what am I? I fought for them, Angel. I fought and I killed and I have to make up for the things I've done. I need to know when I go to bed at night that I did my part. That I tried." He stroked his thumb down her cheek. "I promise I won't leave you high and dry. I'll make sure you're taken care of."

"I don't want that. I want you to love me as much as I love you."

The Scarecrows couldn't have torn him up as much as she did. He *had* to complete his mission. He *had* to earn his honor back. But, by God, he loved this infuriating woman, and knowing she loved him damn near broke his heart. 'Cause he wasn't worth it.

Not yet.

He never should have put his hands on her, not after the things he'd done, the people he'd hurt. He didn't deserve her. But like the bastard he was, he couldn't stop himself from taking everything she offered.

He secured her face in his hands and he sealed her mouth with his, diving in and tasting, trying to be one with her in every way he could. Her hands wound 'round his neck, curling over his skull, trapping him close.

The cuts from the Scarecrows tugged and pulled with each movement, burning and starting to itch, but he ignored the discomfort best he could until Prudence grasped his arm. He pulled away, a shudder of pain rolling through him.

20

Prudence shook her head. "Griff." She cupped his face and kissed the corner of his mouth. "We can't do this. I can't even touch you without causing you more pain."

He didn't seem ready to give up. He turned her around and pulled her closer. His lips skated over her skin and goddess bless him, she wanted him, but he needed to rest. Needed to stop moving long enough to heal.

"Baby, don't. Your cuts." She looked at him over her shoulder.

A blush crept up his neck. At first, she thought it might be the reflection of the water on his skin, but when the red stain hit his cheeks, her lips parted in surprise.

"I . . . ." His gaze wouldn't quite meet hers. "I want to hold you."

After everything he'd done to her last night, he turned red over wanting to snuggle? "Why don't you let me hold you instead? That way, the water can have a chance to work its magic on your wounds." She reclined back on the wall, finding a spot where she could sit, and pulled him back against her. With a little prodding she got him to sink down into the water and rest his head on her shoulder. Stroking her hand through his wet hair with one hand, she asked, "How's that?"

"Nice." He nuzzled her cheek. "'Cept I can't reach your breasts."

She loved this man, every brusque, ill-mannered, passionate, sinful inch of him. Prudence reached down and pinched his ass. "Don't be so plebeian."

He snorted. "It's what I am. You like the way I am."

"Mm. Most of the time. When you're not trying to get yourself killed." She pressed a kiss to his scruffy cheek. "I was so scared."

"Yeah, well, that whole scenario didn't quite go as planned." He put his hand around her arm, stroking her wrist.

She closed her eyes. They were going to have to do it all over in the morning. "How are we going to get out of here?"

"I've got a plan."

Prudence moaned. His plans were scary.

"Hey, now." He lifted up to look at her. "You're killing my confidence here."

"I'm sorry." She gave him a sound kiss and pulled him back down. "What's your plan?"

He waved his hand in the air. "You notice anything unusual about this cave?"

"You mean aside from the luminescent stone?" She cupped some water in her hand and poured the liquid over his chest. "You need to keep your chest covered with water, baby."

He lowered himself until the water lapped at his chin. "Yeah, like maybe how clean the place is?"

Compared to the main cavern, this place was immaculate. A shudder ran through her as she remember things squishing and crunching under her shoes. "The Scarecrows don't come in here."

"Nope. Too much light, maybe." His hand stroked up and down the outside of her thigh. "I say we wait until they're asleep and sneak out. If they're anything like bats, we might get past them without waking them, but we'll take a bunch of these glowy rocks just in case." He let out a lusty yawn.

To her, the whole plan sounded risky. Unfortunately, she didn't have a better suggestion. "Close your eyes and get some rest. I'll make sure you don't sink."

"Don't let me drift off too long. You need to sleep, too." He wound his arm back around her neck and nestled up to her. Within minutes he fell sound asleep. She wasn't surprised. He must be exhausted. Most nights she'd wake up and find him staring back at her when she opened her eyes. He always said he woke when he felt her stir, but she didn't buy it. He was far too paranoid to rest while they were out in the open.

The gouges on his chest looked bad, still seeping a little. She'd feel better if she could stitch him up. She'd do anything for a spare med-wand, but for now, all she had at her disposal was the water.

Goddess, keep him safe. Help him heal.

She held him close while he slept, soothing him through his nightmares which seemed worse than usual, maybe because he knew they were being pursued, maybe because of the altercation with the Scarecrows. Whatever the reason, it broke her heart to see him suffering. If she had her way, she'd find a way for him to live the rest of his life in peace, loving him until he didn't have any space in his heart or mind for the nightmares.

She stroked her cheek against his hair. What might her life be like, living with a man like Griffin? She had a pretty good idea of what the nights would be like, but she'd never seen him at his ease. What kind of job would he have as a civilian? What kind of friends would he choose? Would he be a good husband and father?

Yes. She imagined if he focused all his passion and sense of responsibility on a family, as opposed to his mission, he'd be wonderful. Supportive and protective. He'd fill them up with laughter and love until they were ready to burst. Yes, he'd make a good family man. They'd have a little place—big enough for a family of three or four—close to his brother.

On holidays and birthdays they'd all get together and eat and laugh. They'd be happy.

Oh, yes, she could imagine it all. If only he could.

21

Griffin woke to soft lips nuzzling his chin.

"Mm." He stretched, wincing at the tug on his wounds. "Must be your turn to catch some zs."

"No, sir." She nipped his chin. "It's time to go."

Griffin came fully awake with a curse. His gaze shot around the cave before landing on Prudence. Dark circles smudged beneath her eyes. She looked worn out. He sighed, pulling her close and pressing his forehead to hers. "Angel, you were supposed to wake me."

"I want to live, Warrior. That means I need you at your best."

He cupped her face and kissed her. "All right. Tonight, no matter what, I'm making sure you sleep." His gaze slipped to his hands and he shook his head. "My fingers are so wrinkled, they look like they belong to an old man."

"Yes, but the swelling and redness is gone from around those cuts."

He hopped out of the water and held his hand down to help her up. "What time is it?"

She shrugged. "I'm not sure without seeing the sky, but I'm starting to hear noises out there."

"Let's get going, then. Quietly."

They got dressed and Griffin strode around the cavern, picking up loose chunks of luminescent stone. Prudence made a bed for the rocks in the top of each of their packs and then piled in stones until a beam thick of light shot out the tops.

He helped Prudence shoulder one, adjusting the waist strap around her middle to help distribute the weight. "If they come near us, open the flap. Can you reach?" She showed him she could and he handed her a couple more to hold onto. "Keep these close to your body, hide the light unless we need it." He knelt in front of her and pulled her socks up over her pant legs.

"What's out there? On the floor?"

He shook his head. If he had his way, she'd never need to know. "Never mind that. Nothing harmful. You keep your eyes on me."

Once he had his pack on, he picked up his blaster and they headed out.

The Scarecrows were back in full residence, hanging from their feet with their wings wrapped tight to their bodies. Griffin led the way across the cave. They had to move more slowly this time to keep their shoes from making sucking noises as they walked through the muck. Something slithered up his pant leg and it was all he could do not to react. Damn it, he should've pulled his socks up, too. They were almost across the cavern when something dropped from above, splattering next to him.

Prudence gasped.

The quick, indrawn breath was quiet, but one of the creatures above them shifted.

"Run." He grabbed hold of Prudence's hand and bolted, reaching back to flip the top off his pack. Light lit the cave and a second later it got a lot brighter when Prudence uncovered her pack.

One of the scarecrows screamed.

The sound of fluttering wings filled the cave.

They were only a few steps from sunlight.

Beating wings came closer.

Griffin yanked on Prudence's arm, throwing her past the line of sunlight streaming past the cave entrance. He leapt out of the cave behind her, rolled, and came up with his weapon ready to fire.

Seven Scarecrows flew straight for them.

One by one they entered the sunlight.

And, as they crossed the line of light, one by one, they imploded, their bodies collapsing until there was nothing left.

Prudence threw herself into his arms. "You're brilliant." She kissed him with a resounding smack. "The stones would've worked even better if we had something see-through to carry them in. The flap on our packs kept falling back over the openings. But your plan worked!"

Griffin still stared at the cave entrance. He'd never seen anything quite like that before. There wasn't anything left of the creatures, not even dust. "Did you see that?"

"See what?" She looked up toward the cave.

He started to point, but then shook his head. "Never mind."

Prudence got to her feet and helped him up. "Do you think we can make it over the mountain today? I do *not* want to go through all that again."

"Maybe." There was no way in hell. From what he could see they'd have at least one more night in the mountains. He didn't want her to worry, though. "Let's get going."

"Yes, sir." She shot off a sassy salute and headed up the mountain.

Griffin followed behind, a little worried about her burst of energy. He had a feeling before too long she'd be struggling to keep one foot in front of the other. Sure enough, two hours later, she was dragging. "Come on. Let's have some breakfast." He reached up into one of the nearby trees and pulled down a couple of the brown fruit they'd had yesterday. Hopefully, the sugar would give her a boost.

She rolled the fruit between her palms. "You know what I want more than anything?"

He snorted. "A big, soft bed with feather pillows."

She laughed. "Besides that. I would love some coffee."

"Oh, don't get me started." He'd been trying not to think of all the things they were going without. Now, his mind fixated on the idea of a thick, steamy cup of joe. "Whenever I could get my hands on some, I loved to put a dollop of frosting in it."

"Ooh, that sounds good." She took a big bite of her berriegranate.

Juice dripped down her chin and he leaned forward and licked the sweetness off her skin. "Not half as good as that."

She grinned, kissing him.

Griffin leaned back on his elbow. "Or how about a hover-car?"

"Oh, my feet hurt so much." Her eyes rolled back in a blissful expression. "A ride in a hover-car would be divine."

He popped up a brow. "You never say anything."

"And what would you do if I complained? We're both tired and sore. We have to keep going."

"You got brass, Angel." And God, did he like that.

"You know, I've never quite been able to tell where you were raised."

"Everywhere, USA. I'm a tried-and-true military brat. We moved from state to state on a regular basis. Dad would come home, help us settle in, report to his new C.O., then he'd be off again. Back then, as soon as one war ended, another started."

"I can't imagine if the moving part was rough or fun."

"Lucan hated moving." He finished his first berrigranate and tossed the pit into the bushes. "He's an introvert and he'd just start making friends when it was time to pack up. Me, I didn't mind so much. Kept me from being labeled as a troublemaker. About the time I got in deep shit, it was time to move on and start over fresh."

She grinned, shaking her head. "I can't see you as a bad seed."

He shrugged. "Not that, really. I was always busy, though."

"Now that I can believe. Until last night, I was starting to wonder if you had an off button."

"Yeah, well, if there's trouble around, it tends to find me." He tossed her the liquor bottle full of water. "Drink up."

Prudence stopped with the bottle halfway up. "Oh, wow. Look."

Griffin swung around and came face-to face with a wide, fuzzy head big as a mega-hologram projection. A long, pink tongue lolled out of the creature's mouth and swiped up his arm and head.

Prudence giggled.

He scrambled out of reach. "What the hell is it?"

"I think it's a velocepillar." She stood and walked closer, reaching her hand out. "Look in the book; I know I've seen pictures. If I remember right, it's a pack animal."

He was torn between pulling her back away from the creature and having the chance to get a closer look at the book. The creature's moniker brought to mind toothy dinosaurs. "Weren't veloceraptors dangerous?"

"The raptor part of the name notes the danger. Veloce means quick." She scrubbed her hand through its long, airy fur. "It looks kind of like a spray mum, don't you think? The way its fur sticks out in all directions." The creature closed its big, inky eyes and let his tongue loll.

Whatever it was, it didn't appear dangerous. He pulled the container out of her pack and opened it to get at her book. The hardback cover almost had the texture of cloth and was velvety to the touch. He flipped open the book and found a section on animals. "Do you remember how far into the chapter it was?"

"No."

He paged through, noting some creatures they'd seen and many they hadn't. On the twelfth page in, he found a picture resembling the creature. "You were right. They are pack animals. Says they're vegetarians." He pulled her pack into his lap and stood. "You still have more of those roots?"

"Gah. Yes. I held onto them, though I'm hoping we don't have to resort to eating them anymore."

"Not for us." He kissed her nose. "For him." He found the veggies and packed her book away. "Grab one of those dead branches over there—a long one."

She wandered over to where a fallen log lay over the path and wrestled a branch from the trunk while he took off his long-sleeved shirt and tied one of the sleeves around the veggies. When she brought him the branch, he tied the other sleeve over it. The creature had already scented the veggies. It nudged him back, almost knocking him over as he tried to get to the treat. "All right, big dude, we're gonna see how fast velocepillars are." He thrust his chin to the creature. "Climb on up there, Angel. I'll hand you the packs."

The creature was relentless in his pursuit of the roots. Griffin had to shove him back several times. "You up there yet? He's getting impatient."

She sounded out of breath when she answered. "Yes. I'm up. Give me the packs."

He handed them up, one by one, then handed her the branch. "How the hell did you get up there?"

"I jumped from the tree."

Griffin climbed up the tree she motioned to, needing to pull himself up a couple branches before he could jump onto the velocepillar's broad back. "Well, let's see if this works." Taking the branch from her, he lowered it down until the veggies fell within the creature's line of vision.

They lurched into motion.

"Wait, that way." Prudence pointed to their left.

"On it." He aimed the branch over to their left, bit by bit until the creature headed in the correct direction. "Look there, Angel. You wished for a ride, and here we are. Maybe next time you could wish us into a comfy bed, in a large, well-stocked house, huh?"

Prudence laughed. "I don't know, he's big enough and soft enough to make a comfy bed." She twisted around and looked behind him. "He's moving fast. I bet we'll make it out of the mountains tonight. We won't have to worry about the Scarecrows again."

She was right. The velocepillar raced along, winding through the trees on its tiny feet. The wide, flat segments of the creature's back stayed level even when the creature ambled along on rough terrain. Griffin gathered Prudence's hair in his free hand to keep the silky stuff out of his face. "Lean back on me and get some sleep."

Prudence kissed his chin and lay her head on his shoulder.

Never had he met anyone who was so affectionate. Now that they were intimate, she often touched or petted him, kissed or nipped him. He enjoyed her playful tenderness. He enjoyed her.

But now that they had a ride, their time together grew short. If the field guide was correct, they would reach the spaceport within the next couple of days. When they arrived, he'd have to leave. Griffin tightened his arms around her. Why did they have to meet now? He'd never fallen so hard for a woman, never been the recipient of more than passing sexual curiosity. Lord knew, he had tried not to love her. Caring for his enemy's widow felt like a betrayal to the men he'd lost.

But then, he had no honor.

The closer he came to finding Lucan, the worse he felt. What the hell could he say to his brother? How could he explain that when he'd left Lucan he'd thought he was going to protect those who couldn't protect themselves, but what he'd done was hurt those people? How the hell was he going to look his brother in the eye and explain all the horrendous crimes he'd committed?

Just being with Prudence, finding pleasure and joy with her, made him feel like the lowliest sociopath on the planet. Most nights he couldn't even sleep anymore, the nightmares were so bad. The kids. The explosion. The fire.

His crimes were eating him alive and if he ever wanted a future, he had to make up for the things he'd done.

He couldn't live until he'd buried the dead.

Prudence had slept the day away and woke feeling more rested than she had since arriving in Asteria. The velocepillar's body and airy fur made a cushy bed and the thick trees in the mountains kept her shaded and cool. Griffin sat with his back to the velocepillar's neck with his legs on either side of hers to keep her from falling should she have rolled over in her sleep. His trusty blaster rested on his thigh. He scanned the trees as they passed, searching for threats.

She couldn't comprehend how he could stand to be *on* all the time. In their time together, he'd rarely let his guard down, much less slept. She was grateful for his watchful caution, but she was starting to worry about him.

"Griff?"

He didn't even glance her way.

Were they in danger?

Sitting up, she scanned the surrounding trees and, seeing nothing, looked back over her shoulder. They had made amazing progress through the day, having crossed the span of the mountains and reached the safety of the foothills beyond. She doubted the Scarecrows would come out this far, but as a precaution, he had laid out several of the glow stones, surrounding them in a cocoon of light. He'd also created a brace, using his backpack strung between the velocepillar's antennas, to hold the branch with the veggies steady in the creature's sights.

Prudence refocused her attention on Griffin. He held his body tense and his finger kept stroking across the trigger of his weapon. He didn't appear upset so much as really alert. Getting to her hands and knees, she crawled the short distance between them. "Griffin?" He didn't react when she placed her palm on his face. "Baby?" What was this? He almost appeared as though he'd checked out of his body. It was eerie. How long had he been like this? Her heart sped up in her chest, she shifted her eyes to the gun in his lap, and she had the overwhelming urge to take the weapon from him. She sat back on her calves and placed one hand over his wrist and the other over the gun, trying to ease the weapon away.

He looked at her, but his dilated eyes stared straight through her.

She inhaled a shaky breath. "I need you to give me the gun."

He pulled his arm away, letting the blaster hang down his side out of reach. "I need it." He shook his head, his brows drawing together. "Go back to base, being out here is against regs."

Base? The hairs on her nape and arms lifted. *Oh, goddess help them both.* Did he think he was back on Earth? Back in the Marines? He must. There was no base here. Prudence swallowed past the lump of fear forming in her throat and wet her lips. "I can't. My . . . orders are to bring that weapon back with me."

He shook his head. "That's not right."

"Yes, sir." She slid her hand over his thigh toward the gun. "You don't want me in trouble with the commanding officer, do you?" Leaning over him, her hand wrapped around his wrist. She glanced down to see the ground speeding past as the velocepillar raced through the foothills. If he chose to, he could toss her right to the ground while he was out of it. He could shoot her dead. "Give me the gun, Chief."

"No. I have to be punished."

His face crumple into grief and she realized she wasn't in any danger whatsoever. He was the one in peril. "Why? Why would you say that?"

"I killed them." His raised his hands to cover his face.

Prudence slipped the gun from his hand and pulled him into her arms. "You didn't have a choice. You did what you had to."

"I didn't know."

The sound of his grief brought tears to her eyes and she held him tighter, stroking her fingers through his hair. "I know, baby. You wouldn't have, if you'd known." She had no idea what she was saying or if her words made sense to him. "It's all over now. You're safe. It's all over."

His arms came around her and his wet face pressed to her chest. "Ah, Christ, I didn't mean to. I didn't—"

"Sh. You're going to be fine, baby. Hold on to me and let it all out." Whatever this was, it couldn't be about the shootout between his and his CO's units. Not unless he hadn't told her the whole story. Had he discovered after the fact that the kids in the school were infected from the water? The thought sent a shudder through her. Maybe he'd found out after his CO and the others were dead. Maybe those kids had attacked his unit and he had had to kill them after all. Or maybe they had attacked someone else.

But wouldn't she have heard about such a catastrophe in the States had the water supply overseas been compromised? Wouldn't she have at least heard Alfred and Randolph talking about it at some point? When Griffin had first told her his story, she'd assumed the UN's people had lied to the soldiers about the water. Now she didn't know what to think.

She wanted to ask, but not while he was like this. Right now, he needed to rest and recover from this fugue.

"Come lie down with me."

He shook his head. "They'll be coming for me soon."

"I'll keep watch. I'll wake you before they get here."

He allowed her to pull him farther onto the velocepillar's back. He lay down and covered his red-rimmed eyes with his arm.

Prudence sat next to him, smoothing her hand over his chest until he slept.

This must be some kind of combat related stress. She'd heard the numbers; the UN had used them time and again to plead their case for the need for peace. To show how independent governments were slowly and methodically killing society—because in every war the number of soldiers who committed suicide outnumbered those who died in war. The collateral damages associated with battle lasted years beyond the conflicts, and as those conflicts grew, involving more and more countries, the death toll and the effects on the survivors and their families grew exponentially.

What she didn't know was how to ease him. Would trying to talk about whatever happened make his suffering better or worse? Maybe his brother would be able to help. Or maybe there would be a doctor in Diamond Fjord. Somehow, she'd find a way to help him.

For now, she'd keep a close watch over him.

22

The velocepillar finally got his treat. At some point during the night the big guy curled up like a massive snake and, Griffin suspected, when the velocepillar lowered his head to sleep, the branch slid down far enough for him to reach the veggies.

His shirt was a little stiff from the creature's slobber, but he donned it since there was nothing else to wear.

"Are you sure you're all right?"

Griffin glanced at Prudence while he buttoned his shirt. She'd been acting strange all morning. "I'm fine. The cuts are healing well, I slept two nights in a row, I'm good. Are you gonna tell me why you keep asking?"

She shrugged. "I guess I haven't seen you sleep so much."

"Come on." He took her hand in his and they headed out.

The trees became less frequent until open areas of waist-high blue grass became the norm. Wildlife continued to be a predominant feature of the land—birds and mammals, they'd even seen a few reptiles—little hooded, yellow lizards with salmon pink stripes. Prudence kept her book handy, searching for and naming the creatures and plants they came across, and Griffin entertained her by trying to guess the names before she found them in their book. It was a decent enough game to pass the time, and one that would help her with her life here.

The thing was, he was starting to worry about leaving her behind. Who would protect her? Who would ensure she had a roof over her head and food on the table? Who would make her laugh and cry out in passion? Logic told him she was capable of fending for herself. She'd proven to be strong, independent, and resourceful. He had no doubt she would make friends in quick time and find lovers even faster—if that's what she wanted.

The very thought of her in someone else's arms ate at him.

Hell, maybe it was him. Prudence was the first person he'd taken care of in a long time. He'd come to depend on her friendship. Their verbal battles. The challenge she presented.

He would miss her.

Ask her to marry you.

The thought brought him up cold.

Prudence stopped next to him, scanning the horizon. "What is it?"

"Nothing." He shook his head and kept walking. Marriage? The idea hadn't ever crossed his mind before. Prudence was the first woman he'd known who he could see filling the job. But would she want to?

Hell, even if she did, he had to return to Earth—he had to make things right and by the time he earned back his honor, there might not be anything left of him.

No, he couldn't marry her. It wouldn't be fair. He remembered how things were for his mom whenever his father left. The first couple of weeks she'd cry herself to sleep most nights. After a while, the humdrum of taking care of him and Lucan had kept her from thinking about Dad too much, but then Dad would come home for a few weeks and the cycle would start all over. He couldn't do that to someone he cared for.

"Griff, look."

Up ahead, a tendril of smoke curled up through the trees. After so long on their own, he couldn't decide if he was elated or terrified to see signs of other people in the area.

Next to him, Prudence did a little jig. "Let's go say hello."

He reached out and grabbed hold of her arm, halting her. "Cautiously. Remember your first interaction with the locals?"

Her smile faded and she nodded.

"Good. Keep behind me and when we approach, you stay hidden until I can take their measure. They're less likely to lose their heads around an armed man."

Prudence waited for him to pass and latched onto the back of his shirt. "Give me the knife, in case you need help."

"You keep your head down, though." He pulled the blade out of his pocket and handed it to her. "Don't show yourself, no matter what."

Griffin crouched low, gripping his weapon, and thumbing off the safety. Male voices rode on the breeze as they neared. Beyond the trees, there was some kind of structure. He pointed off to the side at a thick growth of shrubberies.

Prudence squatted down. "Be careful."

He gave her a nod and pushed on, coming out of the trees low, weapon raised.

"Hey, now." A big burly man struggled out of his chair near the fire. His dark hair had a shock of white streaked through it. He held out his arms in a placating gesture. "No need for that, mister."

Despite the fact Griffin aimed a blaster at his middle, the man didn't seem too concerned. The hair at Griffin's nape lifted. Shit, he must be in someone's sites. "Who else is here?" He scanned the camp, taking in the picnic table, the line of rope fashioned into a jump rope. A cabin sat in the background, the windows dark and empty. The whole place was surrounded by trees. Ambush could come from anywhere.

"My family is here. Now, I'm gonna warn you, my eldest, he's got you in his sights, and while I have no doubt there's more than one gun trained on me, I'd rather not die today.

Frankly, I'd rather my boy didn't have to kill anybody today. So, why don't we all lower our weapons and chat."

Griffin glanced around again. "Family. You got women here, then?"

The older man scowled. "None of them would be any good to you, so get the idea out of your mind."

He heard a click somewhere above and behind him.

"Don't want 'em. Just seeing what's what."

"Ah." The big man snorted, his gaze shifted off to the side. "I'm too old now to have much use for a woman, and my boys are too young, if that's what you're worried about." Apparently, he'd decided Griffin wasn't going to shoot him. He waddled over and fitted himself back into his chair. "You're welcome to stay for dinner, long as you quit pointing that damn thing at me. That shit's bad for the digestion."

What the hell?

The big male turned his head toward the house. "Granny? We got guests."

Griffin's attention shot to the doorway of the cabin. A bit of a woman with long white hair appeared on the stoop. Her face was lined and worn thin as a fall leaf.

"Well, what did you do to make him point that thing at you?"

"He's just checkin' us out." The big man reached over and stirred the pot he had strung up over the fire. His gaze never left Griffin.

Whatever was in that pot was making his mouth water.

"I recognize you. News from back home is slow getting here. I wasn't sure at first, but there's no mistaking that face." He leaned back in the chair and shouted over his shoulder, "Kids, come meet a real live hero."

Half a dozen children ages two to almost full grown flooded the campsite. A young man dropped down from the trees behind him, grinning ear-to-ear. One of the younger ones, a little girl with jet-black hair and blue eyes toddled over, tugging Prudence along in her wake.

Griffin lowered his weapon and stared. "What are you doing?"

Prudence shrugged, glancing down at the little girl. "She didn't look very dangerous."

The man laughed. He rapped his spoon against the edge of the pot and set it aside. "I'm Big Jake and this lot here is my brood."

Was he serious? Griffin's gaze shot to the old woman.

Big Jake chuckled. "Granny Nash was my wife's mother. Annie passed away giving birth to this little guy." He reached down and snatched up the youngest of the lot as he tried to run past. "You don't have anything to worry about from us, long as you don't try to steal anything."

Griffin nodded. "We're wanting information."

"Well, now, last I heard, that's free."

The older boy came to stand in front of Griffin. "I'm Rylan. Are you really Chief Payne? How did you survive the fire on *Genesis V*? What did it feel like to kill Alfred Parnell? How come you didn't say nothing at your trial?"

Holy hell. Griffin took a step back.

"You want a drink, little lady?"

Griffin's attention flew to Granny Nash, who motioned Prudence into the cabin.

"That sounds divine." Prudence smiled and headed over.

"'Scuse me," Griffin said to Big Jake. He strode over to Prudence, cutting off her path. "We don't know them."

"I'm fine, Griffin." She patted his hand. "You have to trust somebody some time, and they seem nice enough."

"So thought Hansel and Gretel when they first met the witch."

"Granny, bring some glasses out and you ladies can sit on the porch where we can all see each other." Big Jake was watching him, amusement lighting his eyes. "Come on, Chief, take a load off and tell me about Earth."

With one last, meaningful glance at Prudence, he took one of the seats Rylan brought over. "How long have you been here?"

"Oh, I was one of the first—been here going on five years now. I was serving time for evading duty when the U.N. started grasping for control."

Griffin's gaze shot to his. "Evading duty?"

"War wasn't for me. I couldn't kill anybody." Big Jake shrugged. "Maybe I'd taken too many psych classes. Maybe I'm not tough enough, but when push came to shove, I hesitated. Cost one of the men in my unit his life." He let loose a heavy sigh. "After that, I refused to go out because I didn't know if the same thing would happen again. Better me in the brig than my unit dying one by one because I froze. Yeah, back then the U.S. still said they wouldn't cede control to the U.N., but they were happy to take advantage of exiling prisoner's off-planet. Ol' Uncle Sam liked the idea of a new Australia. Think of all the savings earned from not having to clothe, feed, or house prisoners. The lower crime rate from not having to release us back into the population after we served our time. Asteria was Uncle Sam's dirty little secret."

"You met your wife here?" Griffin glanced around at the kids. They couldn't all be his—more than half of them were older than five.

"Mm." He smirked. "They're not all mine, most of them are orphans. Annie was a Blue Helmet, if you'll believe it. That was back when they still had morals, mind you. Beautiful woman, inside and out." He paused to wink at Griffin. "She couldn't resist my good looks and charm."

Griffin chuckled. Charming, he could believe, but Big Jake was everything but handsome. "What's town like?" He scanned the trees lining the yard. "Why're you living out here alone?"

"Diamond Fjord is a good place now. In the early days, the settlement was filled with criminals, but most of them have been chased out now. Good people live there, we would, too, 'cept I built this house with my Annie and I can't bear to leave. We go down once a month or so. They've got beautiful, modern-looking buildings and all the amenities of a thriving city." Big Jake leaned into his view. "You thinking about settling down with your woman?"

Griffin shrugged. "I'm looking for my brother. They sent him here about two years ago."

Big Jake reached into his shirt front and Griffin tensed. He pulled out what looked like two hand-rolled cigarettes and offered one to Griffin.

"You're shitting me, is that what I think it is?"

Big Jake grinned. "No."

Griffin paused with it halfway to his lips and Big Jake had a good laugh at his expense.

"It's better than tobacco. Stuff smells like a mix between lavender and cherries. My wife, she made me quit smoking, but every now and then I'd sneak one of these babies and to the day she died, she never caught me. I could walk up to her right after I finished and kiss her and she'd have no idea."

"You got a light?"

Jake reached down and plucked a piece of grass, lighting the end in the fire. He lit his smoke and passed it to Griffin.

Griffin inhaled deeply. "Ah, God that's good."

"If your brother is a civvy, Diamond Fjord is your best bet. If he works for the U.N. or spaceport, then you'll be wanting to check out Blue Mesa on the other side."

Two cities, like Prudence had said. "How close are we to the spaceport?"

"'Bout a day and a half, if you're walking. You'll hit Diamond Fjord first. Like I said, the community there is nice, though they don't take a shine to having weapons pointed at them." Big Jake leveled a pointed look in his direction.

"Got it." Griffin took another drag of his smoke, savoring it. He glanced back over his shoulder, scanning the trees.

"Where'd you come from, anyway?"

Griffin sat back in his chair. "Our escape pod landed out in the Black Desert near an outpost."

Big Jake's eyebrows climbed high on his forehead. "Why, you lucky bastard. They take the repeat offenders of violent crimes and drop them off out there in No Man's Land. No one thought anyone could survive crossing the desert on foot. Hell, the Scarecrows in the mountains, they're almost more dangerous than the sun. None of the boys, Merrick—he's the law in Diamond Fjord—takes out there ever come back."

"Yeah, we've had a bit of an adventure."

Big Jake puffed on his cigarette. "Truth be told, you're in for more of one."

Griffin tensed, his gaze shooting over to check on Prudence.

"Not from us, mind you. Blue Helmets been coming 'round asking about a lavender-eyed lady. Seen 'em twice now, but they only stopped once." Big Jake didn't seem to be making a threat. His tone remained matter of fact as he rocked back in his chair and toked on his smoke.

"Yeah?"

"Mm-hm. They're telling the locals they expect them to report any sightings."

"Yeah?"

Ryland had been so quiet, Griffin had forgotten about the boy. "Lucky for you, most of us locals have plenty of reason not to want to help them out."

"Most?"

"Some people are still scared." Big Jake shrugged. "Traumatized. Can't blame them, but you need to be careful. Tell your woman to keep her head down if you go near town.

And you, you need to cover that mug of yours; everybody in these parts will recognize you."

"Well, that's going to complicate things." Griffin took a drag off his smoke. "I can't avoid town. I need to find my brother." He couldn't imagine Lucan would be very happy in a place as violent as Asteria.

"If your brother is a smart man, he's laying low, pretending he doesn't know you."

Shit. He'd have to be real careful. The last thing he wanted was to make things difficult for Lucan, but he had to find him and at least make sure he was okay. Especially now. He needed to reassure himself the Blue Helmets hadn't gotten hold of him. Griffin finished his smoke and flicked the butt into the fire.

"Tell me about Earth."

Griffin looked past Big Jake to check on Prudence. She was smiling, settled back into a big rocker with her feet pulled under her. She seemed relaxed and happy. "It's the same, but then it's not."

Ryland leaned forward in his chair. "How so?"

"Everything is where it should be." He dragged his hand down his face. "The streets and houses and business are all pretty much the same, but the heart's gone. When I came back through Atlanta to find my brother, I kept thinking the whole place was surreal—something out of a horror novel. Everybody was clean and healthy. The streets were pristine. Everything was beautiful. Paradise. Unless you looked a little closer. Then you might notice how tense people are. You might hear whispers of concerns. You might notice that half the population is gone."

Big Jake's head bobbed all through Griffin's report. "My last trip into the Fjord, I heard tale of a revolution on Earth."

"Oh?" Griffin's pulse kicked up.

"Yeah. Seems you weren't the only military survivor. Word is they say they're finishing what you started."

Griffin frowned. "You know about the bombings?"

Big Jake nodded. "Lot of military families here. Always asking the Blue Helmets about their loved ones. Somebody got tired of dealing with it all. They made the announcement several months back. Told everyone their men and women weren't coming back."

"And everyone accepted that?"

"Nope." Big Jake leaned over to stir the pot. "No one has accepted anything. They're just powerless."

Maybe they were, but he wasn't. Except, maybe he wouldn't have to go back after all. If a revolution had already started, maybe it was over. Griffin leaned forward. "Is Parnell still alive?"

"Last I heard."

Damn it. He'd have to go back. He couldn't rest until he made things right. Until he felt certain Prudence was safe. His gaze shifted back to the surrounding trees. Twilight was approaching, leaving too many shifting shadows out there.

"Takes a while to see the news reports. Might not be alive now." Big Jake let his head fall back and he stared up at the sky. "You must be glad to be away from it all."

"I'm going back."

Big Jake's head jerked up. "Well, why would you do a fool thing like that for?"

Griffin laughed. "I was out in the field those last two years when the U.S. ceded. Thing was, they didn't bother telling us grunts. Day after day, we'd go out, thinking we played for the same team we always played for. Completing our assigned missions with no clue that the rules had changed." He met Big Jake's gaze. "I fucked things up. Now I have to un-fuck them."

Big Jake's lips quirked. "How's your woman feel about that?"

"She thinks I'm an idiot."

"Ya are. Let the young pups fight the war, Chief. You've done your part. Every man deserves a bit of happiness. Besides, you leave a woman like that alone and you're gonna have a hell of time keeping her to yourself."

Prudence's laugh drew his attention. Her smile lit up her whole face. "She is beautiful."

Big Jack snorted. "Of course she is. She's Lythonian."

Griffin's gaze shot to the older man. Was he prejudiced? There were still many Earthers who distrusted aliens and half-breeds. "So?"

"They say those ladies give gifts to their mates. Rumor has it that the Lythonian lady Alfred Parnell married gave him the gift of persuasion. Merrick told me that—he was Secret Service, protected the president that last year before we ceded. Anyway, he said the information was redacted out of all their files so he never knew for sure, but as fast as Randolph pounced on her, I'm thinking there might be something to it." Big Jake frowned. "You know, I never met any Lythonians before, but your woman, she looks a bit like that Parnell lady—thinner, has darker, shorter hair. They related?"

Griffin shook his head. Persuasion? Hell, was Prudence the reason Alfred had so many worshipful followers? Was she the reason all these people were stuck here on Asteria? He might have discounted Big Jake's story, except he'd seen the files. He knew large sections of the documents related to Alfred's 'persuasion tactics' were redacted.

What had she told him? *They think I bring them luck.*

Hell, maybe her hands were as dirty as his.

"Well, anyways, men who understand what being her mate means will try to take her from you. You're a right lucky bastard." Big Jake reached over and stirred the pot of food boiling over the fire. "How long you gonna stay?"

Griffin shook his head. He needed to talk to Prudence. Alone. Part of him didn't want to believe any of what Big Jake said, but part of him worried it was true. If it was, there wasn't anything Randolph wouldn't do to get her back. Why hadn't she told him? "We can't stay. I'm looking for my brother and he's not here."

"Well, now, at least share a meal with us?"

He wanted to get away from them; he needed time to think. At the same time, Prudence seemed to be enjoying herself and they both needed to eat. "That would be great. Thank you."

<h1 style="text-align:center">23</h1>

Granny Nash leaned close in her chair. "That's a fine man you have there. Is he a good fuck?"

Prudence's jaw dropped. The old woman said one outrageous thing after another.

Granny cackled. "Oh, I might be old, darlin' but that doesn't keep me from looking . . . or dreaming. So, give me something to keep me warm tonight, is he one of those gentle giants?"

Prudence shook her head. Griffin was far too passionate to be classed as such.

"He's not mean, is he?"

"Oh, no. He'd never hurt me."

Granny's eyes gleamed with an unholy light. "Then what? Is he's a little rough? A bit dirty?"

Prudence's lips twitched. Goddess bless the woman, she was tenacious as a reporter. She cleared her throat, trying hard to ignore the heat in her cheeks. "Yes."

Granny leaned forward more, so much so, Prudence was a little worried she might tumble right out of her chair. "What's your favorite part?"

Oh, boy, she wasn't sure she could talk about this. Everything was far too new to her. "He's, uh, passionate."

Granny scoffed. "I'd hope for that at least."

"And lustful."

"He looks to me like a man who knows his way around a woman." She winked. "So, what's your favorite part?"

Prudence bit her lip. Granny Nash wasn't giving up. "He makes me feel beautiful. He gets so focused on me, becomes so watchful and intent when he's . . . doing things to me . . . I feel . . . loved." When she got brave enough, she snuck a peek to see Granny's reaction.

Granny reclined back in her rocker, eyes closed and a blissed-out smile riding her thin lips. "My Devon was the same. Oh, I think he had a bit of the flair for voyeurism. I think he got off on watching me writhe and beg." Her eyes opened and her pale brown eyes grew misty. "Oh, Lord, I miss that man. Even after he lost his oomph, he liked watching me, and oh, darlin' did I like being watched by him."

Prudence's gaze searched out Griffin. He and Big Jake were deep in conversation—probably planning how to take over the world. She wanted to share the kind of love with Griffin that Granny had with her Devon. She wanted to grow old with him. But she was terrified he wouldn't survive the month.

"You're looking at him like it might be the last time. What's wrong, honey?"

"He doesn't want to stay here. He's planning to go back and assassinate the new PM. Keeps saying he needs to fix things. The whole idea is suicide."

"Can't say I'm surprised, man like him—poor boy looks like he's drowning in testosterone."

"I want him to stay."

"Mm." Granny set her chair to rocking. "You show him the beauty of Asteria. You smile and flirt and bat those dark eyelashes until you seduce those suicidal tendencies right out of him. Men can't resist a strong, happy woman. Don't let him catch you melancholy or clingy. And, of course, driving him wild in the bedroom never hurts."

How was she supposed to do that? She'd never had another woman to talk to. Never had anyone who had similar experiences or who could give advice. Prudence grinned. But she did now. "Granny?"

The rocker stopped. "Yep?"

"Would you give me an example of something that you used to do to drive Devon crazy in the bedroom?"

Granny set her chair to rocking, a broad smile stretching her wrinkles smooth. "Well, now, darlin' have you ever heard of the prostate?"

He had no idea what the hell Prudence and Granny Nash could have in common, but the two of them had their heads together whispering and giggling like teenaged girls. He envied her that. As nice as Big Jake and his family seemed, he couldn't relax. Especially once they crowded into the little cabin for dinner. He felt closed in, claustrophobic. If Blue Helmets showed up, there was no escape.

Christ, it was hot in here. He lifted his napkin to wipe his brow.

Prudence appeared to be having a fine time with her new friend. She acted like she didn't have a care in the world. The food tasted as delicious as it smelled, savory meat and sweet vegetables, but he couldn't enjoy it. The brood of children laughed and teased each other, but he couldn't concentrate on a word they said. All he could think of was getting Prudence out of here. He needed answers. He needed to know how much danger she was in. He needed her someplace safe. Someplace he'd be able to see the enemy coming.

After they finished dinner and the children carted off the last of the dishes, Griffin almost sighed in relief. He stood and offered his hand to Big Jake. "Thanks for everything."

"Are you sure you won't stay the night?"

"No but thank you for the offer."

Prudence shot him a quizzical look but didn't argue.

He turned and there, an oil painting hung on the wall above the fireplace. The scene depicted Mount Rushmore, the faces of four long-dead presidents jutting out from the face of a cliff. All around, trees were visible as if the scene were remembered from a hiking trail.

Griffin stepped closer, checking for the artists mark and sure enough L.R. P., was scrawled in the lower right corner. "Where'd you get this?"

"There's a shop on the waterfront off Main Street in Diamond Fjord—Granny bought that." He looked to the old woman, lifting a brow in question.

"Nice young man runs the place. It's called Visions from Home. You can't miss it."

Griffin nodded. "Thanks for the information. Come on, Angel, we need to head out."

He waited while she said her goodbyes, promising they'd come back to visit and getting promises in return to visit them once they were settled. She was making plans again. For him. For them.

24

—— ◆ ——

Griffin wiped the back of his forearm across his brow. Good God, he was a mess. His hands still shook, he was sweating, and he couldn't seem to catch his breath.

Prudence kept glancing at him as they walked. "What's wrong?"

He continued walking, the tall grass whipping against his cammies. "I didn't feel safe there."

"They seemed very nice. I thought we would stay with them tonight. You know, a real bed. A real pillow. We could go back."

He shook his head. "That cabin only had one door. There were too many people. Too much noise. Blue Helmets have been there twice in the last couple of days."

"Okay." She tugged on his hand to get him to slow. "We're well away from the cabin. Let's slow down before one of us twists an ankle."

He stopped, pressed his hands to his thighs and took a deep breath.

Prudence rubbed his back. "Griff?"

He straightened. "Just catching my breath."

"Okay." She wrapped her arms around him and gave him a hug. "We're safe. Everything's fine now."

Hell, she was coddling him. "Look, I'm fine."

"You're sure?"

He nodded. "We need to talk, Pru." He dropped his pack near a tree and pulled hers from her shoulders and set it down. He plopped down with his back to a tree and patted the grass in front of him. "Come on, sit down."

She sat between his legs, turned and pressed her face to his chest. "What's going on, Griff? Are you sure you're okay?"

"Mm." He wrapped his arms around her. "Big Jake said Blue Helmets have been coming around looking for a violet-eyed woman."

She stiffened in his arms.

He tightened his hold, stroking his thumb over her arm. "You're Lythonian, right?"

Her voice was a bare whisper. "What else did he say?"

"That Alfred's wife gave him the gift of persuasion." Damn it. It hurt to say the words out loud. Had he found out before he'd gotten to know her, he'd have been furious. Now, he was just sad. For her. For him. For everyone else. She started to get up, but he pulled her back down. Kissed her head so she'd know he wasn't angry. "That's what was redacted out of those documents I saw, right? Your gift was his secret?"

When she spoke, her voice was flat. "You won't believe me, but I never gave them anything."

Maybe he shouldn't have pushed her. "Come on, Pru. I know you had it rough." He pulled her closer. "I'm not . . . blaming you. I'm trying to understand. I need to know what's going on so I can keep you safe."

"I have to be in love and loved in return for the mating to happen. I don't have any control over it, not really."

She was gutting him. "You loved Alfred."

She shook her head.

"How did he get the gift if you didn't love him?"

"He didn't."

They were the words he wanted to hear, but he damn well knew they couldn't be true. "How else could he have convinced everyone to go along with his plan for utopia?"

She sighed. "They were desperate."

"Angel, I've told you I don't blame you. I'm not angry with you. I just want the truth."

She pulled away and lifted her shirt, pointing to her birthmark, one he must've kissed a hundred times. "When I give my gift, my mate will take the mark, too. The people on Earth followed Alfred and are following Randolph because they *want to*. No one seems to understand that. Not Alfred. Not Randolph and not you." She blinked back tears. "You men, all you think about is your damn politics and your wars and I'm tired of being caught in the middle."

"Come here." He pulled her back into his embrace. Hell, if Alfred hadn't somehow manipulated the people of Earth, and Prudence hadn't given him the gift of persuasion, did that mean Prudence was correct? Did Earth's citizens actually want the world they'd created? No. He couldn't fathom it. Sure, she seemed to believe what she said, but she must be wrong. Maybe her perspective was skewed. "Tell me from the beginning."

"Alfred picked me out of an orphanage when I was seventeen. Not because he wanted me. Not because he fell in love with me. He didn't even know me, he wanted me because I was Lythonian. He wanted my gift. I told him right from the start that I couldn't give it to him. I wasn't attracted to him, I didn't even like him." She wiped her face with the back of her hand. "He didn't care. He married me and took me home. He wanted a wedding night and I didn't."

Griffin froze.

"He never touched me after that first time. He could hardly bear to look at me. But the next day, Kenya ceded to the U.N. You have to understand, he'd been trying to sell his plan for three years and no one would listen. Kenya ceded and within days several other small countries did the same. He refused to believe it happened for any other reason than because of my gift. He thought I lied about my mating marks transferring with my gift. After he died, Randolph . . . he tried to do what his brother did, but he was so disgusted by me, he couldn't even get it up."

His gut twisted as all the pieces fit together in horrifying clarity and his protective instincts reared up. He knew Randolph had abused her, tortured her at least once—he'd planned to make the son of a bitch suffer for hurting her—but he'd always attributed her resistance to sex to poor lovers and distain for the man who'd killed her husband. His mind rebelled against the idea of anyone violating Prudence. Not his Angel. She was too gentle, too sweet. Just as bad was their making her feel less than worthy. Less than worthy of what? Of rape? That was a hell of a mind fuck. And they kept her under surveillance so she couldn't leave. Couldn't ask for help.

"I'm glad I killed that bastard." If he had half a chance he'd send Randolph to hell with his brother.

He couldn't stand the thought of what those two had subjected her to. She deserved so much more, and instead, she'd gotten him. In their time together, he'd teased her, he'd made baseless accusations, he'd bullied her and, sweet Jesus, he'd been rough with her. Ah, God in heaven, what must have been going through her mind when he'd made love to her? Every time, he'd gotten so overwhelmed by her, he never once tried to gentle her. His face heated with shame.

"You're too quiet. What are you thinking?"

He swallowed past the lump in his throat. "I'm thinking I'm a fucking bastard, Angel."

She whirled around. "What are you talking about?"

"I didn't know, Pru. Do you understand? I'd have been careful making love to you if I'd known how they hurt you. I wouldn't have been rough. Goddamn it, I'm sorry. I just wanted to show you passion."

He couldn't read her expression in the dark and she was quiet and still so long, he didn't think there was a chance in hell she'd forgive him. While he knew their time together was coming to an end, he couldn't bear the thought of parting like this. He couldn't stand the thought that he'd hurt her.

"Griffin, I like the way you are with me. I like the fact that I never have to wonder if you want me as much as I want you. Why don't you show me again?"

"What?"

"Show me again how a man loves his woman."

Unsure what to say, he swallowed. What was she asking him for? He'd give her whatever she wanted but part of him was wary now. What if he did something to remind her of the past? What if he accidentally brought forth bad memories of her time with the Parnells?

She leaned in and brushed her mouth to his. "Maybe I wasn't clear, Warrior. I want you. Uncivilized, uncouth, barbaric you, to pound out any and all lingering memories of the past. I want your hard bits, in my soft bits reminding me why it's good to be a woman."

How could anyone hurt this woman?

Protect. Provide. Cherish.

That's all he wanted to do for her. A shiver of fear snaked up his spine. What happened when he left her to fight with the rebels on Earth? How would she get on without him? How would she get on if he died? For the first time in his life, he feared death. Feared leaving her with no one to care for her—because no one could, not like him.

Protect. Provide. Cherish.

He pulled her up so she stood in front of him, and he got to his knees. His hands shook as he hooked his fingers in her jeans and dragged them down her legs. She'd lost weight. He needed to get her somewhere safe. Somewhere he could concentrate on providing food instead of always being focused on safety. He pushed her back against the tree, burying his face between her thighs before he even had her pants all the way off, licking through her curls while he pulled off her shoe and lifted her bared leg to rest on his shoulder.

He leaned back to survey her. With one leg clothed and grounded, the other naked and held wide on his shoulder she posed an erotic sight. Her fingers tripped over the buttons on her shirt, slowly revealing pale, beautiful skin and he watched, transfixed by the graceful fingers that would soon be wrapped around his cock, the sharp little nails that would scour his back. "Faster."

She'll be all right while you're gone. She's tough and you'll survive, like always.

She undid the last couple buttons and, as she shrugged out of her shirt, he reached up and unsnapped the front closure of her bra. Those glorious breasts popped free, kissed by moonlight and drawn taut by his presence. He reached up and dragged his hands from her collarbone, over her breasts and belly down hips and thighs. Then he spread her nether lips wide. He licked her from ass to clit before drawing that tiny bud between his lips, suckling until she pressed down onto his mouth.

"Ah, Griff."

Already hard and aching, her cry intensified his desire. He needed to be inside her, any way he could get there. He pressed his finger into her tight, gripping sheath.

"Christ, you're wet."

"Yes."

He added another finger, and another until she gasped. He couldn't get enough of her taste, the way she writhed above him. He continued to lap at her, spearing her with his tongue until her thighs trembled around him and she ground herself down on his face and fingers.

She was gorgeous. All tight athletic curves and planes glowing in the moonlight. With her head tipped back and her hands clutched tight in his hair, she was a study in ecstasy. She couldn't hold back, not with him, and those sounds she made—those breathy sighs, husky moans and sharp cries—they drove him damn near insane.

They were his. She was his.

That thought more than anything had him almost coming in his pants. His whole body tensed as he fought against ejaculating. He wanted inside her too much to give into the base urge.

He'd survive. He'd be there for her.

Protect. Provide. Cherish.

Prudence tugged his shirt over his head and her hands stroked every inch of his body she could reach, scored him with her nails, and gripped his hair to hold his head right where she wanted him.

She took.

And he gave.

Her body tensed around him, the leg slung over his shoulder flexing, quivering. He twisted his fingers within her on each slick plunge and sucked her clit into his mouth, flicking the bud without mercy with his tongue.

She cried out in the night, sending shivers shimmying over his skin to gather at the small of his back. Her inner muscles clamped around his fingers, grasping, sucking at him. His cock jumped in response, demanding the same treatment.

Provide. Protect. Cherish.

"Now, Griffin. Your pants."

Her most feminine muscles still flexed with release, but she was impatient, needy.

For him.

His Cargos hit the grass in six seconds flat. He hiked her leg up to his hip as he stood.

"Wait."

All it took was one word and her palm on his chest. His hungry gaze raked over her, but he backed off, ready to stop if she wanted.

She didn't.

She'd been so worried he'd want her gift, like everyone else. Instead, he worried that he'd hurt her. He worried about his behavior. Goddess bless him, he didn't seem to give a second thought to that damned gift.

Slowly, she lowered her leg and walked a tight circle, reversing their positions. She put a little pressure behind her hand until he leaned back against the tree. She nudged his legs apart with her foot. She lifted the edge of his shirt, folding it up to reveal rock-hard abs and nodding in satisfaction. "Yes, just like that." The same position he stood in when she watched him stroke himself off.

His eyes narrowed.

"I watched you that day."

The heat in his eyes doubled, if possible. His eyes dilated.

"I watched you touch yourself and I haven't been able to get the sight out of my mind. You were beautiful." Her gaze wandered down the length of his body. "I've wanted to try something ever since." And after talking to Granny Nash, she knew what to do.

In theory, at least.

His breath was a harsh rasp, echoing hers, but when she sank to her knees, he stopped breathing altogether.

"Angel—"

Her name ended in a strangled moan when she licked him from balls to head.

She wanted this. Needed to give herself to him. Goddess bless them both, did she love him. She loved his fierceness.

His protectiveness. Even his loyalty to his beliefs, misguided as they were.

The broad head of his cock was already wet, slick with his desire. She swirled her tongue over him, savoring the salty taste, before taking in his whole thick length in one long, wet stroke of her mouth. His hands tangled in her hair as she worked him between her lips, occasionally letting her teeth scrape him. Sometimes sucking him hard, then stroking him with her tongue, trying to discover what he liked.

A ragged breath shook from him.

She weighed the heavy weight of his testicles in her palm, fondling him, then tugging her fingers down the center of his sac. She tried to remember every little detail of what Granny Nash had told her to do.

"Angel." His breath came in erratic gasps, as if he'd run miles. "Where'd you learn—"

She released him with an audible pop and sucked his nuts into her mouth.

"Oh, God."

She slicked her finger in the damp desire between her legs, and, as she sucked him deep again, found the tight, puckered entrance to his body and pressed into him, searching for that hidden spot Granny Nash said would drive him crazy.

"Fuck."

Prudence smiled and stroked the spot inside him again.

His legs shook. His whole frame shuddered. His hands became more demanding, clinging in her hair and guiding her into a rhythm over his shaft. Never had she heard him make such sounds. Guttural. Demanding. Begging.

Thank you, Granny Nash.

His hands shifted, gripping her under her arms and yanking her to her feet only to shift positions again and lift her over and onto his cock. He was inside her before she'd even secured her legs around his narrow hips. Her back came up hard against the tree, and his mouth crashed onto hers.

She'd broken past that tight control he had, putting herself into the exact position she'd feared for so long. What would happen if this feral man lost control? Now she knew. He'd take her, hard and hot, but still remember to protect her head with his hand when he slammed her against the nearest surface. She wanted to laugh. She was safe. She'd always be safe with Griffin Jude Payne.

Oh, he'd take from her.

But he'd also give. Fiercely.

And so would she.

The thick weight of him stretched her, pounded into her, and she gloried in the wet slaps of flesh meeting flesh, his harsh breath in her ear, their moans and the thick, musky scent of their desire. He was rough, callous, completely uncivilized and the ultimate gentleman.

Shivers spread over her skin and the winding pressure deep in her belly seemed to expand. She nipped his lip. "Harder."

She needed everything he could give.

Wanted to give him everything she had.

With long, bone-jarring thrusts he joined with her, letting her feel every inch, all his power. Her nails sank into the lean muscle of his neck, and he grunted in appreciation.

"You make me crazed." His mouth seared down her throat.

She arched her back so he could sink deeper, so her nipples stabbed into his chest. "I know." Just as crazed as he made her.

"I can't get enough of you."

She leaned in and bit his earlobe. "Come for me."

"Ladies first." His pace slowed, his hips rotating with each thrust. "You're close."

She nodded, biting her lip.

"Put your legs down."

He helped her ease one leg down, then the other while staying buried deep inside. In this position, the hard, slick surface of his cock rubbed her clit with each driving stoke, sending ripples of ecstasy through her. She clutched at his shoulders. "Griff."

He stroked his thumb over her breast, teasing the nipple to fullness before rolling it between his fingers and tugging. "Come, Angel."

She flexed into each thrust, the shockwaves of pleasure he ignited in her breast sending her closer to fulfillment, leaving her teetering on the edge. This was the best part, the just before. Her whole body tensed, shivers of delight racing over her skin, under her skin and she hung there, suspended from time for a few magical seconds while all his focus was on her.

He pinched her nipple, sending her over the edge into great pulsing waves of ecstasy.

With a shout, he thrust into her one last time as if trying to get as deep inside her as possible. As if trying to touch her soul. He picked her up and her world tilted as he bowed low with his climax.

She laughed. Not since childhood could she remember feeling such a profound sense of pure joy.

25

He pressed his lips to her collarbone and chuckled. "For a minute there, I thought we were both gonna fall."

And that was the thing. She already had fallen. Hard.

The question was, would he?

He gave her a quick kiss. "Let me get the blanket out. We may as well camp here tonight."

She nodded, leaning against the tree and trying to catch her breath.

He wandered around the area, picking up their belongings, at ease with his nudity in the bright moonlight. Had he ever had a moment of self-consciousness? Ever feared someone might not find him attractive? Probably not. He was a beautiful male. She couldn't imagine anyone ever telling him he was too skinny, or that he had ugly eyes.

She almost couldn't imagine anyone telling her those things when she was with him. Griffin made her feel beautiful. He liked the very attributes the Parnells so hated and she was starting to believe, the Parnells had just been plain mean. When she was with Griffin, she felt confident. Self-assured. He had liberated her.

"Come here, Angel." He sprawled out on the blanket and held his arms out to her. She sank down beside him and tucked her head under his chin. The night air felt cool on her skin, but Griffin radiated heat like a furnace. "Can I ask you a question? It's been bugging me all night."

Prudence frowned. There was something else bothering him? "What?"

"Tonight, what in the world were you and Granny Nash talking about?"

She tried to keep from laughing, but her whole body shook with mirth. "Baby, I don't think you want to know."

"I do. I've never seen you laugh so much. Look at you. Just thinking about whatever you talked about is has you in stitches."

"We were talking about our men."

Griffin's hand stopped stroking up her arm. "What do you mean?"

"Granny Nash misses her husband and wanted to relive a little of the excitement of romance vicariously through us. She didn't mean any harm. It was nice to have a woman to talk to. She was very . . . informative."

A groan rolled through his chest. "Why do I have the feeling I'm never going to be able to look that woman in the face again? What did she inform you of?"

Prudence giggled.

"You know, don't answer that, I'm pretty damn sure I already know."

"You liked me inside you." She lifted up on her elbow to look down at him and was charmed to see him blushing. "I liked it, too."

He pulled her down and kissed her. "Hush now, or I won't be able to look *you* in the eye, either."

She snuggled closer, lying her head on his shoulder.

"How does the whole gift thing work, anyway? I'm trying to understand. Is it some kind of ceremony or something? Like a wedding?"

"No. It's emotional. Something not even I can lie about. When I fall in love, and someone falls in love with me, it'll happen. It has to do with pheromones. My mark will go to my mate when they receive my gift." And she would receive her daughter.

"Really?"

"Mm. My mother gave my father the gift of persuasion the night my father took on her marks. He later told her, in the back of his mind, he was worried about how they were going to be together. Lythos had just restricted outsiders to the spaceport so they couldn't be together there. There were laws on Earth forbidding interracial marriages so they couldn't be together there. He said he was thinking about how to convince people to change the laws, because he couldn't imagine being without her. He used her gift to get the laws changed on Earth."

"I'll be damned. Sargent William Brand was your father?"

Prudence grinned. Everyone knew of her father. "Yeah. I guess, because he was such a prominent figure for human-alien rights, people remembered him. They remembered how persuasive he was. Maybe that's how the rumors started about Lythonian women giving the gift of persuasion."

He stroked his hand down her arm. "It's always different, then?"

"From what my mother told me, the gift is tailored to the mate. It's a gift. Something they need. Not everyone needs to be persuasive to be happy, but everyone needs something. My grandfather's gift allowed him to see in the dark—he was a night fisherman on Lythos and he'd been worried about providing for his family."

"I never heard of any of this before."

"You wouldn't have. Lythonians are not fond of adventure and don't leave Lythos and a few weeks after they opened their planet to outsiders, they restricted visitors to the spaceport. The handful of us who live on Earth don't advertise our gifts to protect our families. Who wants to forever wonder if their mate loved them just to get their gift?"

His arms tightened around her. "Thank you."

"For what?" She lifted up on her elbow.

"Trusting me enough to tell me all this." He wrapped a lock of her hair around his finger.

She gave him a kiss before settling back at his side. "Did you enjoy any of your time with Big Jake?"

"What? Oh, yeah."

"Did you get any information on Lucan?"

"He said Diamond Fjord was my best bet, unless Lucan joined the Blue Helmets, which I doubt. Soldiers, spaceport personnel and the like, live with their families on the other side of the spaceport in Blue Mesa."

"Have you considered the possibility Lucan might want to stay?" Prudence trailed her finger down his chest and dipped the tip into his navel. "He's been on Asteria for over a year, right? He might have a family of his own. A job and friends."

"Maybe. I never considered the possibility the people sent here would've built lives for themselves." He let out a heavy sigh. "I'll give him a choice, but Lucan, he never was much for adventure. He always liked to have someone around to do the heavy lifting—which left him time to be the brains of whatever operation he had going on."

She scoffed. "Sometimes I can't tell if you admire Lucan or are annoyed by him."

"We're brothers, so I suppose it's a bit of both." He chuckled. "We don't always see eye to eye, but I love him."

"So if he wants to stay, you'll stick around to keep him out of trouble?" Or maybe stay to keep her out of trouble.

Griffin inhaled a deep breath and let it out. For a long time, he didn't answer. Prudence listened to the steady drum of his heart, tracing circles around one flat nipple.

"Maybe I'll stay for a little while. Or maybe I'll finish my mission so I know where I stand and can get on with life. Big

Jake said he heard some news that a rebellion started back on Earth."

She propped herself up on her elbow. "Then you don't need to go back. The war will be won or lost without you."

He frowned. "I hope to hell the only people thinking that way are on Parnell's side of the conflict."

"Griffin, the whole thing might be over by now. How old is that news? Why travel all the way back to discover you're not needed?"

He shrugged. "Big Jake said he overheard some spaceport personnel chatting in a bar. Could've happened right after we left, or a week ago."

"Griffin—"

"I have to do this. I can't make plans for the future until I settle the past and earn back my honor." He pulled her down to nestle against his side. "Come on, we can talk about this tomorrow. Get to sleep now, we've got a long walk ahead of us."

Typical man, avoiding the conversation so he didn't have to listen to what he didn't want to hear. He was stubborn. Obstinate. Somewhere along the line he'd gotten this hair-brained idea in his head and he was hanging on like a Rottweiler with lock-jaw. None of it made sense to her. Why would he be so willing to risk his life to provide freedom for people who seemed happy without it?

Prudence stared into the night sky while Griffin began to snore. A small smile spread on her face. She must've wiped the poor male out—she'd never heard him snore before.

She sat up and stared down at her lover in the moonlight. *Her lover.*

Who would've thought she'd ever meet someone who could make her love? He was brash and passionate, hotheaded and affectionate. He was one of the most dangerous, notorious men on two worlds—everyone knew who he was, even out here—and he was the only man she'd ever felt safe with. The only man she felt safe enough to fight with.

Prudence's lips twisted into a rueful grin. She'd never acknowledged that fact before, but it was true. Right from the start, even before she'd gotten to know him, she'd stood up to Griffin. She was stronger now. More confident. All because of him.

She stroked her hand down his torso, careful to avoid the healing claw marks on his chest. In the moonlight, his tanned flesh seemed to glow, his musculature standing out in stark relief from the shadows of the dips and valleys of his body.

He mumbled in his sleep and flopped his arm out to the side as if reaching for her.

How many nights did they have left together? And would he live long enough to come back to her? Would he want to?

She didn't think separating would be this hard, but their time together was running out. She'd seen the way he stared at the painting in Big Jake's cabin. He had told her Lucan was an artist and she had no doubt that painting was one of his. By this time tomorrow, they'd be in Diamond Fjord and he'd find Lucan. Would Griffin leave her there? Would he bring her with him to visit his brother? Would he leave right away?

Her gaze ran over him, freezing just below his navel.

Her mating marks.

Two thin, dark lines came down from either side of his navel to twine around a third. He wore her mating marks.

She leaned back, rubbing her hand over her stomach, over the pale, flawless skin. Tears filled her eyes. Though she didn't feel any different than she did earlier that evening, she knew, beyond a shadow of a doubt, she was pregnant.

Would a baby make a difference to him?

Yes.

He was far too honorable to walk away from a child. But would knowing he stayed for the child be enough?

No.

For the rest of her life, she would wonder why he stayed and, he might grow to resent her and the baby. She needed him to stay because he wanted to. She needed him to put the past to rest and choose to live.

Goddess be blessed, she was going to be a mother. A single mother.

She wrapped her arm over her belly. This changed everything. It was one thing to set herself up for the pain of him leaving, of maybe never holding him again or being able to look into his sea green eyes. But she would be damned if her daughter would be raised without her father. Somehow, she needed to get him to see past all the guilt he carried and give him reasons to want to live.

From what Granny Nash said of Diamond Fjord, the settlement was beautiful, the community nice—maybe if he saw what he'd be missing, he could be swayed. Or maybe there was someone there who would know what to say, what to do for him.

Granny Nash was right—she'd never convince Griffin to stay with tears and nagging. She needed to smile. Flirt. Make Griffin see how much Asteria needed him.

How much she needed him.

Then she'd tell him how much his baby needed him.

26

Diamond Fjord was breathtaking.

When they exited the forest and got their first look at Asteria's inaugural settlement, Prudence said, "We're home."

Home? Their journey together was almost at an end. This might become her home, but he had to move on.

Their impending separation was killing him. But Prudence didn't seem to mind. All day long she'd been smiling and flirting. He'd been thinking to stick around and make sure she got settled okay, but now . . . leaving her was hard enough. Seeing how much his leaving didn't seem to bother her—that was downright painful.

He turned away from her bright smile and surveyed Diamond Fjord.

The city—settlement was much too primitive a word—nestled up to towering hills on two sides and an inlet of the Red Sea on the third. Thigh-high bluegrass covered the hills, swaying in the breeze, and the sun glinted off the red-tinged waters beyond where small fishing craft floated. Two- and three-story buildings clustered together at the water's edge, sided in the opaque, gem-like bark that grew on Asteria's trees and caused the buildings to sparkle in the late afternoon sun as if covered in diamonds. In the valley between where they stood and the town, small farms dotted the countryside—a patchwork of fields and fenced areas for livestock. From a distance, at least, Diamond Fjord appeared to be flourishing.

"Don't be hasty, Angel. You know as well as I that the prettiest things can hide the darkest of secrets."

Prudence sighed. "I'm not letting you ruin this for me. Diamond Fjord's beautiful and the people here wanted no part of the Parnells or their dream. It's why they were exiled. I have every right to assume we'll be happy here."

Ah, hell, she kept saying "we." Did she think he might stay? Was that why she acted so happy? The thought made the tightness in his chest ease but was replaced with a knot in his gut at the idea of having to tell her he had to go. "I need you to exercise a little caution, is all. No need getting snippy."

She leaned close and nipped the scruff on his chin. "You'll know if I decide to get snippy, Warrior." She took hold of his hand and pulled him forward. "Come on, if we hurry, we'll get there before nightfall." Turning, she walked backward and shot him a suggestive look. "I'm wanting a real bath and a bed tonight." Her lavender eyes flashed with mischief. "Maybe I'll even share."

Christ, she was so damn beautiful it hurt to look at her. "Careful there, you're gonna end up tumbling down the hill."

With a laugh, she faced forward again. "That painting we saw last night, your brother painted it, didn't he?"

Griffin picked up his pace so he could see her face. "Yeah, that was one of his."

"He's talented."

"Yeah, he always was." Unlike him, Lucan had always had a knack for making the world a little more beautiful just by being him.

She turned sideways to study him while they walked. "Is something bothering you, Griff? I thought you'd be happy know to know for sure he's nearby."

He forced a smile. "I guess I can't get too excited until I lay eyes on him, you know? Maybe he's moved on. Maybe something's happened since then."

"And maybe he's right where Granny Nash said, in a little art studio on the waterfront."

Three hours later, Griffin needed all his energy just to sort out everything inside him. Sadness and fear about leaving Prudence, apprehension and guilt about taking so long finding Lucan, and a healthy dose of suspicion about the citizens of Diamond Fjord—all of it was making him jumpy as hell.

The city itself was indeed beautiful. Everybody bustled about, busy at one thing or another. Main Street was crowded. Shops lined the sidewalks, and hawker stalls lined the streets. A sort of peaceful chaos played out, with vendors and shoppers playing their parts. The whole place seemed crowded and noisy, but then, after being alone with Prudence for a week, anyplace with people felt that way. The scents of various cooked foods, flowers, and live animals hung in the air, adding to his sensory overload. Part of him wanted to find a quiet place to pull himself together, but a more urgent part needed to see his brother and reassure himself he was safe.

A hover car carrying two Blue Helmets edged through the crowd. The way the men scanned the citizens of Diamond Fjord, Griffin had no doubt they were searching for someone. The vehicle had enough jump seats in the back for fourteen more men, and while all empty at the moment, he was sure if they saw something they didn't like, more hover cars would arrive fully loaded. He gave Prudence's hand a squeeze. "Keep your eyes down, Angel."

As the hover car passed, he turned his back, pretending interest in a hawker stall full of live birds. He didn't breathe easy until the craft disappeared farther down the street.

A loud crack sounded behind them, and Griffin spun around, weapon drawn. For a heartbeat or two he was back on Earth, herding a group of people toward a spaceport. Most of the men had already been shipped off by then, leaving women and children and they fought dirty as hell when they needed to.

"You okay, handsome?"

He blinked, trying to focus.

Prudence put her palm on his chest, crowding into him. "All the color dropped from your face."

His attention shifted back to the perceived threat. A kid stared at him with wide eyes, an unused firecracker in his hand and another making sparks on the ground. Griffin returned his weapon to the small of his back with a shaky hand and wiped the sweat from his brow. He nodded, unable to meet her eyes.

He'd pulled his weapon on a kid.

She smiled. "Why don't we find someplace to sit so we can take everything in?"

He lifted his gaze to hers. He found no laughter or admonishment in her expression. Not even a flicker of fear. "I'm sorry."

"There a reason you're showing your weapon, mister?"

Griffin looked to his left, then his gaze crept up to the biggest man he'd ever seen. "Startled. That's all."

The man must've been six-foot-seven or eight and pushing three-hundred pounds of pure muscle. He had his dark hair pulled back in a ponytail. "Then maybe you shouldn't be carrying." He took Griffin's measure through bright blue eyes that seemed to be lit from the inside.

Was he the lawman Big Jake mentioned—Merrick? Everything he wore was black from his boots, to his pants to the knee-length duster. "There a concealed carry law here?"

"New, huh?" He rocked back on his heels and his eyes narrowed. "You look familiar."

Griffin glanced at Prudence, who kept her face downcast. "My friend and I are looking for one of my relations. We're not here to start trouble."

"Got separated during the Expulsion?"

He nodded. "I'm looking for an art studio called Visions from Home."

The big man's eyes widened. "No shit?"

"No shit."

A smile tugged at his mouth and for a minute, he reminded Griffin of a little boy with a big secret. "Follow me."

Griffin took Prudence's hand in his and headed down the street. Even with the crowd swelling and receding around them, there wasn't a chance in hell he'd lose sight of him, he stood a full head taller than anyone else.

Prudence glanced up. "You think we can trust him?"

"Don't know. Keep your eyes open, Angel, and let me know if you see anything odd."

They turned off Main Street onto the docks and were led into a store with an old-fashioned swinging sign out front that read: Visions of Home – Welcome

Griffin stepped inside the cramped shop which was full to bursting with paintings, sketches, and statues. They all held Lucan's unique, precision touch. He'd made it. He'd found his brother.

"Hey, babe?"

Griffin's attention zeroed in on the big man who'd brought them here. *Babe?*

He disappeared behind a piece of cloth pulled over a doorway.

Griffin followed.

Prudence tugged on his hand, trying to stop him. "Griff? Maybe we should give them some privacy and wait out here."

Privacy? What the fuck did they need privacy for? He waved Prudence away and pulled back the curtain.

Lucan sat in front of a large canvas, paint bush in hand. It was him. He was alive. Whole. And if the smile he turned on the big guy was any clue, he was happy. The way he was positioned, he hadn't seen Griffin yet, which was fine, it gave him a moment to study Lucan. He looked older now, his shoulders a little broader. His blond hair was tousled and he wore jeans and a white tee that were both smattered with paint. Christ, he was a sight for sore eyes. All he wanted to do was wrap him in a big bear hug.

"Hey, babe. Someone's here to see you." The big guy put his hand on Lucan's shoulder and bent over to kiss him.

For a heartbeat or two, Griffin couldn't move, torn between walking out and beating the living shit out of the fucking giant touching his brother.

"Griffin, it's all right." Prudence put her arms around his waist.

27

—— ◆ ——

The two men in a lip-lock froze. Lucan spun around in his seat. "Griffin?"

A range of emotions ran across Lucan's face—surprise, guilt, anger. His brother had never been good at hiding what was on his mind and he sure as hell didn't look happy to see him. He didn't look happy to see him, at all. Holy hell, why the hell did he come here? To disrupt his brother's life? And now that he was here, looking at Lucan, he didn't know what the fuck to say. Words wouldn't make up for his not being there.

So he left.

Christ Almighty, what had he just seen? That was his brother. *His brother.* When the hell had *this* happened? With long, ground-eating strides he left the shop and headed down to the end of the dock away from the people, the noise, the . . . *everything.*

He couldn't take any more.

He didn't care who Lucan wanted to be with. He didn't. But goddamn it, he hadn't *known,* and his ignorance of his own brother shamed him. He'd been tight with Lucan growing up, but after leaving for the Marines . . . After he'd been to war, it became more difficult to find common ground. Doing the things he'd done made it harder to look his brother in the eye, much less talk to him about anything important. This was just one more thing to add to his growing list of fuck-ups.

His hands shook and his heart pounded as hard as if he'd traded fire with the enemy.

"Griffin?"

"What?" His reply came out much louder than he intended. He dragged his hand down his face and turned around to face Lucan. "What?"

Lucan gave him a lopsided smile. "Good to see you, big brother."

"Yeah." Griffin ran his hand over his head and turned around to watch the waves roll past.

"You were best man at George and Jacob's wedding. What's got you so freaked out?"

That was Lucan, always going for the clean, logical answer. "I don't know."

"Look, I'm sorry I never told you—"

"Did Mom and Dad know?" He glanced at him over his shoulder.

"They raised us; of course they knew."

The oddest bird—something that looked like a cross between a parrot and a pelican dove down into the water to fish, skimming its oversized beak through the red-tinged water. Damn, he missed familiar things. Everything was different here, even his brother. "Then why didn't I?" Griffin turned around and folded his arms over his chest.

"By the time I was old enough to know, you were gone." Lucan shrugged. "I never dated—didn't meet anyone I liked until I met Merrick—not that you and I talked much anymore anyway."

Now that he'd mentioned it, Griffin couldn't remember ever seen Lucan with a special someone, never heard him talk about anyone he was courting. The thing killing him, though, was *he had never thought to ask*. He'd been too concerned with his own shit. Griffin looked over Lucan's shoulder to where Prudence chatted with the big man who'd brought them here. "Merrick? That's his name?" The son of a bitch was huge and Lucan was shorter than Griffin. He couldn't quite see the two of them together. Lucan was fair-haired, well-built but almost petite compared to the rest of the men in the Payne family. Merrick—he looked like he belonged in some seedy bar protecting someone with a name like Vinnie Two-toes.

"Yeah." Lucan shoved his hands in his pockets. "So, I, uh . . . I saw the holograms of you."

"Damn." Griffin turned away, unable to meet his brother's eyes. All the guilt he held onto for not being there when Lucan needed him bubbled up to lodge right in his goddamned throat. What the hell must he have thought about seeing him kill in cold blood? Griffin hated apologizing and he seemed to be saying sorry a lot lately. "I'm sorry as hell you got sent here, Lucan. The whole thing was my fault. I hope . . . I hope I didn't worry you, you know, when you saw what you saw."

"Worry me?" Lucan's voice edged up in volume. "I thought you were dead. I thought you died in the bombings. Next thing I know, I'm watching my brother assassinate the U.N. Prime minister. Then I'm watching your trial wondering what the fuck the Blue Helmets might be doing to you, because I sure as hell never knew you to hold your peace. Next I hear *Genesis V* is dead in space—no survivors, so for the second time I mourned losing you. Now you're standing here in front of me, won't even look at me, giving me some lame-ass lip service."

For a second, Griffin thought he was walking away. Lucan paced down the boardwalk half a dozen feet, shouted, "Fuck," and came back. "Seriously, this is how it's going to be, now? This whole awkward 'let's-pretend-nothing-happened-and-move-on' bullshit?"

"No." Griffin pulled his brother into a hug and for a heartbeat, he thought Lucan would push him away. He sure as hell wouldn't have blamed him. But just as he released

Lucan, his brother's arms wound around him and hugged him back. "It's all right now."

Lucan's voice shook. "Why didn't you write or call or anything? For two years I got nothing."

Griffin stepped back, jammed his hands into his pockets and stared at the planks of the boardwalk. "They put the military on total blackout. No media, no communications, no leave." He sighed, forcing himself to look at his brother. "I wanted to, Lucan. We didn't know what the fuck was going on. I swear to you, I would've come home no matter what it took if I'd known."

Lucan's face eased a little. "And why didn't you talk at the trial?"

Heat blossomed over Griffin's cheeks. "I couldn't. I underestimated them. Took 'em at face value. I thought I'd be safe in prison during the trial, but they fucked me up."

"How?"

Griffin rolled his eyes. "Come on."

"I have a right to know. What'd they do, break your jaw?"

A sour burst of laughter broke past his lips. "Nah, man. They cinched my shit shut with barbwire. Stuck a piece through my tongue for good measure."

"Shit." Lucan propped his hands on his hips and looked out over the Red Sea.

Griffin looked away. Lucan was an innocent. He was so trusting he didn't even question how a few barbed wires kept him from talking. That was good, though; he didn't want to tell him that the Blue Helmets had taken their neighbor. He didn't want to have to tell him he wasn't sure what happened to the sweet lady who'd brought them food when they'd been mourning their parents.

"You're done now, right? It's finished."

Griffin didn't answer. He couldn't. He wanted to reassure Lucan that everything would be fine now, but . . . .

"Jesus, you're a bastard. Are you at least gonna come meet Merrick before you disappear again? He's had to go through watching me morn your sorry ass twice now. He should at least get to meet you before the next time."

His stomach roiled. Lucan had a special way of making him feel like shit. But his kid brother didn't understand, couldn't understand. Griffin had always taken care to protect Lucan from his life in the Marines. *And you'll continue to do so.* Griffin's gaze traveled back to where Merrick and Prudence sat. They were both staring back at them. "What is he to you? Boyfriend?"

"Husband."

Griffin nodded. Husband. Okay, little brother was married. "He good to you?"

Lucan's face eased into a smile. "Yeah. He is. You don't have to worry about that." He glanced over his shoulder. "What about your lady? She's pretty."

"Pr—" He paused. It'd be up to Prudence if she wanted to share her identity with Lucan. "Angel and I jumped ship together."

"Is that all?" One of Lucan's brows arched. "I'm having trouble imagining you being alone with a woman like that for a week and leaving her alone."

Griffin shrugged. "We're lovers. I'm not sure where we'll go from here."

Lucan's gaze pinned him in place. "Where do you want to go from here?"

"That's a loaded question." He wanted a civvy job. He wanted Prudence to call him babe when she interrupted his work. He wanted kids. He wanted to live close to Lucan and get to know him again. "I've still got a few things to settle."

"Damn it, Griffin, you got to stop with this shit. You do not carry the weight of the world on your shoulders. You don't. You can pretend otherwise forever, but you'll never get a chance to be happy."

Griffin leveled him a glare. "You done?"

"No. I'm just getting started—"

28

Griffin walked past, ignoring Lucan's curse. "Well, I'm ready to meet your hubby." Sometimes that adage about safety in numbers was true. Like when little brothers got too smart for their own good. He must have still had his angry face on, because as he approached, Prudence's eyes widened. She jumped up and rushed over to him.

"Merrick is very nice." She looked up at him with pleading in her lavender-eyes. "Don't hurt him. You'll upset Lucan."

Griffin opened his mouth, but clamped his lips shut again in defeat. Instead, he wrapped his arms around Prudence and buried his face in her hair. Her body went soft against his and she enfolded him in her embrace. For a moment, everything fell into place and made sense.

With her lips to his ear, she asked, "You all right, baby?"

"Yeah."

He straightened and threw his arm over her shoulder, anchoring her at his side, hoping to hold onto the sense of peace she brought him.

Lucan took Merrick's hand and brought him over to where Griffin stood. "So, uh, Griff, this is Merrick."

A smile spread on the giant's face, softening his features and making him appear a bit more human. "Glad to see you in one piece, Chief."

Griffin shook Merrick's hand. "Thanks."

Merrick released his hand and flung his arm over Lucan's shoulders, his gaze full of challenge. "We good?"

Griffin checked Lucan's reaction, but his brother seemed fine with Merrick's possessive act, he even leaned in closer to the larger man which put the remainder of Griffin's fears to rest. "Yeah. Lucan says you treat him well. As long as that remains true, we're good." He glanced at Prudence. "This is Angelica."

Prudence shook both men's hands but held on to Lucan for a heartbeat longer. "Griffin told me all about you. I loved what I saw of your artwork."

Lucan pulled Prudence away and escorted her back into his shop. "You pick out anything you like and it's yours."

Merrick rolled his eyes. "He gives away as much as he sells."

"I believe it."

"Come on in." Merrick clapped him on the shoulder and headed back to the shop. "We live upstairs. You're welcome for dinner. We've got a spare room if you need someplace to stay."

Griffin nodded. "We'd be grateful."

However, when they reached the shop, Merrick pulled the door shut instead of walking through and joining the others. He scowled. "The Blue Helmets are looking for Angelica."

Shit. He searched Merrick's face, but couldn't tell if he was warning him or letting him know he planned to turn them in. "They're looking for a lavender-eyed woman."

Merrick snorted. "There were a lot of Lythonian women on *Genesis V*, huh?"

Their eyes locked, but the son of a bitch wasn't backing down. "Do we have a problem?"

"You're my brother-in-law." Merrick sighed. "Where I come from, family sticks together. We'll keep you both hidden best we can, but eventually, someone's going to see her. You can't hide forever."

"I'm planning to take care of the problem. I had considered sticking around awhile, but I guess I should head out tomorrow. Can I leave Angel here with you?"

"Yeah, but . . . ." Merrick stared at him hard. "Did you tell Lucan?"

"Not in so many words."

Those bright blue eyes turned cold. "You and I are going to have a problem if you hurt him again."

The door opened and Lucan poked his head out. "What's going on out here?"

"We were having a private discussion." Griffin walked into the shop, forcing Lucan to back up. "Never could get any privacy with you around."

"This is my shop, my house." Lucan winked. "My rules. Let me lock up and we can go upstairs. You both look like you could use a hot meal." He locked the door, flipped the sign and as he walked passed, and took Prudence's bag from her. "Holy crap, what do you have in here, rocks?"

Prudence smiled. "Yes. The glowing kind. They did a good job keeping the Scarecrows away."

Lucan stopped and turned around. He appeared incredulous. Him and Merrick both.

Griffin shrugged. "Our pod landed out in the Black Desert near the outpost."

Merrick started laughing. "Those old coots out there have never even tried to cross the desert—they're too damn scared—but you two made it across?"

"Yeah, well, Angel here didn't give me much of a choice." He shot her a teasing frown. "She kept taking off by herself."

"And you couldn't let her go." Lucan shook his head. "Griff's always had a streak of responsibility about ten miles wide."

"Is that what you call it?" She scoffed, shooting Griffin a wink. "He wanted to use me for a hostage."

Lucan's eyebrows shot up. "Did he now?" He put his arm around her and started up the steps in the back of the shop. "Well, you're safe now, sweetheart. I won't let him bother you. Why don't you tell me all about the big bad Griffin?"

Griffin pushed past Merrick and pulled Prudence to his side. "We worked all that out."

Lucan shot Prudence a conspiratorial wink and led the way upstairs. The upper rooms were no less crowded with artwork, most of what Lucan had displayed were pictures of their home and their parents. The stairs ended in the living room with large masculine pieces of furniture positioned in a seating area. Off to one side a door led to what looked like the kitchen and next to that was a dining area. Simple and clean, their living quarters had a homey feel.

"You have a beautiful home." Prudence walked over to inspect a painting of the Payne family, which was so detailed it looked more like a photograph than a painting.

Merrick lowered a tabletop from the wall, and pulled out four chairs from a nook. "Come sit down, babe. I'll get dinner."

Lucan brought them some glasses and a carafe. "Wine?"

They both nodded.

Griffin took his glass and leaned back in his chair. "How long have you been married?"

"Almost a year. We met the day I arrived. Merrick had a little place up the street. He offered me a job."

"How long have you been here?"

"About a year." He sipped his wine. "I was the tiniest bit freaked out when I got off the ship."

Merrick, who must have been listening from the kitchen, laughed. "Is that what you call it?" He poked his head out of the kitchen. His smile faded briefly as he met Lucan's gaze. The little communication was over in done in a heartbeat, but Griffin caught it. "Poor guy still had hibernation sickness, didn't have a damned thing with him but the clothes on his back. He sat down on the church steps off Main Street and I'm watching him stare at one of the vendor carts and could almost see him calculating out how to swipe some food."

Somehow, he had a feeling Merrick was only telling him part of the story.

"Merrick offered me a job—three square meals and lodgings, included with pay."

Griffin frowned. "Doing what?"

Quiet laughter rumbled from Lucan. "Not what you're thinking. He needed someone to do all the paperwork for the town court and jail."

Griffin raised his voice so Merrick could hear. "The Blue Helmets don't take care of all that?"

"Nope. We police our own," Merrick said from the kitchen. "The Blue Helmets pretty much stick to the spaceport and Blue Mesa. I play sheriff and judge for Diamond Fjord."

"You get a lot of crime?"

"Nah. Mostly drunken disorderly B.S., and some property disputes. I think it's just too soon. What happened on Earth is fresh in people's minds. They don't want to make the same mistakes. There's one law here—live and let live. People follow it. They have tolerance. Might not last forever, but I expect it'll last a while longer."

"The town is beautiful," Prudence said. "I didn't expect anything this advanced."

Lucan took a sip of wine. "We've got doctors, architects, and programmers, everything you can imagine. It's just a matter of applying those skills to the resources here on Asteria."

"Food's ready." Merrick served them each a steamy plate before joining them.

Dinner comprised some kind of fish—the meat was yellow and lumpy but tasted buttery and melted in his mouth—a mashed green vegetable which was tart by comparison, and black bread with sweet cream. He and Prudence didn't talk much during the meal, he suspected she was doing the same as he was—savoring every bite.

After Merrick cleared away the plates and Lucan filled their glasses for the umpteenth time, Griffin sat back with a sigh. "My perceptions might be distorted right now, but that was the best dinner I remember eating."

Lucan raised a brow. "Better than Mom's Thanksgiving?"

"All right, second best."

"What about the barbeque ribs Dad used to make on the Fourth of July?"

"Third best."

Merrick sat down and bumped his shoulder against Lucan's. "Babe, stop now while I have a little confidence left."

Griffin chuckled.

Prudence wrapped both her arms around one of Griffin's and rested her head on his shoulder. "I thought dinner was fantastic, Merrick."

"Thank you." He made a little bow. "See, someone appreciates me. I bet your parents were good cooks, right?"

She covered her mouth with her hand and yawned. "Well, no, not really."

Lucan and Griffin laughed.

Prudence rushed to smooth things over. "But I did like dinner."

Merrick pulled a face. "Thanks, sweetie, but you've got nothing good to compare my food to."

She settled back against Griffin and for a moment he was at peace. For a few heartbeats he was content to be here. Sharing a meal and a conversation with family, Prudence right at his side.

But it couldn't last.

He had to head out tomorrow. He needed to make sure Prudence remained safe and he had to earn back his honor. "So, how far are we from the spaceport?" Griffin took a sip of wine.

Lucan frowned. "Doesn't matter much. The place is locked down tight. Merrick can't even get in. Only spaceport personnel have access."

Griffin looked to Merrick. "What about a bribe?"

"With what?" Merrick leaned back in his seat and stretched his arm over the back of Lucan's chair. "He's right. Spaceport personnel have one very good reason to be on guard—their ticket back to Earth. They can't be bribed. Whatever you come up with, I guarantee someone has already tried it. My first two years here, I tried—I'm ex-Special Ops, ex-Secret Service. The place is impenetrable."

"On top of live personnel, they have auto-scanners." Lucan took a sip of wine. "If you're not chipped and you're anywhere within a quarter mile of the place, they'll see you."

"Chipped?"

Merrick grimaced. "Again, I've already tried. Captured a spaceport security guard from Blue Mesa, cut his chip out and implanted it into myself. It was as close as I ever got, and I still didn't get beyond the front gate. After that you still have to pass a retina scan, live inspection, and a DNA scan. You're not getting in."

Bullshit. There had to be a way. "What about maintenance? Don't they ever have locals come do any work?"

Lucan rolled his eyes. "Never. The place is locked down tight."

Merrick shook his head. "Look, even if you got past all the security, you need two key codes entered at the same time—one aboard the craft and one from Earth—to launch the ship."

No place was impenetrable. The spaceport had a weak spot and he was going to find it.

"Why did you come, Griffin?"

Lucan's question jarred him from his musings. "I don't know. I was worried. Couldn't imagine you being happy here. It's stupid, I guess. Now that I'm here, I see you're fine."

"I'm glad you came." Lucan's smiled. "It's good to see you."

Griffin's gut tightened. He was glad to see Lucan, too, but he didn't deserve such consideration from a brother he'd put at risk. He almost preferred Lucan's lecture from earlier to this. Hearing his anger and hurt was difficult, but it was expected. Warranted. Lucan's acceptance on the other hand, left him restless and uncomfortable.

"Angel is out cold." Merrick grinned.

Sure enough, she'd fallen asleep leaning against his shoulder.

Merrick stood. "You want to put her to bed?"

"Yeah. I'm pretty tired, too. Why don't we call it a night?"

Lucan nodded. "Sure. I'm not going to open the shop tomorrow. We can catch up more over breakfast."

Griffin stood and lifted Prudence into his arms. "Where do you want us?" He followed Merrick down a narrow passage with low ceilings. They passed a closed door on their right and paused at the end of the hall near an open doorway. Griffin tried to walk through, but Merrick stopped him. "Please don't leave without talking to him first."

Griffin shook his head. "I won't. I'll explain everything." He glanced down at Prudence. "To both of them."

"Goodnight, then."

"Night."

29

Griffin meant to leave tomorrow.

Prudence kept her eyes closed but heard every word of the exchange.

She waited until the door closed and Griffin bent to lay her down on the bed, before she tightened her arms around his neck and did her best "waking up" routine.

"Didn't mean to wake you, Angel."

"It's okay. I can't go to sleep yet. I haven't had my bath."

Griffin walked into the adjoining bathroom and came back. "No bath, just a little CO2 laser shower."

"Sold."

While she got undressed, she glanced around the little room. They had painted the walls a pale blue and all the moldings and accents white, reminding her of a china plate. A white dresser sat between two windows and the airy drapes hung long enough to pool on the plush carpet. The bed was a deep royal blue, with pale blue and white pillows. She folded her clothes and placed them on the dresser before turning to Griffin. "Please tell me you're not planning to get between those pristine white sheets without cleaning up first."

He gave the bed one last, longing glance before sighing. "Hurry up. I'm right behind you." She'd climbed into the shower when someone knocked on the door.

"I got it." Griffin went into the other room.

The door slid closed behind her, and she flipped the switch and blue-light filled the small chamber. She turned, lifting her arms to shake out her hair while the Carbon-Dioxide lasers did their job cleaning her skin and hair. After a few moments the chamber went dark and she got out.

Griffin leaned against the doorjamb, arms folded over his chest, naked as the day he was born. She couldn't help but admire his muscular physique, and how her mating marks rode low on his abs. Just the sight had her aroused. She liked seeing her marks on his body.

Had he noticed? Was that what had him frowning so hard?

"Who was at the door?"

"Lucan. He's a cheeky bastard."

Prudence's lips twitched. "Why now?"

"He's going to wash our clothes."

Clean clothes? "Praise the Goddess. I love him even more now."

Griffin snorted. "The little shit said breakfast might be more enjoyable if we're only smelling the food."

She gasped. The temperature in her body spiked as a full-body blush engulfed her. *She smelled?*

Griffin crowded into her space, chuckling. "Pink suits you."

"I can't face them again." She buried her face against his shoulder.

His big hands stroked her back. "I'm pretty sure he was messing around, Angel. I don't smell anything."

"Pretty sure?" She groaned. "Of course you don't smell anything. We've been together."

"I'm positive." His whole body shook with laughter. "I swear to God, he was just trying to rile me." He bent to nuzzle the sensitive spot on her neck between her ear and shoulder. "Besides, you're squeaky clean now."

"Oh, go take your shower. I'm going to go hide under the covers."

His laughter followed her into the bedroom. She folded back the comforter and climbed into bed. She had every intention of seducing her mate, but as soon as her head hit the pillow, she drifted off.

Griffin finished his shower and stood in front of the mirror to check on his wounds. He looked like hell. His hair was a bit too long, he was in dire need of a shave and the claw marks from the Scarecrows covered a good portion of his neck, chest, and arms. They were healing, scabbed over and ugly as fuck, but they didn't look infected.

He was turning away when something else caught his notice. Below his bellybutton, he had a mark like Prudence's. He looked down at himself. What the hell had she done?

She'd what, mated him? Weren't the men supposed to do the claiming?

What the hell had she said last night? When she loved someone and they loved her back her mating marks would transfer. Is that what all this turmoil was? Love? Jesus Christ on Sunday, had he known he'd be claimed by some alien mark because of his unspoken feelings he'd have been more careful because she sure as hell deserved someone better than him.

He stormed into the bedroom, ready to give her hell.

She was sound asleep.

All his anger melted away.

He wasn't even sure what he felt. Whatever it was, was tearing him up. Something different than he'd ever experienced before, that's for sure. But the idea of her loving him when he had to leave wasn't a cause for celebration. This whole thing was starting to feel like a Shakespearean tragedy where they'd both end up hurt.

He had nothing to offer her. No home. No job. Not even his honor. For her to give him this—

She jerked awake and opened her eyes, searching for him. As soon as she laid eyes on him, she lay back down and closed her eyes. "Come to bed, Griff. Can't sleep without you."

She was killing him. Slowly, brutally, destroying him.

He walked over and climbed into bed. She draped herself over him, tucking her head under his chin.

God, he wished he could stay. Wished he could marry her and build a home with her. Legally binding her to him would mean everything to him. Having her for his wife would make him happier than he'd ever been. But his very name would cause her endless grief with the Blue Helmets. She'd become as notorious as he. Unless he ended their problems.

Still half-asleep, she shifted, lifting to kiss his chin. "Missed you."

Ah, Christ. Covering her mouth with his, he made slow, sweet love to her. With each touch, every kiss and intimate possession of her body, he tried to express what he couldn't say.

He wanted to stay.

He wanted her love and to love her.

Their bodies breathed as one, hearts pounding, bodies arching and straining, united in their purpose and when bliss took them both, making them shudder and clutch at each other, the release was bitter-sweet.

Goodbye sex always was.

"He's planning on leaving today."

Prudence made that statement as she walked down a back alley with her arm tucked into Lucan's. He'd loaned her his coat which was two sizes too big and a hat which she had pulled low on her forehead. She had to tip her head all the way back to see his expression.

"I know." His eyes were similar to Griffin's, that same sea green. "Look, Angel, I asked you to walk with me because I want to know what's going on with my brother. Merrick thinks . . ." He looked away for a moment. "Well, why don't you tell me what's up with Griffin? Then I'll tell you what Merrick thinks."

Were they still upset over what happened yesterday? "I know he's a bit rough around the edges, but he's a good man, Lucan. Yesterday . . . I don't know what happened, but I don't think it had anything to do with you and Merrick. He's been worrying himself sick—"

"Stop it, Angel." Lucan shook his head, grinning. "You don't have to explain my hot-headed brother to me. I might have a better idea about what all that was about than you do."

"Really?"

"Griffin's always been the responsible one. He's the one who took care of our mom when Dad was away. He took care of me. Then he joined the Marines and he took care of all of us. I don't think he gave a rat's ass that I'm with Merrick or that we're married. What's killing him is that he didn't know. That whole scene yesterday—that was Griffin punishing himself for not being around and maybe waiting for me to punish him, too."

Prudence stared. "Did he say something?"

"Nah." Lucan sighed. "He's just like our old man." He patted her hand. "Now, tell me about things. Does he treat you good?"

"Of course."

"He *is* hot-headed."

She scoffed. "He's all bluster. By our third encounter I figured that out. All his scowling and barking is just his self-defense. All I have to do is put my hand on him and he stops."

Lucan chuckled. "Mm."

"He's always taken care with me. I feel safe with him."

They walked in silence for half a block. She wasn't sure what Lucan was after and she didn't know how to bring up her concerns. So she studied the buildings they passed, admiring the sunlight glinting off the diamond bark walls.

Lucan cleared his throat. "Merrick said Griffin pulled his gun on a kid in town yesterday."

She winced. "It was a firecracker. Startled him, is all."

"Was that the first time he'd been . . . startled?"

She shook her head.

"Nightmares?"

She nodded, stopped, and turned to look at Lucan. "Fugues, too. I'm worried. When we first met . . . I realized he might be suicidal. He wasn't thinking too clearly, but then he was fine for a few days. I mean he was restless at night, but his humor improved. He seemed happy."

He tugged her into motion again. "Did something happen?"

She sighed. "Scanner ships passed us one night. He got moodier after that. Then the next night he had to fight off some scarecrows."

Lucan cursed. "Sorry."

She smiled. "I've been with Griffin for the last week. I'm used to hearing men swear."

"Yeah, I suppose you would be."

They continued to walk. Prudence thought back to the fight with the Scarecrows. Griffin had been in control . . . until the end. There was a moment there . . . . "When the Scarecrows attacked, part of me was terrified for him and part of me . . . was a little scared of him. I suppose he had reason . . . I mean he almost died. Two of them had him in their grasp and . . . oh, I don't know. He got lost there for a few seconds. Had this look in his eyes. Then he was fine. I stayed awake with him that night and his nightmares were fierce. The next day he had a fugue."

"Tell me about it."

"I'm pretty sure he thought we were back on Earth. He kept telling me to go back to base. Said he needed to be punished. He kept saying he didn't know." She stopped walking and faced Lucan. "He had no memory of it the next morning. A few days before he had told me some things that happened while he was active duty. Things that would . . . negatively affect anyone. We can't let him leave. This isn't good for him."

"We're not planning on letting him go anywhere. Merrick's playing along with him. He'll get Griffin's weapons without a fuss."

"Not a chance, Griffin's never without them."

Lucan gave her a wink. "Merrick's a damn fine pickpocket and Griffin's not in top form right now. Merrick will get the weapons."

She felt like the worst kind of betrayer, plotting against her mate. The rational side of her knew this was best; Griffin needed help. She wanted him whole and healthy. But, goddess did she love the man and, doing this, something she knew would make him furious and hurt was one of the hardest things she'd ever done. Prudence nodded. "Then what?"

"Then comes the hard part. We're all going to have to sit down and have a chat." Lucan dragged his hand through his hair. "I went through this with Merrick a while back. It's not fun. He didn't want to listen to reason. God, he was a real bastard, if I want to be honest. There were days I didn't think I could take any more. Days I thought, 'To hell with him, I'm leaving.'" He shook his head and propped his hand on his hip. "Look, I don't know how close the two of you are. You don't have to be a part of this if you don't want to."

"I love him." She pressed her hand to her belly. She was strong enough to do this, as long as it meant there was a chance she'd have a family at the end. "I'll stay."

He grinned. "I was hoping you'd say that. Here's the deal, Angel. He's going to feel cornered as hell, so no quick moves.

Keep your hands where he can see them and keep calm. No matter what he says, or how much of a fuss he puts up, you keep your cool."

Her heart was beating as fast as if she were getting ready to face a scarecrow again. Goddess help them, this wasn't going to be easy.

30

Griffin sipped his coffee while he waited for Merrick.

Lucan had taken Prudence out for a walk, which made him twitchy as hell. He didn't like her out there where people might see her, but Lucan had insisted, and she wanted to go. There wasn't a damned thing he could say to stop her. Maybe it was best. She didn't need to be here while he set his plans.

His hand went to his stomach. He lifted his shirt to look at Prudence's mark. Prudence Angelica Parnell loved him. She shouldn't, but she did.

Merrick walked in with a middle-aged man. "This is Grady. Back when I tried to get into the spaceport, he helped me draw up a blueprint based on what we could see from a distance, memories of those who have passed through, and things we heard about the place."

Grady stood a few inches shorter than Merrick, but his body was rail thin. Thick glasses made his eyes appear overlarge and his movements were so slow as to be almost sloth-like. Even his Southern drawl seemed to creep along. "You Chief Payne?"

"Yeah." He held out his hand and then waited while Grady took hold. Griffin gave the man's hand a hard pump, hoping to instill a little energy into him. "Thanks for letting me take a look at your blueprints.

"'S not much. Drawn from hearsay, to tell the truth. I got true blueprints of every other building for miles 'round. Figures ya'd want this one."

Griffin started to chuckle, then stopped when no one else even cracked a smile. He cleared his throat. "Well, let's take a look."

He had the distinct urge to pace while Grady placed the rolled paper on the table and, methodically smoothed the blueprint out, setting little weights at each of the four corners. Catching Merrick's attention, Griffin rolled his eyes.

The blueprint showed an octagonal-shaped building with two sets of perimeter fencing. "Are those chain-link?"

Merrick chuckled, moving to stand next to him. "Outer fence is electro-wired. Inner wall is eighteen-inch steel, ten feet high with barbwire over the top. Each fence has one opening. The outer fence here." Merrick reached over and pointed to a spot on the map, pressing up against Griffin. "The inner gate here." He did the same thing again when he pointed to a spot on the exact opposite side of the map. "Guards with dogs patrol between the two."

Griffin moved over to give the larger man more space. "You have to be shitting me." He stared at the two men. "Everybody has to walk half the perimeter to get to the second gate?"

Grady rocked back on his heels. "No, sir. There's a moving walkway. Moves real fast, too. We all got to take a ride on it when we first arrived. They took us off the ship, straight onto the walkway and escorted us out. None of us have ever been back in." He glanced back at Merrick. "Ain't that right?"

"Yep."

"Takes about ten minutes get from one door to the next. Here"—Grady pointed to a notch in the inner fence line—"Here." He pointed to the next in the row. There were about twenty little notches between the gates and he had no doubt Grady intended to point out each one.

"Grady, spit it out, man. What do the notches represent?"

"Sniper towers."

Merrick folded his arms over his chest. "And all this is before you even hit the security check points."

Fuck.

Griffin's heart pounded in his chest and sweat broke out on his brow. For the first time, he had to face the very real possibility he might fail. That he might spend the rest of his dishonored life protecting Prudence from a man light years away. Being with her wouldn't be a hardship, but not being able to make up for his sins would make him crazy. "I gotta get in there." He sat down. "I can't—" Even if the rest of his mission failed, he had to take out Randolph if he wanted to keep Prudence safe and that meant he needed to get back to Earth. "He won't stop hunting her unless I make him stop."

Merrick patted Grady on the shoulder. "Thanks for bringing this by. You mind if we hold on to it for today?"

"Nope. I don't need it for nothing. There's nothing on the other side of those fences that's any better than what's on this side." His overlarge eyes seemed to see right through Griffin. "Well, if ya need me, I'll be at Lucky's." Grady meandered out of the room.

Merrick pulled up a chair. "Tell me what's going on. Maybe if we brainstorm this out, we can come up with an alternative plan."

Griffin shifted. He was so wound up he felt like electricity ran under his skin. Worst of all he felt stupid. Naïve. "There's no information about Asteria's spaceport back on Earth. I hacked into the military's system. Everything was redacted." He sat back and looked at Merrick. "I can't believe I fucked up so bad again."

"That's not helping anything. Talk to me. I get that you couldn't make a true plan until you got here, but you had an idea in your head. A goal. What was it?"

"I . . . . I wanted to get to Lucan. When I found out he'd been transported I was terrified he'd been hurt or killed." Damn it, he couldn't breathe. His heart raced in his chest and the whole room seemed to want to close in on him. "I had to see him. I had it in my head that if he wanted to go back to Earth, I'd get him there." Griffin shook his head and wiped the sweat from his brow. His whole body shook. "I lost my base, everything was FUBAR. I went home and he was gone. Neighbors told me the Blue Helmets took him and that he'd been sent to Asteria. I had nothing. My base got fragged. My accounts were frozen. I didn't—"

"Look at me."

The compassion in the other man's expression floored Griffin. Here he was damn near losing his shit, telling his brother-in-law what a stupid fuck he'd been and . . . . And Merrick must not understand. "I went after Alfred because I knew a high-profile crime would get me transported and I hated him. I hated the things I'd done for him. I hated what he'd taken from me and I hated what he'd turned the world into. I've killed a lot of people in the line of duty, Merrick, but I'd never killed anyone in cold blood before and, oh God, I shot him right in front of Prudence." His gut churned. Why had he never thought about that before? She'd watched him kill her husband in cold blood. No wonder she ran from him those first few days.

Merrick's hand closed over his shoulder, making him realize he'd bent in his seat, hanging his head between his knees. "You're safe now. If you want all this to be over, it's okay for it to be over."

Griffin got to his feet and paced. He couldn't sit still. He'd fucked everything up and no one *understood*. "It can't be over. I wanted to make up for what I'd done when I killed Alfred, but I made things worse. You don't understand what Randolph is like."

The other man's gaze was sure and steady. "He is not your problem, Griffin. He's not."

"He is." He could hear his voice edging up, could hear the frantic quality, but was helpless to stop. "My actions put him in charge. *My* actions. I cannot live with myself until I make things right. Do you understand? I have to get my honor back."

Prudence and Lucan came in from their walk and went upstairs. On the way back, Lucan had repeated enough times that everything would be fine until she almost believed him.

However, when they reached the second floor, she took one look at Griffin and her smile faded. The weather was cool enough that she'd borrowed Lucan's jacket, but Griffin was sweating. All his muscles were tensed up and even from across the room she could see how hard he shook. "What's wrong?"

Griffin turned away, but Merrick motioned her in. "Maybe we should all sit down and talk about this."

Griffin met her gaze, his scowl fierce. "It's not up for discussion."

Lucan led Prudence over to the table and pulled out a chair for her. "Quit barking at Angel. You're lucky as hell she's such a sweet lady."

Merrick took hold of Lucan's arm. "Babe, would you bring in some wine? Maybe get something from down in the cellar. I think we could all use a drink."

Prudence watched as some silent communication ran between the two men. In the end, Lucan went downstairs. Merrick gave her a pointed look. Okay. Lucan said if Griffin started getting agitated that Merrick wanted them to keep their voices low, their hands in view. He said not to move too fast or make any threatening gestures. She slid her hands onto the table.

Merrick nodded. "Come on, Griffin. Sit down." Merrick used his foot to slide a chair closer to him. "No one here is going to stop you from doing what you need to do, but if we put our heads together, we'll figure something out."

Griffin sat, but he pulled the chair back from the table first so he sat with his back to the wall. She suspected he wanted to keep an easy escape route. He almost looked the same as he did that day on the velocepillar when he'd had that fugue.

All she wanted to do was go and comfort him, but she couldn't. Not yet.

"So, after you got here what did you expect to happen?"

"I was on the wrong side of things, I guess. I didn't expect any of this." He motioned to the room they sat in. "See, before we realized what was going on, I was hauling people to the spaceport for transport. I saw how scared everyone was. I got to see the dossiers on Asteria describing how inhospitable this place is. I didn't expect to find Lucan working, married, and happy. I expected him to want to go home and I intended to find a way to get him there. I expected typical spaceport security—intimidating but easy enough to breach if you know what you're doing."

"Which you do."

Griffin let out a mocking laugh. "Obviously."

"You got here in one piece." Merrick nodded to Prudence. "You and your lady. I'm pretty sure you two are the first to survive that trek without transportation and heavy artillery. Now, who is looking for Angelica?"

Griffin looked as stunned as she felt.

Merrick smiled. "Before Grady left, you said, 'he won't stop hunting her unless you make him stop.'" He glanced at Prudence and bumped his shoulder against hers. "Besides, I knew I'd seen you somewhere. Can't forget pretty eyes like yours. Prudence, right?"

She nodded and drew in a shuddering breath. "I suspect Randolph Parnell wants me back."

Merrick turned to Griffin. "Which is why you want to get back to Earth to kill him."

"In part, yes." He reached up to rub his temples. "But also to help with the Rebellion."

"I wondered if you'd heard about that." Merrick dragged his hand down his face. "I don't know if my opinion will matter to you one way or another, but I'd appreciate if you'd hear me out anyway."

"What, then?"

"You've gone above and beyond the call of duty. Let it go. The rebels have this. Randolph's days are numbered. Concentrate on you. Get your head on straight and help me keep this town safe. We want you in our lives."

For a heartbeat, she thought Griffin might give in. The way he stared at Merrick suggested he was hearing the last thing he expected, but the expression of absolute shock twisted into something gut-wrenching. She'd seen that particular look once before. The day she'd told him he wasn't a hero.

Guilt tore through her. "Baby, I don't understand why you're still punishing yourself. You are a hero. Maybe you had to kill your CO, maybe you weren't a hero to him, but you asked the questions that needed to be asked. To the men in your unit who were saved from having to kill those kids, you were a hero. To those kids, you were a hero. You've served your time. You don't have to give your life."

"You never give up. Don't you get it?" He held his arms open. "What do you think might have made me start questioning my CO?"

"Don't do this to yourself," Merrick said. "Whatever happened, it's in the past."

Griffin didn't spare him a glance, though. He stood, his attention resting on her. "Go on, ask."

She shook her head. "No. This isn't good for you. Just—"

Merrick eased to his feet, arms held open in a placating gesture. "Listen, man, we don't need to—"

Griffin's voice rose to a shout. *"Ask me why I questioned my CO!"*

Lucan walked into the middle of the tension, carafe in one hand, glasses in the other. "What made you question your CO?" Everyone turned to stare. "What? What'd I miss?"

Merrick swore.

"Since Lucan was nice enough to ask, I'll tell you. See, I went out on border patrol with my unit. We got a call about a terrorist cell on the move—twenty-two of them headed our way in one vehicle, no civilians in the area—can we take them out? Hell, yeah. Ooh-rah. How do you want us to do it? My CO, he didn't care, he wanted them taken out. So, me? I get this brilliant plan to plant heat sensing IEDs across the bottleneck in the road."

Lucan set the carafe down on the table and put his hands on Prudence's shoulders. He gave her a gentle squeeze.

Prudence shook she was so scared. Not for herself, but for Griffin. He was torturing himself over things that were long done. "Baby, you don't have to do this."

"I do." Agitated, he paced in front of them. "You need to understand, Pru. I didn't half-ass the job, I had my team plant six of the damned things, there wasn't a chance in hell anything could get through that bottleneck without hitting at least one of the bombs. Once they hit one, they were all going off. Fucking. Brilliant. We all hunkered down and waited, smoking and joking. Next thing I know, here comes a hover-bus down the road. The driver was hauling ass, big plumes of dust cutting out behind the thing. I'm thinking to myself, what a bunch of fucking pricks to hide in a school bus."

Prudence felt all the blood drain from her face. *Sweet goddess, no.*

"As they get closer, I'm hearing kids singing. At first, I thought they were fucking about—that the cocksucker terrorists were playing a recording or something—part of their cover. But as the bus is getting closer, I'm seeing shit flying around in the inside of the bus. So I grab my oculars and take a peek and you know what I saw? Do you?"

Merrick cursed.

Prudence swallowed past the knot in her throat. "Kids."

"Hell, yeah. Bus full of kids bouncing a holoball back and forth, singing."

For a long time he held her stare, so long she thought he might leave the story there. She wanted him to leave the story there. She already knew what happened. Could see it written plain in the agony of his expression. This was why he was punishing himself. He killed those kids and he couldn't get past it. But she knew Griffin. She knew him and she loved him and there was no way he'd have knowingly done such a thing.

"I couldn't stop them. I couldn't do anything to prevent the bombs from going off. I ran out there, waving my arms like a lunatic and the fucking driver waved back." He blinked hard. "He stuck his arm out the window and waved like he was on a Sunday drive. Next thing I know, it was done. The singing stopped. There was glass everywhere, twisted metal. Toys and . . . bits"—his face twisted—"strewn all over. The air smelled of gasoline and cooked meat. I killed twenty-one little kids and their driver and you know what? I still thought we got a bum scoop. I thought they fucked up. I knew I fucked up. When I returned to base, thinking I was going to the brig, your goddamned husband handed me a medal."

Her hand flew to her mouth. "I didn't know, I—"

"Your husband clapped me on the shoulder, and said, 'I know that must've been hard, son, but you did well.' Did I?" he shouted the question. "Did I do good? Somehow, I don't think that busload of kids singing 'Happy and You Know It' in Swahili were planning to strap bombs to their chests and terrorize the spaceport."

Prudence got to her feet and reached toward him. "Come here, Griff."

He appeared stricken. "What are you doing? Didn't you hear me?"

She nodded, daring a step closer. "What you're saying is awful, horrible."

"Then what are you doing?" His face bunched up. "You can't want me."

"I do." She nodded, urging him closer because she feared if he left, she wouldn't ever see him alive again. "I still want you. I love you."

He cursed and strode out of the room.

"Griffin!"

Lucan stopped her from going after him. "Honey, give him some time."

"I've got his weapons." Merrick held up the blaster and the Swiss Army knife. "He'll be okay for a few minutes."

She turned her face into Lucan's shoulder. "Why does he do that to himself? He didn't know."

"He's always been like that." Lucan shrugged. "For as long as I can remember, he's always had this need to take care of everybody."

Everyone but himself. "I'm afraid I'm going to lose him."

Lucan gave her a warm smile. "Nah. Griffin's smart. He'll think things over and realize you need him more than anyone else does. He'll come around. We'll make sure he gets the help he needs."

Merrick smoothed her hair back. "And if he doesn't, we'll beat some sense into him for you."

Griffin strode down the street. What the fuck just happened?

He'd explained in detail what a dishonorable bastard he was, and she still wanted him.

He'd taken the lives of a busload of youths.

He'd killed his CO and his escorting unit.

He'd survived when his whole base had been destroyed.

And when he'd tried to earn back a little of his honor by making things right, he'd made conditions worse for everyone.

Why in holy hell did she want to even breathe the same air as him?

Anxiety crawled under his skin. Every time he worked himself up to accept the punishment he deserved, no one would cooperate. Instead of going to the brig, he'd been awarded a medal. Instead of a courts martial, he'd survived his base being fragged. Instead of being looked at for the piece of shit he was, a woman far above him in morality loved him.

The thing was, while he didn't want the medal and he didn't want to be the sole survivor, God help him, he did want her love. But if he allowed himself to accept such a gift, wouldn't that make him even more of a monster? Wouldn't that mean he didn't take his past mistakes as seriously as he should?

The noise of Main Street grew louder as he approached and he couldn't bear to be around people right then. Didn't want to see the citizens of Diamond Fjord enjoying their community and the prosperous town they'd built. Doing so would remind him why they were here in the first place—because of him, and men like him, blindly following orders.

Griffin turned down an alley. Even the narrow aisles between the shiny buildings were free from litter.

There was no place for trash like him.

He sat down on a step leading to the back of one of Main Street's shops and stared at the wall across from him.

What the hell was he doing, anyway? Even if he managed to steal a ship, get back to Earth and kill Randolph—who was to say someone else wouldn't rise in the bastard's place?

Who was to say the new PM wouldn't be as adamant about possessing Prudence? Christ, he had to protect Prudence. Maybe there was no hope for him, but he'd make sure she survived.

He focused on the wall in front of him. It wasn't the same iridescent diamond-wood of the others but had been painted a flat white as a base for a mural. With a glance, he knew his brother had created the painting. He must have circled around and now faced the back of Lucan's shop. The left side depicted a war zone, homes and trees burned and Lucan had captured stark horror in the eyes of those fleeing. The scene was dark, the smoke blocking out the sun. Beneath the picture, read: "Society's curse is to bring destruction to individuals."

The first scene blended into the second, the aftermath. The sunlight poured down on the broken remnants of buildings and the skeletal remains of trees. A blackened, twisted swing-set sat in the background and powdery ash covered everything. In the foreground a child poured water from a can onto a bright green sapling. The caption read: "Individuals are responsible for ensuring beauty grows from the ash."

A tremor ran through him and stuck, making him shake like a palsied old man. Tears pricked the back of his eyes. "What the fuck am I supposed to do with that? What's that mean?"

The empty alleyway had no answer, just his shout echoed back to him. He covered his face with his hands, shamed by his outburst.

Behind him, a door opened. Damn it, now he'd disturbed Lucan's neighbor. Without turning, he headed off down the alley.

Someone grabbed him. A bag came down over his head, limiting his vision to tiny pinpricks of light streaming through the material. Struggling, Griffin reached for his weapon, but the blaster wasn't there. Well, shit, that's why Merrick had been crowding into him earlier. He kicked out with his foot, connecting with his attacker's knee. A male shouted.

"Hit him."

Griffin twisted within the grasp of his attacker, arching back with the intention of head-butting the bastard holding the bag over his head.

Something hard wacked him across his skull. Pain burst like fireworks in his head, reverberating down his spine. The tiny beads of light blurred. The hands around his wrists loosened. His whole body jarred as he dropped to his knees. He tried to stop his forward momentum, but his arms wouldn't obey.

The whole world went dark.

31

—◆—

Griffin came awake in degrees.

At first, he noted dread heavy in his gut. He'd fought with Prudence. He'd hurt the woman he loved because he couldn't get past his guilt. More than anything, he wanted to make things up to her. He'd find her, pull her into his arms and beg her forgiveness.

But as soon as he tried to move pain shot through his head, his arms. He squinted his eyes open and after looking at pinpricks of fractured light for a moment, he realized he stared at the inside of a black cloth bag.

Someone had snatched him off the street in broad daylight.

He half-stood, half-leaned against some kind of A-frame. Metal bars rose up at angles on either side of him, meeting where his wrists had been secured over his head. Another bar pressed across his hips, keeping him from sagging and putting all his weight on his cuffed hands. His shoulders ached and his limbs felt as though thousands of tiny needles were being worked under his skin. His legs were spread wide, ankles bound and anchored to the bottom of the frame.

This couldn't be good.

He cleared his throat. Might as well get this blanket party started. "Hello?"

A voice answered from behind him. "Where is Prudence?"

Griffin couldn't see a damned thing, but he'd recognize that voice anywhere. Bronsen. The sick fuck was delusional if he thought he'd tell him anything. "Who?"

A whoosh filled the air. Something thin and hard cracked across his back.

Griffin's lungs emptied of air as pain scorched over his skin. A shudder wracked through him. That would leave a mark. *That's karma for being an ass to Prudence earlier.*

"I'm going to ask nicely one more time. Where is Prudence Parnell?"

"And I'm going to tell you nicely one more time. I don't know who that is."

"Strip him."

Griffin snorted. "Might have been easier had you thought of that before you chained me up, genius."

Seconds later, he decided he should've keep his mouth shut. Two sets of hands went to work ripping and cutting his clothing away. One of the bastards cut a long line down his leg when he sliced through his cargos with a blade. Bit by bit they divested him of his clothes until he stood bare-assed against the A-frame. The only parts of his body even partially protected were his hands at the top of the frame and his stomach which pressed to the freezing cold bar. Blood trickled down his leg.

"You two can wait outside."

The men who had stripped him left the room, the door closing behind them.

"Now, Chief Payne, we found the escape pod you landed in. Prudence was with you; we found her sweaters. I spoke to the men at the Outpost."

"Gee, boss. You already know everything. You must already know that the woman I was with took off while I talked to the men at the Outpost. Haven't seen her since."

"The men said you claimed she was yours." Bronsen made his way around Griffin, his shoes clicking on the floor. "Tell me, how long have you known Prudence?"

"I told you, we met on *Genesis V*. She took off after we landed on Asteria. I haven't seen her since."

"This," he tapped a thin rod against Griffin's hood, "is a bamboo cane."

Griffin heard the thing hiss through the air as Bronsen reeled his arm back. Then he heard it come back. His whole body tensed. Fire blazed across his ass cheeks.

"It's hard not to tense up when you hear the cane sing, isn't it?" Bronsen's chuckle sounded flat, cold. "Thing is, tensing up makes the bite harder."

Sweat broke out over Griffin's skin. "Hey, Bronsen?"

"Yes?"

"Fuck you."

Amusement laced Bronsen voice. "Maybe later. Randolph thinks you helped her plan her trip here. He thinks she fed you information to aid you in assassinating Alfred."

"Bullshit."

Without warning, the cane lanced across his shoulders.

Griffin grunted, clenching his jaw tight. "I acted alone. How the hell would I have helped her from prison? I couldn't even talk. I was never alone." The accusation didn't even make sense, Randolph made sure he was locked down tight during his stint in jail. "I think those reports I read about Randolph being psychologically fragile are making more and more sense."

Bronsen made no response, but he did pause in his endless walk around Griffin. It wasn't much, a missing beat of the clack of his shoes on the floor, but it was a reaction.

Griffin snorted. "Now why does that bother you? Surely, it's no surprise. You were head of Alfred's security. You work pretty close with Randolph. Hell, there were times while I was in prison I was sure the two of you were fucking and—"

Well, shit. He'd been ready to kill the wrong man. Again. "It's you, isn't it? You're listed as the Parnell's head of security, but what . . .? You're their advisor?"

"Nope. Just security." Bronsen continued his circular pacing, and when he stood behind Griffin, he let the cane sing.

A line of fire crossed his back. *Holy hell, that stung.* His body was starting to react, to shake.

"And Randolph's lover. Alfred didn't mind Randolph being around at first." Though he couldn't see, Griffin followed Bronsen's voice, knowing what would come when he reached his back again. "The show of a united family was core to Alfred's purpose. He needed Randolph and I made sure Randolph stayed . . . content."

Whack.

A gasp broke from Griffin's lips as the cane scored his calves. He inhaled a deep breath. "Didn't Randolph mind? I mean his brother was emptying out the loony bins and sending all the mental health patients off-planet. Wasn't Randolph worried he might be next?"

"No. Randolph isn't crazy. It's more of an anxiety thing, but I took care of him. For a while, Alfred forgot his brother had any problem whatsoever."

The cane sang, striking against Griffin's hip. His knees turned to jelly and his gut roiled. It took every ounce of energy to keep his weight off his arms. He blinked away reflexive tears. "For a while?"

"Toward the end, Alfred wanted to clean up the loose ends. He planned to send Randolph away."

Griffin bit his lip, his whole body tensed for the next blow, but Bronsen walked past without striking. Fucking bastard. "But you couldn't allow that." Griffin shook his head. "It wasn't coincidence that there was no security the night I assassinated Alfred, was it?"

Bronsen chuckled. "No. You were tagged, soldier boy. I watched a handful of those who survived. Kept tabs on where you were, what you were doing. It wasn't hard to figure out what you had planned."

"I could've changed my mind at the last moment."

Bronsen chuckled, letting the cane fly.

Caught off guard, Griffin let out a shout.

"But you were there. You were armed. Even if you hadn't been so cooperative, Alfred still would've died."

"And I still would've taken the fall." Damn. Had there been a time in the last two years when someone higher up the food chain *hadn't* been using him?

"Mm. For now, let's talk about Prudence. Then we're going to talk about your pathetic little rebellion."

The cane sang.

Griffin tensed his ass, but this time the cane sliced across the backs of his knees. He bit down on his cheek to restrain a shout. He pressed his face to his shoulder, breathing heavily. He was starting to have trouble focusing. What the hell had they been talking about? "Your mother flogs harder than you."

Bronsen circled him, his shoes echoing on the hard floor. He made one full circle, then kept on until he stood in front of Griffin.

Ah, fuck. Unable to do anything to protect himself should Bronsen strike, he gripped the top of the A-frame in his hands and grit his teeth.

The tip of the cane stroked down his chest, over his abs to his groin. Bronsen tapped the edge against Griffin's testicles. "Are you suggesting my mother is into S&M and that you've had the pleasure?"

His heart thundered in his chest and a hefty dose of adrenaline spiked through his system.

Keep your mouth shut.

He knew remaining silent would be in his best interest, but he'd be damned if he'd let the son of a bitch think he was cowed. "Nah, man. I don't fuck skanks."

The cane sang.

Lucan watched Prudence pace his living room for the umpteenth time. She was a lovely woman, even-tempered, sweet, and head-over-heels for his lunatic brother. What the hell was Griffin thinking? He couldn't want to choose a suicide-mission over a life with Prudence. Could he?

"We're gonna find him, Angelica."

Her lavender eyes were full of concern. "What if he already left? What if he refuses to come back? What if he hurt himself? He wouldn't, would he?"

"Of course not." But he had the same concerns. Griffin never could bear to walk away from a situation where someone was being hurt. The guilt from his time in the military must be driving him crazy. "We'll make him come back. Merrick was pretty fucked-up when we first met. He still had a lot of survivor guilt from his stint in the army. He acted a lot like you said Griffin's been acting. Some days were good, some bad. He started going to Dr. Lambert and it took a while, but he got better."

She paused and put her hand to her stomach. "He's been gone so long. What if he's in trouble?"

Lucan locked onto the gesture. He'd seen her touch her stomach like that quite often in the last twenty-four hours. "Does he know?" His gaze flicked from her flat stomach to her eyes. "About the baby?"

Her hand dropped to her side, before swinging out in a helpless gesture. "I didn't want to add to whatever's going on with him. I want him to want to be with us, but I want him to stay for the right reasons."

While he did understand her concern, he didn't think keeping Griffin in the dark too long would be fair. "But either way, you will tell him?" He couldn't stand the idea of his brother not knowing he was going to be a father.

"Once Griffin has made his choice, I will tell him." She walked to the window and stared out. "If he doesn't want to stay, I'd still make sure he had access to his child."

"Me and Merrick, too?"

A small smile curved her lips. "Of course. I wouldn't deny my baby her uncles."

He got to his feet and walked over to her. "Then let me be the first to congratulate you." He wrapped her in his arms, catching the tremor that ran through her. "Everything is going to be fine, Mama."

The shop door opened downstairs.

"Merrick is back." Lucan released her and went to the stairs, but one look at Merrick's face told him the news wasn't good. He forced a smile for Prudence's sake. She didn't need all this stress, not in her condition. "Angel, I'm gonna go help Merrick. You stay inside and don't answer the door. I don't need to be searching for two of you."

He waited for her nod and then went downstairs and straight into Merrick's arms. For a moment, he took comfort in his partner's strong embrace.

"Come on, babe."

Silent, Lucan followed him outside, surprised when Merrick kept walking. He stopped at the corner and turned to Lucan. "The Blue Helmets have Griffin."

Though he knew something bad had happened, his head still went fuzzy with shock. This hadn't been one of his concerns. "What did he do? Where are they holding him? What's bail?"

Merrick shook his head. "No bail. I'm pretty sure from the background they have him up at the compound outside the spaceport, but I need you look and tell me if I'm right. You're better at noting the details of a place and your memory is better."

Lucan nodded. The compound belonged to the spaceport's commander and chief. Earlier that year, he'd been invited to do a small mural of the Grand Canyon in the dining room.

"I need you to brace yourself." Merrick cupped his cheek, his eyes full of concern. "They're showing him on the mega holo-projector in the square and he's a mess. I need you to focus on the background and tell me if that room is part of the compound. I need you not to react. Blue Helmets are crawling all over the place. You can't let them know he means anything to you."

Lucan's stomach rolled into a tight knot. Though Griffin never spoke of any of it, he knew his brother had been in tight spots before. But Lucan had never witnessed the brutality of Griffin's life—his career—firsthand.

Merrick's hand slid into his and they walked down Main Street to the square. People crowded around in groups of two or three, whispering. The selling stalls were abandoned. The children weren't playing. It was as if they whole town had gone into mourning.

His gut twisted into a sickening knot.

Merrick led the way, walking past their neighbors and friends until they reached a spot where they could see the holographic projection of Griffin.

Lucan bit down on his cheek, his hand tightening around Merrick's.

For a heart-stopping second or two, he thought Griffin was dead. The hologram rotated, showing Griffin secured to an A-frame from every angle. His back, ass, and thighs were raw with a multitude of deep welts and lacerations, several of which bled freely. As the hologram turned it showed the same was true for his front. His chest had turned purple in some places, in others long, deep welts crisscrossed his flesh. His groin had been pixeled-out, but there were long, angry red welts across his thighs suggesting nothing had been spared. The worst, though, was his face, his features were so swollen and discolored, Lucan couldn't tell if he was conscious or not.

Griffin's head lolled to the side and he jolted upright as if waking up, a slurred, "Fuck you," sliding between swollen lips.

A ticker ran along the bottom of the hologram with a picture of Prudence off to one side: *This is what happens to traitors. If you have seen this woman, contact spaceport authorities. Harboring this woman is an act of treason. This is what happens to traitors. If you . . . .*

Merrick squeezed his hand and leaned down. "The background."

Lucan jerked his attention back to the hologram, this time he watched the background as the holo-camera panned around his brother. He didn't recognize the cement floor. The walls were plain white, and could be from anywhere. But when the camera panned across the door, he saw what he needed—the moldings and the door handle—they were unique. The compound had band moldings around the doors with decorative corner blocks and the door handles were silver with marble grips. The compound was the only place in Asteria with fancy Earth decorations.

"I've seen enough."

God, he'd never been so grateful for Merrick's strength as he led the way through the crowd. A few neighbors they were close to, who knew Griffin was his brother, reached out to touch him as they passed, their eyes full of compassion. When they passed Grady, the tall, thin man gave them a nod, slipping a piece of paper into Lucan's palm.

Lucan unfolded it in his hand and glanced down to read the short note: *Let us know when. We're ready.*

Taking a deep breath, he blinked, trying to alleviate the sting behind his eyes. They had friends. Good friends. They'd help get Griffin back.

Jesus, that was his brother he'd seen. That bloody, mangled mess was Griffin. The Blue Helmets had been merciless. When Griffin had been in prison, he'd guessed that they'd abused him, but they had to be careful so the Earthers watching the trial wouldn't know.

The Blue Helmets had no such qualms here on Asteria.

Merrick bowed his head closer as they walked. "Was that the compound?"

"Yeah."

They turned off Main and Merrick pulled him into the alley next to their place. He wrapped him in a warm embrace.

"Ah, God, that was Griffin." He pressed his face to Merrick's chest. "What the fuck did they do to him?"

"They're desperate to get their hands on Angelica."

"Who the fuck is she?"

"Your brother's lover." Merrick tipped his face back and stared into his eyes. "Do we need to know more than that?"

"No. Griffin's protecting her with his life, and so will we."

Merrick tightened his arms around Lucan. "I'll get him back, babe."

"I'm going with you."

Merrick framed Lucan's face in his big hands. "You haven't been trained."

Lucan snorted. "You trained me. You mean to say I'm not experienced, but I will be after tonight."

The set of Merrick's jaw said his lover wasn't giving up. "I've got plenty of men ready to go. As soon as they realized who they were looking at on the hologram they started letting me know they wanted to go after him."

"Grady gave me this." He lifted the note.

Merrick smiled. "See, you don't need to worry about this. I know you're angry with Griffin because you hate that he puts himself at risk, but your brother has earned his place in their hearts. He was the only one brave enough to try and change things."

Sometimes Merrick irritated the hell out of him. While he tended to be the more affectionate of the two, he also had a streak of dominating masculinity. Most of the time, Lucan enjoyed it; today, not so much. "I just got him back, Mer. I'm going, because if he doesn't make it . . . ." Lucan looked away while he tried to compose himself. "I'm not throwing away the possibility of having a chance to talk to him again. He's my brother."

"All right." Merrick pressed his lips to the corner of Lucan's mouth. "Fine. What do you want to tell Angelica?"

Lucan shook his head. "Nothing. We'll head out tonight as soon as she's in bed. I'll tell her we're going to do another round in case he's been holed up somewhere all day."

"Come on, babe. Do you think that's fair?"

"No." He sighed. "She's carrying our nephew."

A range of emotions ran over Merrick's features, surprise, joy, and sadness before they merged into the determined set of his jaw. He looked mean as hell now. "We'll get him back. I swear to God, we will get him back."

Lucan didn't have a doubt in his mind. His concern was whether Griffin would still be alive by the time they got him.

32

Prudence finished the last of the dishes and wiped her hands on the dishcloth.

Something had happened. Both Lucan and Merrick were jumpy. They'd remained quiet throughout dinner. When they thought she wasn't around they spoke in hushed, urgent tones. Whatever had happened, neither of them seemed inclined to share the details, which meant she'd have to find out on her own.

"I'm going to bed."

Both men turned to stare at her but remained silent.

"You'll wake me if you hear anything?"

"Of course," Lucan said.

"Right away." Merrick nodded.

Neither of them managed to look her in the eyes while they lied.

She went to her room, locked the door and went straight to the window. Below, the front awning of the store front stuck out several feet. She climbed out onto the low roof. *Goddess, keep me safe.* Lying on her stomach, she shimmied over the edge feet-first until she hung by her arms, then she let herself fall the last couple of feet.

Only waves and wind dared break the silence of the town. She didn't recall Diamond Fjord being this quiet last night. She had no idea where she meant to go, but she couldn't imagine Griffin had gone too far without his weapons. She walked down to the corner and turned onto Main Street. All the shops had closed for the evening. A few people milled about farther down the street, but the evening had a strange, somber quality. As she approached the square, a bunch of candles flickering in the breeze came into view.

Had someone passed away?

The thought brought her to a halt. The few people still in the square all faced to the left, looking at something she couldn't see. A child wept in his mother's arms.

She crept forward.

Half a dozen Blue Helmets stood at the base of a mega holo-projector. On the hologram, a severely beaten man had been tied to a metal frame and below that, a small picture of her sat next to a ticker: *If you have seen this woman, contact spaceport authorities. Harboring this woman is an act of treason. This is what happens to traitors. If you see this woman, contact—*

With a cry of alarm, her gaze shot back to the man. Her hand flew to her mouth as the holo-camera panned, bringing his swollen face into view. *Griffin.*

Bronsen, the Parnell's head of security, strode onto the hologram, holding a long, thin stick. "Requests for Payne's release have been coming in all day, but as of yet, I have received no news of the woman. Here is my offer, I'll trade him for her. In six hours, I'll hang him."

He strode off the hologram and the view resumed panning around Griffin.

Did Merrick and Lucan know? They must. Merrick had been out here most of the day and he'd brought Lucan out earlier this evening. Why weren't they doing anything?

And what would they do? *Griffin would never forgive them for trading you for him.*

She couldn't let Griffin suffer for her. She didn't want to go back, but Randolph wouldn't dare damage her to such an extent. He thought he needed her.

Bronsen strode back onto the hologram repeating his message. Goddess preserve them, it was a recording. How long had this been playing? Two hours? Five?

Panic welled up inside her.

"Hey!" She walked into the square right in front of the Blue Helmets. "You heard him, he'll trade Chief Payne for the woman. Here I am."

The Blue Helmets stared at her as if she were mad. She must be. Never had she imagined she'd ever go back to Randolph. But she'd escaped once, she'd find a way to do so again. Once they got over their surprise, the men surrounded her and took her into custody. They led her to a nearby hover-car and as they drove off, she looked out the window to see Lucan and Merrick staring back.

Prudence whipped her head around to stare out the back window. Why in the world were they wearing Blue Helmet uniforms?

The compound they took her to was within two hundred yards of the spaceport. As she expected, no one abused her in any way on the trip. They brought her into the front entry of the building and had her wait with a couple guards. The entry was a large room that led to long hallways to both the right and left, but straight ahead the room opened into a massive recreational space for the Blue Helmets who were not on duty. She'd never seen so many in one place before.

This building appeared far more Earth-like than any of the others she'd seen. The walls were plaster and there were real light bulbs lighting the space instead of glow stones.

A man cleared his throat and Prudence turned to see Bronsen. "Prudence, I'm so pleased to see you're safe. Randolph has been very worried."

She gave him a thin smile. "I'm sure."

"I'm not sure if you remember, my name's Bronsen. I'm your fiancé's head of security."

On the surface, he was polite, nice even. She'd never dealt much with Bronsen, though she'd seen him with Alfred and Randolph often. She wasn't quite sure what to think. "Bronsen, I'd like to see Chief Payne."

He smiled and motioned her down the hall. "Of course. This way."

They walked in silence for several minutes while she took his measure. She'd never been too good a judge of character. Humans were far too good at subterfuge to be able to take anyone at face value. They turned into another long, narrow hallway and Prudence coughed to clear her throat. "Everyone in Diamond Fjord knows you have me. They're expecting you to be a man of honor and release Chief Payne."

"He means a lot to you?"

Prudence worded her response carefully. She didn't want to bring any added attention to Griffin. "I don't know him well. But he's the people's soldier. There will be needless bloodshed unless he's released."

Nodding in acknowledgment, he appeared to accept her answer. "He will be released."

Prudence tried not to allow her relief to show but felt lightheaded from it.

Bronsen's hand slid onto her back as he opened a door and ushered her in.

Griffin. She needed every ounce of control not to run to him. He looked even worse in person. Not an inch of his body had been spared. The walls, ceilings and floor were speckled with his blood.

Since she'd last seen him on the hologram, the holo-camera had been removed and an odd-looking table with restraints had been brought in. Several buckets of water were lined against the wall.

Oh, goddess help her, he planned to dry drown her. Her bravery evaporating, she tried to back out of the room, but someone stood right behind her.

She looked up, right into Randolph's eyes.

33

They were releasing him.

Griffin glanced around through swollen eyes. There wasn't a part of his body that didn't feel as if his flesh were on fire. Tears squeezed through his lids, burning trails down his ruined face.

Blue Helmets held him up on either side while they unshackled his hands. Good thing, too, or he would've fallen on his face. He was in a bad way. He was pretty sure both his nose and jaw were broken. Maybe his right ankle and a couple ribs, too. Every breath was painful. Beating him with the cane hadn't been enough for good old Bronsen. The fucker had let his soldiers take turns using him as a punching bag whenever his arm got tired.

The two Blue Helmets turned, giving him a front and center view of the most horrific thing he'd ever seen.

Randolph and Bronsen with Prudence held tight between them.

Lavender tears streamed down her face and a little hiccup escaped her lips. "Chief Payne, the Blue Helmets are going to release you to the citizens of Diamond Fjord now."

Christ. "You turned yourself in?" He didn't think any of them understood what he said, which was good. Last thing he needed was for them to realize how much they meant to each other. The bastards would no doubt use that information in twisted and unscrupulous ways.

Randolph's gaze slid over him, stopping somewhere below his face and narrowing. He staggered in his haste to get closer to Griffin and without warning, he swiped his hand over his stomach.

Griffin winced. He didn't think Bronsen had left an inch of his skin unharmed.

Randolph shook his hand to the side, splattering excess blood and sweat. His eye twitched. A furious blush crept up his cheeks and returned to Prudence. "You gave your gift to *him*?" He pulled his arm back and slapped her across the face, sending her reeling into the wall and to the floor.

Griffin struggled to get free, growling low in his throat.

Bronsen kept Randolph's hand from closing around Prudence's throat. "You need her."

The two men's gazes wrestled for a moment, before Randolph backed off. He turned to a Blue Helmet standing by the door and said something in a low voice. The Blue Helmet left.

Prudence staggered to her feet.

Griffin didn't like the defiant expression on her face at all. The woman looked pissed as a wet hornet. His attention stayed on her, trying without words to warn her against spouting off. Her expression didn't change. He wasn't sure if she didn't understand or didn't give a shit. He had so many questions he wanted to ask her. He wanted to know why she'd come here. Where were Lucan and Merrick? Was there a plan to get them out of here?

Randolph paced the small confines of the room. What had Bronsen said, he had some sort of nervous condition? He was twitchy as hell that was for sure, his eyes blinking in rapid-fire tics. He didn't look good at all. Tired. Thinner than what he remembered. He hoped to hell Bronsen kept his pet under control.

When the Blue Helmet returned, Randolph took something from the young soldier and sent him away again.

Randolph walked over to a low restraint table. His attention snapped to Griffin's. "When we were at the Outpost, I heard all about the items you stole." He held up a saltshaker in one hand and a bottle of liquor in the other. "The men were quite indignant over your theft."

Prudence's voice shook. "You told the people you'd release Chief Payne to their custody if you had me. They'll revolt if you renege on your word."

Randolph's head jerked to the side. "He'll be released as soon as he finishes answering my questions."

Her jaw dropped. "What do you mean? Much more and he'll die."

If she didn't stop, she'd draw Randolph's wrath again. The man seemed to barely able to hold himself together, twitching and blinking as if he had no control over his body.

"Doesn't matter." Lifting his arm, Randolph pressed his eyes to the crook of his elbow for a few seconds. "They said they wanted him released. No one mentioned he had to be alive." A broad smile spread on Randolph's face and he emptied the salt over the slanted table. The little grains slid and caught in the grooves of the slip-proof surface.

Griffin's gut rolled.

"Lay him down." Randolph motioned to the table.

The Blue Helmets half-walked, half-dragged him to the table. He was so weak he couldn't resist. As his raw flesh came in contact with the salt-covered surface, he experienced a whole new kind of agony. He came flying off the table and the Blue Helmets rammed him back down. This time, they clamped his wrists and ankles to the table's restraints.

"Stop it. Leave him alone. He's had enough," Prudence wept.

"Get out."

Griffin wasn't sure who Randolph ordered out, but the door opened and closed while he still writhed in agony on the table.

"Randy, I don't think—"

"You, too. I want a moment alone with my fiancée."

Shit. There would be no one to keep Randolph from hurting Prudence. He forced his eyes open in time to see Bronsen leave, closing the door behind him.

"What good are you to me now, Prudence?" Randolph returned to Griffin's side and held the bottle of liquor over his body. "Why should I give you what you want?"

Griffin turned his face toward her, willing her not to say to anything.

She choked on a sob. "There is no more need for bloodshed. This goes against everything Alfred believed. What would he think of this? He'd be ashamed of you."

"This isn't my fault. You gave my gift to someone else. The only way to get it back is for him to die. This is your fault." Randolph strode toward her. "The only way I see to ensure you don't spread those skinny legs for anyone else is show you what happens to traitors."

She shook her head. "You don't have to kill him. I—I can take it back from him. There's no need for this."

"There's every need. If I let you go unpunished, you'll go fuck around at the first opportunity. You're too stupid to care for your own life. You've never learned any of your lessons when I've punished you. So this time, you'll watch."

Randolph strode back to the table and upturned the liquor bottle, pouring the contents over Griffin's raw skin.

The liquor scorched his wounds like molten lava. A shout tore from his lips, his body bowing off the table only to sink down over the salt in a new position.

Randolph threw the bottle across the room, shattering it against the wall. "Speaking of Alfred, why don't you tell me how you and Chief Payne met?"

She shook her head. "We met for the first time on the ship to Asteria."

"You expect me to believe you happened to run into your husband's assassin while you were fleeing Earth by happy coincidence?"

"Yes." "If you didn't have anything to do with Alfred's death, why run at the first opportunity?"

Prudence showed Randolph the stubborn tilt of her chin.

Oh, Christ, no. She was going to get herself killed.

"Maybe because I grew tired of being used, abused, and raped. Maybe because I wanted to find out what a real man was like."

The back of Randolph's hand slapped across her face hard enough to send her into the wall.

She straightened herself, the tip of her tongue darting out to touch the corner of her mouth which had begun to swell. She must've tasted the blood beading on her lip because she lifted her hand to swipe it away.

Griffin's heart went into overdrive. "Stop it, Pru."

Neither Randolph nor Prudence heard him.

Prudence shrugged. "I can't help it if you don't have the equipment to do the job right."

Randolph struck her again.

"No!" *What in God's name was she doing?*

Prudence glanced his way as she pulled herself off the floor, one hand on the wall to steady herself.

She was going to keep taunting him. Keep drawing Randolph's ire from him. Griffin shook his head. *Don't do it, Angel. Quit poking the bear.* "Stop it."

She turned to look Randolph square in the eye. "Even Alfred was a better fuck than you."

Randolph let out a war cry and tackled Prudence to the floor.

Frantic, Griffin strained against his bindings. He couldn't see them but could hear them struggling on the floor.

The door flew open. Bronsen paused, taking in the scene before launching himself on Randolph. "You need her.

Don't kill her. Save your wrath for Payne." Bronsen wrestled Randolph off Prudence and threw him against the wall. "What are you thinking? She's the reason we're here. You want to kill something, kill him." He waved his hand toward Griffin.

Griffin tensed as Randolph's attention focused on him. "Where's the hood?"

Bronsen pulled the black material out of his pocket and slipped the hood over Griffin's face. A drawstring pulled the hood closed around his neck, securing it in place.

This was it. He was going to die, and suddenly, he didn't want to. Who would tease Prudence and make her laugh? Who would make her scream in pleasure? Who would hold her during the night?

He wanted to be that person. He wanted to love her. He wanted to marry her and get a cramped little apartment like Lucan's. He wanted to do something other than kill for a living. He wanted to see Prudence grow fat with his babies. He wanted to irritate her by playing poker and smoking with friends.

Damn it, he wanted to live.

Cold water splashed onto his chest. His breath hitched as the table lowered on one end so his head and torso lay lower than his feet. His heart thrummed in his ears and a burst of adrenaline released into his body.

Prudence screamed. She struggled with someone, their feet scuffing on the floor. "No, don't!"

Water soaked through the hood, streaming up his nose and flooding his sinus cavity. It burned and his body reacted as if he were drowning. Panic flared, making it impossible to think straight.

He resorted to his training, forcing his body to relax. Sipping tiny breaths whenever the flow of water allowed him to part his lips. The problem was, Randolph wasn't stopping. Waterboarding was most often done to scare someone into talking. But Randolph didn't want him to talk. He wanted him dead. Wanted him to die a slow death while Prudence watched.

With nowhere else to go, the water backed up, dripping through his sinuses into his throat. The urge to cough became more urgent. *Ah, Christ, how big was the fucking bucket?*

Prudence's voice grew hoarse as she sobbed and screamed.

And he realized, beyond a shadow of a doubt, he loved her.

Because as he lay there dying all he wanted to do was find a way to comfort her.

They were killing him.

Bronsen held her from behind, his arms wrapped around her chest, trapping her arms at her side. She kicked, trying to throw him off balance. Forced him to bear all her weight as she arched and bowed over his arms.

But he was far stronger than her.

Tears blurred her vision. "Stop it. Stop. You can't do this. You can't kill him and still be like Alfred. Stop!"

Randolph picked up another bucket before the first finished and as the last bit of liquid poured over Griffin's face, Randolph tossed the bucket aside and started with the new one. There'd hadn't been enough time for Griffin to take a breath if that was even still possible.

Bitterly, she focused on her birthmark, riding low on his stomach. Whatever gift she had given him had been useless. After all the years of suffering because of her precious gift, whatever she had in her was worthless. Her gift hadn't helped him at all.

Griffin's hand, drew her attention. His middle two fingers folded in, leaving his thumb, forefinger and pinky sticking up. Universal sign language.

I love you.

Grief tore through her, bowing her under the weight of what she was losing. Of what her baby was losing. She stared at his hand, dying inside as his fingers relaxed and went still. Randolph released her, letting her slide to the ground. "Ah, goddess." Terrible sounds wretched from her body, making her stomach roil and her body quake.

The men stared at her as if she'd lost her mind.

And maybe she had.

She pinned Randolph with her wrath. "He was going to send you away."

"What?"

She reached for the closest object, a full bucket, and standing, she hurled it at them. "Tell him." She motioned to Bronsen. "Tell him how Alfred wanted him gone." She chased them, grabbing the empties and throwing those, too. Bronsen bolted, opened the door, and pulled Randolph through.

The door slammed and locked, but Randolph's voice carried through. "You're staying in there tonight. Be with your dead lover while his body grows cold."

Prudence pulled the hood from Griffin's face. His lips were blue and he was so still, but she'd seen people brought back before. She'd been brought back before. Tipping his head to the side, she let the water run out of his mouth and nose. She started CPR, sealing her lips to his and breathing for him. His chest rose and fell under her hand with each of her exhalations and rests. She counted the breaths and the started chest compressions. With each compression she winced, praying he didn't have any broken ribs, praying she wasn't making things worse. "Breathe, damn it."

The door rattled and opened, but she didn't stop. They'd have to kill her before she quit. She pressed her lips to Griffin's, exhaling, wishing for all the world she were kissing him instead of trying to breathe life back into him. She pulled away and drew in a deep breath and fed him more air.

When she moved to do the compressions, someone pushed her out of the way. Instinctively, she attacked. Strong arms restrained her from behind. "It's us. Relax, it's us."

Prudence froze at the sound of Lucan's voice.

Merrick took over the chest compressions, then pausing, he glanced at her over his shoulder. "Breathe for him again."

Lucan released her and she pressed her mouth to Griffin's.

He coughed. Water sprayed out of his mouth.

Merrick already had the restraints undone and Lucan helped her sit Griffin up. She held him against her, while he struggled to catch his breath. "You're all right, baby. I've got you." She wasn't sure anyone could understand what she said, she was crying too hard, but she kept up the words of encouragement.

Once he settled into a more normal breathing pattern, she cupped his face. "I love you so much, baby. I'm so sorry."

His eyes were so swollen, she wasn't sure if he could see her, wasn't sure he was even conscious until his lifted his hand to touch her face. He tried to say something and she lowered her ear closer to his mouth. "So . . . much . . . trouble . . . when we . . . get . . . home."

She laughed, which made her tears fall harder. "Oh, baby. You can punish me all you want."

"We gotta get out of here." Merrick pulled one of Griffin's arms around him and Lucan took his other side. Griffin groaned as they pulled him to his feet.

Lucan handed Prudence his gun. "Shoot anything that tries to stop us."

"How do we get out of here?"

"Yeah, same way we got in. There's a delivery entrance at the end of this hall." Merrick leaned out the door to check for Blue Helmets. "Grady and some of the guys from town are waiting outside with a hover car we, uh, borrowed."

She kept her focus trained on the doorways ahead. "Borrowed? Are you sure there's no GPS tracking on that thing?"

Merrick scoffed. "There was."

The hallway was deserted. "Where do you think everyone is? There were quite a few Blue Helmets out here earlier."

Lucan cleared his throat. "Maybe putting out a fire in the courtyard."

She shot Lucan a droll stare. "That's pretty specific for a maybe statement."

"Last door on your right." Merrick nodded ahead. "It's a storage room, should still be empty."

Prudence opened the door, keeping her gun at the ready and searching the darkened corners. As Merrick said, the room contained nothing but shelving filled with dry food stuffs and sundries. They made their way to the back of the room, through the door, and out into the night.

A hover car idling in the distance zoomed up as soon as they were outside. Grady hopped out and helped Lucan and Merrick load Griffin into the back.

Merrick jumped into the driver's seat. "The whole place was empty. How big a fire did you boys start?"

"I may have added a bit too much gunpowder," Grady admitted. "I cut up fifteen of little Liam's firecrackers and aimed my homemade bomb for the trees in the courtyard."

Prudence leaned over Griffin, putting her lips to his ear. "I love you. I'm going to take care of everything, baby. We won't have to worry about Randolph or Bronsen anymore. You've done so much for everyone. It's my turn to do my part, now."

He tried to say something, probably to stall her, Prudence backed away. By the time Lucan turned to check on her, she was back at the compound door.

He jumped out of the hover car. "What are you doing?"

"Ending this and making sure no one comes after you. Take care of him." She slipped through the door and locked it behind her.

Prudence returned to the torture room, locking herself in. She curled up in the corner, hiding her gun in the waistband of her pants and waited for Randolph and Bronsen to return.

34

—⋅—

Lucan started to go after Prudence, but Griffin's whole body tensed up and began to shake. "Oh, Jesus. Merrick! He's seizing."

"Hold on to him, babe. We'll be in town in ten minutes."

Lucan threw his body over Griffin's and Merrick hit the accelerator. "Hold on, big guy. Jesus, don't die on me." He kept up a steady stream of commands for his brother. Panic started to eat away at him and his face twisted. Jesus, he was going to lose Griffin.

Grady leaned over the backseat and handed Lucan a med-wand.

"Where? What body part makes a seizure?"

Grady shrugged. "The brain, maybe?"

Griffin had so many injuries, he wasn't sure the wand would find the right one no matter where he put it. "Front or back?"

"Try the front." Merrick sped up.

Lucan placed the wand to Griffin's forehead and pressed the scan button. Blue light ran over Griffin's wounds. Lucan put his head down next to the wand, listening for the beeps. As soon as the scan finished, he calibrated the wand per the instructions on the display and put it back to Griffin's head.

The seizure still quaked through Griffin. "Did it take? Maybe he's shaking too much. Wait." The violent tremors rolling through Griffin eased, then stopped. He went still.

"Shit. Shit. Stop the car." Oh, God, he lost him. He couldn't feel a pulse.

They came to a halt and Lucan pressed his head to Griffin's chest. There. His heartbeat was faint, but it was still there. Relief made him lightheaded. "We're good."

Merrick took off again.

Worn out form the emotional ups and downs of the day, Lucan settled in next to Griffin and laid his hand on his chest. That made three times now he thought he'd lost him. No more. Griffin would be grounded for a while until he healed, immobile and at their mercy. Whether he liked it or not, whether he thought he needed it or not, the son of a bitch would be having visits from Doc Lambert for PTSD treatment every day. He leaned over the backseat. "Do you think Doc Lambert would stay with him while we go back for Prudence?"

Merrick nodded. "Yeah. Grady, as soon as we get back why don't you round up the others while Lucan and I drop him off with Doc." Merrick met Lucan's eyes in the rearview mirror. "Everything's going to be fine. We got him back like I promised. We'll get Angel, too."

Lucan nodded. He knew they would, but he needed Merrick's reassurance. He settled back into the bed of the hover car and checked on Griffin. "Holy shit."

He jumped back, staring down at his brother. A purple light glowed from somewhere under the sheet they'd covered him with. Lucan pulled back the sheet. A tattoo on Griffin's stomach radiated light. While he could see the radiance from the outside, the light itself seemed to shine on his inside, illuminating the network of veins under his skin until his whole body appeared to be entwined in an iridescent, lavender web.

Grady hung over the back seat, jaw agape.

"What's that light?" Merrick asked. "What's happening?"

"He's lit up like a goddamned glow-worm." Did they poison him? Was it some kind of radiation?

Grady pointed. "Look at his face."

The swelling was receding, the lumps and bruises shrinking. The gash on Griffin's lip sealed up, scabbing and then healing within seconds.

A sense of wonder overwhelmed Lucan, making him grin. "He's healing. He's gonna be fine." He got to his knees and met Merrick's eyes in the rearview. "He's gonna be all right."

Merrick swore.

"What?"

"I have a bad feeling. All the sudden this whole scenario reminds me of Romeo and Juliet." Merrick pulled the hover-car to a stop outside town. "Grady, run and get the boys. Hurry, now, we need to get back to the spaceport before Angelica does something stupid."

Protect. Provide. Cherish.

Griffin stood in the scene Lucan painted on the mural. Everything around him burned.

Even him.

As he walked through homes disintegrating around him, flames licked his skin, scorching him from the inside out. He wasn't worried for himself, though. There was something he had to do. Something important. While he couldn't quite remember what it was, he forced himself to keep going, to keep moving.

The ground moved, the build-up of ash shifting into the shapes of men, women, and children. Their blackened, fisted hands reached out to him. His heart pounded faster, his gut twisted tighter. He could've done more, should've done more to help them. His quest urged him on.

He tried to slip his booted feet on the ground between the bodies, but they were pressed together, covering the ground and forcing him to walk over them to get where he needed to be.

Hesitation made him stumble and fall.

Those blackened fists reached for him. Brittle arms tangled with his and he struggled to get free. When he got to his feet, he ran, which fanned the flames engulfing him and made him burn all the faster.

At last, he broke free from the bodies, his boots connecting with solid ground, but he paused. In front of him, the citizens of Diamond Fjord stood united, blocking his path. Lucan, Merrick, and even Prudence were with them.

As one, they lifted their arms and pointed. They wanted him to go back.

Of course they did. They'd seen him stumbling over the corpses. They wanted him to be punished.

Shamed, he turned back to face his past.

The ashy corpses had gathered behind him, their brittle flesh peeling and sloughing away.

Griffin glanced back over his shoulder. The living closed in, herding him closer to the dead. With nowhere left to run, he stepped into the midst of his sins. The charred faces of the past closed around him, crowding in, their fists held up.

He expected them to drag him down, to beat him, to make him suffer. But they just watched, holding out their fists. Waiting. They must want him to show them he accepted responsibility. They wanted him to participate in accepting their wrath. Griffin opened his arms, holding his palms up outstretched in surrender. One of the dead opened her fist, dropping a tiny green plant into his palm. At first, he wasn't sure what it was, a thick green stalk with two long, thin leaves growing from either side.

Then he remembered Prudence's birthmark. He touched the place on his stomach where her mark claimed him as her mate. Tears in his eyes, he looked up into the ruined faces of his past. "Just like that?"

They all lifted their fists, showing the life they harbored. As they crumbled back into the Earth, their offerings growing from the ash into a lush garden around him and the citizens of Diamond Fjord.

He took a step closer to them, closer to Prudence, but she disappeared. All the others remained, Lucan, Merrick, Grady, and many he didn't recognize. They stayed and they smiled, but Prudence faded from sight.

She was in trouble.

Protect. Provide. Cherish.

Griffin jolted awake, sucking in a deep breath as he sat straight up.

Like in his dream, Lucan and Merrick stared back at him, grinning. A bunch of men he didn't know stood behind them. Unlike his dream they were in Diamond Fjord and it was dark.

He looked down at himself. He was naked but for a sheet pooled around his hips. Prudence's mark glowed purple, the light fading until it once again appeared to be a simple birthmark.

"What is that?" Lucan asked. "The damned thing lit you up and all your wounds faded right before my eyes."

"It's Prudence's mating gift." He closed his eyes and shook his head. "The night she gave me her mark, all I could think about was getting through my mission alive so I'd be here for her." He drew in a shuddering breath.

It's a gift. Not everyone needs the gift of persuasion to be happy, but everyone needs something.

He had needed a second chance.

"Where is she?"

Lucan exchanged a glance with Merrick. Their smiles faded.

The beginnings of panic crawled under Griffin's skin. She couldn't be dead. She couldn't, not when he'd been given a second chance. "Tell me she's not dead."

Lucan rushed to assure him. "She's alive. Last we saw her."

Griffin looked to Merrick, seeking a better answer.

"She went back in while we were loading you into the hover car. Said she wanted to finish it."

She was going to get herself killed. Griffin rubbed his hand over his chest as his heart stuttered in his chest. "I need clothes. A weapon. We have to go back. I can't leave her there." When they continued to watch him in silence, he cursed. "I'm asking for your help."

Lucan opened his mouth, but Merrick held up his hand, staying him. "You'll have all the help you want, providing one thing."

"What's that?"

"Once we rescue Prudence, you go see Doc Lambert every day for a minimum of a month for PTSD therapy before you make any more decisions that affect your future."

Griffin stared. What the fuck?

"I'm serious. Prudence is beautiful, inside and out, and all you can think about is how to go out in a blaze of glory. It's fucked up. You need to quit punishing yourself. We can all see how much you love her. We can all see how much you want to have a normal life. All you need to do is work out the guilt and decide life is worth living. No decisions until you've completed one month of therapy."

Well, shit. "I don't need therapy. I need to find Prudence. We're wasting time."

"He's right, Griffin." Lucan cleared his throat. "I've never seen you like this. It's like something's eating at you from the inside out. It's gutting me; I can't imagine what mom and dad would say."

Griffin spied a pile of clothes near his feet and started dressing. This was ridiculous. He was fine now. He figured everything out on his own, damn it. He'd apologize to Prudence. Everything would be okay. "I don't need to lay on a fucking couch and talk about my dreams." He stood and pulled up the cargos, bystanders be damned.

Merrick pushed him back down on his ass. "If there was still a Marine Corps, therapy would've been part of your exit screening. I'm not asking you to do anything Marines haven't been mandated to do for decades. You have to deal with the past, but not by trying to get yourself killed. You need to face it, talk about it, and let that shit go."

Everything became clear. He remembered lying on the table, knowing he was about to die and not wanting to. He recalled the dream; the dead weren't telling him to choose Prudence exactly, they wanted him to choose to live. They wanted him to face the past and move on. To do good things with his life, and, yes, that included being with Prudence. It had to.

He was letting the guilt of war, the guilt of being a soldier eat him alive. Guilt for trusting those above him for killing, and maybe most of all for surviving. Part of him had been wanting to die ever since they fragged his base.

But now, people were depending on him. Now, he needed to put the past to rest so he could have a life. "That's what's tearing me up. The question of whether or not I deserve such a thing."

"You do." Lucan shrugged. "Everybody's rooting for you. Everyone but you."

"I've messed things up so many times since I met Prudence—"

"And you'll fuck up again." Merrick shrugged. "She will, too. But you love each other, you'll work things out."

Griffin nodded. "Therapy, then. All right. Now, can we go fight the bad guys?"

35

Did they plan to leave her in here all night?

Prudence's eyes grew heavy and she forced herself to get up and pace the small area. It felt as though hours had passed since she'd locked herself in here. She'd counted the blood splatters on the wall. She'd rearranged the broken glass in the corner into a heart shape and stuck the biggest piece in her pocket for an extra weapon. She'd run through several scenarios of what might happen next.

But mostly, she worried about Griffin.

The one thing keeping her somewhat sane was the fact that she still had no mating marks. Griffin would possess the marks until he died, so she knew he lived. But in what condition? Would he have brain damage from oxygen deprivation? What kind of psychological scars would he come away from this with? Would he have physical limitations, now? Sexual limitations? They hadn't spared a speck of his flesh from what she'd been able to see. She'd love him no matter what, but she feared he'd grow to resent her after this.

The lock rattled and Prudence tensed.

A Blue Helmet walked in. His doe-brown eyes scanned the room. His brows drew together. "Where's the guy that was in here?"

She shrugged. "Two Blue Helmets came and got him about an hour ago."

The door closed and locked.

Prudence let out a shaky breath. Now she'd have to wait and see if they bought her lie.

Griffin and Lucan hid behind a cluster of shrubs, peeking out at the compound.

The back door was lit up brighter than Fort Bragg during a Fourth of July celebration. Two Blue Helmets stood guard at the door, but as many lights as they had directed at the spot, he didn't doubt a sniper hid nearby.

"I suspect they figured out we used that door."

Griffin shot his brother a droll stare. "Ya think?" He glanced over his shoulder at Grady and Merrick who had their heads together over a blueprint. "Is there another way in?"

"Yep." Grady cleared his throat. "Front door."

Griffin had the distinct urge to palm his face. "Give me the fucking thing." He waved at the blueprint and the penlight. "Come on."

Grady handed them over with an indignant sniff.

He studied the building. There were no windows on the first floor, and, as Grady said, there were two doors—front and back. Unfortunately, both would be covered by Blue Helmets after their earlier breach. Grady had been correct.

"I don't suppose we have any more explosives?"

"Nope." Grady sucked his teeth. "Used all Liam's firecrackers earlier today. Would've bought some more from old Zeke had I known we'd be doing this twice."

Griffin surprised himself by chuckling. "Oh, God, we are fucked six ways to Sunday."

Eleven men stared at him, waiting. Griffin sobered. Here they were ready to give up their freedom, maybe even their lives and he was taking a piss. "Sorry, just letting out the tension, boys." *Think, you son of a bitch. How do we get in there and get everyone, including Prudence, out alive?* "What do we got? Eleven able-bodied men, eleven automatic assault blasters, one hover car—"

"Stolen from the Blue Helmets," Lucan added.

"I got a grenade." Grady held up the small explosive. It was a fucking antique. "Not sure if it's got any kick left."

"Doubt it," Griffin said. "Though I bet it's still got some shock value."

Grady grinned.

"All right, gather 'round."

The men huddled closer; their intense faces locked onto Griffin.

"Here's the plan. Blasters down your pants. It's gonna be awkward as hell trying to walk with them in your pants, but as long as no one looks too close, we might get away with this." He dragged his hand down his face. "Merrick and Lucan are in uniform. They're gonna drive us up to the gate, saying they caught us joyriding in the stolen hover car."

"All prisoners go in through the front," Merrick said. "They're taken to a holding cell on the ground floor a couple doors down from where you and Prudence were held. I pick them up on Wednesdays for trial and sentencing in Diamond Fjord. Since we're going in the front door this time, we might be better off ditching the uniforms. They're used to seeing me around here. They won't question me bringing in people for holding, but they'll question the uniform."

Griffin nodded. "All right, good. Now, we're gonna try to make it all the way down to here without drawing anyone's notice." Griffin pointed to the room where he and Prudence were held. "But if anyone looks suspicious, pull your weapons and fire at will."

All the men nodded.

"You boys keep your heads. I don't want any friendly fire due to itchy trigger fingers. You watch the man on either side of you. Keep him safe and trust them to do the same for you. You all understand?"

"Yes, sir." The response was weak. They were brave, they were all here of their own free will, but they were scared.

Griffin grabbed his weapon and stood. "Always hug the walls. Keep your body at an angle to make the smallest target possible." He lifted his weapon to the ready position. "Keep the butt of your weapon tight to your shoulder, stay crouched and point the gun wherever you're looking." He demonstrated. "You want to look right, your weapon comes with you, look left, it comes with you. Understand?"

The men nodded.

"Now, before we go in there, I want to thank you all for helping. I couldn't have picked a better unit for this mission myself."

That was what they needed to hear. Their intensity didn't lessen, but, pride and confidence showed in the straightening of their spines. They were ready.

Merrick reached over, plucked Grady's hat from his head and tossed it to Griffin "Put that on, Chief, and pull the brim low so they don't recognize you."

"Thanks." Griffin put the hat on and piled into the bed of the hover car with the others, ready to be a prisoner for the second time that night.

They approached the front gate of the compound five minutes later. The spaceport was like a beacon in the distance, bright spotlights shining up on a spacecraft that stood stories higher than any of the surrounding buildings.

Merrick pulled the hover car to a stop outside the gates to the compound and a Blue Helmet approached the driver's side door. "What's all this?"

"Found these boys having a drunken joyride outside Diamond Fjord. Heard you all had a hover car go missing earlier today. Thought I'd bring it back. We don't have the capacity in town to hold these lot until court on Wednesday. You mind if I take them down to the brig?"

"Yeah, go on, Merrick." The Blue Helmet stepped away from the hover car and signaled for the gate to be opened. "It's Merrick. Let him in."

The courtyard was lit up as bright as the backdoor. Patrols of Blue Helmets walked the perimeter and snipers held posts on raised platforms on the corners of the property. Griffin was sweating bullets. He had no idea how capable these men were. Merrick must be a good shot, he was Special Ops, but he couldn't begin to guess about the others. Didn't know if they'd be able to hit the broad side of a barn from the inside. He might have just signed all their death warrants.

Merrick pulled right up to the front door. Another Blue Helmet approached. "Quite a roundup. You need some help?"

Merrick got out of the hover car. "Nah. These boys won't give me any trouble." He dipped at the waist to look in the car. "You gonna give me any more trouble?"

A round of woeful "No, sirs" came from the men, startling Griffin. Well, hell, with a little luck they could shoot as well as they could act.

"They're good men for the most part. Had a bit much to drink and got a little rowdy. I'm foreseeing community service in their near future."

Grady and a couple of the other men groaned.

The Blue Helmet ducked his head down. "Grady, is that you moaning?"

"Yep, sir."

"You're making a habit of this. Maybe Merrick needs to be a little tougher with you."

"Nope, sir." Grady slurred his words as if he were three sheets to the wind. He hiccupped. "It's like my mama always said, I need to pick my friends better."

The Blue Helmet chuckled. "Go on, get them inside to sober up." He wandered off.

Merrick came around the back of the hover car and lowered the tailgate. "Let's go. Left hand goes on the shoulder of the man in front of you." His tone remained matter of fact and he spoke loud enough for everyone in the vicinity to hear, but not so loud as to draw attention. "Right hand flat against your thigh. There will be no talking, no moving out of line, no pushing. Anybody here deaf?"

"No, sir," they mumbled together.

Griffin stifled a grin and bowed his head. He ended up in the middle of their human chain right behind Grady. Everybody played their part, swaying as they walked, eyes downcast, shoulders slumped.

Merrick opened the front door and continued his lecture as they shuffled past. "Now what do you think your wives will say when they find out you lot are in prison?"

Being inside this place was like being back on Earth. The compound had hardwood floors and white plaster walls with moldings at the top, center, and foot of the wall. Mounted colored photographs of nature scenes on Earth were placed at intervals along the halls.

"Don't got a wife," Grady said.

The front hall was huge, extending far back into the compound and full of Blue Helmets.

"You boys walk along the right wall, keep out of the Blue Helmets way." Merrick walked next to Grady and shook his head. "You do this every time, talking back to me. Am I gonna have to put you in solitary until Wednesday?"

"Nope, sir. Don't like solitary. I meant I don't know what my wife would think 'cause . . . on account of . . . I don't got one."

Griffin listened to the exchange while scoping out his surroundings. None of the Blue Helmets paid them much mind. This must be pretty common, which was a good thing, because if anyone looked too closely, they might notice how their pants and shirts were molded to the shapes of their weapons. To be honest, he didn't know how the fuck no one hadn't noticed yet. Merrick's order to walk along the right wall helped, they all had their weapons on their right, but, Christ, how unobservant could these soldiers be?

"Now, Grady, you did it again. This isn't a conversation, boy. I'm giving you food for thought. Now, don't you be answering me again." Merrick walked farther up the line, keeping pace with Lucan who was second in line. "Take a right at the end of the hall, I'll tell you when to stop." He turned, walking backward to check the line, to scan the Blue Helmets. "All you boys need to think about what you've done. Was your little joyride worth the trouble you're in? No, it was not. You left those poor Blue Helmets without their ride, and what if . . . ." Merrick kept up a steady, one-sided conversation. Must be part of his routine, because the Blue Helmets didn't bat an eyelash in their direction.

They turned the corner and headed down a passageway. The hardwood floor echoed under their boots. There were fewer Blue Helmets here. Three walked past their human chain and headed for the front of the building. Two stood on either side of a door ahead.

As long as they were quiet, they shouldn't draw attention when they took them out.

Merrick turned around again and nodded to Griffin.

Merrick stopped them in such a way that he stood in front of one Blue Helmet and Griffin stood in front of another.

In one swift, silent motion, he slipped out of line, cupped his hand over the Blue Helmet's mouth and put him into a head lock. He flexed his arm around the kid's throat, holding him through his struggles until he went limp. He released him, checked for a pulse, and nodded to Merrick.

Merrick had the other Blue Helmet slung over his shoulder. He pointed to the door and held up one finger. *One guard.*

Griffin pointed to him, and to the door. *You go first.* He pointed to himself and Lucan. *We'll come behind.* He pointed to Grady and put two fingers to his eyes. *Keep watch.*

Merrick passed off the unconscious soldier to Lucan and opened the door. "Hey, Dugan. How's it hanging?" Merrick slipped his hand over the guard's mouth and put him into a chokehold.

This one put up a fight. He was going for his gun.

Griffin dumped his Blue Helmet in the corner and went to help Merrick. He disarmed the guard and held the guy's nose, cutting off his oxygen. "We're putting you to sleep, buddy. Don't make this worse. No one's gonna hurt you."

The man's terrified stare stayed with him until his lids began to sag and his eyes went out of focus. He slumped in Merrick's arms.

Griffin released him. "Lock 'em all in a cell."

As soon as Merrick and Lucan started lugging the unconscious Blue Helmets back, Griffin headed out of the room. He strode across the hall to where he and Prudence had been held and flung open the door.

The room was empty.

His gaze raked over everything, looking for a clue, a hint she'd come back. In the corner, the broken glass from the bottle of liquor Randolph had poured over him had been shaped into a heart.

Lucan came up next to him and swore.

"She was here for a while, at least. Where do you think they took her?" Griffin asked.

"Depends." Merrick said, from behind them. "What do they want her for?"

"Ultimately? Sex."

Both men swore.

Griffin dragged his hand down his face. "Thing is, Randolph was so pissed at her, I'm more worried he'll kill her."

Lucan grimaced. "And you disappearing will add to his fury."

Damn it. He hadn't considered they'd move her so soon. "Where are the private quarters?"

Lucan started walking down the hall. "Upstairs. There's a back staircase near the kitchens, so we can avoid going through the front hall again."

Everyone followed, their shoes echoing on the hardwoods. Grady came up next to Griffin. "How come you didn't kill 'em?"

"A soldier doesn't use more force than necessary. If he fought me, I'd have killed him. He didn't, so he gets to keep breathing."

"Ah." Grady nodded. "Okay, then."

"You got your safety off, Grady?"

"Yep. Sure do, Chief." Grady nodded.

A few steps later, Grady lifted his assult blaster and the sound of the safety clicking off echoed in the hallway.

Holy Hell, they needed a miracle.

36

Blue Helmets came and escorted her upstairs. She had Lucan's gun tucked into her pants at the small of her back. It felt huge, strange, and kept sticking to her sweaty skin.

She'd never killed anyone before.

True, she'd shot the Scarecrow, but she hadn't have a choice; the creature would've killed Griffin.

If you don't kill Randolph and Bronsen, they'll find Griffin and kill him.

But killing was a harder thing to do when she'd had so much time to think about it. Goddess help her, she'd been thinking about it a lot—wondering where she should shoot them. The head? The heart? How big of a mess would it make? Would she hate herself as much as Griffin hated himself afterward? She despised both Randolph and Bronsen more than anyone. She had plenty of right to. Yet, she couldn't bear the thought of causing anyone to suffer. She wanted to kill them quick.

And she didn't want to die. She had her baby to protect. If she played this right, she'd walk away alive and in one piece.

She'd do like Griffin did. Draw, fire, and drop her weapon so the Blue Helmets would have to take her into custody. Merrick was the justice on Asteria. As long as she survived doing the deed, he'd keep her and her baby safe.

The Blue Helmets stopped in front of an open door and took their posts on either side. "You can go in."

Prudence stepped into the room. A long, oak dining table and chairs took up most of the space. There was an archway beyond the right side of the table, with swinging doors that probably led to the kitchens. Two bay windows looked out on the spaceport from behind the head of the table. On the left was a floor-to-ceiling wall-to-wall mural of the Grand Canyon.

Randolph sat at the far end of the table with Bronsen on his right. There was one place setting laid out at the end of the table closest to her.

Randolph motioned to her. "Sit."

She pulled out her chair and sat. This would be the perfect place to shoot them, they were alone. But she wasn't sure she'd hit either of them from this distance. She wiped her sweaty palms on her thighs.

Three servants walked in with trays of plates, their white uniforms marking them as kitchen staff. Two walked over to the men and served them. A young woman approached Prudence and set down all three courses—salad, entrée, and dessert. She curtsied and left without a word.

Bronsen and Randolph began eating, still speaking so softly she had no hope of hearing them. Were they plotting her next punishment? Were they deciding what to do about Griffin's disappearance? Were they planning their trip back to Earth?

Prudence glanced down at her plate and her stomach roiled. She knew she should eat something to keep up her strength, but she wasn't hungry.

Besides, she'd already bitten off far more than she could chew.

37

Griffin took the lead at the base of the stairs, pausing to ask Lucan, "How many doors down?"

"Four. That room leads to the kitchens. Then up one more flight of stairs is the living quarters. We'll come out in the dining room. The private rooms are down the hall."

Griffin nodded. "Stay a couple steps behind me."

He started up the steps and the second floor came into view. Stairs were dangerous as hell because the people at the top would see the crown of his head before he saw them.

"Hey!"

Griffin swung around. A Blue Helmet stood in the hallway below them. He lifted his weapon.

With a curse, Griffin shot him. The discharge echoed in the enclosed space.

As did the Blue Helmet's shout.

"The whole place must have heard that. Let's go." He didn't bother to keep his voice down. He could already hear shouts of alarm coming from different areas of the compound.

They were fucked.

Griffin took the stairs two at a time, cutting down two more Blue Helmets running down the hall toward them.

Half a dozen more spilled out of one of the rooms farther up the hall.

A hand clamped around Griffin's shoulder, pulling him back. "This way." Lucan ducked into a side room.

"We're gonna get pinned down."

"This leads to the kitchens. Follow it around to the left and up the stairs. Merrick and I will keep these guys busy."

Griffin paused. "We should stay together."

Lucan had hunkered down by the door, lining up a shot. "You have to come back this way. We'll be fine. Go."

Griffin wanted to argue further, but Merrick was pinned in the room across the hall, popping out and taking shots at the Blue Helmets. There wasn't a chance in hell Lucan would leave his husband here.

Griffin ordered two more men to stay. "The rest of you come with me. Hustle now."

They made it all the way down the hall without being seen, but the hallway opened into a busy kitchen. A long, stainless-steel counter ran down the center of the room, with stoves, sinks, and storage closets along the outer walls. There must be fifteen people in here, but none of them appeared to be armed with anything more dangerous than kitchen utensils.

A dish shattered, and all eyes turned to them.

"Everybody in the cold storage. Now." Griffin motioned them all toward the back of the room with his weapon.

"Won't they freeze in there?" Grady asked.

"I said cold storage, not freezer."

"Oh, right." Grady moved to the far side of the counters, helping corral the workers toward the back of the room. "You heard Chief, getchyur asses in there quick."

The kitchen staff all squeezed into the small room and Grady rammed his hip against the door until the latch clicked shut.

Griffin wiped the sweat from his brow. "Anyone see the stairs?"

"Over here." One of his men pointed off to the left with his assault blaster.

Griffin jogged over and checked the stairwell. "All right." He turned back to his men, pausing when he realized Grady was eating. "Grady, get your ass over here."

"Sorry." He popped another morsel into his mouth. "Get hungry when I'm nervous."

Griffin shook his head. "Keep your eyes up. Shoot anything you see that's not us." He led the way into the stairwell, making it a few feet before someone opened fire from above. He backed up, waiting for the blasts to stop, before stepping back into the stairwell to fire. The shooter stayed out of sight. Griffin was beginning to think they left, when a blaster appeared over the edge of the banister above and sprayed the stairwell with photon blasts.

He ducked out of range. "Grady, you still have that grenade?"

"Yep." Grady dug the grenade out of his pocket, pulled the pin and handed it to Griffin.

"Goddamnit!" Griffin lunged out into the spray of blasts and hurled the grenade up to the second floor. He glared at Grady. "You hand me the fucking thing live? Are you nuts?"

Grady grinned. "You were right, Chief, damned thing did still have some shock value."

Above them, a blast shook the building. Griffin ducked down with the others, his ears ringing. Flaming plaster and wood rained down in the stairwell. "Come on."

Griffin led the way upstairs.

38

Someone was yelling.

The commotion wasn't coming from this part of the house, but someone sounded upset. Or hurt.

Neither Randolph nor Bronsen had taken notice. They were both still occupied with their conversation.

A few minutes later, Prudence heard gunfire. Her heart sped up. Had Lucan and Merrick returned?

Bronsen lifted his head. "Stay here. I'll see what's going on." He stood, withdrawing his weapon as he walked from the room.

Prudence reached back and took hold of her weapon, keeping her hand hidden under the table. Not a moment later, the whole room shook as an explosion rocked the building. Smoke billowed out of the door leading to the kitchens.

Randolph stood.

With a glance over her shoulder to make sure Bronsen was gone, she rose, too. "Don't move."

Randolph's eyes widened, his head jerked to the side. "What are you doing? Sit down."

"No." Prudence walked the length of the table on shaky legs.

"If you were going to s-shoot, you'd have d-done so already. Put the gun on the table and go sit down. Good God, you're a s-stupid woman."

Goddess, he must be stressed. She'd never seen him like this. Twitchy, pale, now he was stuttering. "No. Not stupid. Compassionate." She stood next to him and lifted the gun. "I wanted to be close enough to make sure I got you with one shot." Prudence flipped off the safety and aimed, trying without success to steady her hand. *Oh, dear Goddess, she couldn't do this. She couldn't—*

Men barreled into the room and Randolph dropped back in his chair.

She shifted her aim, hoping to see Lucan or Merrick. Her heart stuttered in her chest.

Griffin.

It couldn't be him. He was healthy. Whole. Not a bruise marred his face or arms.

Did he have another brother? A twin?

Her moment of inattention cost her. Randolph lunged up and grabbed hold of her, knocking the gun from her hand and pulling her body in front of his like a shield. With dawning horror, she realized he held a blaster.

Griffin and the others froze. For a long moment, no one spoke, no one moved, and the sounds coming from out in the hall grew louder.

Randolph motioned to him with the gun. "You're d-dead. You can't be here."

Griffin began walking down the length of the table. "Hi, Angel. You doin' all right?"

Prudence nodded. "How are you here?"

The corner of his mouth kicked up. "I told you, if you ever disappeared on me I'd come for you myself. Besides, you were about to kill the wrong man."

"What?"

"Good 'ol Randolph here, he won't be a threat once Bronsen is gone."

Randolph fired off a shot. "Shut up. You're lying."

Griffin straightened from where he'd taken cover behind one of the high-back chairs. His smile faded. "Wasn't Prudence who helped me get close to Alfred. It was your lover."

Randolph's arm squeezed tight around Prudence. "You're wrong."

"Am I?" Griffin edged closer. "I'm a tagged soldier, Randolph. Your head of security must have known I was out there. All the rebels, actually. Think about it. Either he's doing a piss-poor job, or he knew we were out there. Where we were. What we were doing."

Randolph backed up a few steps, dragging Prudence with him.

"The night I killed your brother, there was no security. No armed guards. No one swept me for a weapon. They let me walk in, dressed in a Marine's uniform carrying a sidearm."

"I don't w-want to hear this." He pressed the muzzle of his weapon under her chin.

Griffin held up his hand, stopping. "She's innocent. She's done nothing to you."

Prudence cleared her throat. "Randolph, what I said about Alfred planning to ship you away. It was true. I saw the documents. Had Alfred not died, you would've been shipped out on the same flight I took."

"He wouldn't. Alfred created utopia for me. He made everything right, orderly. He did it for me."

Prudence slipped her hand into her pocket, gripping the shard of glass she'd kept from the torture room.

Griffin shook his head. "That's why Bronsen let me in. Whether I pulled the trigger or not, Alfred was going to die that night and I was going to trial for his murder."

"He did it for me, then. Bronsen was protecting me. He must've believed these lies about Alfred and—"

Again, Griffin shook his head. "Remember what I said about soldiers being tagged? Think about the rebels. If

Bronsen wanted to stop the rebellion, he could've. I think he plans to let you die, then take over as PM himself."

"No. He's here to help me get Prudence back."

"For himself. Not for you."

Bronsen chose that moment to walk in. His gaze shot around the room, taking everything in.

Griffin stepped back, pointing his weapon at Bronsen, holding his hand up to stay his men. "Close the door."

Bronsen nodded toward Randolph and Prudence. "He's off his meds, you know. Twitchy as hell. He could shoot her accidently at any time. I'm surprised you haven't taken him down yet. "

Behind her, Randolph gasped. "Bronsen?"

Prudence almost felt sorry for Randolph. He sounded lost as a little boy. Here he was arguing in Bronsen's defense and his lover was urging them to shoot him. Still, she didn't trust him. He had a mean streak a mile wide. She adjusted her grip on the shard of glass.

She shared a glance with Griffin. This could go bad fast. She had a gun to her throat, Griffin was pinned in the middle of the room halfway between Bronsen and Randolph, and the three men he had with him were on the other side of the room, armed, but looking a bit unsure of who to shoot and when.

"Bronsen, they're trying to tell me you've allowed all this to happen. That you could have prevented Alfred's death. That you're allowing the rebellion."

Bronsen shrugged. "You and Alfred both have your talents, but neither of you would be a good leader for the long term. The world needs someone decisive. Strong."

Griffin snorted. "Like you."

"Like me."

Randolph shifted, pulling the gun from her throat and aimed it at Bronsen. "Bastard."

Bronsen swung his weapon around, too. Both fired.

Fire lanced across Prudence's arm and behind her, Randolph jerked. Bronsen took the shot in the shoulder. Not a lethal wound by any means, but as soon as shot went off, Griffin's men fired, too. Bronsen's body jerked several times, before he dropped to the ground, dead.

Prudence jabbed the glass into Randolph's thigh, grabbed his gun, and dove away from him as the men turned toward Randolph. She rolled onto her back, lifted the weapon and fired. Her aim was true. She hit him dead center in the chest.

A look of shock passed over Randolph's face before he slumped to the ground.

"Angel are you okay?"

Prudence got to her feet and pressed her hand to her stomach. *Goddess, that was close.* She'd been so sure she'd been shot. She could even smell burnt flesh. Her ears still rang and smoke filled the room. She stared at Randolph's face, as his lifeless eyes stared unseeing at the ceiling.

"Are you all right? You scared me." Griffin approached her. His worried gaze raked over her before he glanced over his shoulder at the others. "Give me something to tie up her wounds."

But how? How could this be the same man she'd help load on to the hover-car hours ago? "Is it really you?"

He cupped her face and pressed his lips to hers.

Goddess be praised, he tasted like Griffin. She pushed away, searching his face.

"If you tell me you don't at least recognize my kiss, I'm gonna call you 'lady' for the rest of our lives."

Prudence lunged at him, wrapping him in her embrace. He was whole. Not a mark marred his body. "How?" She couldn't stop touching him. She ran her hands down his face, his perfect, healed face. "How many med-wands did they use on you?" She couldn't see him anymore through her tears, but, oh, she was so happy.

"Just your gift." He pressed his forehead to hers. "All I wanted was to survive so I'd be around for you."

That was the loveliest thing he'd ever said. She sniffed and wiped away the fresh burst of tears. "I couldn't kill Randolph. I wanted to. I wanted to make sure he couldn't hurt anyone anymore, but I couldn't and I almost cost us our lives."

"Shh. It's all going to be all right, Angel. You got him in the end." He gave her a quick kiss.

Griffin took her hand in his and began wrapping the slice across her palm from the glass she'd stabbed Randolph with. Another man wrapped her bicep with a strip of his shirt; she didn't pay much attention until he tightened the binding over her arm. She gasped. "I did get hit."

"Hey, Chief, we stay here much longer, we're gonna be in trouble."

"Coming, Grady." Griffin scowled. "You did. We're going to have a long discussion about this later."

The way he growled she had no doubt she wouldn't like whatever he had to say. "I love you, baby."

He winked. "Don't think for a minute that's gonna keep you out of trouble when we get home."

Home. Joy filled her near to bursting. He spoke as if he planned to stay.

"Come on. We need to get out of here."

39

Griffin handed Prudence her gun. "Next time someone points a gun at you, duck."

She pulled a face. "If I hadn't been so shocked by your miraculously healed presence, I would have."

"Christ, you've gotten sassy."

She might have taken exception to his comment but she caught his grin as he turned away.

"Head out the left door, boys." Griffin turned back to her long enough to give her another quick kiss. He took her hand, ready to go but stopped dead in his tracks as he watched Grady leading the men to the doorway on the right. "Military left, you fucking Gomer."

Without missing a beat, Grady turned and led the men back to the correct door.

Griffin hustled past them, taking up the lead with Prudence in tow.

"Ya always this mean when yur in a fight?" Grady asked.

Behind him, Prudence snorted. "Just to the people he likes."

Grady chuckled. "Well, that's all right, then."

Griffin poked his head out the doorway. The hallway was clear, but he could hear gunfire on the floor below. "Let's move. The others are pinned down by some Blue Helmets. I'm hoping this will lead us behind them."

He released Prudence's hand and made his way down the hall towards the stairs. The sound of gunfire grew louder as they approached the wide staircase. "Line up, boys. Mow down anything wearing blue."

Together, they went down the stairs to the smoke-filled second floor. The Blue Helmets had their backs to them. As one, Griffin, Prudence and the others opened fire on the soldiers, dropping half their number before the Blue Helmets even realized they'd been ambushed.

Griffin tried to pull Prudence behind him, but she shrugged him off and continued firing into the fray.

Merrick and Lucan entered the hallway as soon as the shots pinning them down slowed and within seconds, all the Blue Helmets were down.

Griffin glanced around. "Everyone okay?"

A chorus of 'yesses' came back to him.

"Merrick, lead us out of here. I'll take up the rear."

Griffin was impressed as hell with the men. They were all holding their own, alert and reliable. As they made their way through the halls and downstairs, they panned their weapons, shooting any stray Blue Helmets they came across.

Within moments they reached the downstairs storage room He couldn't believe their luck. Had the Blue Helmets taken off when they'd realized they were under attack? "I'm pretty sure there's a sniper watching this door. Everybody haul ass out of here."

Merrick flung open the door and ran out.

The rest followed.

He didn't hear any gunfire, no shouts of warning. *Holy shit, they were going to make it out alive.*

Griffin took hold of Prudence's hand and bolted outside.

And came to a dead halt.

There must have been sixty Blue Helmets out here. All had their guns trained on them. The others had already dropped their weapons.

Shit.

With the spotlights shining on the door, Merrick must not have been able to see what waited for them. They'd run right into a trap.

Griffin lowered his weapon and dropped it to the ground. Prudence did the same.

"Nobody fight," Griffin spoke loud enough for his men to hear. "U.N. law says they can't shoot us unless we fight." He stared hard at Lucan until his brother nodded. Then he glanced at Prudence. "Hey, Pru?"

"Yeah?"

One of the Blue Helmets motioned for them to raise their arms. He complied, though he kept Prudence's hand in his.

"This probably isn't the best time, but I, uh . . . ."

"Don't you dare tell me you love me now."

Griffin jerked his attention to Prudence. She sounded pissed. "What?"

She frowned. "I've been waiting for ages to hear you say it. You will not spoil the moment by saying it now when we're about to be arrested."

"Look, lady—"

Prudence gasped.

"Hey, you two." The Blue Helmet walked their way. "No talking."

They both straightened, keeping their gazes forward.

Griffin scanned the area, searching for a way out of this. The Blue Helmet collected all their weapons—not that having their guns would do much more than assure their deaths at this point. Why hadn't they started cuffing them? He shot a glance at Merrick, who appeared just as confused. They'd surrendered. They'd given up their guns. Why were the Blue Helmets still standing there keeping them in their sights?

The Blue Helmet walked off, leaving them all alone in front of the . . . firing squad.

Another quick glance at Merrick told him his brother-in-law had come to the same conclusion.

Griffin pulled Prudence behind him as the rest of their allies gathered closer.

Grady nodded to him. "It was an honor, Chief."

Shit. "No way, Grady, the honor was all mine."

Prudence ducked under his arm and pressed her face to his chest. "Say it." Her arms wrapped around him and held him tight. "Please."

"Ready." The Blue Helmet's voice rang out. A small spacecraft hovered behind them as if to assure him there was nowhere to run.

They'd been so damn close to getting away.

Griffin looked down into her lavender eyes. "I love you, Prudence Angelica Parnell."

The corner of her mouth quirked. "You've never said my whole name before. I wasn't sure you knew it."

"Aim." The Blue Helmets lifted their weapons.

He smiled and winked. "Political assassins are always known by three names." Griffin cupped her cheek and pressed his lips to hers, determined to go out with her taste on his lips.

"This is the Rebels. Lower your weapons."

Griffin lifted his head. That had come from the spacecraft. He looked up, his eyes narrowing. The unmarked craft hovered lower, causing their hair to whip around their faces. The sound of the ship's gun turrets arming echoed. The speakers on the craft crackle to life. "Blue Helmets, lower your weapons or we will fire." The Marine's Hymn played in the background.

Griffin glanced back in time to see the Blue Helmets drop their guns.

The men around them whooped for joy.

Ropes unraveled from the ship's loading dock and several armed soldiers rappelled down. They lifted their weapons, rushing right past Griffin and the others and headed for the Blue Helmets.

Lucan clapped him on the back. "You recognize that music?"

"The Marine's Hymn." He pulled his brother into a hug. "You did good, little brother."

"So did you."

Merrick shook his head. "That's not the Marine's Hymn."

Griffin tipped his head to the side as he listened. Prudence cuddled up to his side.

"We forged ahead with each decree, killed like your hired guns."

That was his voice coming out of the speakers.

"From ships at sea to each air base, we died in your bomb runs."

He shook his head. "Why the hell are they playing that?"

"You banned our kin from life on Earth, but I'll wash your sins clean."

Merrick grinned. "They call it, The Last Marine's Hymn. It's the Rebel's rallying cry."

"I'm nothing more than you made me, I'm the last U.S. Marine."

"See, baby?" Prudence gave him an affectionate squeeze. "You did make a difference."

40

———— ✦ ————

"Chief Payne?"

Griffin turned at the sound of his name. A big, heavily scarred warrior strode toward him, wearing a conglomeration of uniforms. He'd have been a good-looking guy but for the burn scars covering half his face. "By God, it is you. I swear we all thought we were seeing a ghost."

"Why's that?"

"Word came back to Earth that a fire gutted the *Genesis V* and left her dead in space. You weren't listed among the survivors."

"It was a pretty close thing. Who are you?"

"Chief Donovan Reese." The scars on his face stretched tight as he favored Griffin with a smile. "I'd like to shake your hand, sir."

Griffin stared at the Chief's outstretched hand for a heartbeat before offering his own. "Until a couple days ago I didn't think there were any other military left."

"We were scattered all and sundry. When the bases were taken out, those who survived hid. Well, until we all saw you go after Parnell. You gave us the courage to fight back. Several of us started searching for survivors and acquiring weapons. Took us awhile to be able to put up a decent fight, but five months after you were transported, we attacked. The U.N. folded two weeks ago."

"Glad to hear it. Let's hope whatever government takes over does better this time."

Chief Reese looked mean as hell when he frowned. "You won't be returning with us? We could use your help. With the U.N. gone, the infighting back home is getting a little rough."

"No, sir. As of today, I'm retired."

"I'm sorry to hear it, but wish you well."

Griffin nodded and turned to walk away.

"Attention!"

He paused as the soldiers around the area came to full attention, saluting. For a moment, he thought someone important had walked onto the field, but looking back at the Chief, he, too, held himself at attention, facing Griffin.

Swallowing past the sudden lump in his throat, Griffin straightened himself and saluted back.

It was over. He could sleep tonight with the knowledge that while he'd made mistakes, he had still tried. And he'd made a difference.

Griffin's gaze locked onto Prudence, who stood with Merrick and Lucan. Damn, she looked beautiful. Even with her face bruised and her arm bleeding she was the prettiest woman he'd ever seen.

Lucan pulled away from the group and stepped into Griffin's path. "One month with no decisions."

Griffin opened his mouth to argue, but Merrick cut him off. "You promised."

This was ridiculous, but seeing the worry in his brother's eyes, he knew he couldn't reneg now. He let out a deep sigh. "Fine. One month. Now move."

Lucan got out of his way, but not before Griffin saw his smirk of satisfaction.

Griffin pulled Prudence away from the others. He held her hand, worrying her knuckles with his thumb. "Angel, I've got a bit of a problem I need your help with."

Her brows drew together in concern.

"See, in order to get the others to help me rescue you, I had to make this promise . . . ."

Her gaze cut to the side to where the Rebels were loading Blue Helmets into their spacecraft. "I'm not going back to Earth." She bit her lip. "I'm selfish for it, but I don't want you going back either, you've—"

"No, now, I didn't say anything about that, now did I?"

"No, but—"

"My promise was to stay here and do one month of therapy before I make any more decisions."

She threw her arms around him. "Baby, that's great—"

Hell, everybody thought he needed fixing but him. He pulled back a little and rested his forehead to hers. "My problem is, that means I can't ask you to marry me for a month."

Lavender tears pooled in her eyes.

"So, I was hoping, I might be able to talk you into waiting for me."

Prudence threw herself into his arms. "I was starting to think my daughter and I would be living here alone."

Daughter? They were having a baby? His heart swelled at the idea. She'd have to marry him now. If he had to chase her around the planet twice, he'd badger her until she said yes. He pulled away enough to see her face. "Daughter? How do you know you're not carrying my son?"

"Because I have lavender eyes." She grinned. "Pink-eyed Lythonian women have sons. Are you disappointed?"

"Are you kidding? I'll have two angels all to myself. I'll be the happiest man on the planet."

Epilogue

One month later

Griffin gripped his sidearm in both hands, studying the scene around him.

The compound. He stood in the compound, in the dining room where he'd almost lost Prudence. His heart picked up a beat. People crowded around the dining table, laughing and eating.

A loud pop echoed in his ears and he swung around, weapon raised and ready only to find a waiter holding a foaming bottle of champagne.

Griffin let out a shaky breath. He hadn't fired this time. He was getting better at this. The virtual reality simulator was meant to expose him to his triggers, loud noises, crowds, and stress to give him a chance to practice his self-control. To re-learn how to be a civilian after being a soldier for so long.

The scene shifted. Now he stood in the town square. Blue Helmets mingled in with the citizens of Diamond Fjord. The noise from the hawkers, the crowd, and live animals was almost defending. Bodies pressed up against him as they brushed passed. He felt himself starting to unravel. He took a deep breath, hustling himself to the sidelines where he could press his back against the wall. Better. That was better. He did the breathing exercises Doc Lambert taught him, knowing he was watching.

His heart slowed.

The scene changed.

This was war. The air held the tinny quality of blood and too many photon blasts. Everything looked scorched, and soldiers battled around him. Rockets blasted past overhead. Explosions rocked the ground. Men shouted and screamed.

He knew it was a simulation. He knew it, but his body didn't care.

He lifted his weapon ready to fight.

The scene went blank.

"That's enough for now, we're almost out of time."

Griffin pulled off the virtual reality headgear and stripped off the jumpsuit. He handed both, along with the blaster replica, to Doc.

He was shaking. Sweaty. He inhaled a deep breath and stared at Doc.

He was nothing like Griffin had expected. He'd pictured some polished, refined male he'd have nothing in common with, someone who'd never understand. Instead, Lambert was a kind man with a prosthetic arm and leg. Griffin had never dared to utter the words, "You don't understand." None of them did.

Doc folded his arms over his chest. "You're doing better."

"I didn't shoot." It was an accomplishment. First time in that damn simulator he'd taken out half the town.

The corner of Doc's lips curved. "But you still need the security of that weapon in your hand."

Griffin inhaled a deep breath. Yeah, he was doing better, but he wasn't where he needed to be yet.

"You're doing your affirmations every day?"

"Yeah." As if Prudence, Merrick, and Lucan would let him get away with not doing them. Every time he started getting moody, the least bit argumentative, one of them would bring attention to Prudence's belly. To his daughter. He would be better by the time his little girl arrived.

"Let me hear them."

Griffin fidgeted. While he understood the theory behind affirmations, he felt like a complete idiot saying them. "I have control over myself. My actions are the sole thing in my control."

"What else?"

"I can't change the past or predict the future. I live in the now." That one was important. He couldn't change what he'd done, and if he allowed himself to think about it, he started slipping. If he stayed with the now, he could live with himself.

Doc nodded. "One more."

Griffin's jaw clenched. His throat grew tight. He knew what he was after.

Doc Lambert nodded. "Take your time and breathe. I can wait."

He could. But Prudence couldn't. He was already late which meant she'd be getting worried. He inhaled a shaky breath. "I love myself."

Doc lifted a brow.

Hell. He hated that expression. He cleared his throat and swiped at his eyes. "I love *all* of myself."

Doc leaned his hip on his desk. "You even managed to hold my gaze that time. Maybe you're starting to believe what you say."

Griffin nodded. Maybe. It was getting easier to live in the now. Prudence, Lucan, and Merrick kept him busy. They'd not only accepted him as is, but they embraced him.

"So." Doc stared at him, bobbing his head up and down. "Will I be seeing you Tuesday?"

Griffin restrained the urge to roll his eyes. Today marked one month. He'd made no commitment to therapy beyond that. But Tuesday was group session. Tuesdays reminded him he wasn't alone in this. Merrick went. Grady went. Half the damn town showed up for group session. Big Jake even joined in once a month when he brought his brood to town.

And hell, Prudence made it worth his time, always praising and fawning. Besides, he made a promise to her last night. He sighed. "Four o'clock, right?"

Doc smiled. That was high praise. "And Thursday?"

"Yeah." He pointed to the virtual reality device. "Haven't quite mastered that yet." He wanted to be able to walk through the town square with Prudence without having an attack. He wanted to take her out to eat or go see a show. He couldn't do that unless he mastered that damn thing. Until his screwed-up head figured out the difference between a real threat, and the unexpected noises that went with living.

Doc's eyes twinkled, but he kept his expression blank. "Two o'clock, again?"

Griffin nodded and stood. "You coming?"

"Wouldn't miss it. Go on, I'll be right behind you."

Griffin strode out of Doc's office and into the bright morning sunlight, adjusting his tie. The whole town was quiet. The shops were closed up tight and the shades were drawn on most of the residential windows above the storefronts.

Lucan and Merrick waited alone on the deserted street. Lucan opened his arms wide. "What are you doing? We're late."

Griffin shrugged. "Had to set my next appointment." He strode past his brother and his husband and headed up the street.

Merrick matched his stride. "So, you're gonna keep going?"

He almost growled. They were always nagging and checking up on him. If it didn't feel so damned good to have people give a shit, he might have to do something about it. "Yeah." He kept his eyes forward, trying to ignore their grins.

Lucan elbowed him. "Does Pru know?"

"Of course she does." At the end of the street, he turned left—military left—and headed for the church. Tendrils of apprehension wound tight in his gut. He still couldn't believe his good fortune.

Today, he was going to make Prudence his.

"I still think you cheated," Merrick said. "You weren't supposed to make any decisions until after one month."

"I didn't. I asked her to wait."

"Yet here we are, walking up to a church." Merrick shook his head. "A wedding takes planning, Griff."

"I haven't asked yet."

Merrick snorted.

"In his defense, Prudence and I took care of the planning. She didn't want to give him too much time to sweat over the whole thing." Lucan glanced at Griffin and laughed. "Look at you. You can't tell me you're worried she'll say no?"

No, he wasn't worried about that. Not anymore. Prudence was a sweet, loving woman who told him in a thousand ways every day how much she cared. He was worried this wouldn't be everything she deserved. He was worried he wouldn't be able to make today as memorable as he wanted it to be for her.

They reached the doors of the church and Lucan clapped his hand on Griffin's shoulder. "For God's sake, breathe, man."

Merrick chuckled. "Don't mind him. He might act calm now, but you should've seen him the day we got married. He looked greener than you do."

"I wanted it to be perfect," Lucan said at the same time Griffin said, "I want it to be perfect."

"Perfect is overrated." Merrick shook his head. "Be yourself and you'll do fine."

His brother and brother-in-law opened the doors wide and for a split second, he thought he might pass out. His attention skipped over the citizens of Diamond Fjord crowded into the pews and zeroed in at the end of the long aisle on Prudence. Christ, he was gonna have all those people at his back.

Lucan leaned in and whispered, "We're right behind you, Griffin."

Prudence caught sight of him and grinned. He could do this.

"Isn't this a little backward," Merrick whispered. "The bride should walk up the—"

Lucan wacked him on the chest. "Shush."

Griffin shrugged. "I'm late." He strode down the aisle, Lucan and Merrick hot on his heels and for a second, his mind flashed back to the first time he walked down an aisle through a crowd toward her. A lot had changed since then. They were both different people now.

She smoothed her hands down the pale lavender gown she wore, the color lighting up those gorgeous lavender eyes of hers.

He didn't stop when he reached the bottom of the steps leading to the altar like the others did. "I've got a question I need to ask you, Angel." His voice didn't carry far, but Prudence heard him, and that's all that mattered.

She was wringing the flowers right off her bouquet. "I thought maybe you changed your mind."

Griffin shook his head as reached the top of the stage. The noise from the onlookers quieted as those in the audience tried to hear. "I'm, uh, not a rich man, but see, I've got this plan."

She rolled her eyes. "You're plans scare me, Warrior."

He grinned. "I'm opening a survival training studio next week."

She winked. "Something tells me people will be coming from miles around to train with you."

"I might already be scheduled out through next year. I also have a little side gig helping Merrick out." He shrugged. "But I don't have a big, beautiful house."

"Hm. I bet you've got a nice little add-on attached to your brother's place. Sounds like the perfect home to raise a daughter, surrounded by family and love."

He chuckled. "Smart-ass."

"I'm trying to help things along, I'm running out of bouquet." She lifted the sad little posey for his inspection. "Griffin Jude Payne, did you have a question or not?"

He drew her into his arms, his heart near to bursting from all the happiness swelling in his chest. "All I can guarantee you is that I'll love you to my dying breath the way no one else ever could. So, knowing all that, Prudence Angelica Parnell, will you marry me?"

"Why yes, Griffin Jude Payne, I will."

About the Author

Cara Crescent currently lives in the Pacific Northwest with her children and three overly dramatic ferrets. When she's not writing, you can usually find her curled up with a book, engrossed in a movie, or playing video games with her best friend.

Please visit her on the web at www.caracrescent.com

ALSO BY

The Original's Trilogy

The Beacon

The Shadow

The Knight

Sating Ember Moon

The Last Hero Novels

The Last Marine

Wretched

Other Books

Don't Let Me Forget You